The Hush

EA Mylonas

Published by Inspired Quill: July 2022

First Edition

Content Warning:
This novel contains descriptions pertaining to instances of terminal illness, queerphobia, rape, animal aggression and death, suicide, child death and mob aggression.

Contact the author through their website: eamylonas.com

Chief Editor: Sara-Jayne Slack
Proofreader: Clare Stevens
Cover Design: Daniel Watts
Typeset in Minion Pro

Paperback ISBN: 978-1-913117-13-9
eBook ISBN: 978-1-913117-14-6
Print Edition

Printed in the United Kingdom
1 2 3 4 5 6 7 8 9 10

Inspired Quill Publishing, UK
Business Reg. No. 7592847
https://www.inspired-quill.com

for LK

Out beyond ideas of wrongdoing
and rightdoing, there is a field.
I'll meet you there.
When the soul lies down in that grass,
the world is too full to talk about.

—Rumi

1.

THE LAST TIME the teacher had witnessed a car crash, there had been screaming, and the memory had stuck with her because people were still allowed to speak back then.

Bystanders had yelled and shouted for help. Some had cried even though they hadn't been involved in the crash, nor did they know the people caught in it.

The accident's victims… They had laid on the ground or sat on the curb with their heads hung between their legs. They did not speak, but merely stared at the chaos. The teacher remembered being shocked at their apathy. Their detachment. She imagined the crash had knocked them into a different world. In that world, there were no ambulance sirens. There were no strangers hugging and comforting each other. In that world, they were left alone to deal with the aftermath.

That was then. Twelve years ago, give or take. This time, there was no screaming by strangers. No crying, no yelling. Just two cars colliding with a sound like a bone shattering.

And then silence.

The pickup never slowed. It ran the red light, the only one on Main Street, missing both pot holes, but not the blue sedan.

Glass and errant pieces of metal went flying. The T-boned sedan skidded towards the teacher standing on the sidewalk and, in the time it did, she thought, I'm dead. And, as she did, her body tensed and the cancer in her guts howled with rage at being cheated out of its prize.

The sedan ground to a stop so close she could feel the heat radiating off its surface, hotter than the punishing midday sun, hotter than the dust that seeped everywhere.

For a long moment, there was no other sound in the world than the hiss of smashed engines and the trickling of break fluids onto the asphalt. She was holding her breath. When she released it, she became aware of the myriad tiny holes in the fabric of her jeans and of the pea-sized glass fragments that glistened through them. She poked a finger into one of the holes and found it curious that there was no pain. She leaned against the traffic light, clamping a hand over her mouth. Trapping the whimper that threatened to escape from her trembling lips, for fear that the townsfolk would confuse it for speaking. Twelve years ago, she wouldn't be lynched for speaking. But that was then and this was now. So she swallowed the whimper and the cancer rejoiced.

From the sidewalk, she could see from one end of the town to the other, all three hundred yards of it. Faces came to the windows lining the street, the unrelenting heat rippling off the asphalt distorting their features. It drew townsfolk to their front doors, though most refused to step outside into the sun. Only a few approached and inspected the damage. No words passed between them. No words went out to the drivers. They didn't ask the teacher if she was hurt, nor did they hug and comfort each other.

Among them, a twelve-year old boy with a shaved head.

She recognized his hand-me-downs, because both of his older brothers had worn them to her class, rough overalls mended with patches that weren't quite the right color. He also wore the same facial features they did. Wild dog features. Just like the other onlookers, he observed the damage in silence.

The sedan's door creaked and protested. A boot pushed from the inside until something within the hinges snapped and the door fell off. Out slipped a thin man with cracked glasses, dropping on the simmering asphalt. There he remained, sitting, head between his knees, breath coming in shallow waves. Behind the cracked glasses, his eyes were staring at nothing, as the teacher remembered how accident victims looked in their shock. The thin man was young enough to have been a teenager when language went away, but his skin was old skin. Burned by the sun, scoured by the dust storms and the drought, and turned into tanned leather, much like everyone else's in that town.

None of the townsfolk offered them help, but the teacher could feel their eyes on both of them. Watching from the windows, from the doors, from the street. Watching for any signs that they were about to break their silence and do as humans do when the shock wears off and drool half-uttered syllables. Watching the pair, waiting to intervene and uphold the law. The teacher held her hand tighter over her mouth. *Look*, it said to the townsfolk. *Look. I'm not making a sound.*

The pickup had rolled to a stop on the other side of the street. Its windshield had spider-webbed and there was motion behind it. The door opened and out came its driver, his mouth forming a loose "o", looking around as if uncertain of his surroundings. Upon seeing the thin man on the ground, the "O" of his mouth grew in size. He took a few steps forward and put up a hand as if swearing an oath. With the other, he tapped his chest right above the heart. My fault, my fault, the gesture said in the only way that someone not allowed to talk can ask for forgiveness. *My fault.*

The thin man snarled. Dragging himself first, then limping, he walked with teeth bared towards the pickup driver. Raised fighting fists. They screamed, *how dare you, how dare you.* Still, the pickup driver tapped out his apology on his chest.

His eyes turning mad, the thin man grabbed the pickup driver by the collar. His clenched teeth struggled to keep words locked up inside. All that came out was a jumble of choked consonants and spittle and his face turned a bright red.

There were townsfolk who got excited by the crash and who might have hoped for a long, vicious fight to bring some fire to the lethargic Main Street. They were let down. A single punch cracked the thin man's nose and he hit the ground on his side, bleeding. His glasses went skittering down the road, their black frame skipping to a rest. Above him, the pickup driver stood with a fist still extended and a blank expression. He looked at his hand as if it didn't belong to him, as if it had just grown out of his body, and he shambled back to the pickup.

The crowd shuffled at the windows and doors. Expectation on their faces, eyes eager for more violence. When that didn't come, they melted back into their stores and houses. The thin man cried into his hands, stifling the sound, receiving dirty looks from the townsfolk for making noise like that in front of everyone. The teacher looked over to where his glasses lay with their cracked lenses and wondered whether she should fetch them for him.

"Can't. I can't," the thin man said out loud.

She stared at him in horror. Between sobs and gulps of air, between tears streaming down his face and dusty coughs, he spoke those words over and over again.

"I can't anymore."

With a finger on her lips, the teacher rushed over to him. *Stop it*, she implored him without words by trying to muffle his mouth. *Stop it, they'll hear.*

Heads turned towards them. *Keep quiet, keep quiet*, her eyes told him again and she pressed her hand harder on his mouth.

"Lemme talk," he growled and shoved her cancer-wasted frame away.

She stumbled backwards, her heel caught the curb. Hit the ground hard. If she hadn't been so shocked by hearing words spoken out loud, she would have noticed the pill bottle she had come to town for dropping out of her purse and rolling away. She would have noticed it bounce on the sidewalk and down into a storm drain where it shattered, spilling the painkillers for the cancer beyond her reach.

"I can't, I can't," he said again, as if imploring her to understand. Then, loud enough for everyone on Main Street to hear, "How can they git way wit it?"

Several heads turned towards him with hard looks on their faces, the insulted and the outraged. A woman moved as if in a trance, before breaking into a run towards the Sheriff's office a few blocks away. The rest of the Main Street population honed in towards the thin man. Front doors opened and men and women with their hands curled into fists stepped outside in twos and threes. They merged and formed bigger groups and their faces became a blur of hard lines. More windows opened, revealing heads craning to get a better view. Across the street, two dark-haired children, a boy and a girl with asymmetric faces, smiled and pointed.

Flinching, the teacher crawled away, but her eyes were locked onto the thin man. He continued shouting with an inarticulate voice that croaked with disuse, waving and pointing his finger at the gathering mob. "You're lettin' them git away wit it."

A stone struck the thin man on the temple and he yelped with pain. The boy with the shaved head bent down to pick up another stone, but the teacher soon lost him, the crowd surging forward and swallowing him.

From her spot on the sidewalk, she willed the man to stand, to start moving, to save himself from what was about to happen. Then it occurred to her that, there, sitting on the asphalt, was where he wanted to be. Using his final words to hurl accusations.

He didn't flinch when the mob laid its hands on him.

They pulled him off the ground like a rag doll. Punches and kicks and scratches rained down. They tugged and ripped at his clothes and bright red spots appeared where blood started soaking through. He made an effort to cover his face with his arms, but hands reached out and spread them. A shattering crunch echoed and he howled. Where before they moved with anger, the scream made the townsfolk fall over each other trying to get to him first. Hands clawed at his mouth, holding his jaw open and reaching inside it.

The jaw has the strongest muscles in the human body, the teacher remembered from one of her classes as the mob tore the thin man's away. His eyes opened wide and let out a crawling airless "aaaaaa".

An open-throated scream is the first sound we learn to make, the teacher thought, watching the gaping hole. *It's the natural sound one makes when hurt. It's simple, easy. It doesn't require conscious effort. It doesn't require many muscles to use.* She was certain the alphabet had been born from pain.

The thin man's eyes closed. The teacher hoped he was dead. The mob continued tearing him apart and she averted her gaze.

She rushed to her car a couple of blocks away, still not feeling the glass in her legs. When she got to it, she reached into her purse for her keys, dropping them to the ground twice before unlocking the door and getting inside. The cursing got caught in her throat. She closed her eyes, forced herself to breathe. When she opened them again, the boy with the shaved head was staring at her from a distance. He had a curious expression on his dirty face. His hands were covered by something resembling soot. He seemed puzzled, as if he were asking, *are you alright, Ma'am?* She fought back tears and nodded with the little smile she reserved for a correct answer in the classroom. The boy kept staring, his expression showing a hint of distrust.

In the distance behind him, the mob was breaking up. The townsfolk shifted with lethargic moves now, their energy spent after the climax. Those who had fallen on the ground in their eagerness lifted themselves up. They all appeared to be coming out of a long sleep, looking at each other with a slight sense of confusion, all wild hair and untucked shirts. And then, the celebration. The patting of shoulders and the shaking of bloody hands. The honest smiles, as if they hadn't just lynched a man. Cigarettes and flasks making the rounds. On the ground among them lay the driver's body.

She started the car and rode out of town, up one of its twin hills, never once looking into the rearview mirror. With one hand, she reached into her bag for the bottle of painkillers and found nothing. She wanted to curse to curse to curse, but even in the isolation of her car, ingrained habits won and she bit on her tongue until the urge passed.

The sight of the dirt road turning towards the farmhouse, her home, filled the teacher with relief like a sailor finding a quiet port after a storm.

She didn't enter the house, though. A path took her around it, past the kitchen with its large west-facing windows, past the back porch with the two chairs and the tiny wooden table between them, and into the carious yellow corn fields. The feel of dirt underneath her sneakers felt familiar, safe. She let her purse drop at her feet. Then, holding her breath, she stepped among the stalks. Wandered without direction for a few minutes before she felt safe enough to fall to her knees. She tried to will herself to scream and release the tension, but it was an empty scream that came out, without body or timber or texture, just a ghost of sorrow. *Why didn't he keep his mouth shut*, she thought? If only he'd kept his mouth shut, everything would have been fine.

Hours passed. Pain finally started to set in where glass had pierced her, tiny pinpricks of white heat. The sun lowered on the horizon, casting long shadows, covering the field in darkness. She inhaled, focusing on the smell of warm earth. On the smell that corn husks give off after a full day under the sun. And she focused on an urge that seemed to be building inside her, an urge she thought had been buried and forgotten a long time ago. An urge as dangerous as crying out in the middle of the town after an accident. She breathed out, feeling her muscles unclench with reluctance. When the sky started turning the color of a bruise, she stood up and made her way back to the farmhouse.

Once inside, she stood still, her ears reaching out to the bedroom above and the basement below for her husband's footsteps. She rapped on the dining table and counted to a hundred. No reply came, and she guessed her husband was out working the fields. Satisfied she was alone, she made her way to the staircase leading to the basement and, using the large key hanging from a nail on the wall next to it, she unlocked the heavy oak door. A draft carrying the smell of dry mold reached her as she opened it and, after turning the light on, she descended the few steps.

On the far side of the basement, past propped-up mattresses, rolled rugs, and bulging suitcases, stood a massive red armoire. It took her some effort to open it. She reached inside past the moth-eaten clothes, shifted and contorted her arms, and managed to work loose a panel on the back. Behind it was a large hole in the wall and, inside that, a plastic bag.

She reached inside and pulled out a roll of loose writing paper, covered by dark blotches. Sticky to the fingers. She had secured the pages with a length of twine, as if she were afraid the words would escape and she'd never lure them back again. Words scribbled in longhand full of angles and uneven pressure. Words that hadn't been legal in over a decade. She untied the pages now, flipped through them, and brought them upstairs. She pulled the living room curtains shut before setting the documents on the mahogany dinner table they had bought together. In her husband's ancestral home, a house of old things, of hundred-year old armoires and inherited china, this was the one item she counted as theirs.

She thought that, even years after having written them, she would still remember her own words by heart. Instead, her brain refused to process them at all. She shook the pages, willing the words to make sense. When that failed, she opened her mouth and tried to utter them out loud, as if that would somehow break the spell. Only a sound that was close to a tired sigh came out and she coughed dust. She tried again, concentrating on the form of the letters.

She didn't think as much in terms of words anymore, not like in the past. Now, her mind was filled with images. Sensations, too. The dryness in the air, the acidic bitterness of rationed coffee. Most of all, the constant pain the tumors in her guts caused her. She hadn't tried to speak, not even when alone, in… she couldn't remember how long it had been. Now, when she needed to hear her own words, they eluded her.

Defeated, she fished a pencil from her purse, found the last half-finished page, and paused for a few moments to gather her thoughts.

She thought, *I'm not sure I even understand written words anymore. I know that 'corn' is the name of the plant that grows outside our window, but the word is nothing but random squiggles that make little sense to me anymore. How can I do this? After all this time?*

She rubbed her eyes and contemplated the patterns that surfaced behind her eyelids. They were shaped like a mob with flailing arms. They were shaped like a thin man crying, and his cracked glasses lying on the asphalt. With an exhalation and the pain in her legs rising, she tried to write.

2.

G RAY AND DIRTY red flashed between the corn stalks. The lobos broke their run to peek back at the farmer, then darted ahead with lolling tongues. He led with the shotgun muzzle, pushing the stalks aside. It was hard getting a clear shot at the animals.

Sweat dripped into his eyes and he had to stop and rub them while the lobos ran deeper into the corn field. His breath felt labored. Heavy. Still, he didn't want to take off the handkerchief that covered his mouth. *Damn this dust*, he thought. *Can't it kill those mutts, the way it kills everything else?*

A pair of black eyes glared back at him. He squeezed the trigger. The shotgun thundered with birdshot, cutting down stalks and sending blackbirds squawking into the air. Only two shells remained in his shirt pocket. He pulled them out and studied them, turning them this way and that. He moved to load them into the shotgun, hesitated, and dropped them back into his pocket. Instead, he gripped the shotgun barrel like a baseball bat. He approached the spot where he reckoned he had hit the animal. The shotgun came up.

He found nothing there. Only faint tracks on the dirt. He

slung the shotgun over his shoulder, pulled the handkerchief down and took a deep breath, which gave him a coughing attack. The birds above continued cursing him. Once he managed to get his breath under control, he stretched his aging back, popping and cracking his spine. Every time he did that, he wondered whether he'd slip a disk and fall squirming like an earthworm in the middle of the field, invisible to all but the birds. Then, he thought, *the lobos might come back.* The sun was already on its way below the horizon. Better get going. He'd have to find a way to tell his wife not to wander too far into the fields.

Tracing the way back was easy through half-broken shoots and splintered plants. He knelt. Taking a glove off, he wrapped a meaty fist around a stalk and squeezed. Fibers popped and cracked like his spine had. When he released his grip, the stalk collapsed and sandy powder flowed through his fingers. The farmer wiped his hand against his pants, held it palm up, a beggar asking for rain.

Maybe tomorrow. Maybe tomorrow it'll rain.

It hadn't rained in months.

There weren't many days in a year when the sun didn't oppress the soil and everything that walked on it, burrowed in it, or grew out of it. Seasons didn't matter much anymore. Not even to a farmer. Corn was about the only crop worth a damn, clinging to life in defiance of the sun's tyranny. Good drought-resistant crop. Still, the topsoil was fragile, the drought had seen to that. Strong winds pulled it up in the air, only to bring it down again, choking everything in their path. And they, the farmers? They were left with nothing in the aftermath.

Coughing and spitting dust, he put the glove back on. Next year. Maybe next year would be better.

He walked back to the clearing where the tractor waited for him and where he had found his neighbor's horses.

There were four of them. Two were chestnut with white patches, and the third was the white of dirty skies. The fourth lay on the ground with its guts spilled out where the lobos had torn it open. Its eyes stared at the sky and its tongue was already swelling, covered with flies.

Flies followed the other horses too, a mindless black swarm that bit and pestered them. Other than a swish of the tail or a flutter of the ears, the horses seemed to ignore them. He could count the ribs below their taut skin and see their thigh bones whenever the horses took a step, which wasn't often. For the most part, they seemed content to stand where they were, only dipping their sinewy necks to graze.

Reckon the lobos aren't around anymore, he thought, *or you wouldn't be munching without a care in the world. Not like your dead friend over there bothers you any.*

Half-eaten corn cobs littered the clearing, which in years past would have sent him into a fit of rage. He calculated his profit from dealing with the Party reps and figured he barely broke even, assuming he managed to sell above cost at all. *Why bother*, he wondered. *Let the horses feed*, then added with a shake of the head, *I guess I'm turning into a stoic.*

He opened a pack of cigarettes and lit one to mask the stink of viscera. The horses didn't seem to be afraid of him. He approached them head-on and from the left side where they could see him, like his Pa had taught him. Their bridles were still on, though ill-fitting, dry cracked leather that had once been a shiny black. Taking a good hold of them, he guided the horses one by one to the trailer attached to his tractor. Only one of the chestnut ones, a short mare with an uneven gait, resisted by digging in. The farmer's arms were still powerful despite being a few months shy of fifty.

I like your attitude, the farmer thought while pulling. *But keep moving.*

With a combination of pushing and slapping, he managed to load the horses onto the trailer. It was made to transport crops, not livestock. There was every chance the horses could get spooked by the engine and jump out while the vehicle was moving, breaking a leg. He'd hate to be the one putting them out of their misery, but he also wasn't going to let the horses roam in his fields either.

Besides, he knew who the horses belonged to and he didn't want that man coming onto his property looking for them. They'd had one too many arguments ending in blows. Arguments about land boundaries, and pesticides, and that goddamn stream. Always that stream. Their arguments had always been short. Neither the farmer nor the neighbor had much patience or skill to get their grief across without words. It had always seemed simpler to just punch him, even back when talking things out had still been an option. He'd return the horses, flip him off, and head back in time for dinner.

His fingers toggled switches, going on muscle memory after years of working with the same model. The engine hummed and sent familiar vibrations through the frame. Instead of moving the tractor forward, though, it whined and died with a grinding sound that made him flinch. He grabbed an extinguisher-sized cylinder of compressed air and jumped down. A puff of dust rose out of the hood when he popped it open. Covering his face with his free arm, he blew dust away from corroded gears and shafts. He reckoned he had cleaned the engine only a week ago. Parts needed replacing. His mind went over the cost. That many pounds of corn for that valve, and that many hours of work for that gasket, and that much faith that he could afford it all.

He tried the engine again. After a groan and a hack, it came to life and the farmer eased the tractor into gear.

The neighbor's farm was less than eight miles away. Around twenty minutes at a speed low enough to keep the horses comfortable.

He looked out into the distance at the grain silos and figured he was close to the poisoned stream. One of these days, some poor bastard was going to take a drink from that stream. Yeah, and die a long painful death. That slow dribble had been the good Lord's idea of a cruel joke, but at least he wasn't the butt of it.

One would think that, in times of drought, any amount of water would make the difference between a half-decent crop and bankruptcy. The farmer's family and the neighbor's had fought for three generations over ownership of that stream which ran down the dividing line between their properties, only one item in the long list of grievances between them. No one was sure when or how the stream had started killing everything it touched.

When that happened, there were lawsuits. Fights. The neighbors demanding reparations for the stream wiping out their crops. For the first time in a century, both sides fought to prove the stream wasn't theirs. In the end, the neighbors got stuck with the ownership and the burden, and both families had another reason not to greet each other on the street.

The engine's vibrations and the cabin's swelter led his mind into a meditative state and he quickly found his mind wandering. High above the ground in his tractor, he felt like a captain plowing through an opaque bronze sea, no shore for miles on either side. The anxiety of loneliness was creeping up on him.

He wasn't sleeping well. The previous night, sounds that could have been imagined or real, he couldn't tell, interrupted his sleep. In his grogginess he turned to his wife and thought that he had said something out loud. He drifted back to sleep almost immediately. He couldn't remember what he had said, neither could he remember if his wife, herself caught in that foggy landscape between sleep and wakefulness, had answered back.

He'd like to think she had. It would have been the first time they'd exchanged words in... he couldn't quite remember. Not everyone had obeyed the Hush Laws at first. They themselves had continued speaking behind the walls of their own home for a time after. But the world had changed and they had changed with it.

The horses fussed and pushed each other. The neighbor's farm appeared in the distance.

He brought the tractor to a stop behind the farmhouse, breaking a post of the picket fence. That made him smile. He jumped out of the cabin before the engine had wound down. Wanted the beasts out and to be on his way home as fast as possible. No point in giving the neighbor an opening. That whole mess with the man's wife disappearing back at the time of the Hush Laws made him eager to share his bitterness with the world.

The farmer opened the trailer gate and the horses snorted and strolled out. Behind them, they had left a mess, soiling the bed.

Once the last horse was off, he walked to the fence. He brought his fingers to his mouth to whistle, then stopped himself. Instead, he grabbed a pebble and threw it harder than needed at a window. When no one appeared, he gave the fence a kick, rattling the cans sitting on it. Where was that bastard? He didn't have all day.

Inside the house, nothing moved. He looked out in the general direction of where his own home was. Hunting the lobos had left him drained and he longed to call it a day. He wanted to head back, eat his tasteless meal, and sit on the porch next to her. Then, he'd try to figure a way of asking her how her body was holding up. If there was some way he could save her. He had no idea how he'd do it.

He touched his throat and felt his vocal cords, frayed with the unsaid, and thought, *my world ends where my words die... and the world seems so small now. Before long, I'll forget which words stand for death and which stand for future. Then, it might not be so bad.*

The house remained silent. Behind him, the beasts grazed on weeds. They were good horses. That bastard didn't care for them properly. They'd fetch a decent price, if only they looked healthier. He didn't know who'd buy them, but someone ought to.

He approached them with hesitation, glancing back at the empty house. Grabbed them by the girdles again, and, this time, they didn't resist. He guided them towards the corral he knew would be at the other side of the house. And still, no one ran out of the house to confront him. The gate there was open.

The pump moved without resistance, filling the trough with water that he looked at with suspicion. He searched the barn for hay, but found none. They'd have to graze what they could. He'd done enough already. He locked the corral behind him, testing the gate with his boot. He figured the neighbor was out there in fields that were worth nothing, those fields that were on the wrong side of a poisoned divide.

He climbed into his tractor, ignoring the horses neighing and set course for home.

On his way back, he wondered what to do with the fourth horse's corpse.

The first thing he noticed when he entered his house was that the stereo was turned on, drowning out the TV's static. It was playing classical music, as many radio stations once did, though not anymore. He moved to the windows and checked the fields outside, then pulled the curtains shut. From there, he went to the kitchen and grabbed an old rag to wipe the dust off his boots. Once he was done, he went to the windows again. *There's no one out there, we're alone*, he told himself as he squinted into the evening's dying light, wishing she would stop playing music so often. *We're safe here.*

The second thing he noticed was that she was writing. Sitting at the mahogany dinner table in the living room, her hand maneuvering the pencil, its edge curving deep grooves into paper. The sound of upticks and tight curves, hyphens and crosses, competed with the music. He brushed her cheek and squeezed her shoulders to get her attention, but a frown appeared on her face.

He always thought she had a face that belonged to a painting from centuries ago, severity and serenity coexisting without struggle. The weight she kept losing threatened to upset that balance.

She held a finger up without looking. Her writing picked up pace, until a stroke broke the pencil's tip. Sighing, she leaned back, went over the lines she had just written, scanning them with her index finger.

For a few minutes, she stood still, save for her deep slow breathing. Shaking her head, she turned the pages face down on the table. Then, as an afterthought, she pulled them to herself. He tried to snatch one and she pushed his hand aside. Irritation flared across her face.

She tore a corner of paper and scribbled on it, then held it out for him. When he hesitated, she shoved it into his palm.

picking up book again

He crumpled it and hid it into his pocket, looking behind at the windows.

No point picking an argument, he thought as he felt his cheeks flare with irritation. Not in her condition. The card was in his back pocket inside his wallet, always had been just in case. He pulled the wallet out now, picked the card out from the first slot and tossed it on the table. It sported his picture, a bar code, and the single blue point that marked his place on the Party's hierarchy. High enough to access subsidies. Not high enough for language privileges.

He tap-tap-tapped at it, then pointed at the loose pages. *You can't do that*, he thought. *Don't you know what country you live in? If anyone catches you writing, this card won't save us. We're not the privileged few.*

She ignored the card. Massaged her lower legs with a wince and then stood, went to the stereo and turned the volume up while glowering at him, drowning out the noise from the dead channel on the TV. As if in response, the violins and the cellos reached a crescendo, rattling the windows in their frames. The farmer rushed to the stereo and turned the volume down again, his nostrils flaring. Why was she taunting him? What was going through her head?

Her eyes turned a blacker black, a kind he had seen at the beginning of a thousand arguments, and it was like he could read her mind. *I believe we understand each other*, she'd say.

I'm not allowed to write, yes. I'm also not allowed to listen to music, but here I am running my little rebellion, what's the difference? His own eyes hardened in response. He slammed his hand against the wall next to the stereo, making the music skip.

They stared each other down for long moments, neither one of them breaking their gaze, neither one moving. Without words, the fight went on and on.

It was she who relented. Rolled her eyes and let out a long sigh. She turned the volume down, but not off. She brought the tips of three fingers together, thumb, index and middle, and motioned them towards her open mouth. *Dinner?*

He nodded.

She cleared the table of her notes, the loose pages and her coffee mug, and motioned him upstairs with her hand. He obliged. Upstairs, in the bathroom, he half-filled a bucket with water and soap and scrubbed his grime-covered body.

She is writing again, he thought, staring at the grit flowing along the bathtub's yellowing porcelain. *What's gotten into her? Why is she looking for trouble?* He snorted, splashing water. *Trouble. That word isn't strong enough.*

He arrived in the kitchen dressed in plain jeans and an undyed wool shirt. His fingers picked at the seams of his clothes. The radio was still on.

On the table now sat a large salad of corn, amaranth greens, and okras, some bread with seeds in it, and little else. Most of it came from the fields or their vegetable garden. They hadn't had a single possum or vole attacking the roots in two weeks and he knew that troubled her. It seemed that the rationing would go on forever. Had already gone on for twice as long as last time. The food went to the troops fighting up North, they were told. No sacrifice was big enough for the country's Unity. No sacrifice was big enough in the fight against Division.

Her mind seemed far away. A furrowed forehead, her hands tense. She turned to him and faked a smile, then lowered her chin, her eyebrows forming question marks. *What news*, they asked. He sneered and shook his head. *Same news as every day.* On his chagrined mouth, one could read dying saplings, a murderous heat, and a fading crop. Some men's faces take on a sardonic quality as they reach middle age, a consequence of bad luck and no small amount of self-pity. This quality had become more prevalent in him after every dust storm and drought, after every crop failure.

She stroked his graying hair and cocked her head sideways. There were times when a side glance could convey more meaning than an hour of talking. Spending enough time with a person would do that. They had reached that point long before the law had forced them to go silent.

A change passed through her eyes and her face darkened. Her hand stopped mid-stroke and she looked away with fear. She doubled over, her arms over her guts, wincing. Her face reddened. His own body responded by instinct. He eased her onto the wooden floor and went for her purse on her workstation. In one rough move, he upended it and emptied its contents, sending most of them to the floor. Keys, tissues, wallet… He turned back to her and shook his hands with the palms up. *Where? Where is it?* Shallow breaths came out of her now, her eyes were shut. She tucked her knees in and rested her forehead against the floor. *Looks like she's praying the pain away*, he thought as her tears stained the wood.

The worth of a minute depends on how much one stands to lose in it. In that one minute, he felt he'd lose her. In that one minute and all the other minutes like it.

He helped her sit and held her purse up. *Where are your pills?* She just flicked her fingers. *Gone,* they said. *Gone? Gone where?* She continued flicking her fingers. Her other hand scratched her legs and he reckoned he could see red pinpricks coming through. He didn't press the matter. He rested a hand on her belly, but she pushed it away.

It took several minutes before he let her stand. She was the one who squeezed his shoulder this time. *I'm fine,* her touch said as she grimaced. *Really.*

She motioned for him to take a seat at the table that had been set for one, and pointed to the porch to signal that she was moving there. He didn't react. She repeated the motion again with a roll of the eyes that seemed to him to be more tired than impatient. He nodded with some hesitation and sat at the table as she had asked. With his right hand, he pulled out the chair next to his and raised his eyebrows. *Will you sit with me?*

A bittersweet smile formed on her face and she shook her head. He watched her hobble outside with her arms wrapped around her body, take her seat on the porch and stare out at fields painted red by the last of the sun's rays. Underneath her shirt, he could make the outline of her shoulder bones.

Leftover anxiety formed a knot in his throat and he didn't have it in him to start eating. He did anyway. The greens pricked his tongue and made him purse his lips, but he continued chewing without breaking rhythm. The okras had just started becoming slimy to the touch, but they tasted better. At least they weren't bitter. The corn, he contemplated throwing away, caterpillars had gotten to it first. Instead, he cleared away the worst parts and sank his teeth into the cob, eating as fast as he could, trying to get it over with.

He didn't mind eating alone. He knew she liked to sit outside in the evenings when the heat and the dust became bearable with a tall glass of water and lemon. She added mint leaves when she could get them, which wasn't often. Once the cramps had started, her appetite had disappeared. No point in her sitting around watching him chew.

He used to give her at least an hour alone before joining her. He believed it was necessary for a good marriage to have a date with your own thoughts, spend some time in your own head before coming up for air again. Nowadays, though, that was all most people could do. Kids… They were now brought up in a world that was ready for them, a world where speech and writing were already agents of Division. His generation, though, had struggled. Oh, they had struggled.

And now that the end was near? How could he give her time alone when there was so little of it left?

He finished his meal and washed the dishes while stealing glances at her. She hadn't moved from her spot. At least her arms had slid down to her lap, resting, not clutching at her body. Before heading out to the porch, he paused and felt the cigarette pack in his pocket. Pulled it out, popped it open, and let the lighter slide out. The scrap of paper she had written her declaration on lit up and turned to ashes in the sink.

When he joined her on the porch, stars were coming out. From the farm, they couldn't see the town of the twin hills, and its lights couldn't blot out the night sky. He took his seat next to her and held her hand as she gazed across the thinning fields. He drank her in, her body in tranquil repose, a sheen of sweat on her skin. Her chest rose with a deep steady rhythm and he could hear the suspiration coming out of it, so similar to the sound the fields made as they rippled under a light breeze, and wondered how long they had together before the monster in her guts took her away. How many more evenings? He tried to imagine her empty chair and failed.

Is this what it's about, he wondered. *Is it the cancer that's making her pull this act? Did something happen at the school that's bothering her? What does she mean she's picking up the book again?*

It troubled him that he couldn't remember when she had started it the first time.

The corn stalks swayed like metronomes. The breeze was there, but not enough to give respite from the heat. *Feels like a dust storm coming*, he thought and sighed. *So much for this year's crop. Maybe next year will be better.*

She flinched and looked at him with surprise, then nodded at his hands. He had been squeezing without realizing, a little too hard. He lifted both hands up and shrugged, giving her a little smile until she looked away. The urge welled up inside him to say something out loud, something profound, something caring and at the same time bitter. Instead, he looked away and stared out at the fields. Watched them ripple. He thought, *I need to let her know of the lobos.*

From the living room, the TV continued spewing static.

3.

I T WAS STILL dark outside when she awoke. Echoes of her nightmare chased after her. A wall of hands, hands belonging to faceless men, hands that stank of rust and of the rot underneath their cracked nails, hands grasping at her. Mindless. Rustled and swayed, with a sound like a swarm of insects. She had tried to scream, but couldn't. A hand over her mouth pinned her to the pillow. Terror squeezed at her heart and for a moment she thought her mind would shatter.

Shh, the farmer mouthed over her. In the darkness, she couldn't see him.

She bit down and tasted blood. The farmer grunted and clutched at his hand while she jumped out of bed, her feet thundering against the wooden floor, out of the bedroom and into the bathroom. The door slammed shut. The pipes in the walls strained with low-pressure water, and the house settled back into silence.

By the time she returned, with her arms wrapped around herself and tiptoeing with embarrassment, the sun was crowning over the horizon. Its rays illuminated the empty bed. The smell of rationed coffee wafted from the kitchen downstairs.

She climbed back into her side of the bed and stared at the wrinkles that mapped where he slept. Her fingertips traced and smoothed down the ridges and the creases. Lingered at the spots that soaked his sweat, and their humidity clung to her skin. On her side of the bed, there were spots of his blood.

White vinegar will remove them, she thought. *Or ammonia. Whichever I can get.* She reached for her pill bottle but there was nothing on the nightstand.

Outside, the tractor was gone. From behind the curtains, she took in the fields that rolled outside their home. The corn swayed underneath a cloudless sky, but there was no beauty in it.

THERE WAS ONCE an ancient pharaoh. A king so powerful he didn't think twice of destroying two lives to settle a bet. No story mentions who he made the bet with. No story mentions the names of the two slave babies he bought, nor of the mute shepherd who raised them. Was Egyptian the oldest language in the world? There was a way to find out. Raise two babies in silence. The language they'd use had to be the most ancient one. Had to be. Five years after placing the girl and the boy in the mute shepherd's care, the pharaoh visited them in their mountain lodge. The shepherd didn't recognize him but, looking at the golden jewelry and silk garments, understood who he was and dropped to his knees, his hands trembling. The children stared at him and blathered "bekos". Asking for bread in Phrygian was not the outcome the pharaoh had wanted, and he had the shepherd executed. Historians of the time comment that the great Pharaoh had probably misunderstood the inane garble of starving children for an actual word. Of the children's fate, there were no surviving records.

Many centuries later, another king. This one from Europe. He had an affinity for history, art, and science, but he was also deeply religious and often corresponded with the Pope. He once posed the following question. If a boy and a girl were to be raised in absolute silence, never hearing a human word, wouldn't they resort to using the language that God imparted unto Adam and Eve? Wouldn't two beings raised without language reinvent humanity's first words? It was only logical. The Pope questioned the morality of such an experiment, but the king had already made up his mind. A girl and a boy were locked in a monastery and the nuns tasked with raising them were ordered not to utter a single word around them. The king hoped their unpolluted minds would sprout Jewish, or maybe Greek or Sumerian. Instead, the children slapped their hands and their chests, blew air and grunted, but never used any language that could be identified. It is not known whether the Pope ever found out about the experiment's outcome.

Not long after, yet another king, Scottish, grew up with a passion for languages. He spoke Latin, like all nobility. He spoke French, which helped him communicate with his allies. He was also fluent in German, Italian, Flemish, and Spanish with all its different dialects. He loved literature and poetry, singing and writing hymns. He loved language so much that he wished to discover what would happen to children raised without one. Another girl, another boy. A rock in the ocean became their home. The two babies grew up and reached the age of seven before they died of causes that were of no interest to those recording the experiment. They communicated by imitating the waves bursting on the rocks surrounding the island and the calls of birds that nested there. By the time they died, the king had forgotten all about them.

The teacher looked out at her class. *What must it have felt like raising those children, raising those experiments*, she wondered, not for the first time. *Having them stare at you in silence every day, waiting for you to read their minds. I'm hungry. I'm cold. I'm in pain.*

I am a shepherd, she thought. *And I am a nun, and I am an alchemist too on a rock in the sea with nothing but waves and the birds to talk to. Under orders from kings in faraway castles to create a quiet world for these children.*

She counted heads, five of them. All sitting in a tight group in the middle of a classroom made for twenty. The twins were missing again. She knew they were helping their father coax wheat out of barren fields, but she would make them repeat the year anyway if they kept skipping classes. Everyone else was there. The two girls wore dresses sporting the same pattern of white flowers on a powder blue field, the pattern that sacks of flour came in. From the middle of the group, the boy with the shaved head stared at her, waiting for the class to begin.

Her hand moved over her belly, feeling the constant white noise of the monster gnawing at her guts, while her heart skipped at the memory of the boy staring from the street. And for all the turmoil he caused her, the boy sat there with boredom on his face. Annoyance, even. *Why are you just standing there*, his face seemed to be saying. Which was very close to, *why are you sitting behind the wheel of a car getting all upset? We're just taking care of a talker, is all. Why won't you join us?*

She sighed. Counted backwards from ten, feeling the

tension leave her body. The boy continued staring and scratched the star-shaped scar on his throat. She clicked a button on the presentation controller. On the glass screen behind her, black and white images of Pavlov next to a dog flickered.

Pavlov rang a bell. Pavlov brought out food. The dog salivated.

Pavlov rang a bell. Pavlov brought out food. The dog salivated.

Pavlov rang a bell. Pavlov brought out food. The dog salivated.

Pavlov rang a bell. The dog salivated.

Pavlov smiled.

Light from the screen flashed across the boy with the shaved head, his face popping into and out of darkness. She tried to picture him as part of the mob, brutalizing the thin man with the cracked glasses, but couldn't. Once he got swallowed up by the crowd, he looked the same as all the other faces and they all looked like him. Old, young, men, women. Children. It didn't matter. A mob is the perfect democracy.

The boy had done well. Acted as expected when someone talked in public, which was to shut their ears and seek the nearest adult, then attack the talker. Any of the children in her class would have done the same, she knew, because they held drills every month. Some of them, she led herself.

One of the girls yawned and scratched her identical throat scar, picking at the raised pink flesh. The children were more similar to each other than what their sweat-stained clothes, homemade haircuts, and famished frames suggested. Did they realize they all did that? With her free hand, the teacher rubbed her own throat, unburdened by the star-shaped scar that was so similar to the Unity painted on the classroom wall, three crossed arrows wrapped in a wreath.

Behind the church in town, up on one of the two hills, there was a tombstone in her husband's family lot that was smaller than the rest. Other than its size, it was unremarkable. It had no inscription, but, had it been allowed one, it'd have stated that her boy had lived for fifteen minutes. That was the amount of time it had taken the obstetrician to fail the cordectomy.

Every day, she had to watch the children in her class pick and scratch at their scars. Every day.

She often worried that the Party would change its stance on adult cordectomy. On an intellectual level, she understood the arguments against it and recited them like a litany. Terrible logistics, prohibitive costs, high risk when performed on grown-ups. With children, it was just another item on a midwife's list. Clear the air pathways, snip the umbilical, remove the vocal cords. Present the silent baby to the mother.

The children were lucky to get rid of that troublesome bit of flesh before they could form memories of using it. It wasn't worse than circumcision. Becoming unburdened of speech… The rest of the population would have to continue abiding by the law using power of will. Unless a car accident broke something inside them and pushed them over the edge.

The children paid attention for five minutes before their gaze started drifting off outside the windows. She knew this would happen. Were their heads filled with grunts that somehow made sense to them, this grunt meaning pain and that grunt meaning approval and that grunt meaning I don't care for this class? The first time, she cleared her throat. The second time, she tapped her desk with a pencil. The third time, she slammed her hand down on the desk and stared at them with a menacing look. In the absence of language, the promise of violence was the shortest path to discipline. That's how the Sheriff did it with younger people that couldn't understand her. And, although the teacher hated treating the children like animals, it was good enough for her class.

Diagrams and pictures followed each other. Behind her, Lenin shook Pavlov's hand. The boy with the shaved head fumbled about, then started paying attention again when a diagram of a dog appeared on the screen. She had seen him and his brothers run after strays during recess. Some days throwing stones at them. Other days giving them their lunches. There was a spark in his eyes as something connected. Images making sense, linking cause and effect together, creating new knowledge. The dogs, the bells… Had the blood on his hands bothered him? Had it ever? He had no way of knowing this hadn't always been normal. A time when speaking could be recorded on paper with symbols. That was normal, too. If she could somehow tell him those things, the boy would be horrified. None of them even knew what writing was. How could they? All books had been taken a long time ago. All street signs, every shop name. Gone.

The sudden bell shocked her. Over a flurry of packing bags and shifting desks, she lifted the textless textbook and pointed to the chapter marked with '7', the one explaining the mechanism behind reflexes, all of it in full spread diagrams tolerated for the sake of education. The boy avoided her gaze as he walked out.

In the hallway, he joined his two brothers, each a taller copy of him. They patted him on the shoulder and his shaved head and he playfully punched the older one's chest. Then, he turned and pointed at her. The brothers seemed to understand within their own sort of privacy. Concern flashed on their faces and then suspicion as they urged him away. She waved, but they turned their backs on her and disappeared around the corner.

She saw this every day, this non-language. Like wave and bird noises. She was certain the children weren't even aware they were doing it. Nor were they aware of the widening gap between them and those who still remembered how to speak.

She returned to the classroom and restarted the presentation. She got to the end of it. Then she started it again, judging her work. Rudimentary. Deficient. Unsatisfying. She sighed and turned the screen off. Almost twelve years of teaching in this manner… What she did, what all teachers had to do, was to convey concepts without a word. Couldn't even use simple symbols. To the law, there was no difference, and heaven forbid if one of her pupils was caught replicating the diagrams she used and someone thought they were drawing.

She remembered an old joke from a colleague, one of the last jokes she had ever heard. It hadn't seemed funny to her because it was in reference to getting drunk. *If no one talks about yesterday, did it really happen?* How about ideas and concepts? And what of her tools? Words were instruments of Division, the Party said, meant to spread falsehoods and lies. Silence was the language of Unity.

A knock came from the door and the math teacher' smiled at her, smelling of strong sandalwood perfume, as he waved with one hand. With the other, he held the math textbook close to his chest. His smile faded when she didn't reciprocate. She didn't even look at him. She only stared at his textbook, with its numbers and its circles and lines that were unaffected by the law. Mathematics was considered an amoral truth, separated from the intentions of the men who used it. Words shaped the world, but numbers only described it. Numbers couldn't threaten Unity, couldn't spread Division. They were a bureaucrat's tools and they ran industry, allowed the economy to flow. On the calendar, Tuesday had become 2 and July had become 7, and in the back of her mind she suspected numbers were the one compromise the Party had to make to keep the country going.

Injustice, she thought. *No wonder he's always so happy.* By the time she realized she was being rude, he was gone and she was feeling increasingly aware of how others must have been seeing her all day. Unfocused. *I'll make it up to him next time I see him*, she thought.

The car park was empty save for her own corroded bucket on wheels. She crossed it in quick steps, a handkerchief over her mouth against the dust. Despite the heat, she kept the windows rolled up, turning the car into a furnace on her way to town. She had at least fifteen minutes at a decent speed before she got there. It wasn't unusual to not see another vehicle until Main Street. Still, she preferred not taking chances when she turned on the radio.

She scanned the spectrum for a pirate station playing music. She yearned for the timbre of violins or cellos, for guitars or drums, for anything coming out of the speakers. But what was music, if not a conversation between the instrument and the heart, and therefore condemnable?

God, just plain talking would have been fine. She wished for a brave soul to speak stream of consciousness into the microphone of a self-made radio console, for someone to risk it all for an opportunity to bare their souls to strangers who couldn't answer back. It was a foolish thought, but she needed to hear someone reaching out, someone not afraid. Someone alive.

She wished to hear him, most of all. His voice had always felt familiar, yet she couldn't place him. How many people lived in the town of the twin hills these days? She must have met them all at one point or another. He only spoke for five minutes every Monday at roughly the same time. He spoke about everything and nothing, about the heat, crickets, the decreasing amount of sugar in rations, how rare it was to see a plane in the sky these days.

He sometimes talked about other countries. Their neighbors. How 'bout them, he'd say. How 'bout them other places, beyond our borders, the ones we don't interact wit' no more. Where was they when the silence came about? Did they ever reckon it mightta been a good idea to lend us a hand, like good neighbors oughtta, or did they decide to jes close their eyes and ears? Pretend it was someone else's problem? Bet they was glad to look the other way.

It wasn't much. But at least he was there for her. Usually. He'd miss a week here and there, but she hadn't heard his voice in months.

In the end, she grew tired of the static and turned off the radio. Only the sound of the engine accompanied her thoughts, painting them with its monotony.

She drove along endless fields of desiccated corn. In one of them, she saw kids driving a pickup truck, the horn going off without stop, leaving a trail of vaporized plants behind them. They were hanging through the windows and their mouths were open in a semblance of laughter. Kids got their amusement where they could, and beatings from the Sheriff be damned.

When that happened to their own fields, her husband would punch the walls and kick chairs until he exhausted himself. Then, he'd sink into the couch, catatonic for hours before shuffling into bed at dawn. She thought it made no difference. No one was losing a fortune on dying corn. She only felt sorry for his hands and the blood she had to clean off the walls. Still, it had been months since any of his outbursts. He'd gotten mellower with age. *He's gotten mellower after the diagnosis*, she corrected herself. Like those quiet moments without pain, the world felt odd without his moods.

The road snaked on, more potholes than asphalt, crumbling away at the edges. It took her past small farmhouses and the old industrial mill with its single stack, up and down sharp declivities. She reached the top of one of the twin hills, where the posts that used to hold the sign with the town's name rusted. The town itself lay nestled in the valley below. She slowed down as she passed the first buildings. Single-floor houses whose facades were smudged with dust and age, where plastic bags and broken bottles littered their yards. As she rolled by, a girl no more than five wearing only grass-stained briefs watched her with insolent indifference from the side of the street, picking her nose.

Had the town name sign still been around, it would have stated that around two thousand souls lived there. She didn't know how many lived there now, though they seemed fewer and fewer every year.

The car turned into an empty Main Street, past the large wordless posters that advertised the country fair for Unity Day. As she drove along the road, she lifted her eyes to where the loud neon hardware store sign used to be. Even after twelve years, the elements hadn't erased its rectangular footprint that remained a shade lighter than the surrounding wall. None of the signs on Main Street had been replaced once words had been taken away. They had just been removed. One had to know their way around town, but, after having lived here for fifteen years, the teacher thought of herself as a local. Once the travel ban had been enforced, she figured she didn't have much of a choice on the matter.

She parked and killed the engine. Looked out at the road that seemed to vibrate under the sun, the air shimmering with the heat, to the distant handful of people shuffling their feet without purpose. She had driven to the town for a reason, but now that she was there, her hands couldn't let go of the steering wheel.

She couldn't shake the sight of the thin man with the cracked glasses.

A bell rung over the pharmacy door as she pushed it open. The smell of sterility and antiseptic hit her nose. Less obvious, but still distracting, was how surfaces felt as she trailed her fingers along them. A thin layer of resin that stuck to the fingers. On the wall, Unity stared down at her.

She stood in line behind a woman with a wracking cough. Silence brought a certain madness to the face after a few years. They all had it. Her husband had it at times and, she suspected, she had it too. It hollowed out the cheeks and thinned out the mouths and gave people an air about them as if they were fighting a million urges, making them jittery and chewing their lips raw. Except for the children, who had never known a different world.

The woman in front had that permanent worn out look about her, greasy hair swaying as she shuffled and, through the holes in the sleeves of her sand-colored cardigan, sores and green-blue veins showed.

Behind the counter stood a man a good head taller than most, with a hewn face and an unkempt chevron mustache decorating it. He disappeared for minutes at a time and re-emerged with bottles of this or boxes of that. He appeared stiff-jointed and rigid, though there was an economy in how he moved. Barely visible behind his collar, he had the same star-shaped scar on his throat as her students. Some of the townsfolk had tried to spare themselves the burden of speech, showing up at hospitals asking for a cordectomy. But mutilation required a different kind of courage than lynching a lone man.

On the counter sat a catalog containing a few dozen yellowed pages. When the teacher's turn came, the pharmacist motioned for her to approach. She opened the catalog and went straight to page eight, where the painkillers were. She pointed to the picture of an orange bottle. Its label did not have the drug's name printed on it. Instead, a constellation of atoms showed the bottle's content. She tapped at the picture again and gave the pharmacist the prescription. A single barcode was printed across its length. The pharmacist examined the stamp, the date, the numbers that did not hold any significance to her, but which told him how she was dying. Holding the piece of paper close to his face, he moved down the row of shelves that stood behind him.

More people shuffled in, sun-blistered, dazed. She exchanged glances with them and tried to recall if she had seen them at the driver's lynching.

The pharmacist tapped on the counter to get her attention. Unsmiling, the piece of paper with the barcode in one hand, he pointed at the door. *What's wrong, why,* the teacher asked by lifting her hands palm up. She pointed at the catalog again. The pharmacist shook his head and motioned at the door with a curt wave of his stiff fingers, then motioned for the next person in line.

Breathe, the teacher recited. *Breathe. This is just a misunderstanding that I know how to set straight. Breathe.* She stuffed her hand down her handbag, bringing out a pill bottle identical to the one in the picture, though this one was empty, fished out of the trash. The label was peeling at the corners, but the chemical compound that kept the pain in her guts in check and stopped her from shitting blood was clear. She held it aloft for the pharmacist to see and shook it with frantic eyes. *What's wrong, why?*

The pharmacist looked around him as if for an answer, twitching his nose and frowning. He pointed at a date underneath the barcode, a couple of months in the future. *But I need it now,* the teacher thought.

She felt the hand on her shoulder asking if she was alright. *No, I'm not,* she wanted to answer. *I'm not alright. How can I be alright?* She snatched the prescription out of the pharmacist's hand and ran out of the door.

Outside, she walked with her head down, coughing from the dust and feeling the same desperation creeping up on her as a few months earlier, when a doctor had pointed at her belly with an apologetic look on his face.

The cardiganed woman was standing on the corner with her neck craned up, her eyes narrowed, a sun-worshiping statue. The teacher approached her and smelled the sweat soaked up by her clothes. She made to continue down the street, then changed her mind. That way was the Sheriff's office. She didn't want to come across that woman, not in this state. She took a right turn instead, down the road the cardiganed woman was facing, down towards the Town Hall.

There, swaying from the traffic light, was the driver's body. A slipknot had been pulled tight around his torso. The body did not resemble anything that could have once been a human being, its proportions violently altered. It had ceased being a person and had become a thing.

A twinge in her guts made her double over. The teacher held her breath and wondered how many days she was away from writing the final word. She felt suspended over a hole in the ground whose bottom she could not see, floating and wondering when she'd plunge straight into its maw. Details of the world washed away in waves. The maw widened.

She lowered herself to the sidewalk and hung her head between her knees, focusing on breathing. The cardiganed woman coughed and the cadaver creaked as it swayed.

The radio remained silent on the drive home.

SHE SCOWLED AT the manuscript. The page sitting on the mahogany table in front of her had very little text left that was not crossed out. The lines ploughed into the paper, almost tearing through it and continuing into the wood below. Broken graphite littered the table, ground into smudges beneath her elbows. The TV hissed from the corner of the living room with dead channel noise.

She wrote

They

They ~~hushed~~

They hushed her

then crossed it out.

She leaned backwards, crossed her arms and tapped the

pencil against her shoulder, then hunched over the page again.

They hushed her
They hushed her existins.
Sole
Her soul

She scrunched her face. Rather than crossing off the last sentences, she ripped the page off the notepad, let it float to the floor, and held her head between her hands.

After the car crash, she had felt the words form inside her brain, piling up. But they wouldn't come out. She begged them. Dropped to her knees for them. Chased them, flirted with them, bit them, gave herself to them, promised them her soul if only they helped her out and laid themselves into neat sentences that spoke truths. Just the truths. But they refused her. Slipped right past her. Like the silver-skinned fish in the ocean off her family's home back west that bit at her as she swam.

She looked at the growing pile of discarded pages and felt the words burn inside her.

The pencil hovered a few inches from the paper and there it remained until she dropped it in an act of surrender. It rolled away, fell off the table, hit the floor, and ended deep behind the cupboard with the good china.

With her eyes closed, she thought, *God, I need to write this or I'll go insane. The words, they'll kill me if I don't let them out. They poison me.*

Pain twisted her insides.

She only opened her eyes when the driver's face appeared behind her eyelids again. She wanted to yell at him, *leave me alone. Stop torturing me.* But the driver didn't answer. Only opened his mouth with an airless aaaaaa. She crawled onto the floor and retrieved the pencil. Couldn't waste a good pencil. Not when the school kept an eye on how many she used for fear that she'd hoard them.

It hurt her to admit it, but the Party's policies had worked better than she had thought. All those years without uttering a word. Without writing a word. Her ability to put thoughts onto paper had once been passable. Now, it had atrophied and shriveled and made her incapable of expressing her frustration at the world.

That man with the glasses died because he had been frustrated for years. How long before she exploded too? Before she stood in the middle of the town unable to hold her tongue anymore, screaming accusations until they tore her apart? Things that needed saying had a way of forcing their way out. Didn't matter who wanted them hushed. She recalled his words. *You're letting them get away with it.* He had addressed it at no one, but she felt it was meant for her alone.

She slammed her pencil against the table. She didn't like feeling passive. It insulted her.

The story lay on the table, unfinished. "Every fiction is a lie that hides a bigger truth". That's what she had told herself when she'd started it all those years ago. She had wanted to say something about the silence of her world, to make a statement. To point her finger. Then, what? She had never figured that part out. There was, perhaps, a hope—a heroic vision—of printing copies of her book and reaching out to others. Just like the man on the radio reached out to her. She imagined those people reading and recognizing a bit of themselves in her words and feeling a bit lighter knowing they were not alone.

That had been a long time ago.

She was on the verge of abandoning all hope of a productive evening, when the TV called out to her. Static died, giving way to long beats of silence. She hadn't noticed the sudden emptiness, or that the dead-channel static on the screen had been replaced by black. When the whistling sound came from the set, it made her skin crawl. It followed the first few notes of the party anthem, all minor dissonant keys full of edges. She approached the screen, light-headed and weary, and she thought of Pavlov's dog salivating at the sound of bells. She raised the volume and the Party anthem's opening bars filled the house. The image cleared, giving way to an intertitle with Unity in its background.

PARENTAL ADVISORY: SPOKEN CONTENT
REMOVE ALL CHILDREN FROM THE ROOM

Then, a switch to a silhouette standing in a studio.

First, the outline of the Mouth of the Party appeared. He was recognizable despite static obscuring his features, the familiar bald head and the backswept ears. The picture continued clearing and the round glasses and knowing half-smile appeared. As always, he was dressed in unassuming black clothes with a simple pin depicting the three crossed arrows wrapped in a wreath. A red ruby shone at the Unity's center. A small, unassuming thing that placed him in a different world to hers, the world of the few who could still talk, could still write without fear. Fear. That's what that red ruby was. Freedom from the fear of opening your mouth.

Around him, the studio lacked any decoration. The Mouth stood behind a podium with a single microphone that could pick up the shuffling of paper, the buzz of studio lights, and a large audience waiting in silence off-screen. A video feed of the capital's skyline was projected onto the wall behind him. The camera zoomed in.

Then, the Mouth began to talk.

"My dearest citizens. We have great news to share with you. There's been tremendous progress in the war effort in the North. Your generals commanding your armies have scored a major victory against the aggressor, whose name does not deserve to be uttered. Your armies have secured areas stolen from you at the end of last year and have exacted revenge for several atrocities carried out against you in the years since this defensive war was forced upon you. The enemy has brought war to your doorstep and they will not stop there. As of now, you have mobilized an additional three brigades that are on their way to the front. We call on every responsible citizen to continue working hard in the fields and the factories to feed and clothe your soldiers, the only line of defense between you and the aggressor."

As the Mouth talked, a window appeared over his right shoulder with shaky images of battle. Helicopters unloaded soldiers who grinned at the camera. Night skies lit up with tracer rounds. A Unity flag waved atop a bombed-out shell of a building. Graphics showed arrows moving North across a map without town names.

"Your soldiers are doing their job of protecting you from external enemies. Your job is to protect them from our internal enemies. Be mindful of provocateurs, infiltrators, and fifth-columnists. They seek to sow Division with words and pollute your Unity. Do not allow them. You guard the home front. It is the duty of every citizen to take drastic action. Neutralize those who would seek to divide your society, to splinter it as before with rhetoric and demagogy. Zero tolerance. Every word that comes out of their mouths puts you in danger. Action must be immediate and absolute."

Cartoons of people whispering to each other, their angular features and crouched forms marking them as villains. The image switched. The villains were now faced by a crowd of square-jawed citizens with violent intentions. The teacher felt nauseated. *The man with the glasses had not been an insurgent*, she thought.

The Mouth paused and dipped his chin. The fierce intelligence burning in his eyes reached through the screen and into the living room. When he spoke again, his words came out coated in honey, with the unhurried delivery of addressing a lifelong friend.

"The day when I am no longer needed is close. I can already see that fine day when the general public will no longer live in fear of Division through language. This country's transformation over the past twelve years has been nothing short of remarkable and it comes down to your personal accountability. You, my dearest citizens, you have trusted the Party to speak for you. You have delivered the voices of the next generation to the Party. A necessary sacrifice, not to be taken lightly."

The teacher's hand moved to her throat of its own accord. *A couple more decades and there won't be anyone able to talk. There will only be those with scars on their throats and those who can no longer remember what words were.*

"This sacrifice will one joyful day release me from my duties. I will miss serving you, but will be content in the knowledge that, all across this great nation, there will only be one voice, that of Unity. Protect it, at all costs. We are One Nation, we speak with One Voice. Good night."

The screen faded and static came back into view. The teacher had to lower the volume again. There was no power button. No mute button, either. Her husband would be back from the fields in a while. She walked back to the mahogany table and her step was a little firmer than before. Instead of avoiding him, she brought the thin man with the broken glasses back into focus. Forced her mind's eye to take in every detail. The defeat in him. His nullification. One hand went over her belly. She took her seat, pulled out a fresh page and started putting words to it. Outside, the corn rustled as the wind picked up.

4.

S HE WASN'T ON the porch when the farmer got home. As the first stars appeared in the sky, he had expected the house lights to shine in the distance. It was only when he drove closer that he noticed the living room bathed in the TV screen's blue light. He maneuvered the tractor onto a patch of dirt by the porch and killed the engine. Through the window, he could see her sitting at the dining table, a small desk light next to her and her face lined with concentration. At least the stereo was turned off.

It took more than an hour to hose down the filth from the trailer. All the horse blood and the bits left by the carcass which was now buried by the stream. It had been a hard decision getting rid of all that meat, but the maggots had gotten to it so fast.

At the door, he heard the sound of paper being crumpled and he figured she had been absorbed by her story. God bless her, the little he had read over her shoulder didn't make a lick of sense to him, rumbling on and on without anything happening, just people talking for pages about nothing, as if they spouted the first thing that came into their heads. He had never read so much nothing written so well.

He removed his work boots, put on his sandals and entered the house. Stashed the shotgun above the cupboard with the good china. There she was. Hair in a tight ponytail, attacking the pages with her pencil. Tendons ridged in her writing hand, her eyebrows had converged into a frown. She looked like she was trying to scare the letters to do her bidding.

He flipped a couple of switches on, filling the house with light, which made her flinch. Still, she didn't lift her gaze. He waved to catch her attention, but she ignored him. Puzzled now, he approached her and put a hand on her arm. She pushed it away and he felt her hands shaking. She let out a long breath, grabbed the paper and vanished into the spare room, while he, clueless and flushed, remained still and staring in the direction where she disappeared, scratching his head.

Now what, he thought. *What did I do now?*

Washing just gave him more time to stew. The sounds of paper being shuffled and crumbled and the snapped tips of pencils didn't stop when he returned. There was something of the tempest in her posture lately, a sense of unrest at odds with her cheekbones becoming more hollowed every day, and her skin that grew thinner.

It was all causing him a headache. Now, it was he who frowned. He rummaged through the refrigerator, not really seeing, letting his hands do the guiding and selecting.

There was not much to choose from. As he chewed on yesterday's leftovers, he felt like they had just had an argument.

He would remember the exact words that had ended the last one, their last real argument, until the end of his days. He had picked them for their barbs and their thorns. It wasn't out of spite, but he had been getting tired and wanted to put an end to the fight, or at least that's how he had justified it to himself later. He had thought his retort was clever and witty, despite having nothing to do with their quarrel. That had been good enough, because his only goal had been to win. Still, his words had lacerated his throat as he spewed them out. He had regretted them the moment it had become too late to reel them back in. So much more vitriol than he had intended. In a way, he had won. But it hadn't felt like it.

The fight had been about her damn book. And now, years later, it bothered him that here they were again. He just couldn't see the point of picking it up again. They had a few months left together, if they were lucky. By winter, she'd be gone.

He scratched his scalp until the skin broke. Everything incensed him. His dinner, her writing, the stench of dead horse under his fingernails that he couldn't get rid of. He stomped to the TV set, turning the volume as low as it would go, which wasn't enough to kill the noise. The power cord was welded into the socket, still he tried to pull it out. First with one hand, then both, grimacing. He braced against the wall and tugged, stopping only when he felt his back pop. Pain shot up his spine and he clamped his mouth shut by instinct, stifling a scream.

He dropped the cable. Anger drained away as fast as it had taken over. He rested one hand on his knee and another on his lower back, massaging the part where it hurt. *Stoic, my ass*, he thought and shuffled back to the chair where he collapsed.

There he stayed, losing track of time and listening to the ocean of silence between them. Silence, accentuated by cicadas and time ticking away and the blur of a TV set that couldn't be turned off.

The screaming startled him.

It drifted again through the open kitchen window, over the porch and the vegetable garden, through the fields. Protest and panic. The teacher hesitated on her way out of the spare room, as if hypnotized, her hands rubbing each other. She slouched and looked at him, raising her eyebrows. He felt the muscles around his belly clench. It seemed he weighed a ton when he stood, and his back protested.

He retrieved a flashlight and the shotgun from above the cupboard, and stepped out onto the porch. The screaming continued. "Move" it begged. "Go". The farmer held his breath as he crossed the threshold into the fields, diving into the sea of corn and crushing stalks beneath his sandals. He had to stifle the voice before it brought the authorities here. To their house. He wouldn't let them take her away. He wouldn't let her die away from their home.

Who could be foolish enough to shout out here in the open? What if the neighbor was about, looking for his dead horse? What if he'd heard the voices coming from their farm? The neighbor would find that hateful bitch, the Sheriff, and give her the opportunity she had been looking for all these years to destroy their lives. The Party membership would count for nothing. No bribe would convince the Sheriff to look the other way. Not her. Not with the amount of hate she had for him.

There were two voices, a male and a female. She urged him to run faster. He hurled curses in a foreign language. How far were they? He could hear stalks breaking.

There was something else in the fields with them. Dozens of feet moving in the same direction. His skin crawled, imagining a pack of lobos. He turned and waved the shotgun around him in a wide arc. Nothing but corn, corn everywhere. Out in the distance, the voices moved away.

He stopped and willed his heart to calm down. The voices came from a different direction now. Off to his right. Could it be he had passed them without realizing? He couldn't see much other than his house's roof behind him. Only the stalks right up to his face illuminated by the flashlight. Had his fear made him lose track of both time and space? Above, the stars glinted like shattered glass. The farmer turned to the right and continued, his feet more cautious this time.

✕

hey easy now

                                                  please don't hurt us

hey no

sirs we don't want any trouble please

 don't point those guns at us

  please we're just moving through

                                      what do you want from us

 if you could just let us go

we're not hurting anyone

                         take it it's just food just take it let us go

please listen don't point that

                                            no

                                leave him alone

let go

let her go she hasn't done anything

  you got me let her go

    come on

    get your hands o

                                         no

                                      stop

                                    christ

                                       no

                                    stop

                    for pity's sake, say something

                                    no

                                    please

                                    please

                                    stop it

stop it

you fucking animals

stop it you're killing him

what the fuck do you want from us

stop

baby no

no

baby

baby?

look at me

look at me

baby?

I lo

✕

FROM THE OPEN living room window, the teacher listened to the screams. A man and a woman begging and pleading and denying, all Please and Nonono. And then came the shotgun blast. In the darkness, the flash reached her first, with the sound barking right after it, making her jump and clutch at the front of her shirt.

Then, a wail. An endless open-mouthed wail that made her skin crawl. A mind coming loose.

When the second flash reached her, she counted the heartbeats to the blast, like she used to during thunderstorms.

Silence rushed back in again and she knew the murder was over. She creaked the back door open and crept outside. Took a deep breath and stood on the porch with the fields in front of her rippling.

Corn stalks swayed, metronomes keeping time to a dirge. The porch lights painted them yellow, the landscape stirring as it breathed. In the distance, one, then two, then three beams pierced the vegetation. One of them scanned from left to right, while the other two stood still. Then, in unison, they all pointed and moved in the same direction. Towards the farmhouse.

The stalks facing the house swelled and her husband broke through, panting. Eye contact was quick. *What happened*, she pleaded with her eyes. *What did you do to those people?*

He shook his head coughing into his elbow. *Wasn't me.* He motioned with the shotgun at the light beams that were coming closer. *Not me. Them.*

His shaking hands nudged her towards the door. *I'm not going anywhere*, she thought. *Whoever's coming here, I'm not going to hide, waiting for them to break the door down.* The more frantic his moves became, the more determined she was to stand her ground. She could see him losing his patience. Twisting his mouth and breathing heavily. He stared at her the way he did when he had enough of asking, with his just-do-as-I-say look. He put the shotgun down, brought his thumb and index finger together and pretended to write in his palm.

The manuscript.

Before realization set in, before she thought of rushing inside to hide her manuscript, the beams reached the edge of the field. Men and women strode out of it, about a dozen, old and young and even three teenage boys. They all carried knives, some borrowed from their kitchens, and guns for farm vermin.

She recognized a trucker who lived in that big house out of town whose kids and wife died when the dust started turning bad. There was another farmer she recognized who raised chickens and whom everyone envied, as well as a clerk from the town hall who had been born mute and who had adapted better than anyone. The pharmacist was towering above all, cradling a hunting rifle in the crook of his arm. The boy with the shaved head, he was there too. He and his two brothers carried shotguns too big for them. She knew them all. Law-abiding citizens.

The mob fanned out. From the corner of her eye, the teacher noticed the two older boys disappearing around the house. The pharmacist himself made a beeline for the short steps that led up the porch. The farmer stepped forward to block his way and pointed at the hunting rifle. In response, the pharmacist, thick chevron mustache covering his upper lip, did a stiff little bow and rested the rifle against the steps. Only then did the farmer move aside and let him pass.

The pharmacist nodded a greeting, which wasn't reciprocated. Regardless, he tapped his neck with two fingers, then held his hand palm-down about four feet from the ground. *We're looking for a talker, about yea high.* He left his hand hovering.

When the farmer lied, he always exaggerated his

movements. The teacher hoped the pharmacist didn't realize that. Her husband tried his best to act incredulous and shocked. *What kind of crazy talk is that*, he'd say if he could. *A talker? Here?*

A door opened and slammed shut again from deep inside the house. The farmer raised his chin up once with enough disrespect to make his point understood, then waved the pharmacist away. But the pharmacist didn't move. Instead, he nodded at the house and tried to move past the farmer. Somewhere in the living room, glass broke and footsteps echoed up the staircase.

Both the teacher and the farmer moved to block the pharmacist. As they did, the teacher noticed her husband's face, going from furious to shocked. A muzzle poked his back. The boy with the shaved head looked at her with uncertainty over his oversized shotgun, then his face hardened with a sense of right-doing.

The farmer let go of the pharmacist and turned to eye the boy, pressing into the shotgun with his chest and pushing him backwards. The pharmacist patted the boy's shoulder and lowered the barrel. He motioned with his other hand. *Calm down.* Then, after taking the farmer's shotgun away, he leaned back and waited.

The door to the back porch opened. The boy's older brothers came out and shrugged.

There was a long moment when the pharmacist eyed both of them and the teacher thought he was trying to read their faces, looking for a clue that they were lying. Disappointed, the pharmacist motioned for the mob to move. He grabbed his rifle on the way down and nodded at the teacher and the farmer, raising a hand again in apology. One by one, the mob disappeared back into the fields.

The two of them looked at each other for a long moment. Then, he frowned and she could tell he was mad, because he wouldn't look at her in the eyes. He only hung his head and shook it with his fists clenched.

When they went inside, she ran straight into the spare room. The manuscript was still there, as she had left it. She gathered the pages into her arms and ran downstairs into the basement to hide them, ignoring his stares. The boys must have come across it. Had it been one of the older members of the mob searching their house, one of those who still remembered what letters looked like instead of the two boys, it would have gone bad for them. She'd admit to it. But the mob wasn't looking for writing. They were looking for a child, and it made sense to send children inside. All they had found was incomprehensible squiggles.

When she came back upstairs, the farmer still avoided her. His neck skin was red where he had scratched himself raw. Not for the first time, she was glad they couldn't talk to each other. He'd have a point to make. But she wouldn't stop, no matter what he said. The silence just spared them the argument.

5.

I T WAS THE teacher who discovered the girl in the morning, sitting on the dusty concrete floor of their basement underneath an open window too high for her to go back through again. If the teacher were to come across the girl outside, sitting by the road, she'd keep her distance. There was a certain kind of savage sorrow in the youngster. The kind that demanded to be handled in solitude and which, when not respected, had a tendency of lashing out.

Two things stood out to the teacher. One, that this was the healthiest almost-adolescent she had seen in a while, healthier than any of the children in her class with their rail-thin legs and twig arms. The town's children all had a tendency towards being wiry, as sugar and chocolate and most other pleasurable things made it into the rations only on Christmas and Unity Day. This being a farming community by and large, they still got something in their bellies. It was never enough, though. This girl was taller than any of them, and sturdy.

The other thing, and the one that made her almost gasp with surprise, was the smooth skin on the girl's throat. A throat that screamed and yelled with a clear, loud voice.

"Let me go," she demanded and flung a pot lid at them. The farmer pushed the teacher behind him and raised his arms, asking the girl to stop, but his wife pulled them down and advanced. She reached back to her training. She wasn't going to let a child push her around, in or out of class. Her index finger speared the air and she stared the girl down. In response, the girl unscrewed a bottle of motor oil and mock-lunged forward.

"You want this, mutes? Huh? You want it?"

There was no imitated bravado or second-hand attitude in her. The teacher noticed her husband wince at the words, but he held himself together. She was grateful to him for that. Hurt tinged the girl's rage. Her trembling lip was full of sorrow that she fought to conceal, but she delivered every word with a sharp enunciation that drove them back.

A girl who talks, the teacher thought. *A girl that hasn't had her voice cut out, right here in our own basement.*

Underneath every question that surfaced in her mind bubbled another and another, layered with excitement and peril.

But a girl who talks…

Her ears hurt, just as her heart leaped. For the first time in days, she felt no pain in her guts reminding her of her mortality. There was no thin man, bloodied and torn. Only potential.

Folks had once tried to run away from the silence. Not in waves or in masses, but in trickles, one or two families at a time. Both she and the farmer had come across them once it got through that the Party was serious about having language gone. With the travel ban in place, the safest way North was on foot through the countryside. The last of them had been years ago. The subject of leaving was never brought up in their own home. She didn't need to ask his whys. Knowing that this land had been in his family for generations and that most of them had been buried behind the town church had been enough. Home was home.

"Let me go," the girl wailed and her voice broke. She lunged again.

Getting covered in oil wasn't the worst that could happen to them in this situation. Yet the teacher didn't want to have to get to that.

"Let me go," she said one last time and tears streamed down her face. Her shoulders lost their pride and she slouched, the fight gone out of her.

The teacher saw her opening. She swiped her index finger down, over and over, using the sternest face she could muster until the girl lowered the bottle. The girl wrapped her arms around herself and sank onto the mattress in the corner, then let out a frightened squeal. The farmer was moving with his handkerchief in his hands before his wife had realized what was happening. He grabbed the girl by the cuff, shoved her face down into the mattress and held her there with a knee between the shoulder blades.

"Get the hell off," the girl screamed. The teacher could see the struggle in his face, how he fought to shut out her words. His hands worked the ends of the handkerchief and he reached forward, missing her mouth and scraping her nose instead. Her screams turned from indignation to shrill yelping, discomfort turning into pain. Terrified that he had broken her ribs, the teacher waved her arms to get his attention. When that failed, she rushed him, putting her weight behind her shoulder and pushing him off of the girl.

What are you doing, his eyes demanded. She shook her head and rubbed the girl's back as the girl brought up her knees and curled over, crying out a litany of ow's.

He reached over once more, trying to tie the girl's mouth shut and the teacher put her own body between them. In their struggle, his elbow caught her on the chin. Only then, as she staggered, did he pause.

Dropping the handkerchief, he knelt by his wife, his eyes wide with shock. He touched her shoulders and his face took on an apologetic look.

Go, she waved him away and exhaled in slow measured breaths. *Just go.* He looked at her with confusion for a moment. A series of pops and cracks emanated from his back as he stood. He launched the handkerchief at the wall and stormed up the stairs and out of the basement.

His exit sucked the tension out of the room and only the girl's low whimpering broke the silence. Above them, heavy footsteps paced back and forth, then grew distant. After a while, the front door slammed shut.

The teacher tried to caress the girl, but stopped when she squirmed away. Instead, the teacher leaned back against the wall and studied her. The girl's hair was a tangled mess, more thorn bush than anything. Even drenched in tears, she was a badger, all snarls and defiance. A canine was missing from her thin mouth, while one of the front teeth was chipped.

She stood, making the girl retreat even further into the corner. The handkerchief lay on the basement floor where it had landed amongst dust bunnies and webs. *No need for muzzles,* she thought as she picked it up. *All it takes is a small procedure to cut a voice away. No worse than circumcision.* She touched her own throat.

The girl was eyeing the handkerchief. The teacher quickly tossed it into a box with junk and wiped her hands, exaggerating the moves. *That's that,* she thought. *Let's not bring this terrible thing out again.* She brought her thumb, index, and middle finger together and motioned them towards her mouth. Her other hand rubbed her belly in a circular motion.

"You won't let me out, will you?" the girl asked.

The teacher tried to smile.

SHE RUBBED HER dry, restless hands together. The hands of someone who had been a farmer's wife for longer than she cared to remember. Covering her mouth and nose against the dust, she went outside to the vegetable garden. The tractor wasn't there. She looked over the garden with her hands on her hips and sighed. There were a couple of wild onions, a half-rotten head of lettuce and wilted tomatoes. There were several roots underneath the soil, but she knew they weren't ready yet. She cut the wild onions, returned to the kitchen, and stared into the refrigerator.

There wasn't much she could put together, except for old grits. There were some slimy okra, two potatoes from that week's ration package, and a hard-boiled egg. She chopped the food and mixed it up in a bowl while the TV hissed static, and took it downstairs to the basement. The girl had fallen asleep. She left the plate on a stool close by and went back upstairs.

Her next stop was the master bedroom. She moved the heavy iron bed frame with some difficulty, putting her decreasing weight behind it. She had to find a better hiding place, she thought. All this moving was curving grooves into the wooden floors. She gave up halfway through and flattened herself underneath the bed instead. There were several books under the loose plank, but from this angle she couldn't see which one she needed, so she took all of them out.

She formed the books into three small stacks on the floor. She spent several moments reading the titles on the spines, allowing herself to become re-acquainted with them, her lips shaping the words. It took effort to concentrate on the letters and even more to understand them. In the end, she picked two of them and sat on the bed.

Bridging the Gap: A Practical Guide to Understanding and Teaching Challenging Students, 2nd Ed.

Introduction to Grief Counseling for Children, 5th Ed.

Both were hard cover copies, all broken edges and wrinkles. The pages crackled and complained as she turned them. Her handwritten notes decorated the margins. She was surprised at how hard it was to make out her own words, by how alien they now felt. Wide, open curves danced across empty spaces, ignoring their confines and spilling onto the printed text, a single letter taking the same space that three of her current ones would. The strokes forming the T crossbars shot across entire words and the arcs in the m's and n's swooped down in dramatic bends.

She read all through the morning and well into the afternoon until the sun started throwing long shadows. She thought of her classes and felt lucky she didn't have to face the boys that day.

Halfway through the second book and with the sky turning into a swathe of violets, she went down to the basement. Half the potato was gone, and the grits had shifted around a bit, and that was all. She picked up the plate and looked at the girl.

"It doesn't taste of anything," the girl said.

The teacher sat on the stool and started peeling the egg. She offered the plate to the girl once more, who shook her head. The teacher finished the food and then sat next to her. Thoughts swirled in her mind.

A girl who talks...

She pointed at the girl, then spread out her fingers. The girl looked, trying to understand what she meant. The teacher pointed at herself and counted fingers. One, two, three, four...

"I'm almost twelve," the girl replied.

The teacher smiled, then looked up to the ceiling in search of her next question. Her stomach fluttered, but it wasn't the monster that ate at her. It was the feeling of rushing downhill, enjoying the speed. The thrill of flirting with tragedy. She thought back to her manuscript that, by now, had more strike-throughs than finished sentences. The tangled mess inside her head throbbed.

"I wish you'd just say what you want. I can't read minds, you know," the girl said. The teacher shrugged and wished the same. A knot tightened in the back of her throat as she tried to will words to come out. There would be no undoing years of silence in the space of a day. Language was a muscle and hers had long since withered.

She picked a corn kernel from between her teeth and cleared her throat, then rubbed her temples with her eyes closed. In the end, having made up her mind, she turned to the girl and pointed at her with a questioning face.

"My name?" the girl hesitated.

The teacher nodded.

"Corvo."

The name brought a smile to the teacher's face. She stood up and opened the red armoire. From behind a panel that opened into a hole in the wall, she pulled out her manuscript.

"What's this?" Corvo asked when the teacher presented her the pages. She spent a few moments reading it with squinted eyes. "Is this a story?"

The teacher nodded.

"And you want me to read it?"

The teacher nodded again.

6.

O F THE THREE bodies that hanged from the traffic light, two were fresh. There were bruises on their heads and limbs, and the cuts and scrapes on their skin were turning black. On the asphalt beneath, there were pools of darker hues where they had bled out. A woman wearing a cardigan full of holes and a foggy look stood close by, observing them. She pointed a stubby finger at the bodies, her mouth gaping.

It looked like a man and a woman. Broken corn stalks still clung to their clothes. It made them look as if they had been removed from shallow graves. One of the woman's eyelids was swollen shut, the other torn off.

While her features were recognizable at least, the man's face didn't resemble anything human. The farmer could only tell the husk was a man from the shoulders and the cut of the clothes. The head had swollen to the size of a small pumpkin, the flesh puffed up and distended.

Fighting against his stomach, the farmer forced himself to keep staring. *I can see it*, he thought. *Not on him, ain't nothing to see on him, but her. Same nose as the girl, the same cheekbones, the same Asian eyes. Hard to tell with what they've done to her. But I can see it, alright.*

Close by, the cardiganed woman coughed loudly without covering her mouth. The farmer turned and, with a gloved hand covering his own mouth from the stench and the dust, he walked away.

The gray silence washed over the town and its twin hills in waves, heavy and leaden and miasmic. This town made wading through it a labor of will. He walked past the sign for Main Street pointing down the road, blank save for a fat, faded arrow. A few figures appeared outside doors, distorted by the haze emanating from the asphalt. Most of the townsfolk would be hiding inside from the sun.

He walked and he seethed, his lips quivering with the feeling of having gotten into a mess with no way out. His wife probably thought she was doing the right thing, but she was putting them in danger.

And for what? He avoided looking through the pharmacy window, though he caught sight of the pharmacist's tall figure standing behind a counter.

What have we done?

Some way down the street stood a storefront without windows or a door, its stucco walls blackened a long time ago. Part of it was covered with posters announcing the country fair for Unity Day, a simple drawing of showmen, confetti, and a date. He reached out a hand as he walked, touching and peeling off plaster, revealing blue and yellow and pink fragments underneath the soot.

We lived in caves once, the farmer thought. *Naked and scared of snapping twigs and rustling leaves, because we knew what made those sounds. We knew what lay in the darker corners of our caves, those black places that smelled of wet fur and broken marrow. And so to survive we became scarier still. We formed mobs. To the monsters, we appeared a mass of arms and legs and snarling faces. A single mass that barged into their abyss and dragged them into the burning light, out into the angry sun, we tore them apart limb from limb and hooted over their corpses.*

A girl appears out of nowhere, a girl that talks, together with her parents. Criminals. Menaces to how the world has learned to live. A threat from the dark places of the world. And so a mob forms. It gushes out of its homes and its shops, out of its fields and out of its sheds, and chases them down. A monster with dozens of feet and arms and eyes. It finds them. And, when it does, it makes sure that it won't be threatened by them anymore.

Now, the girl is in our basement, the screaming kicking little shit. The farmer looked at his hands.

But she's just a girl.

But what if they come for us?

How his heart had skipped, how his guts had frozen solid when the girl had spoken. When one is used to only hearing footsteps and breathing, a clear voice can shatter bones. Even now, he could hear her and his fists clenched, wanting to shut her up.

The talkers must have come from far away. The land was fields as far as the city on one side and as far as the desert on the other. He'd heard them struggle. Begging for their lives as loud as they could, drawing all attention to them and away from the girl. Brave. He'd have done the same thing. But, now, the burden of the girl was on him and his wife and he didn't like that one bit.

Below the anger and the fear, another feeling rose inside the farmer. Guilt. Deep down he knew that, had he found the girl in the fields first, he'd turn her in to the mob. She would have been up there next to her family. And he would have been relieved. They'd be safe, and he'd be unable to look at himself in the mirror.

He scratched his head until his skin bled.

A bell rang over the door when the farmer entered the workshop. A bald man appeared from a back room. He smiled through his tired, dust-irritated eyes. They shook hands, and the bald man brought out three hard-bound dossiers, covered in faded leather. He set one of them on a swivel book stand and turned it around. The farmer flipped through it.

Carburetors, fuel injectors, spark plugs, all labeled. Years, specs, batches. All numbers, no words.

The farmer shook his head and the bald man nodded in a silent display of service honed over many years. *Let me see what I can do*, his gesture said. He opened the second dossier.

The farmer pointed at an engine gasket with a large red X over it, showing it was out of stock. With his other hand, he pulled out his wallet and showed the bald man the member's card. The bald man nodded several times. When the spare part arrived, the farmer would have first right to it. Member's privileges. The farmer rubbed thumb and forefinger together. In response, the bald man took a calculator from under the counter and offered him a price.

200

The farmer seemed to consider it for a long moment. He ran quick mental calculations of future produce and how much profit he stood to make, the cost of fuel, the cost of repairing the tractor, then went back to the profit he expected to make and inflated it for it all to work. The bald man waited with relaxed shoulders, his gaze resting out on the street out of politeness.

The bell rang over the door again. The bald man perked up. There was a flash of recognition between the two, the bald man and the teenage boy that had stepped through the door. The boy stood with his hands at his sides, just staring at the bald man. Just staring. No nods, no moves, and no indication of what he wanted. In the past, this would have warranted a rude response from the shopkeeper. Even now, annoyance flashed through the bald man's eyes. But this was a different time. What was once insolent was now normal. The bald man took another look at the teenager and walked away from the counter, disappearing through a side door. His footsteps echoed through the wall as he climbed a flight of stairs, then across the floor above them.

A walking contrast, the farmer thought. *That's what he looks like.* The teenager wore clothes that were too large for him, drenched with sweat. He ran a finger inside the collar which was buttoned all the way to the top and rubbed against the scar on his throat.

The teenager noticed the farmer staring and he stared back without malice.

How old was the kid? The farmer guessed sixteen. Probably couldn't remember no one else talking in his life, save for whatever words they could overhear the Mouth saying on the TV. Too old to have had his cordectomy at birth, too. *That's when they do it, right when you pop out. Before, you'd baby-proof the house, stock up on formula, then hope the crying wouldn't drive you nuts. These days, you'd have to keep an eye on them constantly, no other way to tell if they're hungry or sick or they've shitted themselves.*

The farmer rubbed his neck, and for a moment he imagined himself in the boy's place, twelve years ago, being dragged to the doctor by his parents. It would have made him four years old. Old enough to have learned to speak. And then, he thought of the boy he himself had lost. His wife, always the braver of the two, had wanted to give birth at home and spare their boy the cordectomy. But things hadn't gone the way they had planned.

The footsteps above them doubled. Both the farmer and the teenager looked up, following them along the ceiling and back down the flight of stairs until the side door opened again. Behind the bald man came a skinny thing the same age as the teenager, with straw blond hair tucked behind her ears, and the same long nose and chin as the bald man. The teenager stepped forward and took the girl's hand, waiting for a reaction. The girl looked at his reddening face and his downcast eyes, looked back at her father and even at the farmer. Sweat ran down the teenager's forehead in fat drops, but he stood straight. The girl pulled his hand and led him out of the workshop. The two exited and turned a corner, disappearing from view.

Life went on for all of them. Each year was getting warmer, each year becoming harder to coax corn out of the ground. But people were people. They dated and fooled around and kept on popping out babies, even if they couldn't say much to each other. The farmer shook his head and remembered the girls he'd lost because he couldn't keep his mouth shut.

The bald man stared at the street in the direction where the teenagers had gone. The cost of parts must have left his mind. He tossed the calculator across the counter. The farmer didn't envy him. Didn't envy the gap between him and his girl that would only get wider. Was he the lucky one for never having become a father? He couldn't imagine raising their boy, the boy they had lost, with the patience silence demanded.

The farmer thought for a few seconds, reached for the calculator, but changed his mind. Instead, he nodded and shook the other man's hand.

The teenagers weren't on the street when he stepped outside.

He had one more stop to make before leaving town. He crossed the street towards the bar. In the half-light, the place looked empty. Old spilled beer, so close to the smell of urine, and acrid tobacco hit his nose. As his eyes adjusted, he saw smoke dancing over the booths. There must have been about five others in the bar, sitting in ones and twos, staring down at the bottom of a glass. There was little difference between the way they looked and the cardiganed woman. Wild hair and cancerous complexions. Empty stares and hacking coughs.

No one lifted their heads in welcome. When he met their eyes, they averted their gaze, and from the back of the bar someone spat on the wooden floor. A man with glazed eyes glared at him, before going back to nursing his drink.

The farmer smiled with bitterness. There was a time when people would greet him anywhere he went. Would shake his hand. But that was when crops were still good. *I know you*, he thought. *I know all of you. I went to the same school as you and you. And you there, I hired you when you was starving. You there, sucking on the gut rot, I gave you good work when the desert took your land, though I was not obliged. One good combine is enough for the harvest. Never needed you yet I gave work to y'all. Not my fault you chose to put your faith in cotton and almonds, only good for dying in a drought. You filled your bellies thanks to my corn. And now you avert your eyes? Like it's my fault you didn't become members when you had the chance.*

If they wanted him to answer for his good fortune, they'd be disappointed.

The farmer went to the bar, sat on one of the stools and waited. The owner, a man that resembled a tower of barrels, tossed a menu with pictures of drinks on the counter. The farmer disregarded it. Instead, he pointed at a bottle of whiskey.

He drank, and then he drank again, and, when he felt his mind loosening, he thought. On the wall behind the bar were framed photographs of lynchings, the townsfolk at the foreground posing as men and women hanged above them.

What was she thinking? Throwing herself over that girl to protect her. It wasn't his fault. The girl was squealing like a piglet. Not his fault. He was trying to shut her up. He was doing it for their sake. What business did she have protecting the girl? What right? What right? They'd both be hanged because of her.

His thoughts went on and on in a loop until they blurred together. He felt small. He felt like they'd had a fight and he had been in the wrong.

His mind foggy with alcohol, the farmer stepped outside. Eyes were on his back. Angry stares, ungrateful stares, and he felt happy to leave them behind.

Alcohol made the world a shade less harsh and the heat didn't seem as relentless. He looked up to the sky until his vision washed out. The smell of stale beer still hung about him, as did the tobacco, only now it mixed with the dust, with the sweat clinging to his skin, and the stink of dead bodies left under the sun. The town's breath reeked and he took it all in. This town… If only the dust buried it.

Under the hanged bodies, the Sheriff stood next to the

cardiganed woman, pointing at the dead and whispering into her ear. And the woman, she cowered and trembled.

The Sheriff talked in short sentences followed by long pauses and every word was an act of violence. Her skin stretched almost painfully over her strong features, all sharp angles. They accentuated a jaw that clenched whenever she paused, and exaggerated the grinding of her teeth. The cardiganed woman had squeezed her eyes shut, hands raised to protect herself from the words that stabbed at her.

In the end, the Sheriff pointed with her chin and mouthed a single word. Get.

Free, the woman shuffled away as quickly as she could. Later, when the farmer replayed the scene in his mind, he cursed himself for being too slow to disappear down a side road himself while he had the chance.

The Sheriff stared at him a good while. There was hesitation, but also a feeling that she was assessing him.

Her fingers uncurled from the fists they had formed and she walked towards him. Keys jingled with each step. On her chest was her badge, a star, and on it three crossed arrows wrapped in a wreath. In the middle of the wreath, a single red ruby.

She leaned into his ear.

"Good mmmorning...," she said, lock jawed. He could smell good government-issue coffee on her breath. Soap on her skin. He avoided looking at her face, but could hear her sniffing the alcohol on him.

"I ain't goin ta cause you trouble. Believe me or not, it don't makkke a difference. But it'd be a lot better if you did."

The farmer nodded. The woman's jaw muscles tensed even when she wasn't speaking, even when she seemed to be at rest.

"How's your wife?" she asked.

When the farmer didn't answer, her face hardened and her voice took a harsh tone.

"I hear there's been some shootin on your property," she continued. "Do I understand correct, jes nod yes or no."

The farmer nodded.

"Themmm two fellers swingin up there," she pointed, though the farmer didn't look up. "Did you witness the accct?"

The farmer shook his head. Then, as an afterthought, he tapped his ear.

"Mmmust've been loud, mmm."

He pressed his elbows closer to his body, willing himself to become smaller. *Yes*, he nodded. *They were loud.*

She wasn't asking questions, the farmer understood. Just confirming what she already knew. Nothing stayed secret in a town like this, even if no one was allowed to talk about it.

He imagined the pharmacist, that tall man with the stony face driving into town with the girl's parents in the back of a pick-up truck. He saw him pulling over in front of the Sheriff's office and knocking on her door. Talkers, he'd mime by tapping his throat. He hadn't done it for any reward. Duty was its own reward. The Sheriff would have recognized them for out-of-towners. The clothes, the items in their pockets and rucksacks. She would have then brought out a map for the pharmacist to point where the mob had found them. And then, he'd offer a final piece of information. He'd point at the two still-warm bodies and hold three fingers up, then turn the hand palm down and bring it to about waist-height. When the Sheriff would ask, where is the kid, he'd shrug.

The farmer thought he could see curtains twitching.

"Did you see anyone else? A kkkid, bout yea high.

Lookkk, I would appreciate some respeccct by lookkkin at me when I talkkk, mmm? Please."

Of course she knows, he thought and it became a little harder to breathe. *Of course she knows. The woman who silenced this town years ago knows all of its secrets.* He shook his head.

She stared at him long and hard. In the stillness of the town, her rhythmic breathing and the tapping of her boot created a cacophony. He turned to face her and shook his head again.

"I ain't your enemmmy, mmm," she said and sighed. "I ain't. Ya wanna believe otherwise, that's on you. I could've business wit you, would have every right. But I don't."

Something ugly must have shown in his eyes, because the Sheriff gave him a smile full of good government-insured teeth. Her gaze went to the strung up bodies. A couple of carrion birds fluttered around them, squabbling. Below them, the cardiganed woman had returned and stood with her arms up, fingers clutching at the birds. The Sheriff sighed in exasperation.

"Half the town's gone dummmb as dirt..." she said, staring at the cardiganed woman as she hooked her thumbs in her belt. "Other half's lookkkin fer an excuse to shed blood. That mess up there, that's what? Secccond lynchin in as many weekkks. Haven't had that mmmuch butchery since the early days. You know, it's gettin folks all riled up and eager, gives them somepin else to think than dead crops. Now we're missin a fugitive. Last seen on your property."

She paused and leaned in closer.

"You know them folks. They'll takkke matters into their hands and comme a-knockkkin, eventually. Remember Tommy the mmmute, the barman's kid? The one they kkkilled cause he spoke sign? That was before sign got banned too, they kkkilled him jes in case. Jes in case. Mmmight do the same to you. Can't cccontrol these animals. Not really. Wish I had the nummmbers."

The town seemed to be coming out of its slumber. Doors opened and townsfolk peeked their heads out in curiosity, roused by her voice. The Sheriff inspected their audience with no apprehension on her face.

There was safety in being with the Sheriff. His mind knew that. Another part of him, the primitive lizard part soaking in whiskey, screamed in panic. *Get out*, it said. *Get out.*

The Sheriff leaned in, that smell of coffee again.

"How many talkkin kids are there in this town, mmm? How many?"

The farmer nodded. He thought of better times. Of a time when seeing the Sheriff made him smile instead of sending him into a panic.

"Listen. Listen. If you have the kid, I'll takes care of it. On mah word. Won't involves no Party bastards. You won't have nopin to hide. Hey now, don't let them catch you, mmm?"

Lies. Damn lies. Acting like she wasn't the Party's emissary. Like it hadn't been her who had stolen the town's words all those years ago, like it hadn't been her who had fed people to the Party's maw because they refused to stop talking. All the blood on her hands was the blood of her neighbors, people she had known their entire lives and had sworn to protect. Give her the girl? He'd love to. But then he'd be admitting to harboring a talker. And he'd sooner trust the lobos in his fields than the Sheriff with keeping her word.

He put on his best ignorant face and shrugged his

shoulders at the Sheriff.

"Now, don't be lyin to mmme, you hear? I catch you wit a talker kid, I gotta bring you in. All three of you, in fact. Gotta involve the Party. Then, the kid gets hanged anyway. Can't do nopin bout that."

The farmer shrugged again.

"I'll take care of the kid. Promise, mmm. No one will know."

The farmer averted his gaze.

"Mmm-mmm," came the sound from the cardiganed woman. She pointed at the birds picking at the hanged woman's lidless eye. She shook her head with a pained expression on her face. A closed-mouth wail emanated from her, her lips shut tight into a thin line. "Mmmm-mmmm," came out. Low and agonized. The town stirred.

"Look what this silence does to us. Come the end, we'll all turn like her."

She headed to the woman.

"Psst," she motioned at her and motioned with her cupped hand over her own mouth. "Shut it."

The cardiganed woman pointed at the birds. Tears were streaming down her face, confusion in her eyes. *No*, the farmer thought. *Not all of us go mad in this silence, though that would be a blessing.*

The Sheriff approached her, shoulders squared off. Stumbling, the cardiganed woman reached for the Sheriff's revolver. A quick sidestep and the Sheriff had a hold on the woman's wrists with one hand. The other covered her mouth.

"Hush, sweetheart. Hush now. Don't give them the pleasure," she whispered into her ear and embraced her. "You wanna die already? You're not leavin this hell so easy. Hush, now. That's enough kkkillin. Why don't you keep me commmpany? Mmm?"

Gathering his courage, the farmer turned and walked down the street. He resolved to continue moving, no matter what. He'd keep his head low and his eyes to the ground. The barked command to stand still never came.

The drive home was filled with glances into the back mirror, but he only saw the asphalt rearing up in the heat and nothing else. The hair on the back of his neck began to prickle with static electricity. *Dust storm*, he thought.

7.

ABOUT A YEAR ago, a new pesticide hit the market. The new chemical killed most parasites, so everyone used it. No one could afford not to. Margins were tight and every rotten carrot and maggoty peach was a sin to ponder over. The Ministry of Agriculture promoted its use with vigor. Do you want to hold back the war effort? Do you want the bank to take your land? Do you want to be taken off the list of approved suppliers? They came to the farms and spread their gospel, arguing with farmers who couldn't argue back. And so, the farmers switched to the new pesticide. Besides, no one minded being pushed around when the pesticide was that cheap.

One day about a year ago, the teacher ate a piece of lettuce that had been sprayed with the new chemical. She ate it together with boiled potatoes and a fried vole she had killed with the shovel in the vegetable garden. She worried a bit about ticks on the rodent. She never thought the lettuce could harm her, though.

Somewhere past her stomach, past the small intestine and in the large one, the chemicals absorbed into her bloodstream. One cell. That was all it took. One insignificant cell amongst trillions that went mad. It divided, just as it had thousands of times before, but faster and farther, giving birth to more flawed copies of itself. Hungry for space, the mass ate holes in her and pushed against her liver and right lung.

That was when the bleeding started.

✕

THE PENCIL TIP hesitated over the paper. It seemed to consider whether the words it would produce would be a waste of time. Whether it should go back into its case with the other hoarded pencils until smarter ideas demanded to be written or more elegant expressions came together. It seemed to consider all that and still it hovered, uncertain. It traced a circle in the air the way buzzards do, buying time. Then, holding its breath, it plunged.

She was writing.

The words didn't seem to struggle as much as before. There was no breaking-of-the-dam experience. Today the words were just a little more eager than yesterday. A little less reluctant to hide in the tangled mess of her mind.

The small words unfurled first. Then, a couple of the longer ones. The teacher put them down on paper and marveled at how her writing hand didn't hurt with tension. After a few minutes, her thin lips worked themselves into a smile. Impatient and unable to hold back, she attacked the page.

It works, she thought.

When she failed, she didn't mind as much as she used to. There was no sense of panic this time. No urge to walk away from the page and do something, anything, other than struggle with her thoughts. The words were in there, had always been there, tucked away and forgotten in dusty corners. Now, she knew how to cajole them out. It would take perseverance, but that was fine. She had the girl that talked and that made all the difference in the world.

She mimed her questions. Simple ones. *Are you hungry? Do you hurt?* And the girl replied. "Yes," and, "a lot."

And that interaction had been enough. The act of listening to the girl talking coaxed out verbs, nouns, and wild adjectives.

Letters lost their angles. Every so often, they exploded into familiar flourishes and arabesques, galloping along the page. At one point, brimming with haughtiness, she stumbled over her words and the pencil tip broke. She slowed, then picked up the pace again. And, for the first time in a long while, she saw meaning even as the monster in her guts reminded her that it, too, was there.

No, she muttered at it, *you will not ruin this. Time is on my side, for once.*

Are you certain? It whispered and twisted her insides with malice. The pain made her double over and drop the pencil. In her purse on the table close-by, the pill bottle still lay empty. The monster smiled.

You will never finish what you started.

Breathe, she told herself and dismissed the voice.

Stop wasting your time.

Breathe.

It's not good enough.

B… Breathe.

You're dying.

But I can still write.

And who will read it?

The teacher felt her throat tightening and the monster

grinned.

If no one reads it, does it matter?

We'll see, thought the teacher. *Can't give brain-room to who will read it right now. What matters is that I can write and the words flow. The pain... I am fine with it. I am. See, I have the girl now. Corvo. The girl that screams in a world that was hushed. And how she screams.*

At last, the pain faded away and she smiled. The words were flowing. The words were flowing. And at least one person would read.

When she became exhausted, she set the pencil down. Grooves marked her fingers where they'd held the stylus. One by one, she put them into her mouth to soothe them, tasting graphite. Outside, a slight wind had picked up. Ripples ran over the fields, gentle waves. Far off in the distance, their scarecrow's lonesome silhouette stood stark against a steel blue sky that was beginning to turn gray at the edges. Desaturated. As if the TV static from the living room had seeped into the world. The more she stared through the porch windows, the more her vision blurred, filling out with tiny black spots. Crowding, until she could see nothing.

When she came to, it was almost dark. Her face ached, a dull throbbing where it had hit the table. From somewhere deep inside the house, someone was knocking on a door. With some effort, she pushed herself to her feet. Nausea hit hard. She had to concentrate to not vomit.

Once her vision cleared, she saw red spots on the paper she'd written on, seeping into the words. She touched her mouth. Her fingertips came away bloody and a wet cough sprayed more blood onto the paper. She took out a crumpled tissue from her pocket and wiped her lips.

As she shook her head in denial, a thought kept

repeating. *It's spreading. It's spreading.*

The monster laughed without a sound.

Another knock on the door. She spat into the tissue, hoping the blood would stop. And every time it appeared she lost a little more of her composure.

"Mmmm," she moaned with her hand over mouth and looked around for help. "Mmmm-aaah."

Screaming is such an easy sound to make, she thought. *It's the natural sound one makes when hurt, when one dies little by little, torn apart from the inside.*

She dried the tears on her cuffs. Then, as fast as her knees could carry her, she stumbled to the basement door. She tapped it twice and the knocking stopped. Only the static from the living room filled the void. With some hesitation, she put one ear on the door and listened for a long beat.

"I'm hungry," came the voice from the other side.

The teacher swallowed blood. She tapped the door again, a wordless confirmation, and staggered away, one hand against the wall for support.

In the kitchen, she spat into the sink and washed the blood away. She took a few deep breaths and stood a little straighter. Held her head a bit higher. Exhaled slowly.

It was becoming difficult to feed the girl. Wherever she came from, she was used to eating more often and better than the teacher and her husband. The teacher could see in Corvo's eyes what she made of their food.

The teacher suspected she had lost her sense of taste a long time ago. *One adapts*, she thought. *One adapts, or one goes mad.* It had always been her belief that, given enough motivation, humans could adjust to any misfortune, any shortage. Not doing so was a matter of choice, not of weakness. Children without vocal chords knew how to communicate with a glance, or a subtle flick of the wrist. No one had taught them that. She had seen it evolve in front of her eyes. They needed a non-language, a patois of silence, something that didn't count as a horrible attempt at Division, an affront to Unity. So they created one.

She wondered how far the non-language would evolve when she wasn't around anymore. Did those abandoned children in the shepherd's hut talk to each other with the angle of their chins? Had their first non-word to each other been a nod? Were her words becoming obsolete, at last? What is the non-word for "I'm dying and I'm scared"?

In time, the Party would wise up and ban this non-language the moment it started looking real enough to be a threat. Twins made up their own languages all the time, at least the ones in her class did. Sometimes without anything resembling words, just tongue clicks and mirroring body language. This too would happen here. If only she could live long enough to see it…

The dish she managed to put together was a pile of garden herbs, collard greens and fried dough, all cooked together in an iron skillet with tallow. The pile had taken an off-green color. The teacher lifted a bite with her fingers and tried it. Not finding any flavor, she judged it a success.

Carrying a food plate on a tray, she moved listless towards the basement as if the cancer had robbed her of all substance. Not even making the ancient floorboards creak. Almost a wraith already. She managed to open the door with one arm without spilling everything and then lock it behind her again.

The girl was sitting on her mattress in the corner, arms around her knees. Her gaze followed her as she descended the stairs. The narrowed eyes and the furrow on her brow issued a warning. The teacher approached. She put the tray down by her side, then retreated to the stool. From there, she returned the staring.

They sat in silence. Corvo scrunched her face at the sight of the green lump with the chunks of fried dough. She looked again at the teacher with incredulity. The teacher kept a neutral expression.

She nodded at the food and waved at the girl. *Go ahead, eat.*

"Don't you have any spam?"

The teacher didn't react. Only continued staring at her. *My lungs don't hurt*, she thought. *But it's spreading. It's spreading.*

The girl shifted her gaze to the ground. It didn't take long before her resolve broke and she was eating.

Every few minutes, she stopped and set the fork down with a grimace of disgust. Then, after a minute of staring at the food with hatred, she continued. The silent dinner went on until she emptied the plate. With a sigh of exasperation, she dropped the fork and pushed herself back into the corner, back into sulking.

The teacher brought her fingers together and kissed them, then raised her eyebrows.

"No. It tastes like lawn."

The teacher patted her belly.

"Whatever you say."

The teacher reached into her mind and tried to remember what it had felt like uttering words. For her, pencils spoke easier than tongues. Always had. Now, she doubted she could recall what her own voice had sounded like. Over time, her inner monologue had gone as quiet as her home. Silence had become her native language.

When the monster started twisting her guts, it brought with it a new vocabulary of feeling. Pressure turning into the tip of a knife. Muscles contracting to a pinpoint. The last time she had visited a doctor, he had held up a scale from one to ten, with one being a happy face and ten being a tortured wreck, and he had asked her to point on it. She jabbed at ten repeatedly, until he put it away and gave her a prescription for painkillers.

Now, with the girl in her basement, she felt her own voice returning as a distant murmur. Enough to convince her she could finish the story.

She retrieved her manuscript from upstairs, minus the parts she had bled on. She smoothed the pages and spent altogether too much time adjusting them, before offering them to Corvo.

"I don't want to read your stupid story, I want to get out of here. I need to find Mom and Ali."

The teacher wrote on a blank page.

Where came from???

That mistrust again in the girl's eyes, like a wild animal's.

"South. We came through the forest."

The teacher smiled. There hadn't been a proper forest around these parts since the desert started creeping in.

And then?

"What do you mean, and then?"

The teacher nodded encouragement. The girl sighed with weariness and nudged the plate with her foot.

"There was a boy sitting up on a tree. I think we scared him because we were talking, he almost fell off when he saw us. Ali tried to calm him down. Mom told him to grab the boy, but the boy was too quick. He jumped off the tree and disappeared into a patch of weeds. Ali went after him, but couldn't find him. He wasn't going to hurt the boy. We just wanted to… talk to him, tell him that we were just passing through and we'd be on our way. We didn't mean trouble. Ali couldn't find him. He returned without the boy and Mom yelled at him and told us to get moving faster and then we started running. I fell a couple of times. That's where I got this," she said and pointed at a thick scab on her elbow.

The teacher shook her head and sighed while she fumbled with a button. It felt wrong asking the girl for details. It felt wrong, because she could guess what had happened, but needed to hear the girl talking. Anything to hear her talking. The girl's voice shook the foundations of the house with a whisper.

"Two women showed up. They were far away, and at first they were just two small dots. We could see them because they wore red scarves around their lower faces. Ali didn't think they were anyone important, but they moved in our direction and they didn't stop. They were so far away and we were running so much. But they kept coming after us. When it got dark, Ali said we would be fine. That the two women were so far away. But Mom made us move. My legs hurt, so Ali carried me. I don't remember much, but…"

The teacher lifted her eyebrows.

"Ali woke me up, because he couldn't carry me anymore, and there were more of them. Lots more. We could see their faces, they were angry at us. And they carried things in their hands. Axes and hammers and some of them had guns."

The button came loose in the teacher's fingers. She considered touching the girl's shoulder, but changed her mind.

"They didn't stop, so we kept running. And then, we got here."

Where's home?

The girl exploded. "Let me go," Corvo yelled and jumped up. "Let me go, I can't find them down here, how am I supposed to find them when you won't let me out?"

Her voice splintered and cracked and she collapsed on the mattress just as fast as she had erupted, sobbing into the sheets.

"I heard the shots. Alright? I need to know they're okay. You can't keep me here. How am I supposed to find them?"

Blood rose to the teacher's mouth again. She wanted to explain what had happened to the girl's parents. She wanted to tell her it was pointless waiting for them, but every time she thought she'd muster up the courage to do it she saw the driver with the black-framed glasses who couldn't take the silence any longer. She saw his head hanging between his knees with tears in his eyes and a dozen arms pulling him apart and she knew that she could never explain lynching to an eleven year-old girl.

"They're looking for me, I have to get out," she repeated until she couldn't utter a word through her exhaustion. "I'm telling you, I need to find them, you can't keep me in here."

But you make the words flow, the teacher thought and touched her lips. *And you can read. How can I ever let you leave?*

Everything the books said about guiding the girl through her grief, everything she believed she knew about handling children was pushed aside by a single burning thought. *I need you. I need you. Who will read the story, but you? It won't matter if no one can read it. When those monsters seemed to be just beyond the curtain of stalks, did your mother push you away? Did she send you to me? Telling you to run as far as you could and not look back? Did she tell you they'd find you? Of course she did. I would have.*

Safe here
Can't leave now
Not safe out there
Not yet
We wait here
For Mom and Ali
We wait here

The girl sat up, pushing the teacher's hands away when she tried to wipe her eyes. Instead, she nodded.

The teacher pointed at the food and rolled her hand in a so-so motion, while scrounging her face.

"It doesn't taste good."

The teacher shook her head and smiled.

"You got to let me out."

Soon
When it's safe

She offered her pinky to the girl. Corvo matched it with her own without enthusiasm. Regardless, it made the teacher smile. She motioned for Corvo to wait and went upstairs, returning a few minutes later with two slices of toasted bread on a plate with tallow spread thin on them. While the girl nibbled on the bread, the teacher took a seat next to her.

Once Corvo finished, she gave the first two pages to the girl and waited for her to begin. The girl wiped her hands on her jeans and picked up the first page. Brought it close to her face, then placed it on the mattress. With the tip of her index finger, she traced the words.

The longer the word, the more she dwelt on it. Sometimes, the finger skipped words altogether. Other times, when a word was misspelled or unusual, she seemed to be summoning all her energy to decipher its meaning.

The teacher tapped her on the shoulder.

Your parents taught you?

"Ali did. The others at the compound didn't have the time."

The teacher gave her a blank face. *Compound?*

"The compound. Like a little town. Our home. I don't get this, who's this girl in the story and why won't anyone listen to her?"

But the teacher wasn't looking at the girl anymore. Her eyes were pointing up, at the stair landing. Floorboards groaned with familiar footsteps tracing circles through the house.

"Anyway. I don't get the story. It's like nothing's happening half the time," the girl said.

It's okay, the teacher thought as she stared at the farmer on the landing high above, harshness in his eyes. *It's not finished yet.*

"Just this girl talking to people and people not listening to her. It doesn't make a lick of sense."

I suppose it doesn't.

"I don't like it."

That's okay. It's not finished yet. She picked up the empty plate and went up the stairs.

The farmer stood aside to let her pass, his eyes going

from her to the girl to her again. He clicked the basement door shut behind her, locked it, and turned to confront her, but she was already on her way to the kitchen. He followed, sandals shuffling along the floor.

The teacher grabbed a cloth and wiped the plate clean while leaning against the dining table. Standing across from her, he continued to stare. She avoided staring back. If she had, she would have seen his nails dig into his palms, drawing blood. She would have seen his eyes turning red with the effort of not falling into pieces. A few times, he opened his mouth, but closed it again. He fumbled with his hands, wiped his brow.

Then, the farmer's face turned harsh. His lines deepened and his jaws locked together. He pointed at the basement, his index finger tense with hatred. With one big sweeping move of his arm, he dragged his finger through the air until it pointed at the fields. Repeating the motion, he made his mind known. *Out. We need to get rid of the girl.*

The teacher finished wiping the plate and set it into the dish rack. When she returned to the table, she shook her head.

No.

He repeated the move. She stood unmoving, unflinching, feet rooted in place like ancient stone. Impervious to his silent arguments. The look on her face told him to stop wasting her time. The look on her face said, *I'm done here.*

With thundering steps, he closed the space between them. He opened his mouth with wild eyes as if to yell and his drawn-back features made him look like a dog. She recoiled, wincing away and bringing up her arms to protect herself. For a moment, he was teeth and snarls, and mad. Mad and hurt, because all madness comes from grief.

Just as fast as he had exploded, he turned and left, and bitterness hung in the air in his wake. The porch door slammed and the tractor engine spurted to life. Bright lights flooded the fields. Before long, the tractor's whine had disappeared into the distance.

For long minutes, the teacher remained in place, arms folded over her chest. *How can I begin to explain this to you,* she thought. *How can I make you see how important this is? How important she is. The monster has spread. I have no time for your blindness.*

She went back to the basement where she joined the girl.

When he came to bed much later that night, he smelled of earth and sorrow.

8.

T HE HOURS AT school dragged on. Her thumb clicked the forward button on the presentation controller as if by its own will. The slides behind her flashed on and on, but none of that registered with her. In the room's half darkness, she couldn't see the scars on her students' throats, but she imagined them nonetheless.

There were four in her class today. All of them huddled together. Her eyes rested on one empty seat in particular. She wondered about the boy with the shaved head, but was grateful for his absence. Relieved, even.

Her husband's side of the bed had been empty in the morning, his imprint covered in sweat. No body warmth left.

The presentation continued.

Seven monkeys in a cage with a bunch of bananas hanging from its roof and a ladder leading to it. The monkeys rushed up the ladder, but they were hosed down with water. Shocked, the monkeys huddled in a corner, looking miserable. Soon, however, they turned their eyes back to the bananas. A couple of monkeys broke away from the group and tried the ladder again. Once more, the entire group got drenched in water. Not just the ones that tried the ladder again, but all of them.

That was repeated again and again until the group had had enough. The next time a monkey went for the bananas, the group grabbed it back and beat it.

In the end, none of the monkeys cared for the bananas anymore.

The researchers removed one of the monkeys and replaced it with a new one. The new monkey, seeing the bunch hanging from the roof, rushed up the ladder. The others, the monkeys that had been there from the start, grabbed the newcomer and beat it, because they knew what would happen. Another original monkey was replaced and the new monkey rushed immediately towards the ladder. The original monkeys plus the first replacement attacked the newcomer, until it, too, stopped eyeing the bananas.

And on and on it went, until none of the original monkeys remained and none of the monkeys in the cage knew why none of them dared to go for the bananas. Only that they were off-limits and that violence was the punishment for breaking that rule.

At some point, the bell must had gone off and, lost in her thoughts, she hadn't even noticed. The children had left, and at no point had she realized she was alone.

It's spreading.

The words echoed in her mind. She touched her lips and stared at her fingertips. *How long,* she thought. *How long before I can no longer write? How long do I have?*

The darkness remained silent.

She almost screamed when she felt fingers on her shoulder. Dropping the controller, she covered her mouth and stumbled backwards, catching the edge of her desk. The light turned on. An amused expression danced across the math teacher's face. Stinking of sandalwood, he mock-scolded her by shaking his finger and pointed at his watch. But she wasn't paying attention. She grabbed her bag and fled the classroom, feeling blood rising into her mouth.

9.

FROM HER CORNER in the basement, Corvo regarded the mute and debated with herself whether it was alright telling her plans to this woman. She had seemed nicer than her husband. Still, could she trust a mute, any mute?

Neither of their faces was right. The wrinkles around their twisted mouths were too many and too deep and interspersed with sores. Tensed up. Broken sun-beaten skin. And their eyes roamed, unable to find a fix, unless they stared at each other.

She waited as the woman scribbled something onto a piece of paper.

Where you going? With your parents

The girl coughed and rubbed her eyes. Breathing felt heavier away from the compound. More labored. As if the gritty air sanded the insides of her lungs.

"North," she offered. "We're heading North. They'll take us in there. They take anyone who makes it to the border."

The teacher nodded and looked away, folding her notes.

Why?

"Why, what? You mean, why leave?"

The teacher nodded.

"Everyone is gone. Everyone's dead. They found us."

The teacher frowned with confusion.

"You people did."

The teacher pointed at herself and her eyebrows formed question marks.

"Why don't you talk? Huh? Why are you mutes? You people don't talk to anyone, that's what Mom told me. No one talks to anyone anymore and you don't want us to talk to anyone either. You want us to go all Major Tom, just like you."

The teacher leaned back as if she were pushed. She tried to jot down an answer, almost losing her pencil in the process.

The law
No talking

The girl's tone rose. She assaulted the teacher with her voice and the more the teacher shriveled away the louder Corvo spoke.

"That's not our law, it has nothing to do with us," the girl spat. "Now everything's ruined, because you won't leave us alone. Everyone's gone. Everyone from the compound is dead and I'm stuck in this stupid basement when Mom and Ali could be out there, all because of your stupid laws. I bet you could be dying and you wouldn't even call out to your man for help. You're all just a bunch of monsters with stupid lives and you want to make everyone else miserable too. Why are we leaving? Are you kidding me? We're leaving because we don't want to be like you."

Silence hung in the air. Corvo's eyes turned from

triumphant to regretful. Then, they turned dismal. She opened her mouth to say something, perhaps an apology, but closed it again. Instead, she stood up and paced the basement, running her fingers along its walls and dragging her feet across the ground. Behind her, she could hear more scribbling, though slower this time.

North
There's war there
Not safe
Here is safe

Corvo considered that for a moment, then pushed it away from her mind. *Can't trust a mute. They are either evil or, like that woman, clueless.* She turned her back to the teacher and there was a sense of finality in that gesture that signaled the discussion was over.

While she brooded, the teacher tried to continue her story. The pencil tip hovered over the top left corner of the page in front of her for long moments. With a snort of surrender, she lowered the pencil and continued watching the girl.

Corvo picked up the handkerchief, turning it over in her hands and feeling its rough fabric, holding it up to the light coming in through the narrow windows. She put it across her mouth. It became a bit harder to breathe, but it stopped some of the dust.

The house
Want to see it?

She took the handkerchief away from her face and regarded the teacher with suspicion. "Sure," she answered.

The teacher stood and straightened her clothes, then offered her hand to the girl. Corvo ignored it. Instead, she ran past her and up the staircase. Sighing, the teacher followed. She unlocked the door, swung it open, and let the girl pass first. Corvo took a few steps, then looked back over her shoulder, expecting the trap to spring shut, but the teacher gave her a smile and motioned her forward with her hand. *Go on.*

And she did.

While Corvo ran her fingers over the dining table, the cupboard with the good china, the hissing TV set, the teacher followed her. It made her uncomfortable. She couldn't understand the excited look on the mute's face. Reluctant to let her guard down, she shifted from one leg to the other, instincts on alert. But when nothing happened, she began to relax. Became bolder. Curiosity took over. She walked up to a light wooden trunk and pointed at it. The teacher nodded permission. Inside, there were thick quilt blankets. A warm scent emanated from them that reminded the girl of something she couldn't put her finger on, but it made her feel safe.

She opened drawers and looked inside cabinets and under tables.

"It's different than the compound," she said with a sense of profundity. She picked up a white-and-blue porcelain cup and turned it this way and that, feeling its weight and its cool surface. "Most of our things were made out of plastic," she added. "Plastic doesn't ruin easy."

That's china

"Like the country?"

Once in the kitchen, she went straight for the refrigerator. She sighed with disappointment once she saw how empty it was.

The teacher waved her hand over its contents, prompting her to pick whatever she wanted.

Instead, the girl closed the door with a soft sound and continued her exploration.

She approached the TV and looked mesmerized at the snow. When she touched it, the screen made her fingertips tingle and the hairs on her arm stand, which amused her. She looked at the teacher and smiled. As she did, the TV stopped hissing and its screen turned black. A few bars of music played, the Party anthem echoing through the living room. The girl looked at it in alarm, unsure of what to do. She jumped with a start when the intertitle appeared—PARENTAL ADVISORY, REMOVE ALL CHILDREN FROM THE ROOM—, followed by a creepy bald man with round glasses, who seemed to be staring straight at her.

The teacher covered her smiling mouth with her hand. Taking large strides, she grabbed a quilt from the trunk and threw it over the TV, covering the screen. She then went ahead and turned on the stereo. Music flooded the house, drowning the man's words as he began to say "My dearest citizens".

The girl looked confused and panicked, as sounds of war flooded and mixed with the music, explosions and piano keys and buildings ground to dust.

"I know what a TV is," the girl seemed embarrassed.

She tried to put on an air of apathy and continued exploring.

The spare room with handwritten pages scattered throughout. The bedroom with its cotton sheets and the metal filigree bed. The low attic with cobwebs thick with dust. The girl roamed through the house with the teacher a few steps behind. She ran to everything that caught her attention and placed her hands on it, memorizing its shape and reading its texture with her fingers. Wood. Lace. Rattan. Burlap.

Finally, the girl returned to the living room and stood behind the porch door. She put her hands against the insect screen and stared out at the fields. The corn undulated in the breeze and the world seemed, somehow, to grow quiet despite the music. Only the whispering conversation between the wind and the fields broke the stillness. With a deep breath that seemed to echo throughout the house, the girl pushed the door open. She stepped outside and felt her hair sway against her skin, the sun pulsing. She stood motionless, save for her eyes that scanned the horizon for Mom and Ali.

After days in the basement, the open vista took her breath away. For a moment, she felt alone in the world.

"Where are you?" she asked the fields. "Are you out there?"

Heavy hands grabbed her by the shoulders and lifted her. She protested, kicking and swinging her arms, but it felt like she was striking a wall, and then the floor was over her head and her feet were in the air. The farmer turned off the music with his free hand, carrying Corvo down the basement staircase so fast, the girl got scared they'd both fall. Instead, she found herself tossed onto the mattress, his seething face over her. He pointed and fumed, shaking his head in disbelief, his cheeks pulsing red under the deep tan. With an exasperated huff, he walked back up the staircase. Before the door closed, Corvo caught a glimpse of the teacher. Her hands were over her mouth, eyes pleading for understanding.

Deep inside the basement, the girl stared at the door and listened to the heavy staccato steps behind it. Steps of how-could-you and of what-were-you-thinking. And throughout it all, the bald man's speech rambled on, muffled and distant. Shadows flickered underneath the door, arms waving and hands gesturing. There were no words from either of them. No shouting. That's how mutes were. When Mom and Ali were angry at each other, they shouted. They screamed. Sometimes, they cried. Then, their voices turned back to normal, even if they were a little hoarse.

But not mutes.

Mutes couldn't argue. Not with words, anyway.

Still, silence had its own intonation, its own accent. And what she heard in it was hurt.

THE TEACHER WOKE up in the morning aware of his sleeping form beside her. His back was turned to her as if still mad. For her interaction with the girl, for leaving notes everywhere, even for dying, presumably. She slipped out of bed feeling static prickling her skin. A headache pounded between her temples and she needed a moment to steady herself once she stood up. In the bathroom, she chewed on two aspirins without water. She was glad for the country fair. The school would remain closed. She'd spend the day sitting with the girl in the basement. Corvo would talk and she would listen and write until late in the evening. *Progress*, she thought and allowed herself a smile which died almost at once. She'd have to find a way to make it up to Corvo for the previous day. The word "apology" had more syllables than she was comfortable with, but she owed it to her. As for him, she'd have to bear his grudge.

She hadn't expected him to be back home the previous day, not that early. She had been careless, she knew that. But how could she explain it? How could she begin to explain anything to him, words or no words? Silence had its own comfort. In time, her ability to bare her soul to him had atrophied and she was sure he felt the same. She was also sure that, for most of the time, neither of them minded.

Having changed into her clothes, she made her way down the stairs. Still sleep-blind, she put the kettle on for coffee and set the pan on the stove. Other than the headache, nothing felt out of place. No blood in her mouth. The monster in her guts was quiet. Outside, the scarecrow shook its head, caught in a rising wind that pulled dust up from the ground and left it suspended in the air. While the water boiled, she went to the basement door and gave it a gentle knock.

When no reply came, she knocked again and went back to the kitchen. She felt the aspirins doing their work, blunting the pain and clearing her vision. Once the pan started smoking, she poured fat into it and then dough. There was a half-pack of sugar in the pantry she kept for special occasions. Once she finished with the frying, she'd sprinkle some of it on the dough and let the heat turn it into caramel. *An appropriate way to apologize*, she thought. And then, she'd ask her to talk about her plan to go North.

There was nothing North but war and misery. They were

more likely to die than set eyes on the border. Or maybe they were planning on taking advantage of the chaos to slip through. Still. To escape into enemy territory, and then what?

She thought of those things, of the impossibility of covering the distance on foot without being noticed, of the sheer luck they'd need to not get caught in the crossfire. She also imagined herself in their place, fleeing this town, and felt a sense of lightness. North. Her mind was already preoccupied with a deluge of single-syllable words.

Hope. Write. Death.

Our home is here, she thought. *The fields are here, such as they are. Here is where his family is buried, where our boy is buried, and where we'll both be buried when the time comes, in the same cemetery on the hill behind the church.* She tried to look out of the window that had become dustier than normal since she had woken up. *They still talk in the North, she thought. And read.*

With the breakfast in one hand and a mug of black coffee in the other, she went back to the basement door. She turned the key with one hand, but the door was already unlocked. *We never locked it*, she realized.

Dropping the food, she ran through the hallway, through the living room, and out onto the porch. She flung the door open and looked out over the fields, searching for the girl. Beyond the corn that cracked and swayed in the wind, a dust storm painted the horizon red.

10.

B EFORE THE SUN came up, Corvo sneaked out through the front door. With the farmer's handkerchief over her mouth and nose against the dust, she stole up the dirt driveway. The road's crumbling asphalt extended forever, until it faded out of sight. She squinted into the distance. No cars. The yellow dividing line along the road's middle had faded to ashen gray a long time ago and chaff from the fields rotted between the cracks.

A deep breath. Then, she darted across the road, plunged into the dead tree thicket on the other side, and disappeared.

She never looked back. Fear gnawed at her mind that the moment she turned, they would be behind her. The woman with her story, always her story. The gorilla that twisted her bones and bruised her. Both of them chasing her, wanting her back in the basement, away from everyone that mattered.

And, if not them, then the other mutes would be after her.

"Go North," she kept telling herself. "Go North". That was the agreement with Mom and Ali. If any of them got separated, they'd continue North and wait for each other at a safe place. If they were still alive, she'd find them.

Without warning, the thicket parted and she found herself in a withered wheat field. Only then did she slow down.

The fields extended to the hills that rimmed the horizon. A breeze was picking up. She searched the horizon for the rising sun that would guide her. Instead, she saw a sky smeared with dirt. Dust clouds hung heavy, dragging over the earth. They were too far away for the sound to reach her, but static electricity prickled her skin.

Without the sun to guide her, she kept the storm to her right and continued.

After a couple of hours, a depression in the ground opened without warning and she stumbled in it. Her right knee hit the ground hard and became wet.

I'm bleeding, she thought.

Her fingers went to her leg, but, when she looked at her hand, there was no blood. Only water. Below her, she was sunk knee-deep into a stream that flowed in a lethargic driblet. Without thinking, she pulled the handkerchief down and drank drank drank, tasting bitter grit in the water. Corvo became aware of how thirsty she was. How hungry. She had nothing with her other than the clothes she wore.

She tugged at her t-shirt as, around her, wind-blackened trees stood out like lone stick figures. Every time the wind picked up, tiny pieces of bark flew off and danced in the eddies and vortexes between the branches. Roots like arthritic fingers grasped at the soil, fighting to keep the trunks upright and losing, losing, losing.

Corvo coughed dust and stared at them with hatred. Everything in this land was broken. Everything was poisoned. She imagined the mutes spilling venom from their mouths, because they couldn't release it with words anymore, and the venom seeping into the ground, rotting it from the inside out. The land loathed her as much as she loathed it. Her coughing got worse and her eyes itched. She kicked at the plants, shattering them into pieces, raising dust that never settled down again.

In the late morning, sharp pain in her belly forced her to stop. She checked a spot for snakes, pulled her pants down and squatted. While she did her business, she kept an eye out for mutes and didn't notice the blood dripping between her feet. And, when she was done, she covered her mess with dirt like a cat, not leaving any sign that she had been there and not noticing anything amiss.

It's the food that woman's been feeding me. It's giving me the skitters, she thought and kicked more dirt. *Keep going. Keep going.*

She ran-walked through what used to be wheat and oats and alfalfa, always keeping the growing dust storm to her right. The farmhouse ruins were easy to spot in the distance. She picked up the pace when she noticed its skewed form, shifted off its foundations. A chimney lay collapsed on the ground and the hole in the roof where it had once stood gaped wide open. Shattered glass glinted on the rotten porch.

Safe place. Safe place. They had to be in there. She knelt among the weeds and observed it, trying to spot movement through the windows, her stomach rumbling but not out of hunger.

Despite wanting to run inside, she held back, observing the ruin, cautious of mutes. She remained still, fighting both her impatience and the rising nausea.

When her legs started going numb, she made her move.

There were moments when the house disappeared from sight, even while she stared right at it. Her legs still moved, but she had no control over them. A blink and the house was ten paces closer. Another and it was to her right as if she had veered off course. Beneath her clothes, she could feel her belly distending. Why were her knees going loose? When she fell, she didn't cry out. She laid there on the ground and closed her eyes, her forehead burning up.

When she came to, the light was different. The dust storm was closer and now she could hear a low animal rumble coming from it. She pushed herself up and vomited, pain shooting through her head.

A car approached, moving through the field. She crouched down again between the wheat, listening.

The car stopped next to the house and two doors opened. Footsteps echoed on the house's porch, breaking glass underneath them. Then, silence.

She remained hidden in the wheat, observing the black beetles that swarmed over the vomit. The pain in her belly came in waves. She bit her lip. It was difficult to tell whether the heat she felt in her head came from the sun or from a fever.

When she could no longer sit still, she saw them coming out of the house. Two teenagers, him with a shaved head, her with thin straw blond locks behind her ears. They adjusted their clothes and as they did, he kissed her neck. He cupped her breasts and she squeezed his hands tighter against her body. Then, she broke away from him and ran to the passenger door. They paused, the girl's posture going rigid, and they stared at each other over the car. To Corvo, they appeared to be reading each other's faces, seeking words in each other's features. They didn't smile, nor did they frown.

Corvo understood that a silent conversation went on between them. She tried to imagine it, but she wasn't raised a mute. She was raised normal, around normal people who didn't go all Major Tom because they forced themselves to stay quiet.

The girl's posture relaxed and she let out a long sigh. The boy smiled. Whatever conversation had taken place between them had ended. They both entered the car and drove off.

After she lost sight of the vehicle, Corvo stood and walked to the house where she dragged herself up the stairs onto the broken porch.

The air inside was stale and musky, with the sour smell of spilled alcohol punching through. Crumpled pieces of wall plaster littered the ground. Mom and Ali weren't there.

She kicked at a pile of old clothes in a corner. Amongst them lay an oversized navy blue sweater. She lifted it out of the heap, shook it free of dust and rolled it under her arm.

To her relief, the stairs to the upper floor were solid. She walked through its empty rooms. One of them had a soiled mattress on the floor, the cheap sheets covering it all crumpled up. The room smelled the same way that Mom and Ali's bedroom did after they had sex. Through the window above the mattress, she could see crops for miles. Wheat and hay and beans all turned yellow as the sun burned down on them.

Corvo used the sweater as a comforter and laid on the mattress. Sleep came over her the moment she closed her eyes. She had no dreams.

✕

SHE WOKE UP in parts, slowly enough that she didn't realize at first that she was awake. Not even when she felt teeth pulling at her foot. Not when she saw that foot disappearing into the

animal's mouth. She rubbed her eyes and, with consciousness, pain also set in.

So much soot and dust covered the animal's fur that it
was hard telling what breed the dog was, but she thought she
had seen its sort in picture books. They were meant to be
kind.

"Stop, stop," she shouted. The dog paused its pulling, as
if surprised to hear words. With her shoe and foot in its
mouth, it stared back. It seemed puzzled, as if asking "You
talk?" With her other leg, the girl kicked the animal once in
the snout. It reared up and snarled, snapping teeth at her. It
bit at the blue sweater, shook its head left to right.

Screaming, snarling as the dog did, she kicked it again,
this time with both feet.

Again.

Kicking. Crying.

Again.

Letting her grief out. Emptying her lungs, finding solace
in the violence.

The walls echoed.

The dog fell backwards pulling the sweater with it,
whining. For the briefest and the longest moment, an urge
tugged at Corvo's chest, to reach and grab the sweater out of
its mouth. It seemed vital, somehow. Then, the clicking of
claws on wooden floors. Then, terror.

There's more of them.

Instead, she ran outside as fast as she could, ignoring the
pain shooting through her ankle. Behind her, the clicking of
claws on wood echoed through the house, coming from the
bedrooms, from the kitchen, from the basement. From deep
inside the house came deep full-throated barks. Several blurs
scrambled over furniture to get to her. She crashed through

the door and tripped over broken planks on the porch, tearing a gash in her right leg. Losing balance, she stumbled over the porch steps and smashed into the ground with a loud cry as the air got knocked out of her.

She wanted to cry, to scream again and release the pain, but she couldn't. Instead, she gasped and braced herself.

The cavalcade of clicking drew nearer. The dogs spilled out of the house. Her hand curled around a stone, and she launched it at them. It caught a brown flat-faced brute on the forehead and sent it whimpering away. The rest reared back and barked. Seeing her opportunity, the girl picked up another stone and made a show of raising it high over her head, baring her teeth and huffing, slapping the ground with the other hand.

Still barking in frustration, the dogs retreated back into the house. Not letting up, she hurled the stone through the door, sending the pack scattering. Corvo picked herself up and limped away.

She set a course towards the closest hills, ignoring the storm heading in the same direction. Behind her, the dogs stared. One by one, they jumped off the porch and disappeared into the wheat.

Through the stalks and the husks and the seeds, flashes of fur accompanied her, flanking her and kept pace, all lolling tongues and ravenous panting. She could see the light glinting off cracked teeth, and smell the soot on their pelts. And the more her heart raced, the louder the excitement came from across the divide, starved and impatient. The dogs refused to attack just yet and, through her pain, she realized why. She would slow down sooner or later. She would stop and drop to the ground in exhaustion and helplessness. In the end, she'd give up and they wouldn't.

Her foot throbbed. She looked down at the mangled shoe, blood caking around the ankle, and pain shooting up with every step. "So stupid," she sobbed. With effort, she picked up a stone and threw it. A soft thud and a yelp came back and she grinned through her tears.

When the panting grew nearer and she thought she'd have to make a stand and fight, the fields started to thin out. Houses appeared, their rooftops bathed in the evening light. She headed straight for them. Behind her, the dogs pricked their ears and sniffed the air. A few of them turned in circles around themselves, hesitant to follow. The girl limped on, ignoring chills as both the wind and her fever picked up.

One by one, the dogs abandoned the hunt. By the time Corvo reached the houses, only a single dog remained standing in the distance, slurping at her blood on its mouth. It was still looking on with the soot blowing away from its fur in gusts as she ducked down a back alley.

As adrenaline subsided, the pain came flooding in to fill the void. She bit her lips. *I can pass off as one of the mutes*, she thought. *As long as I don't talk.*

She walked close to the walls, avoiding windows where she could. Still, the houses seemed dark and empty, save for the glow of TV static.

She heard the crackling sound even before she approached Main Street. Then came the smell, that odor that crowds exude. Sweat mingled with dust. Breaths stinking of dry saliva and infection. Dried piss.

There were other smells there too. Frying oil. Fizzy soda. The warm yeasty comfort of baked bread. Corvo made her way towards the bustling.

The street was full of mutes. There were people with their families and there were carts with sugared apples, stands with colorful drinks and sugar cane. On each cart, she could see the same symbol. Three crossed arrows wrapped in a wreath.

The entire town must have been there. Yet there was no talking, only the humming of generators, the sloshing of food being prepared, and the din of feet hitting asphalt.

She should have been feeling alarmed. She should have hidden, or better yet, turned around and ran straight out of that town, taking her chances with the dogs. Yet with her dirty face, her muddied clothes… even the limp, she looked no different than most of the townsfolk, save for the fact that they were skin and bones and she wasn't. Save for her eyes. She pulled the handkerchief tighter and let her tangled hair cover her face. Hid her body in a ratty oversized shirt stolen from a backyard clothesline. And she slipped amongst them.

She kept what distance she could from the mutes, walking along building walls, and they paid her no mind. Not enough to tell she didn't belong. She studied their faces. With the exception of the couple that had locked her up, it was the first time she had been so close to mutes. None of their faces were right either. Too long or too wide on the forehead, or with uneven eyes, or all of those together. She saw other things too. Arms that were too short or too thin, swollen legs. Toothless mouths, twisted and warped as if they'd been interrupted mid-speech and never got to finish. And star-shaped scars on their throats. All the younger mutes had it, but only a few adults. She adjusted the handkerchief now, trying to make it cover her throat, conscious of the smooth skin there.

All of the food was free. All she had to do was wait in one of the long queues together with the mutes. When they received their share, they wolfed it down, then made their way to the back of the queue again. A couple of kids tried to cut in line. A woman in a Sheriff's uniform walked up to them and, without warning, smacked them loudly upside the head and nodded to the back.

Corvo didn't dare get too close to the mutes or the Sheriff. Instead, she snuck behind one of the stands and grabbed a few sugared apples from a crate. As she was sneaking away, she spotted a mute girl staring at her. Thinking quickly, she tossed one of the apples to her, and the other girl flashed a crooked smile before running off.

With a sugared apple in each hand, Corvo found a quiet corner in an empty lot and ate them behind a half-built cinder block wall, away from prying eyes. Despite being happy that she was eating something other than bland greens, she couldn't concentrate. Her fever had dropped, but the chills worked their way through her body and she shivered. She wished she had the sweater the dog had taken from her.

Besides the food stands, there were small stages along the street. They were wheeled, made for traveling from town to town. On one of them, a dog with two heads scanned the audience from inside a chicken wire cage. A man tossed raw scraps of meat and gristle at it and the two heads fought with each other over them. At the other side of the street, a man stood with another diminutive version of himself straddling his shoulders. Turning his back to the audience, he let his loose shirt drop to reveal he was attached to the smaller man, or rather the smaller man was attached to him. The homunculus pulled his lips back in a toothy grin. He put two misshaped hands on his bearer's head and forced him to dance, a disjointed prance that enthralled its audience.

Corvo enjoyed the sight of the woman that covered

herself in hairy spiders and, when no one was looking, the girl got close enough to the donkey with the six legs to touch it.

One stand piqued her interest more than others. A thin white sheet stretched over a wooden frame the size of a bed. It reminded Corvo of the TV back at the compound. Her Mom had told her that, a long time ago, one could turn a TV on just like the radio and see what folks from distant places were doing right at that moment. Corvo had asked if mutes had TVs. Her Mom had stopped smiling and nodded. "They do," she had said. "But you could only ever see one person on them. And you could never turn them off."

As the evening wore on, a crowd formed in front of the sheet-stage. She stood at the back, keeping her distance from the other children.

A light trembled into existence behind the sheet. Shadows of figures and buildings, vehicles and other objects appeared, lit from behind. They faded in and out. There was no narration, but Corvo could understand the story. She could comprehend poverty, power. Division and Unity. She could recognize all that and, with every shadow that appeared on the sheet, the story became clearer. And when she did piece it together, her heart grew cold.

IN THE BEGINNING was the Word. But the Word lived in the hearts of men who were not worthy of it. Just as it can soothe and becalm, so can it poison the mind. It can make brothers lift their hands against each other in anger, and cheat the guileless out of their livelihoods. It is only natural. The first word was made to deceive. And so, the Great Crisis arrived.

The poor wailed in the streets. Millions were jobless. Those who did not respond with violence, starved. Those who did, filled the prison cells. And all the while the false parties raged on, waving and pointing their fingers at each other. Measures were taken to protect society. Thieves were executed on the spot like dogs. Beggars were dragged away. But, when the poor starve, what else is there to do but eat the rich? Over thirteen days, streets drowned in blood in an event termed the Fears. And still, the rhetoric ensued. From their safe mansions, the false parties, together with their collaborators, called for reason. They called for peace, even as they manipulated the poor, sending the police and the army, poor people themselves, to restore order. It would have been the end of the nation. Those who sought to destroy it counted on discord. They counted on words of Division, seeded like rotten kernels. The Party's strength was that it did not comprise only of the poor or the rich or the strong or the downtrodden. It included everyone who was not an enemy of the people, whose interest was Unity and not mutual destruction. The greatest thinkers formed the one true Party and led the nation through the Great Panic, bloody as it was. Yet, it was a blooding that led to rebirth. Nations have but two rights when their existence is challenged, annihilation or greatness. The Party showed the way to greatness. The truth liberated the people. They had been coerced to the brink by false words. There had been many voices where only one mattered. And so the people made a decision. The Party would speak on behalf of the nation. The Party would become the Voice of the nation. The Fears would forever stand as a reminder of Division, a reminder of a time when the nation was almost drowned in its own noise. There would be Unity. One voice. One nation.

✕

THE AUDIENCE WATCHED with eyes wide open. When the army descended on the civilians and executed them, they stomped their feet. When the Party intervened, they clapped in unison.

Corvo watched all that and frowned. Her stomach turned, as much by the lies as by the nausea. Skeletal silhouetted figures roamed the silhouetted streets with babies in their outstretched hands, while corpulent pig-faced figures towered over them and argued with each other, their jowls quivering under the light. Sharp shapes tumbling out of their mouths represented words. They spilled out and rained like bombs on those dying below them. Other figures, made of rigid squares and walking in lockstep in tight formations, pushed the poor before them. The poor pushed back in a terrible black wave, and the stage plunged into darkness.

The light of a single candle danced into existence. Specks fell through that single point of light. Magnified, elongated and distorted, until they regained their true shape. Human forms tumbled through the air, the myriad dead of the Fears. Hollowed ruins appeared on the stage's wings. The human deluge bloated the sky and still the light brightened. In the end, it swallowed the stage. The dead, the ruins, the sky. When it dimmed enough for shadows to become visible again, tall father-figures came into focus. They extended their arms, gathering the broken people around them. Members of the false parties shed their pig-faced masks and joined their ranks. Their heads were bowed, but the Party embraced them all the same. Instead of punishing them, the tall figures reached down and handed them tools, then directed them back to the destroyed buildings. The people opened their mouths and the words flowed out of them, joining into one big swirling cloud that condensed into a revolving sphere. The sphere rose far above the crowd. The audience watched in rapture. A single figure rose higher than all the rest and took the sphere within itself. In the beginning was the Word. Now, the Word was with the Party, and the Party spoke for all.

The audience broke into applause. Tears streamed from the eyes of a few.

When the clapping died down, the story continued.

The true enemy revealed its face.

The North had had a hand in the Great Crisis. The words of Division had been their words, whispered into the ears of those who were easily fooled. War was now a matter of survival, of ensuring the Fears would never be repeated. Corvo watched shadow warplanes scream through the skies and rain bombs down on demonic shapes full of teeth and claws. Troops paraded through enemy cities, their inhabitants welcoming them as liberators, showering them with flowers, while, back home, the people supported the war effort with their labor in the fields and the factories.

Corvo crossed her arms over her chest and refused to clap. *That's not what happened,* she thought. *It didn't happen that way, Mom told me the truth. Ali told me the protests were against the Party.* None of the other things happened, yet the mutes were applauding. At the same time, doubt crept into her head. If they *were* at war with the North, how could they reach it? Would the North still take them in? She stared at the screen and felt torn. How much of the play was a lie and what part was true?

When she noticed some of the children staring at her, she slipped away. The sun dipped ever-lower to the horizon.

Her shivering became more violent. She rubbed her arms, but couldn't warm up. She needed to find a safe place and sleep.

She stumbled down Main Street on her bloodied and swollen ankle. Mutes had stopped what they were doing to point at the dust clouds that had gathered close to the town, reaching high in the atmosphere. Some of them started to run.

She turned the corner. There, a pack of children threw rocks at three shapes hanging over the only street light in the town. Three of the children looked almost identical to each other, although they were of different ages. Their features and their shaved heads betrayed them as brothers. The younger one swung his arm in wide circles before releasing his stone. Every time he hit one of the shapes, he looked at his brothers and they raised their arms in triumph.

She didn't recognize Mom and Ali at first. Their faces had become deformed. Their skin had dehydrated, stretched tight over cheek bones and shin bones and collarbones under the sun, turned stone gray. And yet, it was them.

The world went as gray as their skin. She stumbled towards the group of children, got close without paying attention. Shot an arm out to steady herself, pushing the younger boy, who stared at her as if he were trying to place her. Someone grabbed her arm and at that point she wanted to scream louder than any of those mutes had experienced in their pointless lives. She wanted to turn them into dust, them *and* this town of theirs, and blast everything into the wind. A hand covered her mouth and muffled her crying. She thought of Mom and Ali being grabbed by dozens of arms and pulled into the fields, sinking into the darkness.

She was picked up by rough hands and dragged into the side streets away from the hanging bodies and the crowds.

She heard labored breathing above her and her heart beat even faster. The farmer stared hard as he carried her, while the teacher ran ahead and opened the car door. She tried to fight when she got tossed into the car. From the driver's seat, the farmer turned to face her and held a finger to his lips, his eyes cursing her. The teacher sat next to her and closed the door, pushing her head down.

The car peeled away and left town.

Everything around them turned red all at once as the storm descended. A curtain had dropped over the world. Behind them, the town's lights vanished. The fields on either side of the road took an alien feel.

"What's happening?" the girl asked through her delirium, but no one answered her. "Mom, Ali," she shouted. "What have they done to them?"

The girl tried to stick her head out of the window, but the teacher pulled her back inside. A shocked expression crossed her face as she brushed the girl's forehead and felt the fever.

"What have you done to them?" the girl muttered and her eyes rolled back into her head.

The storm shook the car, lifting it before dumping it down again. When the farmer touched a button on the dashboard, a spark hit his finger and he grunted in pain.

The car pinged with tiny impacts and the girl caught glimpses of the window turning opaque with dirt, as if a decade had passed in the space of a few seconds. Flashes of light cast harsh shadows on their surroundings.

In the fields, sparks flew between the branches of the wind-blackened trees, and, one by one, they burst into fire.

The car drifted at the turn to the farmhouse, pushed by the wind. They came to a stop outside the door and the teacher covered the girl's head as the farmer carried her inside. Rushed down to the basement and locked the heavy oak door behind them. For the first time since she had arrived in the farmhouse, Corvo was thankful for the silence.

11.

WHEN THE TEACHER was diagnosed with the monster in her guts, she refused treatment. She had seen what fighting terminal cancer had done to her mother-in-law, who wasted away until there was nothing left of her dignity. A life like that was not worth clinging to. The farmer brooded when he found out, but he seemed to understand. At least, that's what the teacher assumed.

Painkillers were the only thing the teacher conceded to. But these took time to act.

As the teacher waited for the pills to work, she learned that controlling her breathing took away the worst of the pain.

In the basement, she showed the girl how to breathe.

Held her hand up.

Counted to four, inhaled.

Then, held her breath. Another count of four.

She released her breath. Unrushed, taking her time. Feeling the pain exit.

Then paused her breathing. Keeping her eyes closed. Letting the pain ebb. Another count of four. Then, starting over again.

They did this together, until Corvo followed the rhythm by herself. Soon, the girl closed her eyes and fell into a deep sleep. Her forehead still burned, but a stillness descended into the basement, even as the dust storm wailed outside.

The farmer stood apart from them underneath the windows, trying to peer past the thick layer of dust to the fields. He kept scratching his head. When she caught his eye, he looked away, as if embarrassed, and his face became stony.

She had showed him the empty basement and insisted they go out and look for the girl by pulling him towards the door. He had crossed his arms and stood his ground, only relenting when she got into the car alone and started the engine. Silence by resentment smelled different than the easy silence of comfort. It smelled of sulfur and it filled the space between them, first in the car and now here in the basement.

He stared out of the windows, but she could tell his eyes were not seeing.

She inhaled while counting to four.

12.

T HE DAY THE words were taken, the four of them were
sitting around the mahogany table. Across it laid potato
salad heavy with mayo, casserole, dark bread and blonde
beer. Roast pork slices dripped with juices next to the gravy
boat. Not a cob of corn in sight.

They ate and they drank and they laughed. The glow
through the windows lit the corn fields outside, thick and
green and healthy.

"Everything alright?" the journalist asked.

The Deputy was checking her phone. Her fleshy fingers
typed a message in a flurry.

"Yeah. Kinda. Don't know," she said, distracted. "Boys at
the station got a package by courier. From County.
Instructed to be opened in thirty minutes."

"Sounds important," the farmer said with a mouthful of
potato salad.

"It's outta process and mighty abnormal, is what it is. No
wine for me, thanks," she said and pointed at her not-yet-
showing belly.

"You don't hafta leave, do you?"

"Naw. Hope not. Only if it's an emergency or somepin.

They'll call me if it is."

The teacher didn't respond. Her attention was on the TV blaring out the news.

The farmer took a swig out of a beer bottle and pointed at the images of masked rioters clashing with armored police, throwing stones, launching Molotov cocktails, kicking shop windows in. From the helicopter shot they seemed like ants, black dots swarming the capital streets.

"Look at them. Fuckin savages. Like that's gonna solve your problems. Morons."

He eyed the journalist and pointed a fork at him.

"We checked your article—"

"Editorial."

"The whatever you wrote last week."

"Didn't know you read me."

The farmer smiled. "Course we do. I don't think you're being fair."

"I've been called worse than that."

"No shit. That's not the point. The point is, people read you. You're riling them up by tellin them non-truths. Tellin them the Party—"

"Oh, so it's just 'the Party' now? That was quick."

"Telling them the Party is some boogeyman slashing liberties left, right, and center. That's not fair. Then, this happens."

The journalist glanced over at the Deputy who was still texting. He rubbed puffy, red-rimmed eyes and cleared his throat.

"All I'm doing is pointing out the implications behind the elected government absorbing the other parties. You don't see anything wrong with that?"

"Getting things done fer a change? No arguing, no

bickering, no unnecessary discussions? No, I don't see a thing wrong with that."

The journalist shook his head. "How about other opinions?"

"There's your other opinions," the farmer said, pointing at the TV. On screen, a car burned in the middle of an abandoned boulevard, throwing harsh shadows. "Do you enjoy this?"

"I don't see anything to enjoy. People are angry and angry people take it out on anything they can."

"You're the one makin them angry with your articles, instead of writing 'bout the good the Party has done. The public works, the economy."

The journalist shrugged. "I don't condone viol—"

"No, don't say that. Take responsibility for your words."

The Deputy put her phone on the table and stroked the journalist's head, her wedding band disappearing into his curly hair. "Folks usually pay him fer his opinion, mmm?"

The farmer reached into his back pocket. "Sweetheart, have you seen my wallet? I'd like to hear what this man's gotta say."

The teacher rolled her eyes and continued watching the TV with a glass of wine in one hand.

"Are you gonna pay him fer real or just wave that stupid Party card around again?" the Deputy said.

"Hey, it's cool," the journalist lifted his hands. "It's cool. I think that if intact shop windows are the problem, we are solving it in great style. I'll concede that."

"Can we please not talk about politics over dinner? You're already getting cross at each other again," the teacher complained.

"We're having us a civilized discussion," the farmer

replied.

"Nobody wants to hear about that."

"What?"

"We're having a good time and you're bringing up work."

"We're just talkin."

"Okay. You're just talking."

"Maybe he wants to talk."

"Sure."

"Why are you—If he doesn't wanna talk 'bout—You know what, never mind."

"No. Forget what I said. Talk if you want."

The two couples glanced at their plates, moving around potatoes and making patterns in the gravy. TV noise filled the room.

"But, to be honest," the journalist mercifully interrupted the silence, "nothing I say really matters for long, so I don't see why you're getting all riled up about it. I give it three weeks before it all blows over, tops. Same thing happened when the Morality Board got introduced. Travel quotas, same thing. Oh, I'm consistent, me. I was running the same arguments back then as I do now. People," he waved a hand at the TV, "bark and rage for an average of twenty-one days, sometimes less if holidays are around the corner. There's research backing this up. The National Unity Party does not respond, which is smart. It doesn't even acknowledge there's a reaction. It ignores us, refuses to engage. The public runs out of steam. In the end, everything goes back to normal, because people realize they can survive whatever gets thrown at them. Besides, they got bills to pay. Rioting is a lot harder with a mortgage. My writing is me doing what I have to do and I've stopped pretending it'll change anything. There will always be a backlash. Just don't count on it lasting for long."

"What I think," the farmer said, "is, you destroy someone's property, you should get shot. On the spot, no questions asked, no due process. Destroying someone's property, how does that make them any different than common criminals?"

The journalist threw his hands in the air. "We're not even having the same discussion here."

The farmer turned to the Deputy. "If someone breaks into somebody's business, you shoot him. Right?"

"Shit, yes," the Deputy said. "Standard procedure. Maybe chuck a coupla grenades at them too."

"It's a serious legal question."

"Then, here's a serious answer on behalf of your local law enforcement. We protect the people. All of them, even from themselves. It's right there in the law in black and white. Alright? Anger makes people stupid an' there's lots of it pent up as is. Why, I ain't gonna shoot every angry person I see or this place would turn into a ghost town real quick."

"Angry my ass, just want to ruin other people's property with impunity. You're excuse is not accepted, Madame Deputy."

"Hell, I'm in a foul mood myself most of these days, amount of interference old man Sheriff gets from the Party. Telling him how to run things in his own town."

The teacher didn't follow the back-and-forth. Her eyes remained glued to the TV.

Lowering his head, the journalist spoke almost inaudibly. "It's the official narrative that matters. I'm going to keep writing my opinion. Whether anyone acts upon it, is a different matter."

The images on the TV of raging crowds, of burning trash

bins rolling through the streets, of police carrying shields and batons cut to suited men and women sitting at a conference table. They were discussing in low voices and passing notes to each other, their faces tight and determined under the flash of cameras and studio lights.

At their head sat the Party's Spokesman. His was the only easy smile, one arm thrown behind his chair. With the other, he scanned a document line by line, making corrections here and there with a pencil. Without warning, he raised his eyes and looked straight into the camera. He smiled that half-smile of his that had been his trademark since the election, together with the bald head and backswept ears, which had given political satirists and cartoonists an easy shorthand to mock him.

Other Party members looked into the camera lens with slight annoyance and awkwardness.

"Speaking of writing, how's yours going?" the journalist asked the teacher.

"That guy," the Deputy pointed at the Spokesman as the camera zoomed in on him. "His smile creeps me out."

"I gotta tell you," the farmer interjected, ignoring the Deputy. "The plot is a little frou-frou for my taste, but if people pay to read it, you won't hear me complaining none."

The teacher bit her lower lip. "It's going," she answered. "It's a slow process."

"Like wading through mud."

"It must be easy for you. You've written two books in the time it's taken me to write one chapter."

"Apples and oranges," the journalist said. "I don't have to be creative, just need to give my opinion."

"I wish I could bring you to the school and have you talk to my class."

"I'd like that too. Just… not right now."

"Still?"

"I don't have many fans at the moment."

"Seems it's been like that since I've known you."

"And for a good deal before that, too."

The Deputy squeezed his hand. "Let's make a list with all the people that hate you, all the people who've ever threatened to kill you, and I'll mail them a thank you note for sending you out here in the boondocks and straight to me."

The journalist smiled, then pointed at the TV. "Ah. More measures," he said, and the farmer gave him the finger.

Now, all four of them dropped their conversations and focused on the screen. A news ticker at the bottom counted off a litany of locations across the country that citizens were advised to avoid due to riots.

A number of shushes from off-screen, and silence fell in the conference room on the TV. The Spokesman stood, buttoned his jacket and, carrying a single sheet of notes, moved to a podium with the Unity Party logo on it.

"My dearest citizens," he started. "We have extraordinary news to share with you."

WHEN THE DECISION was announced, they all stared at each other, but couldn't find the words to describe their thoughts. Only the journalist fumbled with his phone.

"I need to check in with the paper," he said and left the table.

The farmer excused himself. He went upstairs to the bedroom and closed the door behind him. He stood next to the window overlooking the corn fields and fished his own phone out of his pocket. Quick-dialed. After several rings, a rumbling baritone answered.

"It's me," the farmer said. "Jes wanted to hear how you and Ma are doing. Are you watching the news?"

A long sigh from the other side. "Ma is Ma. You don't worry 'bout her, she's tougher than both of us together and then some. She don't complain. Folks here is treating her nice enough. 'Specially this foren nurse. Been giving your Ma foot rubs, helps relieve the pain. And, yes, we're watching the news. Can't help it. Entire hospital's watching."

The farmer tapped the window with his nail. Outside, the cobs lay heavy, making the stalks bow. Calculations ran in the farmer's head. He could see two new tractors in the new crops. An extension to the house. Paid medical bills.

"And? What d'you think?"

Silence from the other side and the sound of moving, of looking for a private spot.

"Hang on… Can you hear me?"

"Yeah."

"Okay. What do I think," the voice now came low and it sounded like Pa was in a bathroom. "I think you don't have to worry 'bout a thing. Just keep your head low. There'll be folks riled up, as usual. Let it blow over."

"Pa, they're asking people to not talk anymore. No, there's no asking. It's a law. Done deal. Ain't it too much? This can't happen here. Maybe in some shithole of a stan country where they treat people like cattle, but here?"

"Now, you listen to me. Things are gon' change. Okay? Things will change 'round here. But fer the better.

"Pa… That's not why we voted for those guys."

"We're on top, now. Okay? Son, we're on top. Yeah, bunch of folks will suffer, but it won't affect us. We're members, son. We'll get back t'all them bastards that ruined the country and let it go to the dogs. The ones that…"

A long pause. When his father talked again, it was with a terse whisper, anger behind it.

"The ones that let your Ma and all the others at the cannery get sick, then hung her out to dry when they shut the place down and painted her as a liar. The ones that take us for a bunch of uneducated idjits that don't deserve a voice. Now, we're taking theirs. Let them see how they like it."

"Pa?" the farmer rubbed his forehead. His throat felt dry.

"This, this is nopin," the voice continued over the phone. "The fambly is good and safe, is what matters. We're Party members. We're on the inside. Our people run the country now. They used ta tell us we don't deserve ta vote, because we're all backward. Us, the backbone of this country. Where's the justice in that?"

"You're telling me you're good with what just got announced? This ain't a tax hike, Pa, or even queers marrying each other."

A sigh from the other side.

"It don't matter none. It won't apply to us. We're members."

The farmer felt a headache beginning to develop. His free hand rolled into a fist.

"Can I talk to Ma?"

"She's sleeping. Jes got outta chemo. Lemme call you back when she's feeling better. Yeah?"

"Sure. Okay. Look, I gotta go. Got guests over. Jes called cause I don't know what to think 'bout this whole business. Talk to you soon."

"Alright, son. Keep that member's card safe, you hear?"

"Yessir."

The farmer hung up. When he returned to the table, he found the teacher alone staring at the TV. The Party members were now shaking each other's hands. The spokesman beaming in their midst. The news ticker at the bottom of the screen had disappeared.

"Where's everyone?" he asked.

"He's driving her back to the station," she answered without taking her eyes off the screen. "State of emergency."

He took his seat next to her and they both watched the news for a long time without saying anything. When they caught each other's eyes, he reached out and took her hand and she squeezed his fingers in hers.

13.

ORNING CAME AND went without anyone in the town
realizing. The townsfolk remained in their homes
with the curtains pulled shut, while outside the screaming
darkness continued to blot out the sun. It was as if a fairytale
wolf had come into their town and prowled the streets,
howling, rattling the boards on the windows. At night, the
stars remained hidden.

And yet, most of them felt calm. The constant scratching
and scouring filled their minds and chased away stray
thoughts.

By noon, the wind had diminished. Blinding patches of
blue appeared here and there in the sky. The mad howling
turned down to a tired yell and then into a whisper.

And then, just as it had started, the dust storm ended.

The townsfolk didn't come out at once. A few curtains
parted with hesitation. A few doors cracked open, letting the
dust inside. First one, then another, they shuffled out to
inspect the damage.

Only tattered ribbons hanging from a frame were left
from the shadow theater sheet. The storm had overturned the
food carts and the stages. Underneath the only traffic light,

the three ropes dangled free. The cardiganed woman waddled underneath them, lifting her arms, fists curled, her mouth twisting.

Outside town, the farmer jumped onto his tractor and drove off. He needed to inspect the damage. Needed to get out of that basement.

He had spent the night pacing in a black mood. It wasn't the girl's fault, he had tried to reason. She wanted to get to her folks, to her own. You couldn't fault her that. Family is all that matters. And yet, he had continued stewing at the danger she had put them in while the dust storm battered the house.

The girl has cursed us, he concluded. *She's better off gone. Better off away from them, away from the town, from any people that are not her own. Maybe she'll find what she needs up North.*

Especially now that they had been seen with her. Someone was bound to come asking questions. The faster they got rid of her, the better. If only he could have let her talk and damn herself, she wouldn't be his problem anymore, but his wife had forced his hand.

He punched the tractor's steering wheel, once, twice. *So little time left. And she's wasting it on that girl.*

He drove on. From the tractor cabin, all he could see was a dull monochromatic landscape that stretched out in every direction. *It'll be alright*, he thought. *Ain't the first time. Won't be the last.* Still, as he inspected the damage, something inside him cracked. He stopped the tractor.

He stayed in the driver's cabin for several long minutes, the sound of his breathing filling the silence. Sweat ran down his forehead and stung his eyes. Acres of flattened corn lay all around, as far as the horizon. Only frayed cracked fronds remained standing. He jumped down. He was careful with where he placed his feet, avoiding stepping on the plants in case they were still alive. When he found a seedling still standing upright, he knelt and removed a glove. He palmed it, squeezing it in his naked, callused hand. When he opened his hand again, the plant crumbled into dust.

Calculations had already started in his mind. Adjusting this year's profit over and over, playing with the numbers, doubling them and tripling them, hoping they'd work out. The new pesticide's price. Spare parts for the tractor. Selling for silage. He begged the numbers to add up until all hope was lost.

Next year, he told himself. *Next year, the crop will be stronger.* He told himself those things, but still he felt diminished. Small. Could anything be salvaged? Did anything separate him anymore from all the other men in town that had lost everything?

Standing, he noticed a furry mass curled up in the poisoned stream. There, sand running out of its nostrils and mouth, lay a dog. Flies covered its black eyes and its belly was distended with corpse bloat. The farmer sighed. *I reckon I took you for a lobo once*, he thought. *Fairly certain I almost shot you, too.*

He reached down and his fingers wrapped around a collar made of cracked leather. He pulled the lifeless dog out of the ditch. Then, taking a few steps, he dragged it deeper into the neighbor's land and left it there for the crows.

He drove past the stream and kept on driving until he reached the neighbor's house. There, he jumped off the tractor and walked straight to the barn without hesitation.

Something about the empty house hadn't seemed right to him when he had returned the horses. Over the following days, he had parked at a distance and observed. The animals had remained in the corral where he had left them, weak and starving. No one was coming for them. On the third day, he had brought a bushel of corn and led the horses into the barn, away from the sun.

He checked that the horses were still alright in there. The white one turned to look at him and went on chewing corn together with the other two. Satisfied, the farmer made his way to the house's front door and tried the handle. It was unlocked.

For as long as he remembered it, the neighbor's house had seemed uncared for from the outside. White paint flaked off the walls. Shingles littered the ground below the roof. As a child, he and his friends would dare each other to sneak all the way up to the fence and give it a kick before running, barking with laughter and sending the buzzards flying. Even back then, it had seemed run down.

Yet, the house inside was a different creature. Floors were the deep burned brown of massive wood. The farmer ran his hands over the beams supporting the low ceiling and felt their immovable weight. There wasn't much in the way of furniture, but the little there was seemed handmade.

The photographs captured and held his attention. On the coffee table, on the otherwise empty bookshelves, hanging from the walls. Most of them were black and white. Others were yellowing and fuzzy, past generations captured on film.

On the older pictures, faces stared out refusing to smile. Here and there, something in their features would trigger a sense of recognition, the way certain lines curved on either side of a mouth like a parenthesis, the shape of someone's eyes. Through time, postures became looser, shapes became sharper, colors blushed into existence, and faces became more familiar.

He picked out the neighbor himself almost at once. The eldest of five children, he looked like a finer, more delicate version of his father: the same expression, the same odd vertical wrinkle at the corner of his eyes, the same slant of the shoulders. He followed him as he aged through the photographs. The face filled out, the hairline receded. Wrinkles. Fashions changed and finally a woman appeared by his side, her smile an explosion of energy reaching out of the picture. In every single frame she was in, she held the neighbor tightly by the arm and her beaming smile spilled into everyone else around her.

The last picture had been from twelve years ago. And then, nothing. He scratched his head and thought of the journalist who, like his neighbor's wife, had disappeared at around the same time. Them, and others. He'd liked the journalist. Couldn't agree on most things and their arguments could get heated, but he respected the other man's willingness to discuss anything.

THE FARMER GUIDED the horses out of the barn and fought back a coughing fit. Led them to the corral, worked the pump until he filled up their trough with muddy water, and set off on his way back.

As he drove close to his house, music from the stereo drifted to his ears.

He could see the girl now, sitting on the porch steps side by side with his wife. The girl looked pale and hollow. Her foot was bandaged and she leaned onto her knees. Listless. He gripped the steering wheel and braced himself for what he knew was the right thing to do.

They've seen her, he was certain. *And they've seen us take her. If they find her here...* The image of three dead bodies hanging from the post came to his mind. Only it wasn't three strangers that he saw, but him and his wife on each side of the girl.

Both the teacher and the girl now looked up as the tractor came to a rolling stop.

The farmer pushed his door open and stepped down onto the sand-covered ground, first one leg, then the other, taking his time. There was no rush, no sudden movements. The girl pulled her knees a bit closer. The teacher put an arm around her shoulders.

He approached and pointed at the girl. Then, he pointed North.

The girl looked from the farmer to the teacher.

"What's he saying?"

The farmer snapped his fingers in front of her face to force her attention and pointed North again. He grabbed the girl by the hand and forced her up.

"No, no," she protested, making him wince. "No, please. Don't send me away."

She reached out for the teacher and grabbed hold of her shirt.

"Please, let me stay. Tell him to let me stay. Tell him."

The farmer scanned the buried fields around, scared that someone might hear her. He motioned his free palm downwards to shush her. *Stop it. You're safer out there alone. We're safer here without you. Go North. They'll take care of you there. This isn't a place for a talking girl. Just leave.*

"Please, don't send me away. No," the girl screamed.

The teacher held the girl's other hand and eyed the farmer with a severe look, but he didn't flinch. He repeated the gesture again to the girl.

For all of our sakes, you have to go.

"Please, don't."

Shut up.

"Don't."

Why don't you understand me?

He grabbed the girl by the cuff and dragged her along the wooden porch, leaving tracks through the dust. Ignored the wailing that hurt his ears, ignored his wife clapping her hands behind him demanding his attention, ignored his own thoughts asking if he was going too far.

"I got no one else. I got no one else," the girl begged.

When they reached the tractor, he set her upright and pointed away from the house with gnashing teeth. *Go. Get lost. North's this way. Don't stop, don't turn around, don't even think of us again.*

The girl swung and kicked him between the legs with her good foot, collapsing them both to the ground. He remained there, wincing and doubled over, one hand on his crotch, another on his mouth to muffle his grunting. Finding an opportunity, the girl pushed herself up and limped back towards the house, past the teacher, and upstairs. A door slammed like an exclamation mark and sank the house into silence again.

The little bitch, he thought, and rolled over onto his belly, snorting sand and coughing into his hand. At the porch door, the teacher stood facing inside the house. She glanced over at her husband struggling to stand. Her hesitation surprised him. In the end, she took a step back and headed after the girl.

14.

THE SUN SANK into the West and the stars came out.

In the twilight, the fields were a mess of jagged edges and odd angles. The scarecrow still remained on its cross, its bowed head examining the disaster below.

From the still dusty porch, the farmer sat with his hands steepled and waited. Waited for the mob to surface from the ground, ropes and blades in its many hands. He expected it to rush into the house, shapes without voice or shape bursting doors down and swarming in.

Taking her away.

When the last light disappeared and the nocturnal creatures slithered from their holes, he heard the girl tip-toe down the stairs and rush into the basement. His wife followed soon after.

Her footsteps paused behind the porch door, then moved away. The basement door closed shut soon after. She was still down there with the girl when he went to bed.

Sleep wouldn't come to release him from his thoughts.

The girl.

She's cursed us.

She's put both of us in danger.

This whole damn town knows. They've seen us.

They'll hurt us because of her.

They'll make us suffer.

Make her suffer.

And for what?

For what?

15.

THERE WAS A joke the teacher had once heard in the teacher's lounge. It might have been the math teacher who had said it, she couldn't quite remember. She hadn't laughed because it was in reference to getting drunk. The joke went; if no one talks about yesterday, did yesterday ever exist? A couple of the teachers had chuckled.

A few months after the Hush Laws were announced, the joke had resurfaced in her head. It had become a reminder of how strange the world was about to become. If no one talks about yesterday, will we forget it existed?

Letters and words became instruments of Division, meant to spread falsehoods and lies, forbidden messages and radical ideas. That's how the Party had justified it in their directive to the school. Sign language would also be banned at a later stage. It was too close to speaking without speaking, it couldn't be treated any different. How they were thinking of stopping people from using their hands to point and threaten and provoke, she couldn't tell.

We are not unreasonable, Party representatives kept saying until it became a mantra. There will be time to adjust. Directives will be sent to all authorities and the public will be informed in due time.

On the same day the law passed, the directive arrived at the school from County. Pages and pages of verbs written in the passive voice. The measures will be imposed. Speaking will be forbidden. Offenders will be punished. Always concealing who was doing the imposing, the forbidding, and the punishing.

This is the way forward, the directive insisted. We are not unreasonable, they repeated. We are not. It will be difficult to adjust, but the measures were created to promote Unity, with a capital U. In the end, there will be One Voice. One Nation.

At least math teachers everywhere had been spared. Numbers were still kosher.

Not many people were smiling during those days. No one was making jokes. People had started to hunch when they walked, their gaze fixed on their shoes, avoiding eye contact with strangers and neighbors because that would have meant seeing their own distress mirrored back at them. Only the children didn't seem to grasp the implications of the Hush Laws. As she walked through the school corridor, they mocked-mimed and pulled faces at each other, sneering at the unfathomable.

And it was so quiet. Scuffling feet, lockers closing. Classroom doors screeching on their hinges. Outside in the practice field, a whistle would go off every now and then. But no words.

There was a transition period. All the brochures on the new ways of being that appeared in the farmhouse's postbox, she dumped into the trash without reading. On the day when silence became the official language of the country, the principal asked to see her.

He motioned for her to take a seat across his desk and scribbled on a legal pad with small tight letters.

no-talk deadline is today
You've been telling your class not to comply
parents have been complaining

She gazed at the pad with hesitation. Silent now, because she couldn't muster the courage to say something. Her own pupils had been telling on her. Had it come to that? She grabbed the pad and wrote her answer, feeling ridiculous for carrying out a conversation in that manner.

How the hell am I supposed to teach like this?

She held the pad up for the principal to read, then changed the page and attacked the paper again.

We are not dogs they can shush
even animals are allowed language
the bastards will dare take that away from us

Then, on another sheet of paper;

There's a reason language is the first thing we fight
to learn

The principal read her words, black circles around his eyes.

"I'm a literature teacher, for Pete's sake," she whispered.

The principal reached under his desk and retrieved a book with a Unity symbol on its green cover.

"Why are you giving me this?" she asked as she flipped through wordless pages full of diagrams. Digestive systems, plant roots, and dog skeletons. "I don't teach Biology."

You do now
biology or you're fired
not my rules
but
your choice

Then, right below;

Forgive me

He let the pad sit on the desk between them. She didn't make an effort to pick it up.

"Listen to me. You can't ban language. You just can't. You might as well ban breathing. You stop people from talking to each other, they will either figure out some other way to communicate or they'll go insane. Okay? This won't last. It can't. We are not meant to be locked up inside our own heads."

The principal crossed his arms and looked away, and the teacher wanted to yell at him, *See? You're talking to me right now, even though you don't want to. How are they expecting to kill language?*

After a few seconds of non-reaction, she shoved the biology book into her bag and left the office, hearing the sound of paper crumpling behind her. She made a mental note to hoard as many pencils and as much paper as she could over the next few days. Just in case. Just in case.

On the way home, there was nothing but static on the radio. Her hand twisted the frequency dial, working the stations, being rewarded with hissing snow. There were still a few stations that operated, but they only played instrumental music. She continued searching. She needed to hear someone, anyone, talk. Frustrated, she switched to the AM band.

"—strange times, indeed," the man on the radio said. "But I promise y'all, I'll do mah best ta keep you company through 'em, until they shut me down or I somehow lose mah tongue."

She would continue listening to that station for the next twelve years.

NO ONE TALKED about yesterday anymore. And, when people started disappearing, no one talked about them either. One day, they were there. The next, gone. People she used to come across at the general store, or at the PTA meetings. People with names she couldn't speak in public anymore.

At first, she didn't think much of it. When a couple of the teachers didn't appear one day, she went to the principal looking for answers, but he refused to see her. Their classes went to other teachers and everything continued as normal.

So, when one day the Deputy banged on her front door in an urgent barrage, the teacher half-expected why.

"Listen, I know you're not allowed to talk. I'm not allowed to talk either, but I need you, somepin terrible's happened," the Deputy had said in a single breath, her eyes red.

If the teacher hadn't already known, she wouldn't be able to tell her friend was due in two months. The three-sizes-too-big uniform hid her pregnancy. It was also a mess of wrinkles. Sweat stains had formed under her armpits and she could smell days of work on her. Despite the pregnancy, she was losing the roundness of her cheeks, her skin starting to stretch over her bones.

She motioned for the Deputy to enter the house and locked the door behind her.

"What's going on, honey?" the teacher said while hugging her. She tugged at the excess fabric of her friend's uniform and sighed. "There's a lot of weird laws shoved into our faces right now, but cordectomies are too much. This can't... It won't happen. You don't have to hide the pregnancy."

"I'm not taking any chances, no one's touching mah baby. Look, I know things are crazy right now, but I need to ask you a favor. You won't get in trouble, I got your back. I got ol' man Sheriff's ear, at least fer now."

"Well, sure. Anything. What's going on? You're scaring me." If her friend had influence, the kind that could shield from bad things happening, why did she need her help?

The Deputy opened her mouth, but only a sob escaped. The teacher gave her time to compose herself. "They took him. He's gone. I got home today and the door was in pieces and he was gone. I called the paper, they've grabbed a bunch of others too."

"They? Who's they?"

"The Party. Come on, you must've seen their thugs, they're not subtle 'bout it."

"The editorials?"

"What else? He was just trying to do the right thing. Give his opinion. And they took him for it."

The teacher motioned for the Deputy to wait for her and went to the kitchen. She returned with a glass of water with lemon juice and mint leaves. The Deputy drank it in one long gulp.

The Deputy had been the first person who had made her feel welcome in the town of the twin hills. The Deputy who'd felt the new literature teacher needed instructions in navigating streets that didn't always have names. So much had changed since.

"Honey," the teacher started. "Honey, out of anyone I know, you're the only one who has any idea what's going on. The one with the most authority."

"Your man is a member, ain't he? It's his home team that's lording it over us."

"Well, yeah, but he's just a farmer. He got a piece of plastic from his Dad years ago saying he's a member and that's it. I mean, do those things come with privileges?"

"You're not listening," the Deputy hissed with her jaw clenched. "Your man, I don't care if he digs dirt. The way things are going, the way things *will* go, he owns a license to do what he pleases. Do you understand?"

She took a couple of steps towards the teacher, who retreated.

"He and the people like him can do whatever the hell they want. They're sitting in mah office right now, telling me who to arrest, who is allowed to talk, who ain't, telling me how to do mah job. Me. And there's fuck all I can do 'bout it. I don't know these people. They don't wear no uniform, they don't wear no badge, they just wave their credentials and muscle in and ol' man Sheriff tells us we should jes let them and say please and thank you very much, only we're not even allowed to say anypin anymore. I want your man to do what's right and tell me where mine is."

"Please, calm down. You're scaring me."

"*I'm* the one who's scared," the Deputy exploded.

The Deputy stared at her for a long time, then walked over to the dining table, pulled a chair out and sat down, staring out into the distance with a hand on her belly. The teacher joined her and rubbed her shoulders. There they remained for a long time before either one said anything.

"I got a duty," the Deputy broke the silence. "I'm sworn to uphold the laws of this country and to protect the people of this town with mah own life if need be, but right now doing one means not doing the other and I'm about to go nuts. It don't matter though, 'cause I can't even protect mah own man. I can figure it all out later. I jes need you to help me find him first. Your man has authority. He can help."

"He's just a farmer," the teacher repeated, her voice sounding tiny in the room.

"That's not true."

"Please—"

"That's not true."

"It is," the farmer's voice broke into their conversation. He stood at the back door with a wrench in his grease-covered hands, his boots covered in mud. "I don't know where you got that idea from. I don't even know other members," he said, approaching the teacher.

"You need to help me."

"No, you need to leave," the farmer said. "I ain't got no authority, but we're on top now. I'm sure the boys down at your office won't respond well to threatening a fellow member."

"But I ain't threatening you."

"Git out." Then, as an afterthought, "Please."

The Deputy pushed herself out of the chair. As she straightened her back, she seemed changed. The muscles in her jaw stretched as she ground her teeth. Her arms hung stiff by her sides. She looked each of them in the eyes and walked out of their house. In the stillness, they heard the cruiser crunch stones beneath its tires as it sped away. The engine sound grew more distant and then vanished altogether.

Only then did the two of them breathe out. At first, they looked at each other, then forced themselves to go about their day, to do normal things.

The teacher retrieved a pail from underneath the kitchen sink and filled it with water as she eyed the muddy footprints on the hardwood floor.

"What the hell was that? She's our friend, why are you treating her like that?"

"She wasn't getting it. I got nopin to offer, but words weren't getting through."

"And you have to throw her out of our house like that? Do you at least know what happened to him?"

"Now, how the hell would I know that?" he replied without looking at her. "It's strange times. Things will change 'round here. I mind mah own business."

"What?"

"What do you want me to say?"

"How about your own words, rather than your father's? For Pete's sake, these people are our friends."

"I know."

"Oh, you know? That's it? That's all I'm getting? Did you always have this feeble side?"

"Just what do you want me to do? People are disappearing and you want me to go out and look for them? Old man Sheriff himself has no say in what's going on anymore. Sweetheart… What. Do you want me. To do? I go outta mah way to look fer her man, I bring this thing on our heads. We can't be seen to be associated with enemies of the state."

"Of course. Let's look out for our own skins and damn

the rest. Let's throw our friends to the wolves when things get tough."

"You're making me sound like some goddamn coward. Like you don't know me any better."

"I know you're not. Which is why this burns me so much."

"And, hey, I didn't hear you offering any real help, and I'm the bad guy here?"

"You know what? Fuck you."

"Oh, fuck me? Did you consider that maybe, just maybe, he brought this on himself? With all that criticism, all those articles—"

"Editorials."

"The whatever."

"I thought we had freedom of speech."

"Yeah. Had. Look, things have changed. You need to start changing the way you think, too, or we won't make it. 'Freedom of speech', hell. Until the storm passes, I have one priority. Making sure none of it touches this fambly. End of. Anypin else is none of mah business."

"Can't you make it your business?"

He remained silent for a long moment, wiping his hands on a cloth and looking at her pregnant belly. "No," he said and left.

The teacher ran after him. "Will you wait for a minute?" she said. "Please, talk to me." But he was gone.

16.

THE YEAR THEIR boy was born had been the hottest in recorded history up to that point. There would be more hottest years in history after that, but that particular one burned itself into the teacher's memory. The year they lost language. The year she lost the Deputy. The year they lost their boy.

By the end of the summer, the teacher had been two weeks overdue, the boy refusing to come out. Sitting on the sofa in their home with her hands laced over her belly, she stared off into the distance as the farmer pleaded with quiet whispers.

"Least let them monitor you," he said. "There's no point taking risks. Lemme take you to the hospital where they'll look after you."

"And the cordectomy?" she asked.

He scratched his head and went silent for a long time. He took out his member's card and turned it in his hands, then put it back into his wallet. Restrictions kept being announced. No speaking. No writing. No traveling without permission. A long litany of No's. No exceptions for Party members of his rank.

"No point taking risks," he repeated with a voice that was small, almost inaudible, and sat next to her. "Least the boy will live. His voice is a small price to pay."

Later that night, her water broke and still the boy wouldn't come out. The contractions never arrived. She refused to look into the farmer's expectant eyes. She felt a stillness that became heavier as the hours passed, until, after the sun had gone up and back under the horizon again, she allowed him to lead her to the car and to the nearest hospital, two hours away.

Once there, they rushed her into the operating room with a towel over her mouth to muffle her cries of pain. No one told the farmer he couldn't follow. So when they stopped him at the entrance, clumsy as he was to speaking his mind without words, he used the only other language he knew and tried to shove his way inside. They shoved him back and he fought against the urge to curse out loud. In the end, snorting and puffing, he turned away and stood in a corner of the waiting room, unwilling to sit.

The doctor and nurses prepped the teacher without a word, manipulating her arms and legs. Medical equipment arrived without being called for, shiny scalpels and drips and other devices that she didn't recognize and which nobody explained to her. The doctor and nurses moved in a well-practiced dance.

When they cut her open, she decided that the C in C-section really stood for the shape of the incision that gaped in her lower abdomen and through her uterus. With the local anesthetic numbing her from the waist down, she only felt distant tugging and pulling. Then, a sudden pressure that increased, filling her up, and then disappearing. The boy came out covered in blood and mucus. The doctor cleared the boy's nose and mouth, and tapped his back until a cry emanated from his lungs, closer to a rabbit scream than a human voice, desperate and urgent. It filled the room, covering the scuffling of feet and the sound of machines beeping.

The doctor wrapped the boy in a blanket. Then, instead of handing the boy over to the teacher, he took him to a table and leaned over.

The doctor held his hand out for a scalpel and wiped the sweat from his eyes. He examined the one he received, made to hand it back, then changed his mind and waved the nurse away. The teacher craned her head and wanted to say, *is he alright? Is he healthy? Why is he screaming?* She felt a gloved hand press down on the towel over her mouth, stopping the words from coming out, and the smell of its fabric filled her nostrils. A tugging again at her belly, this time pulling her flesh together and sewing the C shut.

The doctor leaned in, holding the scalpel the way one holds a pencil. He lowered it and touched the boy's neck, then retracted and winced as sweat got into his eyes. The gloved hand over her mouth tensed and relaxed, tensed and relaxed, following the rhythm of her breathing. She was aware the nurses had stopped their dance and were staring at the doctor too. It had been half a year since cordectomies had been introduced. On an adult, they would take place from inside the throat. On newborns, it was faster and safer to cut from the outside in. The rabbit scream continued to fill the room.

The doctor's body went rigid for a second, then he lowered his hand again and cut into the boy's neck, right below the apple.

His hand didn't seem to move at all for whole minutes.

The teacher continued watching, breathing in the fabric.

This time, instead of wincing, the doctor's eyes opened wide.

Red spurted down his hands.

The teacher inhaled and held her breath in as the boy breathed out and stopped screaming.

THEY BURIED THE boy next to the farmer's parents behind the church on a quiet Sunday morning. When they returned home from the service, the farmer shuffled through the house without aim, running his fingers along the walls or staring through the windows while she, still weak from the operation and the mourning, sat on the couch with her eyes half-closed. He asked her if she wanted a drink and she replied, yes, some water would be good. He brought her a glass of warm water with lemon and mint leaves.

"It's fixing to be a bad harvest," he mumbled. "Too hot. Ground's gone all dry. Corn won't make it."

The teacher held the glass with both hands and nodded.

"There's always next year," he continued. "Next year might be better. Oughtta be better."

He continued stalking through the house. When she finished her water, she stood and got to cooking. They didn't say much else to each other for the rest of that day.

THE FARMHOUSE BECAME quiet from there on. Not entirely silent as it was obliged to be, because he kept insisting that the Hush Laws wouldn't, couldn't apply to members. He asked her in hushed tones if there was something he could do for her and she would answer in a voice like the rustling of curtains that she was fine or that she was tired and needed to rest her back. She asked him if he had a good day and he'd reply with a neutral mmmm that didn't mean much to her but at least it meant nothing horrible had happened either. As far as they were both concerned, nothing horrible happening was good enough. If only life was filled with nothing horribles.

One late night, while they both slumped in front of the television watching wordless news of riots being quelled with the volume turned down low, she pointed out without thinking and close to sleep, what fools were those who had voted for the Party to believe anything good would come from it. What fools ruined their own country and ruined it for everyone else too. With her eyes closing, she said, our boy died because of them.

She felt him tense up next to her. He sat a little straighter. In the end, he didn't say anything and soon after they went to bed.

For the rest of the week, though, she felt his grievance as coldness. In how he turned away from her when the lights turned off in the bedroom and how he didn't much smile when she touched his cheek. The snapping, Lord, the snapping, like a prissy little pup. It bothered her, but she responded by ignoring him. She took to taking longer walks into the fields. Even after dark, though she knew he didn't approve.

Most of all, she kept her mind occupied. With her classes, and the vegetable garden she had been planning for some time. With rumors of martial law and of war. With the Deputy's pregnancy that surely must have come to term by now. With anything but the man she shared a bed with.

This quiet continued until, against the whims of the weather, the next harvest was rich and his good mood infected her for a short while.

✕

INTIMACY CAME BACK into their lives in parts.

Inquisitive glances. Touches that tested the waters, when before a certain look was all that had been needed.

When they removed each other's clothes, it was slow. The movements awkward and devoid of their old playful flair. A certain amount of shyness had crept in. They got reacquainted with each other's bodies to the sound of dying riots from the TV and of the world going quiet. Stretch marks, loose skin. Strands of gray.

When his body rubbed against hers, the wine-red scar on her lower abdomen itched, and, when she pressed against him, it bled. The constant sweating annoyed her. By that year's sweltering winter, her movements had slowed to match her mood. First in bed, then out of it too.

When they finished, they'd stand up without fanfare, wash separately, and slump on the couch in front of the TV an arm's length away from each other.

"How could they do this to me?" the farmer would whisper every day while watching the news. "I'm a member. I got a member card. It oughtta count fer somepin. It oughtta."

She never responded.

"We're members. How could they do this to us?"

She never was sure if by 'this' he meant losing their boy or being treated like everyone else.

The teacher wasn't a member. She'd never been a member of any party, never had any interest in politics outside of literature. What came out of the TV was noise and she found herself zoning out. She didn't care. She knew the

Party was responsible for ruining her career. Taking their son away. That was all she needed to know. Understanding it any further was a waste of time.

ON THEIR FIRST date, her husband had breached a cardinal rule and asked her about her politics. She had shrugged and answered with honesty. I don't follow any politics. Don't care. Still, that hadn't been enough. He had grilled her about her beliefs, and she had become defensive. After five minutes of deflecting his questions, she stood up, muttered an apology, and left.

Right after the first date fiasco, he had called to apologize. Don't think about it, she had answered and tried to hang up, but a stream of consciousness from his side had stayed her hand. It was a small community, he had argued, and it wasn't every day that someone from the city arrived. There had been trouble before. He had just wanted to find out if she saw him as a country bumpkin, uneducated and crude.

Again, she had answered him with honesty. He didn't judge people before getting to know them first. Their second date had taken place a month later. Her condition was that they didn't talk politics.

On that second date, she had noted how gregarious he was. Sitting at the bar, several people had come up to him, big smiles on their faces. He had greeted every single one of them by their first name, more people than she had met in her few months in the town of the twin hills.

Later, after they got married, the same people would come to her at the school or in town and shake her hand, asking her how her husband was and inviting them to their homes. She chose to forget most invitations, because she preferred her quiet evenings, but somehow they still found their way to him. At their homes, he became the center of attention, a role he took over without effort.

"Things were supposed to be different," he continued every day, pounding his fist on his knee. "We're members." And some days, he would add, "Are you still writing?"

She could no longer remember what she had once started writing about. After they lost language, it didn't matter. Amidst the silence, she felt compelled to say something about it. Her writing had become about something else. Had mutated. In the end, she felt that it had always been about the silence.

She'd had a story tumbling around in her brain since the Hush Laws were announced. The story of a girl named Parrhesia who could only speak the truth.

She spent longer stretches of time inside her head than out of it, slaving over the pages and working out the story. Days went by before she came up for air. Days spent with only basic replies. Yes. No. I'm fine. I don't want anything. I'll come to bed later.

In the meantime, he raged on, always careful to check out of the window first and keep his voice low.

One day, as they were sitting on the couch, him watching the news, her writing, he started talking with a voice small with fear.

"I went to town this morning," he said, his eyes glued to the TV. "Had to pick up somepin fer the earworms, found a bunch of them in the fields, getting all fat on the corn."

He seemed to hesitate. His eyes drifted to the side.

"There's work crews taking down signs all over the goddamn place. Unscrewing them and throwing them in the back of trucks. Street by street, even the shop signs. Don't replace them with nopin. A man can't find his way 'round here no more, unless he's local. Shit, ain't that big a town neither, and we got the church on the hill to tell left from right."

That hesitation again.

"Somepin horrible's happening," he said, deep in concentration. "Madame Deputy's lost her goddamn mind."

"Why?"

"She's gon' round, picking off people for talking. TV says there will be fines and prison time fer folks still talking. Fair enough. We knew this was coming. But the folks she's arresting are ending up dead. You hear? Dead. Folks are switching side of the road when she approaches. She's grabbing them off the streets and outta their homes. Then brings them out and makes the townsfolk beat them to death. She makes them. All fer talking. You hear?"

She could feel his eyes on her.

"She's lost it. Her man's gone and she's taking it out on the world." He paused. "She brought out this kid, mustn't have been older than sixteen. All fuzz and pimples. She brings him out, throws him to the ground, and vanishes. Boy throws his hands up in the air and starts wailing. Admitting to talk, to conspiring against Unity, ta being a traitor. Didn't believe half of it, mind. Seemed to me the boy woulda admitted faking the moon landing had you asked him."

The teacher wanted to ask him how the boy looked. Was he in her class? She didn't open her mouth.

"Before I know what to think, someone walks up to him and kicks him and suddenly folks rush in. And Madame Deputy just sits at the back watching."

The farmer paused and looked away.

"I think the boy is gone."

She noted his choice of words. Not dead, not killed. Gone.

He let the silence hang between them and fiddled with the remote control. On the screen the Party's Mouth smiled and waved as a rally of thousands applauded him. Behind him, Unity loomed large on a banner.

"She got the townsfolk to do what they did to the boy, then she looked at me, straight in the eyes," the farmer continued. "I got outta there. She's lost it."

The teacher sighed and put down her pencil without lifting her head. "Maybe you should have talked to her when she came begging for help."

"You're not listenin'."

"I heard you fine."

"You wanna go over this again?"

"As many times as it takes for you to get it."

"She's getting folks killed. There's nothing to get."

"Okay."

The farmer stared at her hard. When he opened his mouth again, his voice was close to breaking.

"What the hell's wrong with you?" he said.

She grasped the pencil again and made to write, but couldn't, and he stood up and left, taking his words with him.

✕

SUMMER CAME AGAIN, though no one had realized it had gone in the first place. Plans to make adult cordectomy mandatory were rejected. Too expensive. Too dangerous. Impossible logistics. By that point, the silences between them had begun taking on a comfort the teacher didn't always feel like interrupting. On most days, she didn't care for the quiet to end. It was peaceful that way. Conflict had no place in a vacuum and who would want to ruin that?

On the fifth day of a silent stretch, a man had knocked on their door. Dressed in overalls with a Unity on his chest, he confiscated their TV and replaced it with another, blockier sort, which he welded into a power socket. This one showed only the state channel. When they tried to turn it off, they found that they couldn't. The volume could be turned down, but not muted.

The farmer had punched walls and kicked chairs and, when he got exhausted, he sat and glared at her with storms in his eyes. His hurt pride was howling. Part of his mood had been her fault as well, she realized. Her manuscript pages were spread out on a table in the spare room, just out of sight. It had been luck that the man with the overalls hadn't seen them.

She continued writing as he glared. Part of her wondered if she wished for the fight she knew was about to start. She could have a fight for any number of the silent transgressions that passed between them so easily these days. Small, pointless sins. Like his constant misery and his aimless walking around the house that grated on her nerves.

When they fought, they danced. Tip-toeing around the point, taking shots at it but never addressing it. With him, she wasn't confrontational. It wasn't that she was afraid of it, not by any stretch. After they fought, though, electricity always hung in the air between them, giving her a headache for days. She didn't have the energy for that. It was easier to avoid his jabs than to reply with her own.

Besides, he never went full out either. After their fights, even if they were resolved, he would hide from her in the basement, shifting through old junk without looking for something specific. No, it was more practical to swallow their clever arguments, their need to dominate. To point the finger at each other and gloat in victory. They followed the old adage. They could either be right or be married. Never both.

But this time, something was going to be different. There would be no dancing.

"I need you to stop that book you're writing," he'd said with a voice hoarse from disuse.

"My writing is not negotiable."

"I'm not asking you."

"Wouldn't care if you did."

"I'mma gon' pretend those words didn't just come outta your mouth. Wouldn't care? What am I, some kinda stranger to you?"

"You expect me to be nice when you boss me around?"

"This isn't a debate for the sake of mah feelings. Did you see what almost happened? They catch you writing a book, we're screwed. So stop it. Please."

"I can't. I won't. Honey, I don't feel like trading words with you right now, but I don't understand how you don't see this. You have your fields. They will always be there for you. I got nothing. Everything I am has been taken from me. I can't let this go too."

"I get it. I do. But, you gotta try see this my way for once, just once. We disagree more often than not, but I'mma gon' need you to work with me. I'mma gon' need you to burn this book, bury the ashes where no one can see, and pretend it never happened."

"Or what?"

"There is no 'or what'."

"So, that's all? Are you not going to threaten me? Force me to shut this down?"

"You know, I only ever supported you in this."

"Supported me? How exactly do you support me other than talking about how much you support me? You haven't lifted a finger to make this easier on me. You've only ever supported me as long as food, laundry, and ass have been on time."

"That's how you want ta talk to me? Hmm? Just stop it. Please. 'Fore someone sees you and we both end up hanging from a rope."

She exploded, and it stunned him. As she described to him how furious he was making her, he just stared, slack-jawed and unable to react. She would never stop the book, never, not for him, not for anyone, so he'd better get it in his thick redneck skull. Then, he leaned back in his chair, crossed his arms, and smiled. Like a prize fighter, he let her exhaust herself while looking for an opening. When she stopped to catch her breath, he countered.

There was no reason in his argument, no rebuttal. No point. Only poison and thorns. He delivered his insults as if he had been practicing them, nurturing them for this moment. He denigrated her as only a husband could, reaching deep into her wounds and twisting.

It didn't startle her. Somewhere deep in the back of her mind, she was nonplussed that his attack didn't shock her to silence. Words now came out on their own. She gave them permission, go forth and eradicate. No Howdareyou's, or demands of apology. No sorrow. If they both were made out of glass, she'd gladly shatter him with her own shards.

She wouldn't back down. This woman who felt far more comfortable in the quiet.

She punched him. He shoved her. She tripped backwards and hit her head on the wall, leaving a nickel-sized red spot on the plaster.

As if a spell had been broken, he rushed to help her up. Instead of taking his outstretched hands though, she kicked his shins. Through hair that had fallen across her face, she stared with rawness. Seconds passed and his concern turned back into derision that dripped from the corners of his mouth.

Neither of them said anything. She searched the back of her head for blood with her fingertips, wiped it on her pants, and got up.

"I guess we're done here," she said.

The farmer shrugged, going to the basement where he spent the rest of the evening.

When he came out at some point after midnight, he found her pretending to be asleep on the couch in the common room. He approached in the darkness and stared at her for long moments. In the end, he muttered something to himself and went to their bedroom where he fell asleep in his clothes.

He was up before dawn. Not bothering with breakfast or even a cup of coffee, he went straight through the door and off to work.

When the tractor's noise died away, the teacher got up. She made her way into the bedroom where she kept the manuscript in the nightstand. Holding it, her fingers curled into fists, crumpling the paper between them. No more writing, she thought. I can't. There's nothing worth saying anymore.

When she uncurled them, words appeared in graphite smudges on her hands. Terrified, she ran into the bathroom and didn't come out again until her skin was bright red from the scrubbing. The first thing she did was to stash the pages inside the hole in the basement behind the armoire and try to forget it ever existed.

✕

THE NEW SILENCE that followed festered first for a few hours, then stretched to several days. The silence from outside, spread into their home and settled, getting snug into the recesses and the cracks of the farmhouse. The world had changed, they thought. They told themselves they were changing with it. Months later, both of them realized they couldn't remember the taste of each other's names. Or of any other word. But the thought did not take root as their minds wandered through teaching materials, and seeds, and grades, and soil, and the war with the North, and corn prices, and absenteeism, and tractor parts, and stationary orders, and that goddamn heat, and the dust the dust the dust, and the new government-issued TV that couldn't be turned off or muted.

And on the silence went.

17.

THE SHERIFF PULLED over at the side of the road and killed the cruiser's engine, letting the fields fill her ears with their threshing. In the backseat, behind a metal mesh partition, sat the math teacher. She eyed the driveway leading to the farmhouse. At the far end spreading behind the house, corn stalks broke through the dust.

She turned back to her passenger and regarded him.

"You two work together, do I understand correct? She teaches biology, you teach…"

The math teacher raised trembling fingers as if counting. One, two, three, four, five.

"Mmm, mmmath… But, you do workkk together. True?"

The man nodded several times. He loosened his collar, tried to wipe the sweat gathering on his mustache with a sleeve. The Sheriff's eyes wandered over him. She broke him down into details and clues, pieces of evidence. His crumpled yet expensive clothes. The veins on his nose broken by whiskey. The beads of perspiration running down jowls few men could afford, and he stank of sandalwood that became unbearable in the heat.

"Teachers rattin on folks, you know this town's gon to hell. You rat on your kids too?"

She didn't expect an answer. He just stared at her and continued sweating.

The Sheriff knew every single informer in the town of twin hills. It was fortunate that she could spot them with a single glance, but there had been official lists. Sometimes, tired of waiting for a Party membership, townsfolk presented themselves, hoping she would honor them with a membership card for the tips they brought her. The desert outside the town was littered with the bodies of informers she had driven out.

"Hope you're not this loyal t'all your friends," she said and read the way his fingers fidgeted with each other. "I'mma go in there and have mmmahself a chat wit your friend and her worse half. Bout that girl y'allegedly saw them wit."

She opened the door and stepped out. When the math teacher tried doing the same, his door didn't budge and neither did the window.

The Sheriff leaned down to face him.

"Reckkkon I'll be back in a few. Try not to sweats too much in mah car, mmm?"

The Sheriff approached the house, taking in the dust that had settled between the roof shingles. She reached over at her shoulder mic and clicked the receiver a number of times. After a few seconds, the speaker responded with a chatter of clicks, her deputies acknowledging her.

She rapped on the front door and listened in. Steps approached behind it. First curious. Timid. Then frantic. The gun pressed heavy against her thigh inside its holster. She banged on the door with her fist this time, shaking it in its hinges. When no one answered again, she moved around the side of the house. Kneeling, she tried to peer through the basement windows, but they had gone opaque with dirt.

She continued to the back porch, nudged the back door open with her shoulder and stepped inside.

Dust hung in the air and grit crunched underneath her shoes. The TV played static from the living room. But the house wasn't empty. She could hear footsteps from distant rooms and the groaning of old floor planks.

On the dusty floor itself, she could see paths; tracks blending, moving from room to room.

How little had this house changed. She lifted a plate that had been set upside down on the mahogany table and studied it, bringing it closer to her nose. The footsteps continued. One pair came from the floor above, another heavier one from deep inside the house. She opened the refrigerator. The milk and butter were almost finished even though rationing was only two days ago.

She ignored the teacher when she appeared in the entrance to the kitchen. The Sheriff continued her inspection, opening the pantry, going through the drawers and studying the cutlery.

Another set of footsteps grew louder and now the farmer joined the teacher. He took her arm, trying to grab her attention, but she wrenched herself away and pointed at the Sheriff. He hunched and his limbs seemed to shrivel against his body.

"Y'all didn't hear me knockkkin?" she said without turning. "Gone deaf as well as mmmute?"

The couple looked at each other, sharing a quiet communication that she didn't miss. She approached them. They appeared like two overgrown children lost in the forest, skittish and jumpy. She dragged a chair from the dining table and slumped down on it. Words or no words, anything coming out of them would be a lie. Their posture said as much.

"Pardon mah mmmanners, mmm," she began. "I tend to get all riled up when I see you. Even after all this time. I've come here on account of a citizen reportin possible harborin of a terrorist elemmment," she said. The official words came out muffled by her strained enunciation, the tension on her jaw. "That citizen bein one of your colleagues," she nodded at the teacher who looked confused.

"I'd be careful of the commmpany I keep if I were you. There's somepin awful that's gotten hold of folks. Not knowin who to trust is a terrible thing."

She turned to the farmer.

"Fetch me a glass of water. Mah throat gets parched wit this dust."

The farmer stared at her for a moment, then shuffled to the sink where he started filling a glass with water.

"I've missed ya," the Sheriff said to the teacher. "But I hope y'understand why I don't visit. Came across your mmmedicals. I'm sorry. Why aren't you takkkin the chemo, mmm? Your man is a mmmember, you coulda taken the chemo if you wanted to. Why isn' he doin' somepin bout it?"

The teacher put a hand over her belly and shook her head. The farmer handed her the glass of water, avoiding her gaze, and she drank it all at once.

"Much obliged. Now, you," she pointed at the farmer when she finished. "We had a talk not so long ago, us two. In the sense that I did the talkin and you me in your thoughts."

The farmer shook his head.

"Wasn't askkkin. Course you cursed me. We had that talk and I remember askkkin if you had a talker hidin in here.

A talker shows up in your property. Fair 'nough, don't mean mmmuch. Then, they see you grabbin some girl from town and drivin away through a dust storm. You mmmust think mmmighty low of me, think I can't put one and two together. You lie. And still, I forgive you. Jes as I forgave you before, when you wouldn't help me find mah man. It was tough times. I get it. Past's the past and dwellin on it is a sure way to have no future, mmm?

"'Who is a God like ye, who pardons sin and forgives the transgression of the remmmnant of his inheritance? Ye do not stay angry forever, but delight to show mercy'. Wise words. Words I heed and you should do well to not mmmake me forget."

She watched the farmer squirming in the long pause that followed. Sometimes, silence was just as good as any speech when she wanted to make a point.

"Now. I don't always manage the not dwellin part. Of this, I ain't proud. Every day is a struggle."

The Sheriff coughed. When she opened her mouth again, her words came out mournful.

"But, it gets lonely. Havin no-one to talk to. There's me in this town and there's the Mayor, and that's it. Haven't seen the Mayor in months. Could be dead fer all I know."

The teacher's face hardened and the Sheriff could tell she was steeling herself, ready to resist. She had hoped it wouldn't come to that.

"You have a girl that talks. Hand her over. I'll proteccct her better than you two. Why, half the town suspecccts. They'll come a-knockkkin fore long. She still young, they'll cut her voice out, make her one of them. You two, they'll hang. Nough killin, ya hear? So, hand her over."

They both remained silent, gazing at the floor, letting the

TV static fill the emptiness.

"No?" she said and sighed, straightened her posture, resting her hand on her gun. "You won't interfere in the search fer said terrorist elemmment and y'will assist as required," she continued in a monotone and stared at them, waiting for a reply. Both looked up and nodded.

"Oustandin," She pointed at the cupboard where the fine china was stored. "Start by throwin the contents of that cccupboard to the floor. When you're done, empty all food outta the back and bury it."

The farmer lifted his hand, drawing the Sheriff's attention to it. Then, in a long slow move, he reached to his back pocket for his wallet.

"You show me the mmmember card, I'll tear it in half, I swear. Could've done some real good wit it. Mmm. Won't even take care of your sick wife, you don't deserve it. You don't. Now. The cccupboard, please."

Her callousness in searching the house was calculated malice. She put a knife into their hands and forced them to tear open the sofas. Shred their clothes. Shatter windows and toss plates through them. Only the mahogany table escaped, unbreakable as it was.

The damage was unnecessary. If they had the girl, she knew where they'd be hiding her. Yet, in her mind there were dues to be paid. For lying. For disrespecting her. For not seeing sense.

And throughout it all, they remained compliant. Unwilling or unable to resist, she didn't care which.

When she got to their bedroom, she commanded them to pick up their photos and smash their frames. Then, when they thought that had been it, she made them overturn the heavy iron bed and pry the loose board underneath it open.

She had seen the grooves on the floor. That there was nothing inside was irrelevant. She was making a point. Nothing could be hidden from her.

The Sheriff left the basement for last, marching down there and ordering them to stand in the middle of the room. Her eyes took in the dirty windows, the junk gathering in piles. She also noted the absence of dust in the corner, a clear rectangle on the concrete floor in the rough dimensions of a mattress. She walked over and stood in that space, hands on her hips and measured the ground with her eyes.

At once, she ordered them to turn over every heap of rusting tools, to empty the buckets of paint onto the floor where it smothered the spider webs.

Across the corner and against the wall stood an old red armoire, scratched up and leaning, uneven, on a worn-out leg. The Sheriff approached it and threw its doors open to reveal an anarchic mount of clothes, all frayed ends and faded colors. She tossed them to the ground and stood observing them, as if willing the girl to materialize through their fabric.

Her mood turned sour. The more time went by, the more destruction she demanded. And yet, with every shattered glass or smashed chair she understood that the battle was being lost. Despite everything that broke, she wasn't breaking them. She could even swear she saw the trace of a smile teetering on the farmer's lips.

"Nough," she commanded and pointed upstairs. She marched them to the dining room and had them stand again, as if she was lecturing them. She paced, though her eyes were now unfocused and her shallow breathing betrayed her mind.

"What's this?" the Sheriff pointed at the stereo.

The Sheriff sauntered over to the old wooden stereo,

taking in its faded lettering and worn out lines, running a finger over it that came up dustless. Then, she pressed play.

A cassette inside the unit rolled, its spools engaged. The house filled with singing. The Sheriff's hand rested on the gun handle.

The farmer and his wife lowered their eyes, full of guilt, or maybe they were upset at not being more careful. The Sheriff did not care.

"You two have to be idjits to think I wouldn't notice this. Runnin round behin closed doors, hidin who knows what else and leavin this, *this*," she said and knocked the stereo with the gun, smashing it against the wooden floor. The cassette flew out, brown tape trailing it like a comet. She picked up a broken corner and hurled it at them.

"The only language animals understand is violence," she growled and walked up to the farmer as he winced. "Call her."

"Call her," she repeated into his face, spittle collecting at the corners of her lips.

"Call her," she took out the gun and pressed it against his guts.

The farmer closed his eyes.

The Sheriff looked down at her arm, shaking. It felt like a prosthetic, not her own flesh and blood. I warned them, she thought. They're forcing my hand.

Fingers wrapped around her wrist. The teacher moved between her and the farmer, pulling on the gun arm and forcing it against her own body. The Sheriff tried to pull back, but the teacher kept it in place.

"Stop pullin, you idjit, it'll fire," the Sheriff said, unable to stop panic from forcing itself into her voice.

The teacher's face, all angles and shadows and frailty,

told her to leave as she pushed against the gun with her body. The Sheriff resisted. She tried to pry the teacher's hands away, but the teacher kept pushing. Get out, she told the Sheriff with her eyes. Get out.

"Gimme the girl," the Sheriff commanded again, now forced towards the door. She tried to let go of the gun, to move around the teacher, tried to get back to the farmer, but the teacher held on tight. Her friend squeezed her fingers together and the Sheriff felt the trigger shifting. Gears rotated within the gun. A bullet clicked in place.

"I'll go," the Sheriff said. "I'll go. Stop pullin, I'll go."

The teacher's fingers relaxed, but didn't release the gun until they reached the threshold. There, the teacher let go and shut the door.

The Sheriff threatened and cursed and swore they'd regret it if they didn't hand over the girl. That she could lock them up for the stereo, though she knew she'd never do that. In the years serving the town of the two hills as a Sheriff, she had never arrested anyone for breaking the Hush Laws and she didn't intend to break her promise to herself. Not for them, not for anyone.

She continued punching and kicking the door, but the house remained silent. Holstering her gun, she stormed away.

THE TEACHER WATCHED the Sheriff enter her car and turn to speak to the figure in the back seat. She couldn't tell who the person was from that distance, just that the Sheriff was pointing, jabbing fingers, shaking her head and leaning closer to the mesh partition with hunched shoulders. How like an animal she had become.

The figure burrowed deeper into the seat, trying to shield themselves. Their hands were covering their face. A sigh and a shake of the head and the Sheriff brought the cruiser to life, rolling it back into the street.

The teacher waited until the cruiser disappeared and then she waited some more, until the tree shadows shifted. From inside, she could hear the sound of broken wood being picked up and thrown into a pail. She could hear his sorrowful, humiliated steps.

It's a pity, she thought. *There's not even enough wood left out of the stereo to build a bird house. I'll miss the music.*

His hand, thick calluses that she could feel through the fabric of her shirt, touched her shoulder and squeezed. She felt an apology in him that she would not get to hear. For not resisting the Sheriff. For their torment. *They are just things,* she thought and squeezed back. *Just things.*

She pulled herself away and descended the basement stairs, tip-toed around the spilled paint, and headed straight to the half-open armoire. Its contents remained piled up onto the ground. She knocked on the back panel with her knuckles. It shifted and warped as if swallowed into a fold in space and then opened to reveal Corvo nested inside the wall behind it. The space was no bigger than a laundry basket and the girl stretched out her injured foot with a wince. Still, she was safe. *You're still with me,* the teacher thought and smiled. *The girl who talks. The girl who can read.*

The girl wiggled out. Behind her, the manuscript pages lay rolled in a loose bunch next to the teacher's books.

"Wow," Corvo said as she took in the disaster and looked at the teacher with apprehension and guilt. In response, the teacher cupped the girl's shoulders into her hands and squeezed gently.

It's okay, the teacher thought and nodded a reassurance. *Just things. A small price to pay.*

Behind her, the farmer turned his back and shambled up the stairs.

18.

H E SAW HER smile and it made him anxious.

Sitting in the ruined basement next to the girl, her writing hand relaxed around the pencil, she emanated a sense of ease and contentment. A calm smile crossed her face without effort or pretense.

There was life.

She reminded him of rare vacations spent next to the lake before it dried up.

Of easy mornings.

And easy laughter.

She reminded him of how little his world made sense anymore. Of the schism between them and of how incapable he was of bridging it. Of how much he could hurt her by trying.

And he felt anxious.

He scratched the palm of his hand and frowned.

It takes a certain kind of person to coax corn out of the ground. A person able to wake up long before sunrise and plow through the harsh soil, his mind empty of all but routine, over and over and over again. It takes a person trusting that the seeds he plants won't be picked clean by the birds, that rain won't rot them, that the sun won't kill them where they lie. It takes someone able to look upon disaster and shrug, muttering, next year, next year. Next year the rains will fall just so and will turn the land fertile and giving. Next year, the corn will grow taller than a man and it will sway with cobs the size of footballs. Green and gold will cover the earth. Our pockets will be filled. Our table will never empty. And life will be good. Next year, next year.

Yet, he looked at her write and smile.

And he knew there wouldn't be a next year.

19.

P IPES IN THEIR house were an odd thing. A word spoken in the basement would travel through them and echo between the bathroom walls where the farmer stood, reaching his ears as a half-imagined whisper. He heard the girl's voice coming in short, clipped sentences. Even though he couldn't make out the words, he could make out cadence, rhyming.

Poetry, he thought and tensed. She's reading poetry. Yeats, that his wife liked so much.

"Had I the heaven's embr… Embroidered cloths…

En… Row… Enwrought. With golden and silver light,

The blue and the dim and the dark cloths

of night and light and the half-light."

Looking into the mirror in his boxer shorts, he mouthed the words. Vowels stretched his mouth open. Consonants made him bare his teeth, and digraphs had him biting down on the tip of his tongue.

"I would spread the cloths under your feet:

But I being poor… have only my dreams.

I have spread my dreams under your feet."

He stared at his mottled sagging skin, destroyed by a lifetime of working the fields. At the wrinkly part over his upper lip where a finger is meant to rest while whispering hush. At the tired eyes that he relied on to do the talking for him. When was the last time he had seen himself speak?

"Tread softly."

The words trailed off into sobs.

He cracked the bathroom door open and leaned his forehead against the cool frame, eyes closed. The sound of turning pages came from the bedroom where the teacher lay. *This quiet is a terrible kind of violence*, he thought. He turned back to the mirror and tried to speak. His mouth opened in a grotesque grin, tendons tensing in his throat.

"Kkhh... Khhhh..."

All he managed was choking on his spittle. He wanted to say something true. To speak his piece and to speak his peace, even if no one else heard him, for his own soul's sake. That muscle, though, had gone numb with disuse. The girl's reciting mocked him. He asked himself, *how can I stand straight if I can't even say the word "pride"?*

He entered the bedroom and climbed into the heavy iron bed the Sheriff had made them overturn, on the other side of the book barrier she had raised. He eyed the books as they lay open along their spines. Child psychology, development. Her old teaching manuals from before they forced her to switch from Literature to Biology. Yeats. All illegal now. He hadn't known she had kept them.

He remembered desire but couldn't remember how it worked. Only its burning felt familiar. Even though that burning was now tainted with something bitter. Frustration, dread. Wounds that gaped open.

This used to be so easy.

The divide between them had increased every day. Since the girl had arrived? No, even before that. Since she refused the chemo that was her right, only accepting the painkillers. She had offered no explanation and he had asked for none. No pleading. No argument from his side, silent or otherwise. He understood dying with dignity. After the chemo, after the radiation and the drugs, his own mother had been left with none. But, no. The divide had started even earlier than that. He just couldn't tell when.

He reached over the book barrier and placed a hand on her thigh, feeling the sweat on her skin beneath his fingers. No response from her. Just the turning of the pages on Introduction to Grief Counseling for Children, 5th Ed. He let his hand roam, hiking up the hem of her nightgown and exposing her hip. Without taking her eyes from the book, she put a hand on his and squeezed it. For a moment, he let his fingers intertwine with hers, but soon they were wandering again.

What's so special about the girl?

He stared at the familiar curve of her neck and the starburst of freckles on her nape, the swollen twisted veins in her legs and the dark spots on her hands, as his own hand slipped underneath the elastic of her underwear. Her chest rose and fell faster. For the first time since he had entered the bedroom, she faced him. She pushed his hand away and pointed downwards. *The girl. She might hear.*

Why are you spending your time with her and not me?

He leaned in to kiss her, but she moved away. His hand reached out to grab hers, knocking books aside. He pulled her closer. There was irritation in the way she jerked her arm out of his grasp, at the way her half-turn told him to stop.

You have so little time left. Why her and not me? Because she talks?

He reached over again and tried to pull her towards him and, when she resisted, his fingers dug into her flesh.

Why her and not me, he asked, grabbing her wrists and pinning her down. Her kicks scattered the books onto the floor.

How much is this silence worth? he demanded as he mounted her. *Say something, damn you.*

At first, she didn't seem to understand. More annoyed than anything, she brought her knees up between them and tried to push him off. He moved one hand down again, brushing against sagging breasts that he had, in the past, licked with tenderness. It continued south and caressed the wine-red scar across her womb just above her coarse pubic hair. He used his fingers the way he remembered she liked, but didn't feel her going wet. Struggling against her, he pulled her cotton panties to her knees, then pushed his own boxers down just enough and forced himself inside her. She squirmed and pressed her mouth shut with her hand by instinct. There was pain there for him too, his body unused to expressing his eagerness, though he would never admit it.

He forced his lips against hers, bit her, and he tasted the salt on her skin. He thrust, not stopping even when she grunted and tensed with pain. She felt foreign to him. Like her body didn't slip in to occupy the space underneath his the way it once had. It made him want to tear her from the inside, even as he begged her to split open and swallow him whole, to pull him into her warm center and make him part of her.

I wish none of this had happened. I wish you were already dead so I wouldn't hate you. He lifted himself up and put both hands on her face, cupping her cheeks. Her red eyes didn't seem to recognize him.

Look at me! he wanted to scream at her.

She struck him on the throat. He let go of her and fell back, coughing and already limp. There was confusion on her face, and fury, fury. She straightened her nightgown and pulled the sheets over her legs.

There they remained, staring at each other. Each trying to find an explanation in the others' eyes. From the basement, the sobbing had stopped.

20.

D URING THE SECOND winter after the Hush Laws, there were a couple of days' worth of drizzle and that was it until spring. Everyone knew something was happening. Had been happening for some time. Even the poisoned stream marking the boundary between the farmer's land and the neighbor's had been shrinking. And everyone complained about the weather, about having to rely on expensive irrigation systems to draw enough groundwater out of a thirsty soil.

Still, what were the farmers to do? They couldn't well stop. Only shrug in the manner that farmers do and mutter "next year" to themselves low enough so that no one overheard them.

The farmer realized then that one goes broke gradually. First, your savings, then, your borrowings. Then, you start staring at walls. A lot of folks had stared at walls until the bank took those walls away from them too, together with the land and the livestock and the equipment. The only thing left for the farmers to take was their own lives. Those who didn't go mad with despair, or weren't too proud, came to work for him. Come harvest, a lot of people he knew worked for him.

Every time someone shuffled to his doorstep, he thought the same thing. Better you than me. That lasted until he came close to joining the ranks of the newly-impoverished himself. He had an ace up his sleeve though. He was a Party member. Had been one since the early days. The member card had been a gift from his Pa, God rest his soul. Not that the farmer believed in the Party, but membership had its benefits.

The little card sitting in his wallet kept him on the approved corn supplier list. It allowed a man to go places. Opened the way from a blue to a red Unity and the right to use words again. To him, though, that wasn't important anymore. Spare parts for the tractor were. Grants. Seeds. If others wanted the card to get their words back, that was their problem. He reckoned he'd never speak again and he was, after struggling with the injustice, at some sort of peace with it.

That little laminated piece of paper was his trump card. One couldn't just become a member these days. The farmer was lucky. There had been a time when the Party would welcome anyone. There had been a time when the Party had begged for members. But that was then. No matter how bad things turned, he wouldn't trade the card. With it, he could always rebuild. Damn the words. He could always rebuild.

Hell, maybe he could buy up an acre or two on the cheap now that folks were desperate.

During that winter, sex with the silver-haired woman was short and desperate.

He met her at the Town Hall, where she had an office she'd use whenever she was in town doing business for the Ministry of Agriculture. Before anything, before kissing or undressing, he always tried to talk to her. Nothing serious. He didn't care for the sound of his own voice, but for the sound of someone else's responding to it. Even a simple good morning would be enough. It had been so long since he had last spoken with his wife that it felt like it had always been this way. Talking had been easy, once. He wouldn't know what to say anymore.

Every time he tried to talk to the silver-haired woman, though, she would lay a finger to his lips.

"No, no, no. You're not allowed to," she would say and the grin would widen, while locking her legs around him and drawing him in.

Short and desperate. When they finished, he tried to come up with something smart to say. Instead, he avoided her gaze and let her do the talking. And she did. She talked for hours about her work, about the state of the world, about things he neither knew nor cared about.

"You wouldn't believe how…"

"Just the other day, I got to know that…"

"Could you imagine that, they have little chance of…"

"Statistics tell us that this is a simple matter of…"

"What is the point of proposing a fucking law if you know that there is no measurable…"

"Very few people are aware of how little there is to know…"

"Fortunately, it's a well-known fact that if you add…"

He didn't pay attention to the content of her words. Only that she talked.

But this is a real woman, he thought. *One who talks when the whole world is hushed. Who curses, who mocks, who speaks whatever's on her mind, and damn everyone else.*

This is a real woman.

✕

ONE LATE EVENING, after a day spent with the silver-haired woman at her office, he came home, and moved to take a bath straight away. From the corner of his eye, he caught the teacher staring at him as he made his way upstairs, but ignored her. He took his time, scrubbing his body clean. Then, he shaved, put on clean clothes, and came downstairs to eat. He filled a plate with ham casserole, the last he'd have before the rationing was announced, and sat at the mahogany table across from her.

He pretended not to see the shocked realization on her face. He nodded with pleasure as he wolfed down his meal and concentrated on the chunks of fat on his plate. When he lifted his head again, she was staring through the windows at the fields with a blank expression. That, he ignored as well. He ignored the suffocating air between them over the next few days, how she would stare at him when she thought he wasn't paying attention, and how he himself would avoid eye contact. A few weeks later, he ignored the unfamiliar scent of sandalwood on her clothes. Ignored the late hours she was spending at the school.

It was long after the silver-haired woman made the one-sided decision to stop the affair and long after the teacher stopped coming home smelling of sandalwood that they sat next to each other again and let their skin touch without flinching or moving away. They remained there, touching, not saying anything, not looking at each other, until the sun came up again the next morning.

<h1 style="text-align:center">21.</h1>

T HE BOY WITH the shaved head stared at the farmer from
the debris pile.

The farmer recognized him as the youngest of three
brothers that his wife taught. The boy was squatting on his
hams, arms elbow-deep into the pile of broken wood and
shattered glass. Leftovers from the Sheriff's visit. The farmer
had heaped up the debris where the driveway met the road,
hoping someone would take it. For firewood, maybe, or as pit
fill. He had expected, perhaps, to find a vagabond sorting
through it. Instead, he found the boy, bicycle lying on the
ground a few feet away.

*Didn't you hold a gun to my head once, you little shit? In
my own house?* The farmer mimed holding a shotgun to his
temple. There was no response.

The boy's face provoked him with its nonchalance. Every
time the farmer came out of the house with another load on
the wheelbarrow for the pile, he eyed the boy, but the boy
returned the stare without malice, without intent.

What language do these kids think in, the farmer
wondered. *Soon, this will be a country of idiots. My world
ends where my words fail. Where does your world even start,*

boy? If I were to crack that shaved skull of yours open, what would I see inside? I bet it's full of a big old nothing. Eat, sleep, shit. Maybe hold a shotgun to someone's head without understanding why. Because someone made you. That's what you are. Empty.

The boy stared with curiosity.

Get lost, the farmer kicked a stone at him. The boy snarled, showing crooked teeth and, when he pulled his arms out of the pile, he was holding a sharp piece of wood held like a knife. In response, the farmer drew a thick rod from the wheelbarrow and pointed it straight at the boy's head. A few steps forward. Now the rod's end quivered a couple of inches from the boy's nose.

I've been having a hell of a year, boy, and I don't see you carrying today. Don't test me.

Still snarling, the boy dropped the piece of wood, jumped on his bicycle and pedaled away.

The farmer watched him cycle down the long narrow road. He tossed the rod onto the pile and picked up the piece of wood the boy had dropped. The station dial was still on it. Springs and wire hung from one side and, when he twisted a knob, he could make out the mechanism moving, tiny gears rotating. That part, he pocketed. He'd have to bury it where no one would find it.

He'd also have to keep the girl inside, away from prying eyes. Enough close calls.

In the distance, the boy had stopped in the middle of the road to stare at him.

Anything broken during the Sheriff's destruction ended up in the pile. Anything. The girl helped. Using a broom and a dustpan, she collected the wreckage and dumped it into a bucket, which the teacher then emptied into the wheelbarrow. There were no words from the girl. She was all furtive looks and making herself small and useful. Even when she cut herself on a piece of glass, she stuck her finger into her mouth and said nothing. She still limped slightly on the wounded ankle. Yet, she didn't complain.

What part of that was humility and what part was mourning, the farmer couldn't tell. Perhaps a bit of both.

Another load. He took out the remnants of the china cupboard. Tipped the wheelbarrow, and glass and wood tumbled out with porcelain flowing in between like blue and white scree sliding down a mountainside. When he looked again down the road, it was empty. No boy on his bicycle.

When he returned to the house, he found the living room empty. The dustpan and the broom lay on the ground beside the pail. A faint cry reverberated off the now naked walls. He followed the mewling to find the girl curled up on the floor in a corner of the kitchen, the teacher sitting in front of her, stroking her head. The girl talked low, words that he couldn't hear, couldn't understand, but his wife nodded. Words like a low murmur, tree leaves rustling. Then, they hugged.

The teacher helped her stand. Hand in hand, they passed by him and went back to the living room. The sound of sweeping continued.

The junk in the basement would be harder to sort through, but it had to be done. The girl needed the space.

And so he steeled himself and plunged through memories, bringing them out piece by piece and dumping them into the open for passersby and bone pickers to pore over.

There was a plastic neon yellow umbrella he and his wife had once bought at the country fair when the skies had opened without warning. The umbrella had collapsed the moment they had tried to open it. No refunds were given.

The remains of a dirt bike that he had destroyed as a teenager. Ruined it when he had tried to jump over the poisoned stream on a makeshift ramp, cracking the engine block and two of his ribs. For years he had thought he could resurrect it, but he had a better head for tractors than dirt bikes.

A box of toys he had bought for their son, which he avoided dwelling on. The girl wouldn't like them anyway. They were for babies.

There were also piles of the Party magazine from the last few years that appeared in their mailbox at irregular intervals. He had never subscribed to it. Flipping through one of them, images of smiling families flashed from the pages, smiling soldiers at the Northern front, smiling workers, smiling doctors and their cancer patients smiling as they died, smiling sheriffs and their smiling deputies, smiling teachers in classrooms filled with non-grieving smiling children, smiling farmers in their healthy corn farms who may have been Party members. Earnest, beaming smiles everywhere and not a word written on any of the pages. Just everyone being happy in silence.

OVER THE NEXT few days, as the farmer brought out more of the wreckage and things that had outgrown their use, he'd notice the boy pedaling down the road too far away to make eye contact with. On other days, he'd be just arriving to catch him sorting through the pile, his arms scratched up. As soon as the boy saw him, he'd drop whatever he was holding and speed away. The bicycle now had a small trailer attached to it, little more than a box on wheels. A length of rope tied it to the handlebar. The farmer didn't fail to notice that the toys he had left out were gone.

Throughout it all, he never looked at the teacher in the eyes. Not for lack of effort. Her gaze seemed to be focused on the work in front of her. On writing. On the girl. Not him.

He felt a need for her acknowledgement. For her to give him a sign that everything between them was intact. That it was as before, before he had messed up by trying to reclaim her from the girl in the only language he felt he had left.

His eyes followed her as she wandered through the house and he begged.

Look at me. Don't cut me off. I didn't mean to hurt you. I'm just drowning.

As days went by, the basement took shape. The teacher sat at her writing desk, which she had moved next to the girl's cot. The girl talked to his wife in a hushed voice. He couldn't quite make out what she was saying from the head of the staircase where he observed them. He could figure it out, though. The teacher showed the manuscript to the girl, and the girl responded. And his wife smiled or she nodded, or crossed her arms with her chin resting on her fingers.

Late one evening, he descended the stairs, clearing his throat. The teacher glanced at him before looking back to the manuscript. The girl regarded him with what he hoped was respect. When he tried to smile at her, she turned around and continued reading from her book.

He approached his wife and squeezed her shoulder.

Please, look at me. Make it okay for me to still be yours.

She didn't react. Only continued writing, ignoring him, possibly remembering that pretending he didn't exist was a bigger punishment for him than any word she could utter in anger. She had done it before, when he had gone too far, when he had messed up so badly he didn't dare stare in the mirror.

He remained over her and tried to sneak a peek at the manuscript.

He read the story of a girl, a girl called Parrhesia, who was cursed by the Gods to talk nothing but the truth. And the more truth she spoke, the more she was hated. There were those who did not want her to speak of them. They knew they had benefited in life by acting in dishonorable ways. Self awareness brought them shame. Still, it was shame they could live with as long as their neighbors remained silent. If no one talked about their deeds, it was as if they hadn't existed. Parrhesia's every word, and she was unable to keep her mouth shut, was a condemnation against them and their way of life. And that meant she could not be allowed to talk.

He read the story and did not understand. *Why would you write something like this, something so obvious? And who will read it? Are you so eager to have our lives destroyed? To have what little of your life remains thrown away? I cannot protect you from this. I can't protect you from anything anymore.*

When she caught him looking at her words, she gave him a firm push, still refusing to make eye contact. There was disgust in that motion, loathing. He made himself feel every last bit of it, deserving it all.

Next to her, the girl sat with her hurt leg stretched out. She read from a thin book whose brittle pages turned with a scratching noise. Along the spine, half-faded letter spelled the name W.B. Yeats. The farmer picked it up.

"Hey, I'm reading that," the girl protested.

The farmer ignored her. He leafed through the book, straining at the letters, the simple words that echoed dissonant as he read them. He mouthed the words, his tongue going dry. Next to him, the girl looked to the teacher for help.

The farmer read in silence.

And I took all the blame out of all sense and reason,
Until I cried and trembled and rocked to and fro,
Riddled with light. Ah! when the ghost begins to quicken,
Confusion of the death-bed over, is it sent
Out naked on the roads, as the books say, and stricken
By the injustice of the skies for punishment?

He re-read the passage, trying to derive meaning. A man could lose himself in such nonsense and never find his way out again.

He could feel the girl fidgeting and his wife glaring. He handed the book back to the girl and patted her, roughing up her hair. On his way up from the basement, the farmer heard his wife sigh.

Evening came. He tipped the wheelbarrow's contents into the pile and wiped his brow. Down the road, long shadows fell across the asphalt. The boy was nowhere to be seen. He looked behind him, down the driveway and past the house, at the fields. Once the last of the wreckage had been cleaned, it'd be time to consider what to do about the dust in the fields. He'd have to start from scratch. Plow everything. Then, he'd have to beg and borrow to get more seeds. He thought of the silver-haired woman from the Ministry of Agriculture, whom he still did business with whenever she came into town. She would help him if he asked. She never said no to him. She'd get him the seeds and maybe secure him a grant. Those were hard to come by, but she had her ways.

He leaned forward and rested his hands on his knees, feeling weariness pull him into the ground. *What the hell's the point?* he thought. *There will be no next year.*

Leaving the wheelbarrow in the driveway, he walked up the steps to the porch. There, his wife sat with a glass of plain water. No lemon or mint. She had her eyes half-closed and her head tipped back, her fingers intertwined over her belly. It was the moment when the temperature changed and the fields seemed to breathe a sigh of relief. He took the seat next to her, feeling the salt and the grime on his skin. Inside, their house looked abandoned. The girl was gone, back into the basement probably.

His wife took a deep breath and a rattle came from deep within her lungs. He looked at her belly and imagined a clock counting down days, minutes, moments. The curve of her neck was sinew and veins, and even a hint of bone where once was muscle and healthy skin.

He reached over and touched her hand. She pulled away.

He sighed and closed his eyes. He tried to remember her name which he hadn't spoken in years. And realized he couldn't.

"Kkcan… we talkhh?" he rasped.

Something inside the house braced. She opened her eyes and stared at him.

"Can… we ttth… talk?" he continued, reaching out with his hand again.

She stood up with a wince. Her horrified eyes looked away.

"Can we tth… talk?" he repeated and his words shredded his throat.

She turned and bolted into the house. His voice pleaded

with her and, as it did, it burst. It ruptured into splinters of wood, into shards of glass, into fragments of blue and white porcelain. He chased her with his voice and she ran from him, covering her ears.

When he caught up with her, she had paused at the basement door, her hand on the handle, panting. He rushed up to her, stood close, his face so close to hers he could smell the dust on her lips. Dust.

"Can we talk?" He whispered. Then, as an afterthought, "Puh… Please."

She opened her mouth, but nothing came out. She shook her head and entered the basement, locking the door behind her.

22.

THAT BASTARD, THE teacher thought. *That goddamn bastard.*

He banged on the basement door again and again. Each knock howled and begged, rattling the door on its hinges.

The teacher stumbled down the stairs and slumped against the far wall, burying her face into her hands. Her chest convulsed in silence.

Breathe Breathe Breathe. She inhaled and tried to count to four, but failed.

This is what seeing a ghost must feel like, the teacher thought.

As if in response, the knocks came louder, faster now, more urgent.

Corvo half-raised herself in her cot, a book in her hands, and stared up at the basement door.

"What's going on?" she asked the teacher. "What's happening? Why is he pissed off? I haven't done anything, I swear."

No, don't, the teacher begged and tried to smile. *Don't be upset. It's fine. It's fine.*

The hammering at the door continued until, with a

single desperate punch, gavel-like, it ceased, plunging the basement in silence. For a few minutes, she could hear nothing but her own breathing. Then, dragging steps moving away from the door. They grew distant, roving across the floor above them. Now, he was in the living room. Now the kitchen. Then the steps grew louder, until they echoed right above them again.

A shadow appeared under the door. Pressure against it, making the wood groan, and the hollow thump of a body slumping down. And then, nothing.

The only thing the teacher wanted was for him to leave, to go upstairs to the bedroom they had shared for years and fall asleep, leaving her in peace. She would deal with all this in the morning. Not now.

Yet the minutes came and went and still he remained on the other side of the door. The girl leaned back again and leafed through the book the teacher had given her.

Why was he doing this to her? Why? Was the other night not enough? Was *anything* enough for him? She just wanted to finish the story and do some good before she was gone. Why couldn't he let her die in peace? What more could she give him that he hadn't torn out of her already?

What more did he want? What more did she have to give? She stood up, opened her hiding place behind the armoire and retrieved a new pencil, then moved to the cot next to the girl. Corvo gave her space, moving her hurt leg out of the way.

The teacher motioned for the book of poetry Corvo was reading, opened it, and wrote in the margin of a page with a pencil.

Tell me a story, please.
Your home.

Corvo gave her a blank stare.

"My home? The compound?"

The teacher nodded.

Corvo wedged herself deeper into the corner, and winched at her injured leg. Her eyes seemed to lose focus as she stared somewhere beyond the basement walls, beyond the farmhouse and its surrounding fields. The teacher lay on her side on the cot, feeling the girl's residual warmth against the mattress.

"The compound was in the forest. We had our own house, Mom and Ali and me. It had a gas kitchen and a living room with a sofa and a radio, though there was never any music on it. I had my own bedroom too, which was nice. In our last home, we had to sleep on the floor, Mom said, but I can't remember it because I was still small back then."

The girl's brow furrowed in concentration.

"Our house was next to the chain fence. Mom always said we were lucky to live there because it meant we only had neighbors on one side. The fence was really tall, almost as tall as our house but sometimes the tree branches from the other side bent over it and scratched our roof. Sometimes, squirrels would jump off the branches and wake me up by tapping on my window.

"Mom's job was in Maintenance. She went around peoples' houses and fixed leaks and broken lights and stuff like that. She really liked it, especially when Bonnie was with her, they were really good friends. Bonnie would come over in the morning to have tea with Mom and they talked until it was time to go to work. Then, they would go around the compound from house to house, knocking on doors and asking people if there was anything broken they could fix.

There was always something, they said.

"Bonnie told me once that the houses were super old. Soldiers used to live there before people went mute. Bonnie said she was my age when her family found the abandoned compound and she knew every building in and out, including the dining hall and the laundry room, and had fixed everything in them at least ten times each. When I asked Ali where did Mom and Bonnie get all the things they needed to make repairs, he said the Party was kind enough to lose a few things now and then.

"Ali was an engineer. We had these rusty generators he took care of that broke every few weeks and some of the houses would lose power. Whoever lived there would go visit other houses that still had electricity for a couple of hours until Ali fixed them. Once, we had to walk across the entire compound to find a house with lights still on. Ali said he sometimes took longer to fix the generators on purpose so I would have plenty of time to play with the other children."

She smiled at the memory.

"My job was to go to school. Mister Lakshman taught our class. He taught all kinds of things, like math and engineering. He also taught other boring things like history, which is just about a bunch of dead people, anyway. It's easier reading numbers than words for me. Mister Lakshman didn't know how to help me read, because letters dance when I look at them and words don't always make sense. Ali didn't mind staying up late with me until I could tell what the words were supposed to say.

"There weren't many children at the compound. There was me and Polly and the twins and Isaiah, but Isaiah doesn't count. He came to school but he never understood anything. Ali said there weren't many children in the compound because we didn't have a doctor and having children without a doctor is dangerous. I asked him if he meant that children would turn out like Isaiah and he said that Isaiah was lucky to be alive.

"Some days, the Hunters would return from beyond the fence and, instead of birds or deer, they carried these metal rings the size of a pumpkin that had a," she held an index up and moved it in circles. "They had a rotor. And they flew. When the Hunters found those, we all had to cover our houses with green nets that had leaves in them, make the compound look like the forest, and stay inside real quiet until someone came and knocked on our door to tell us it was safe again. I didn't like the staying quiet part, but Ali and I had a game about who could stay silent the longest, so it wasn't too bad. Ali said that those things flew through the forest and had tiny little cameras on them for pictures. I asked him who were the pictures for, but he went very quiet and didn't want to talk about it anymore. Then, my Mom told me to stop asking questions that upset people, so I stopped.

"One day, all the grown-ups gathered at the gate and had a big argument about opening it and letting someone inside. The stranger on the other side had a weird voice and it was difficult to understand him. He shouted help, but it sounded more like aelp, aelp, and some of his a's sounded like o's and he swallowed his letters. Like, he'd shout Op'n te dowr, I'm starv'n, and it took me a few seconds to understand what he was saying, you know? Ali didn't want him inside. He said he didn't sound like someone who had everything in the right place, he didn't sound all there.

"Some of the others, some Hunters and his friends from Generators, agreed and wanted to shoot the man because he was yelling and the flying machines would hear him. And others got angry and said that some people didn't want to let Ali in when he first came to the compound because he sounded like a Haji, and where would he be now? That really upset Ali and it scared me. Ali never got upset.

"Eventually, the grown-ups decided to let the man inside. It was Missis Cohan's decision. She is, was, the one who decided who got what house and what kind of job people should be doing. She was very good at it. She used to organize people for a living, she told me once. It's easy, she said, all it takes is to make people see they need to do something for their own good and they'll go and do a fine job out of it. People always want to do the right thing. They just need direction.

Corvo narrowed her eyes and looked out into the distance again.

"He lived with us, in the compound I mean, but his face didn't seem special. He was sort of sick-looking, he had a bunch of scars on his skin, and he looked down a lot so his hair fell in front of his face. And he had this strange walk, as if his left leg was heavy. He wouldn't look at you when he talked. Someone asked him what his name was, but he said he couldn't remember it. That we could call him whatever we wanted. They opened the gate and they let him in and a lot of people clapped his back and shook his hand, even Ali, although he didn't smile like the others did. That first night after he arrived, he came into the dining hall and it was like everyone suddenly stopped talking and eating and stared at him. I remember Ali left the dining hall early that night.

"Mom and Ali argued a lot about the stranger. The Hunters found more of the metal rings with the cameras out in the woods and Ali blamed it on him. Ali told Mom she forgot easily and Mom said he was being unfair, that everyone had lost people. That we should give the stranger a chance to prove himself.

"They put the stranger in one of the empty houses close to us next to the fence. There had been an old couple living there, though I can't remember their names. They never went out much. One day the wife died and then the husband died a couple of days later and no one lived in there since. Everyone said the house smelled weird. The stranger, though, he said it was a good place, that the smell didn't bother him, and he kept murmuring, 'obli'ed, obli'ed'. I don't think Ali liked having him so close, but he never said so. Mom went over once to say hi and to check for leaks together with Bonnie and she said he slept on the floor, even though there was a perfectly fine bed for him.

"Once, on a Sunday, I was playing outside with Polly and the twins. It was Polly's idea to stand on the firewood box below his bedroom window and spy on him through the window. The stranger was sitting inside his house, staring at the wall. He gave me the creeps. He wore a pair of pants Mister Lakshman gave him, but nothing else.

"The skin on his back looked like old tree bark with scars all over. He was missing a few teeth and Polly said he was missing some toes too, that's why he walked the way he did.

"Then… he saw us. I froze, but Polly ran away, leaving me there by myself. The stranger stared at me. I could see his ribs, every single one of them. Then, he stuck his tongue out. It looked like someone had taken a chunk out of it. When I still didn't move, he let out this horrible screech. I ran away and never went to his house again and me and Polly never talked about it.

"After a few days Missis Cohan put him to work to get folks used to seeing him. She put him in Maintenance, but

Mom said some people complained and he was moved to the Builders instead. Ali said that, as long as they didn't give him a gun and kept him away from his generators, he was fine.

"Mom found out about me and Polly. Polly's Dad told her. She yelled at me and pulled my hair. Ali told her to stop, then she told him to mind his own business and to stop telling her how to raise me. When Mom gets mad, she's not herself. She says and does things she shouldn't. She started talking about Ali's family, about how I wasn't his daughter, that his daughter was gone, and that he needs to stop treating me like I'm her. Ali never said anything when Mom was angry. He just crossed his arms and stared at her until she calmed down and apologized. But Mom didn't calm down then. She screamed at him and hit him and called him a son of a bitch, but still he didn't move or say anything. He let her scream and scream, and call him all kinds of things, until her voice got tired and then she couldn't talk anymore. And when she got exhausted, she stopped. Then she apologized, even though it hurt her to speak, apologized for talking like that about his family, and he hugged her and kissed her and said, you're my family too, and that he was going to talk to the stranger, have a chat about how he was freaking people out. Mom said he shouldn't have to. That she was going to take care of things, but he wanted to do it, wanted to do things properly, to take care of us, and Mom apologized again, and Ali told her it was alright and he hugged me too and said it was fine, that it was all going to be just fine.

"They went to see the stranger together. When they came back, they were silent. I didn't ask them why.

"After that, they didn't chat with the others in the dining hall like before, didn't laugh at jokes. We all left early after dinner and Mom and Ali locked themselves in their bedroom and whispered.

"A few weeks after the stranger had moved in, Mom woke me up at night. She had her hand over my mouth and told me to be quiet, that I had to listen and do exactly as she said. She told me to put as much food and clothes as I could carry into my backpack. I asked if we were leaving Ali like we left Dad, but then I saw him walking up and down in the living room and carrying things, so I guessed they weren't fighting. When he saw me awake, he came over and winked and asked if I felt like making a bet with him, we'd go on a walk through the forest and first one to talk was a loser. He didn't smile the way he had when we'd made the bet before, but I still agreed.

"When we left the camp one of Ali's Hunter friends was outside the gate guarding it. We hid and waited until he moved away and then sneaked through. When I looked behind, the compound was gone. We went so far into the forest that I couldn't tell where we were and then I was sure we had gone farther than I had ever been from the compound, far from the fence, far from everyone.

"Some time later, I heard a rumble. I looked behind and saw flames above the trees. It smelled like a bonfire. Both Mom and Ali looked scared and confused. I didn't care about the bet anymore, so I pulled at Mom's arm and begged her to go back and help the others, but she kept pulling me along and when I begged Ali instead, she slapped me. Ali didn't say anything.

"We didn't stop walking until the sun came up. I sat down and when I couldn't stand up again, Ali lifted me and carried me on his back. He said not to worry about the bet, he was pretty sure he had talked first. We stopped at a river to rest and eat some of the smoked meat Ali had brought with him. Mom went down the river bank to get water. Ali asked me how I felt and I said tired. Then, he asked me if I understood what had happened. I said that someone had found the compound and torched it. He nodded and chewed on a piece of deer jerky. He asked me if I understood that we were never going back again. If I understood that we were never going to see the people we lived with at the compound, that Polly, Mister Lakshman, even Isaiah, were dead. I said yes. I asked him if it was because of the stranger and he didn't say anything for a long time. Then, he said no. It was because of the people that had convinced the stranger he was doing the right thing.

"We sat and ate and rested for a bit. Then, Ali asked me if I wanted to go and see what was taking Mom so long.

"We went down the bank together. Mom was kneeling with her hands in the water. I went closer and called out at her but she didn't hear me. There were black logs going down the river and she was staring at them. I put a hand on her shoulder and it made her jump up. She said the water was not good and pushed me back. When I looked over her shoulder, I saw a burned body coming down the river that looked like Bonnie.

"We walked until the forest stopped and a valley started. Mom wanted us to go North, across the border. Mom said we'd make it. We just had to get there, because they take in anyone who reaches the border, doesn't matter where they come from or whether they are mutes or still talk. As long as they get there. We didn't know there was a war going on.

"Ali stopped talking a couple of days after we left the camp. He said he was just tired, but then Mom said we were all tired, and then he told her to get off his back and then neither of them talked for a while. So, I stopped talking too.

We walked faster that way, but it wasn't easier. I don't know how you mutes do it. Not talk when you are mad at each other. Don't you burst from all the words?"

<h1 style="text-align:center">23.</h1>

A HOUSE SETTLES into stillness like it settles into its foundations, full of groans and protests until its walls find a comfortable way to bear their own weight and the beams that hold it together have warped as much as they're going to.

From the mahogany table where she was writing, the teacher observed Corvo working around the farmer. The farmhouse was empty now after the Sheriff's destruction. Its bare walls echoed as Corvo unloaded the last bucketful of debris into the wheelbarrow, then rushed ahead to the front door. There was visible tension on the farmer's face. He motioned for her to get away from the door, not caring one bit that the girl hadn't been outside in days.

In response, she lifted her hands and shrugged with an annoyed expression. *Why not?* it said. She pointed at the wheelbarrow and made a throwing-away gesture. *Why can't I help?*

The farmer motioned her away again, brow furrowed. He didn't open the door until Corvo had moved away, all rolling eyes and hands thrown up in the air and wordless huffing and puffing. There was the suspicion of a "come on" and a "just want to help" coming out of her, that she uttered while covering her mouth. The farmer pushed the wheelbarrow outside, checked that she wasn't going to run out, and closed the door behind him.

The girl picked up a broom and began sweeping, shoulders slumped and mouth half-open. Baby fat had begun to melt away from her face. The first hint of sharp shadows appearing below her cheeks, the kind the town's children grew into early on.

Yes, the house was settling once more. This new stillness had a specific taste that did not bear any comfort, and it filled the farmhouse to the rafters. Only the girl's feet scuffling along the floor interrupted it.

The teacher shook her head. Tapped a pencil against the table and nodded to the girl to come over as she wrote a question on a piece of paper.

How's your leg?

Corvo took the piece of paper and turned it over. She reached out for the pencil, but the teacher held it out of her reach.

"It's fine," the girl said narrowing her eyes. "Still hurts a bit."

You've been quiet
I miss hearing you

"I got nothing to say today."

You've been quiet for a couple of days now

The girl shrugged. The teacher continued watching her as the girl picked up the broom again and wandered through the house, sweeping places she'd already swept before. *Music would have been nice now*, the teacher thought, and looked over to where the stereo used to be.

What she wanted to ask the girl was, *do you hurt?*

A long time ago, she had concluded that pain was the death of language. When the farmer's mother got cancer, the old woman had tried to explain what it felt like. The physicality of pain. Compression, constriction, contraction, she had said and pointed at various parts of her body, at the organs that were failing. None of those words meant anything to the teacher. She'd never understand what that woman felt, even if she went through the exact same experience.

In time, the farmer's mother stopped talking about it altogether. She had said in her tilled earth accent, "you wouldn't understand and I don't care to give thought to it. So forget about it, and maybe we can pretend it ain't all that bad." One could spend years in silence, pretending like her mother-in-law. Then, one day, run a red light and get into an accident and find out you can't keep silent anymore. Not because you have something to say, but because the pain means you can't not speak anymore.

And this girl will try to keep it all in, the teacher thought. *Will keep it all in, because everyone else does it. Because the only other two people left in her life won't tell her otherwise. Only she won't make it. In her throat, she still has the capacity for words, and, one day, they'll spill out too. It could be years from now, years after both the teacher and the farmer are gone. But the moment will come. Words shaped by pain tend to find their way out and they don't care how much damage they do.*

In front of her, the pages were waiting. Only a few were

missing from the story, she felt, and she'd be done. She held the pencil over the page, impotent and unable to write another word.

She had been working on that book since she had arrived at this glorified village, so that must have been... Fifteen years? At first She had started because writing had been a better waste of time for a literature teacher than staring at fields. Then, the Party took over and she had something to say.

The Party hadn't been elected to power as much as it had slipped through the cracks. On the year of the worst voter turnout in history, the few that made their way to voting stations had been enough to bring the Party to power. The Party must have been as surprised as everyone else.

When the Party started intruding into their daily lives, she felt compelled to mutate the story and have it reflect her experience. When the Party took her words away, she felt justified. She wanted to make a point. Not for other people, but because she felt she'd burst if she didn't say something.

Why the devil is this book so damn important to you? the farmer had asked her. Why is it important enough to risk our lives? It's just words on paper.

She had looked at him with weariness. You're saying that, she answered, as if words on paper can't tear the world apart or put it back together.

She went through the pages, though the story was so familiar by now she barely needed to.

There was once a girl named Parrhesia, who was unable to speak anything but the truth, the story went. Her mother had offended the gods by refusing them their offerings. Not out of laziness, but out of poverty. When, perplexed and offended, the gods questioned her about her lack of faith, she argued that mighty beings such as they couldn't possibly notice her insignificant offerings anyway. The gods cursed her for that moment of honesty and the girl that was growing inside her became incapable of telling a lie.

The girl grew up with her mother in a cabin in the woods. They never visited the nearby village, never spoke to any of the villagers. If they chanced upon them foraging for mushrooms or hunting deer, they hurried away, covering their faces with their shawls. For food, they relied on their little garden and what the forest could provide. Their clothes, they made themselves. If they needed something they had to buy, they did without.

When Parrhesia questioned her mother on why they avoided the villagers, her mother's mood turned dark. People love a comfortable lie more than a harsh truth. And her words held such bitter conviction that Parrhesia never questioned her again.

One day, the woman fell ill. She lay in bed and wheezed, barely lucid and muttering to herself. Disobeying her orders, Parrhesia left to get help. Upon reaching the village, her inability to say anything but the truth turned the villagers against her. Villagers who were offended when she pointed out how cruel they were to each other, how lying to others came to them as easily as breathing. How easily they lied to themselves. Every single one of them lied, telling themselves stories and making excuses for their actions so they could continue living easy lives.

They tried to hurt her for her comments. Threw her in a cell despite her pleading, despite her begging for someone to help her mother.

They released her only when she agreed to never come to the village again. When Parrhesia returned to the cabin, she found her mother dead. Overwhelmed by pain, Parrhesia cut out her own tongue. *Better to remain silent,* she thought as she reached for the shears. *Better to say nothing and live in peace.*

The teacher had used broad strokes in her story, not caring for subtleties. Stories travel faster than manifestos, she had justified it to herself. She would find someone escaping North and ask them to take her manuscript across the border. Someone would be interested, she reasoned, in what this country's silence had to say. People would understand the allegory, she was certain. They'd see the finger-pointing towards the self-righteous Party, they'd identify its savage practices underneath the paper-thin layers of metaphor. And they'd understand the plight of those who lived in this country South of their borders that risked their lives every time they spoke out loud.

And then, slowly and all at once, hers and the farmer's personal hush had taken root, and writing no longer seemed to have a point.

As the teacher re-read Parrhesia's story, the Party's anthem played on the TV that couldn't be turned off and the Mouth appeared. Animated sequences of terrifying Northern soldiers played on the screen, demonic faces full of fangs and forked tongues. She tossed her pencil on the table in frustration.

For all its pretty words and years of effort, the pages said nothing of the real pain she felt.

When the farmer returned, he went right past her without making eye contact and washed his hands in the sink. Then, as he had done so many times, he took to wandering without purpose through the house. She stalked him with her eyes as he dragged his feet along the floor, arms stiff by his sides. Shoulders pulled down by gravity.

Look at me, she called out to him without saying a word. *Raise your head, you bastard.*

The scuffling of his feet merged with the girl sweeping.

She continued staring, hoping he would look back. Hoping he would talk again. If he talked to her again, she wouldn't run off like last time. She would answer him. She was done nursing her pain in silence.

Instead, he rounded a corner and disappeared. His steps grew smaller as he descended the staircase to the basement.

She stood up and felt her belly, then her chest. With slow, lazy moves, she picked up the discarded pencil and put it back into its case, ignoring Corvo's questioning look.

She went outside and covered her mouth and nose with the top of her blouse, before entering what was left of the fields. Dust crept into her mouth every time she sighed, with its argil flavor. So much of the world was dust. She felt the monster that had spread inside her tightening, squeezing her guts and lungs. She ignored it, like she ignored the chaparral that scratched her legs and the chamomile sap that brushed against her bare feet.

Farther and farther, she walked into the fields. Even out here, with the dust choking everything and the dead corn between her toes, she felt her mind clearing. She needed to be away from the farmhouse. Away from her husband's suffocating presence and the girl who pretended her language had burned out just so she could fit in.

She started coughing. Winced and clasped her side, choking and spitting red on the ground. A few more steps and she reached the scarecrow. She slid down at its base and closed her eyes, counting her counts of fours while her lungs filled up with dust and blood.

Eyes closed and head up, she faced the sun.

If no one talks about yesterday, she thought, *did it ever happen?* If she never said out loud that their baby boy had died, would it matter? Or would the words just fester? Do they, like all the things she never said, turn into a cancer and eat her from the inside? And all the transgressions that passed between her and him. Never acknowledged. Never answered. He had committed one last offence when he had forced himself on her. So close to the end, she shouldn't have to hate him in such absolute terms, but he had made it so. Confusingly, profoundly. And she wouldn't say a word to him about it. Couldn't.

We really messed up, didn't we?

She continued gasping for breath and didn't smell the wet muzzle until it was close, didn't hear the panting coming from behind. Between coughs and the sound of her blood dripping on the ground, footsteps approached, claws digging into the ground. The dog sniffed her nape. Tugged at her hair with its canines.

The teacher leaned forward and sucked air, abandoning her counting. Embracing the pain instead of avoiding it. She remained in that position, feeling the dog's rotten-meat breath behind her ears. With her left hand, she grabbed a fistful of dust and threw it into its snarling mouth. The animal flinched and staggered away, shaking its head with a violent hack. The teacher turned around and spat blood into its eyes, and the dog ran away, dragging its head along the ground.

Night fell. When the sun disappeared below the horizon, she heard the porch door swing open and him coming out of the house. Short, frantic steps. Him slapping his chest, hitting hard, making noise. No words anymore. Whether because he was afraid someone would hear him or because he didn't dare use words with her anymore, she couldn't tell. Her arms felt like they were made out of lead. She lifted them with effort and clapped once, then once more before dropping them. His pace picked up and before she knew it he was carrying her back to the house, back-glancing at the red she had sprayed around her.

Holding onto him, she leaned into his ear and mouthed. *All the words in all the languages of the world don't contain half of the meaning to understand the you and me.* Feeling her breath, he half-turned and stared at her, for a moment forgetting his shame. But, by then, she didn't have the energy to hold her neck up anymore.

The memories behind the source of their dysfunction were fading in her mind, she realized, leaving only the dregs of bitterness behind. Their boy. The cheating. So many things, they seemed to bleed into each other, leaving just resentment.

I think I've figured what I want to say, she thought. *I've figured it out.*

24.

THE TEACHER OPENED the manuscript in front of her in a hundred-page tarot spread. She read through the story she knew by heart.

Upstairs, she could feel him staring at the ceiling. Below, the desolation that grew inside the girl.

She read through the story again. Then, she picked up her pencil point-down in her fist like a knife and carved large X's across every page. When she reached the last one, she balled them all together, took the mass under her arm and walked through the porch to the edge of the fields. There, she dug a shallow pit and dropped the mass in it.

Can we talk?

Odd how three words and a punctuation mark can split the sky apart.

She lit the pages on fire and watched as the ashes rose. Before the funeral pyre had consumed the paper, she turned her back to it. *I've been chasing the wrong ghosts*, she thought.

Back inside, she took her seat again at the mahogany table and stared at the blank page in front of her. She picked up the pencil.

And she proceeded to write anew. Not fiction this time,

no layers of metaphors and symbolism, but something simpler. Their story.

The pages filled out fast. She hadn't expected the truth to be so easy to write. She wrote and only stopped when her hand got numb and her sight blurry. Only then did she join him in their bedroom.

She slipped in next to him and crossed her arms over her belly, knowing he was only pretending to be asleep.

25.

T HE GREATEST TERROR the Deputy had experienced in her life had involved a transient. A drifter that had looked like an old torn jacket riding a stick. When she had asked him to pack and leave town, he had taken offense. That's when he'd pulled out a gun on her.

Her mind had gone blank, though she did remember the rabid blackness in that man's eyes had twisted her insides with a death grip. Hadn't let go until much later, after her patrol mate had beaten him senseless, after she had been ordered to go home and get some sleep, after she had taken her pillow and crawled into a closet, muffling her mouth with it as she wailed.

When the words were taken away and she barged into the townsfolk's homes or snatched them from the street, it struck her as odd that she was the one a hair away from losing her mind to terror. The violence she inflicted brought back the same feelings of blackness. And throughout it all, she kept thinking, *who's barging into the homes of my loved ones?* As if in answer, the baby inside her stirred, hidden by extra layers of baggy clothes.

"Please," they stammered as she took them away. "I was

jes talkin' on the phone."

"Why are you doin' this?"

"Are you gon' have us killed?"

"I hope they do the same to you."

She kept her mouth shut and repeated the same thought. An order is an order is an order.

Every day, as her concealed belly grew, she brought talkers to the Party thugs at the station, unable to tell them how sorry she was, that this wasn't her fault. And, every morning, when the townsfolk came out to the Main Street to work and shop and loiter, the thugs dragged one of those talkers out.

The man who led them, she called him Red on account of the red stone at the center of his Unity. No black clothes and polished jackboots on him or any of his thugs, no shaved heads or tattoos.

Red himself had the power to be forgotten. His features were plain and his dull gray eyes were unremarkable. Neither too tall, nor too short, or fat or thin or anything that would make him memorable in any way. A perfect everyman.

When they brought out a talker, the thugs moved like wolves. Unpinning their Unities, they disappeared into the crowd. Red's everyman features transformed as he slipped on a mask of incredulity and indignation. He went up to each person in the street, grabbing them with alarm on his face, until he had a good crowd going, and pointed at the talker with an accusatory finger. The other thugs maneuvered within the crowd and feigned the same outrage until, like a virus, it spread from person to person. To the wheat farmer, the pharmacist, the clerk from the town hall.

Few talkers kept their mouths shut when brought out. Most blathered at the top of their lungs, hoping Red would keep his promise and not hurt their families if they owned up to their crime of talking in public. They lamented and sniveled until veins popped in their necks.

As they talked, Red's face filled with rage. He gesticulated and frothed and the color of his cheeks matched his name. He moved with the skill of an orator who didn't need words to convey his message. Soon, the crowd was hypnotized. He opened his arms wide, as if to embrace every man and woman, making eye contact with every single one of them. Soon, their arms and faces twitched in imitation of him.

When Red took a step away from them, the crowd shifted forward, their feet moving on their own accord, trying to remain close. Those who wouldn't budge, the Party thugs forced with a shove and a punch in the kidneys. From beyond the half-circle that formed, more townsfolk gravitated towards the mass. Red was leading the townsfolk on a dance. When someone tried to break away, Red pointed at them with derision and disgust, shaming them back into the group.

The crowd seethed. Soon, their faces were the same furious mask Red was wearing. Those who most resembled him moved forward, pushing their way to the front and, as they did, the ones in the back shifted with distress at being left behind. No longer influenced by the other Party thugs, but now acting on their own volition.

Red worked the crowd to a climax. At that point, he gave the thugs an imperceptible nod. They rushed forward, dragging the townsfolk with them. They rained down blows on the talker, punching and stomping, hitting harder as the talker cursed the world for bringing him to that moment, cursed his own mother for bringing him into existence, until his voice was drowned out.

When the mob, thugs and townsfolk alike, exhausted itself and lucidity returned, they stared at the broken body, half in fascination and half in befuddlement. A few of them lifted the arms they had broken and touched the face they had mangled. Others went through the dead person's pockets. There were a few who took souvenirs. A broken crown. Pieces of a cauliflower ear. In that moment, they would have done anything Red asked them. Would have, in their guilt, followed him to the gates of hell had he pointed the way.

Instead, Red approached them all one by one and clapped their shoulders, embraced them. The townsfolk then congratulated each other, repeating the gesture. Soon, a celebratory atmosphere took over. Content and pleased, they dispersed with smiles on their faces. There were still others who did not smile, but seemed dazed and confused. Those, Red signaled at the Deputy to keep an eye on.

When the street in front of the station emptied, he nodded at his thugs and they dragged the talker's body away. Then, he approached the Deputy and, leaning into her ear, he whispered.

"Good work. Go find us another."

To have an effective state, the Party directive to law enforcement declared, the population needs to do the right thing most of the time when no one's looking. How you train them to do that is by being unforgiving. In time, conditioning would pay off. Law enforcement couldn't be everywhere, but the people would police themselves. A perfect state.

Red and his thugs left the town three years after they first set foot in it and the Sheriff passed away in his bed within the same week, although his spirit had died much earlier.

By then, the Deputy's uniforms felt loose on her. With the pregnancy flab gone, she expected she'd be down to her usual weight. Instead, plenty of fabric bagged around her chest and over her ribs. As she buttoned up in front of the mirror the morning after they buried the old man, she made a mental note to have them adjusted, then shoved the extra material into her pants and pulled the belt tight.

The palm-sized box had arrived at the station the day before and she had been fingering it in her pocket through the funeral. She brought it home with her, leaving it on top of the TV that wouldn't turn off. Such a small thing. It caused her a long, sleepless night, until she gave up and got out of bed before dawn.

She opened it and ground her teeth. Nestled at the center of the golden Unity was a flaming carmine orb, much like the sun when it came down over the hills. She picked it up and felt its cool metal against her forehead. She could have done good things with it, great things. Not just for her, but for the entire town. But the town hadn't spoken in three years and there had been plenty of murder staining its soul. Red had broken it. *She* had broken it.

She removed the Deputy's Unity and pinned the Sheriff's to her chest, but the badge pricked her and a drop of blood bloomed on her tan shirt. *Too late to change*, the Sheriff thought. *No one can see it, anyway. The badge will cover it.*

Inside the box was also a thin strip of paper with six digits. Those, she memorized and burned the paper, as instructed.

"Good mmm… mmmornin," she said to her reflection, staring at her tense jaw muscles. "Good. Mmmornin. Mmmornin. Good mmmornin. Good. Good mmmornin, everone." She tried to loosen up her mouth. Shed her tension.

The more she tried, the tighter her lockjaw became. She gave up with a grunt.

Before leaving, she went to the kitchen and filled a tray with several glasses of water and a bowl with mashed vegetables. Took the tray downstairs to the basement and left it next to Zachariah's bed. She watched over the three-year old sleeping, thumb in mouth. The windows up on ground level were blacked-out with tar and several layers of soundproof insulation covered the walls.

"Your Ma's goin up in the world, bean," she said in a low voice. "Your Ma's allowed to talk now. She has authority now. It don't count for much, but I won't say no to it. You'll see, bean. Things will get better fer us. You'll see. I'mmm in ccc… I'mmm in cccontrol now."

She wanted to run her fingers over his smooth throat, feel the unspoiled skin she had fought so hard to protect. It had been in that corner where his bed was now that she had given birth to him, squatting over a pile of musty towels, biting down on her duty belt. When she collapsed on the floor, after a night and a day of him tearing his way out, she touched that tiny intact patch on his quivering newborn throat and swore she'd split the earth in two to keep it that way.

"Never again a viccctim," she muttered to herself. "Never again." She sewed herself back together with fishing line and held him, unmoving for days, lying in her own dried blood, until she found the strength to stand up again. No one would ever find out about him. No one would take his voice away.

She moved a strand of curly hair away from his forehead and kissed him. He stirred, but didn't wake up. She stayed for a few moments longer, then she locked the door to the basement, covered the TV that wouldn't turn off with a thick blanket, and drove away in her cruiser.

She didn't enter the station right away. Instead, she parked and walked down the road towards Main Street, past the only traffic light in town. Her town.

She knew the buildings by the people who occupied them as well as she did by their street numbers. Their business, their family names that didn't matter anymore, their transgressions. Around her, the townsfolk went about their day. The pharmacist nodded at her as he unlocked his doors. Two farmers without a farm entered the bar, despite the early hour.

Standing in the middle of Main Street, it was almost as if things were back to normal. As if she'd be able to open her mouth and strike up a conversation with anyone about the Indian summer they were having or about last week's Party-sponsored football game that had taken place in a silent county stadium. The townsfolk were silent, but Main Street was far from it. Car engines and shoes on asphalt. Store doors opening and closing. Words were gone, but life would carry on without them.

There, surrounded by the people she served, she took an oath. She wouldn't arrest anyone for talking again. The town's soul was long gone, the townsfolk too conditioned and damaged. But she wouldn't contribute to their damnation any further. Every stinging thought that screamed how it was too late for that, that her hands would be forever red no matter how much good she did from there on… All those thoughts, she pushed down down down until they no longer tormented her.

When she got to the station, the two Deputies stood and nodded. She nodded back with a modest smile.

Their masks were good, but they had their tells. She

could no longer rely on people talking themselves into a dead end, so she relied on reading their body language. She took note of which one didn't look at her in the eyes. Which one exaggerated their smile. If they chewed on their lips.

"Good mmmornin," she said with a weaker voice than she intended, and those two words made the Deputies freeze in place. Neither of them had ever heard her voice. After a moment of indecision, they gave her slow nods and went back to their business. That, too, she noted.

Of the old man Sheriff's deputies, she was the only one who survived Red. The others couldn't obey, and so he had thrown them to the mob. She always thought that, when it came down to it, she'd stand up and do the right thing like they had, consequences be damned. When she heard of genocides and oppression in other parts of the world, she told herself she wouldn't keep quiet if it happened to her. That she'd do the right thing.

Only she didn't. She told herself she might have, if she had only herself to worry about, that the baby inside her was innocent. That swallowing her pride was easier than getting both of them killed. And what was one person supposed to do when everyone else complied? It wasn't that simple.

There were sleepless nights and there were nightmares because the Sheriff's honor was a difficult creature to muzzle. But her boy was still alive. In the end, that was the only thing that mattered.

She sat at the Sheriff's desk, her desk, and ran her fingers over one of the two computers left in the town, the other one sitting a couple of buildings over at the Town Hall. Both of them connected to the Party headquarters in the capital. Queries flowed to the Party. Info flowed in the opposite direction, if she was allowed to see it. Or at least, that's how old man Sheriff had explained it to her.

She pressed the power button on the side of its bulky frame and it hummed to life. A single blinking green cursor appeared on the black screen. Without hesitation, she typed in the six digits that had come with her new badge. The cursor disappeared and a query box replaced it.

They had a number of names over the past three years. "Unofficial Collaborators" was one. Before that, it had been "Secret Informers". Early in the Party's rule, they had simply been called "information people", without capitals. Somewhere, in a terminal deep within the Party headquarters, sat a digital list of everyone who was keeping tabs on their neighbors.

In time, she'd go through each and every name. First, though, she'd allow herself a single indulgence. She figured the universe owed her this much.

A few keystrokes and she got the name she was after. She was surprised to find out it hadn't been the farmer. He wasn't on the collaborator list at all. When he refused to help her, she'd been certain he had something to do with her husband disappearing. But she had to be sure. A picture stared at her from the monitor. This was the one who had led the Party thugs to him. It was a woman, barely. Just out of her teens. She touched the monitor and tried to find something in the woman's bio that stood out. Membership to the Party, or perhaps a criminal record. There was nothing. In front of her was a person so utterly unremarkable she thought she had made a mistake. All her searching and interrogating through the past three years, all her secret evidence-gathering and red tape…

Her husband had moved to this town to get some privacy, he had claimed. Soon after they met, he opened up about the death threats by people whose interests he had hurt. Politicians, entrepreneurs. Heads of state. He joked about them, but still went around town using a fake name. Good manners meant folks kept their noses out of the business of outsiders. For the most part. Still, someone had figured out who he was. Any one of them could have pointed him to Red. But it hadn't been anyone. It had been this woman, and he had been only one of many.

She drove to the woman's house the next day. It was a few minutes out of town, at the edge of the old forest. She parked the cruiser on the road shoulder, some way off the house. With some hesitation, she took her gun out of its holster and locked it in the glove compartment. Then, she cut her way through the forest.

Splashes of red, orange, and blue paint marked the trees. Here were the ones to be cut down, here those to be left alone. The property itself had been raised at the forest's far end during the town's founding. It had belonged to the most introverted of the original fifteen families that had settled in the area. Their names were once commemorated on a plaque outside the town hall, now gone. In time, the house had changed hands, then changed hands thrice over again. It had been renovated and extended and parts of it replaced. She had come across it as a child collecting mushrooms with the aunts that had raised her and never thought much of it. This house had two floors, like most other houses. Flaking paint, like most other houses. Hushed stories of drunken wife-beating, and bastard children, and the occasional self-inflicted gunshot filed as an accident for the sake of a proper burial. Like most other houses.

She could see it now through the forest, even though it was still far off. Little foliage remained on the evergreens to obscure her sight. Most of it lay scattered on the ground, singed and brown, crackling underneath her boots.

Something was wrong with the world. Even she who had never worked the land could tell as much. Rain came after longer and longer spells and, when it did, it wasn't enough. What would happen to the crops the town depended on? The sweet decaying smell of moss and fungi growing on rotten wood that she remembered was no longer there. Only dried mud and dust.

When she reached the edge of the forest, she pressed her body against a tree and watched the house. She waited, unmoving, for an hour, observing the dirty windows and the door with its flaking yellow paint before *she* appeared. Wiry and blond and no more than nineteen. It still surprised the Sherriff at how young she was.

She tried to imagine this woman keeping a list of names and addresses in a simple lined notebook, a single page at the end of hundreds of other blank pages. She tried imagining her approaching Red and his cabal and handing them the list, knowing what would happen to the people the names belonged to. Maybe she didn't care. Maybe she cared, but did it regardless. It bothered her, knowing her husband's own name had led to him being erased from the world. If only he had been merely a title, journalist, father, something, anything that did not mark him out. He would had been alive and able to hold Zachariah during the fits the boy suffered, and whisper in her ear in the middle of the night, with the lights turned off and his stubble scratching the back of her neck. If only he had been never given a true name, he'd be unknowable. Untouchable. And still hers.

The girl worked on her garden with a spade for the better part of an hour, unearthing roots and cutting vegetables. An older couple came out of the house and smiled at her before leaving in a car. The Sheriff could see the woman's resemblance to both of them, in the arched eyebrows of the older man and the long limbs of the older woman. Once she finished digging the garden, she removed her gloves, took a few steps towards the forest, and stood looking in the Sheriff's direction. The girl lit a cigarette. The Sheriff clenched her jaw and ground her molars so hard it hurt. The girl couldn't have seen her.

She stood watching the girl smoking cigarette after cigarette, unmoving. *You're the Sheriff now*, she told herself. *Act like it. Do what must be done. What is right is not always legal, and what is legal is not always moral. Do it. No one will know.*

But she didn't move until the girl tossed the last cigarette butt away and went back inside through the flaking yellow door. The Sheriff waited for another hour, staring at the house, then melted back into the forest.

When she got back home after dark, she fed and bathed Zachariah, told him about her day without lying for his sake, and, when he got tired, she tucked him in. When he was born, she had considered not giving him a name at all. Crouched in the corner with the sleeping baby in her arms, she had felt his little life slip out of his body several times. Every time he went still, she had held her breath until his chest moved once more and only then had she dared exhaling. She had thought that, if he didn't have a name, no harm could come to him. And, if something were to happen, it would happen to no one. She wouldn't have to mourn for no one.

In the end, because she felt uncomfortable thinking of him as the Boy, she named him Zachariah, after the martyr who had refused to speak when Herod's soldiers had demanded to know where his son was hidden.

SHE RETURNED TO the woman's house at the edge of the forest the next day and the day after that. Always approaching through the dead forest. Every time, she felt a little bolder, but couldn't bring herself to approach the woman yet. She hid behind the same tree. Each day, the woman came out at more or less the same time to work her garden. On her smoking break, the woman always stared in her direction, as if she knew the Sheriff was there. After a few minutes, she'd go back inside. Then, the trek back to the cruiser would start. The gun always remained inside the glove compartment.

ONE NIGHT, THE Sheriff stayed late at the station. After the Deputies nodded their good nights and left, she searched for her husband's name on the computer. She came across several dead ends, obstructions, and restrictions. There was the date he was arrested, which she already knew, and the prison he was processed in, but not much else. Nothing useful. Nothing to goad her into doing what she needed to do.

In the end, a random query for medical equipment led her to a manifest for body bags, which led her to marching orders, which led her to a death list. His name was on it. The same blackness took over as all those years ago. She had accepted he no longer lived. At best, she had hoped for a quiet death, but she had served Red and his kind for years. She knew they did not afford such luxuries.

For the next hour, she went through the ugly nakedness

of his end. How they skinned him, starting from the toes. The chemicals they used to turn his mind into dust. The systematic sodomy. None of it necessary. He gave up all the information they asked of him without resistance. Contacts and sources. Names and addresses. It didn't matter, they tortured him anyway.

She didn't manage to sleep that night, nor for many nights after that.

Early in the morning of the third day after she had read the report, she put on a uniform that fitted her well after the adjustments. It took her longer than normal to button her tan shirt, her fingers constantly slipping. When she pinned the Unity to her chest, she drew blood again. She almost dropped one of the water glasses as she took them to the basement with the mashed vegetables. She didn't caress Zachariah's forehead while he slept, nor did she kiss him goodbye. Instead, she just watched him breathing. Then, she locked the basement, threw a thick blanket over the TV and, instead of heading to the station, she drove towards the woman's house. This time, she didn't pull over at the shoulder. She went on until she found the dirt road leading right to the door. She let the cruiser roll into the empty driveway and got out. This time, the gun didn't stay inside the glove compartment.

The Sheriff walked towards the garden where the woman was working. She whistled at her to get her attention and tapped at the golden Unity with the red stone set in its center. The woman acknowledged her and nodded towards the trees.

They walked, the woman leading the way. From up close, the woman looked different to her picture. Her hair hung lifeless behind her ears and brown patches stained her skin. They went deep into the woods, the woman shuffling her feet through the pine needles. Above them, heavy branches creaked by a sudden gust and pine cones dropped around them with echoless thuds.

When they reached a fallen birch, the Sheriff ordered her to sit. The woman complied without hesitation. She kept her back straight, placed her hands on her knees, and stared at the Sheriff. *Such nonchalance*, the Sheriff thought. *As if I'm not using every shred of my being not to reach out and feel that smooth throat of yours snap underneath my thumbs.* She took two steps and stood over the woman.

"Do you know why I'm here?" the Sheriff asked, and ground her teeth.

The woman didn't reply.

"Been lookkkin fer you for a long time. You took someone from me. Can you guess who, or do they all becccome a blur after a while?"

The woman crossed her arms and looked up at her with a cold, distant look.

"Twenty-eight deaths cause of you. Will you not defend yourself?"

She stared straight into the Sheriff's eyes. Her chin held an angle loaded with irreverence. It said, here sits a woman whose world does not have room for doubt, who stands by her actions.

"I see. By the end of the day, I will have words outta you. I prommmise. Mmm?"

The Sheriff took out a picture from her breast pocket with slow, deliberate moves and showed it to her.

"This," she whispered, "was mah husband. You knew his real name and took him from me."

The woman squinted at the picture, not showing any signs of recognition.

"Didn't do no harmmm to no one," her voice trembled.

"I'm sure you had your reasons fer doin what you did. I'm sure you've thought them through. But I don't care. I'll watch you die like a dog. You won't get buried behind the church. I'll make sure of that. I'll drag your corpse through the fields and watch the lobos tear it to pieces."

More silence. A dried branch snapped and dropped somewhere deep inside the woods, and the woman stared off into the distance.

"Look at me," the Sheriff growled and grabbed the woman's face. "Have you got nopin to say? Mmm? All this mmm-mess you've caused and you've nopin to say? If I don't get you apology, least I demand your respect."

The woman struggled and punched at the Sheriff's arms, then tried to reach for the gun in the holster, but the Sheriff held her at a distance. With a final shove, the Sheriff let go of her. The woman looked at the Sheriff now with hatred in her eyes.

"Finally, a reaction," the Sheriff said and tossed a pair of handcuffs at her feet.

The woman weighed the handcuffs, then put them on. There was something of the wounded martyr now in how she held onto her dignity.

"We're going into town, where you will confess what you did to the townsfolk."

The woman questioned her with her eyes.

"Oh, got your attention now, don't I? Mmm? 'Proccclaim the truth and do not be silent through fear. Nopin great is ever achieved without much endurin."

A snort and a shake of the head. That was all she got.

"I'm not askin. Not askin."

There was plenty of disrespect in the way the woman made herself comfortable on the fallen trunk and crossed her cuffed hands over her lap.

"When you die, and you will be dead once all this is over, I'll head back to your house and wait there for your Pa and Ma. Tie them up and take them wit me. There's an abandoned mill some ways outta town. There's a cement mmmixer in a shed at the back, with bout a dozen sackkks piled next to it. Ten pounds of lime down their throats oughtta keep them good and silent, mmm? I'll do it. See if I don't. I'll hate mahself fer it, but I'll do it. Or confess. Tell the townsfolk how you took their husbands and wives and children away. Let them hear it from your mmmouth and I swear I'll leave your parents alone."

The woman looked at her with eyes that did not understand.

"Party's done a fine job turnin us into animals. Townsfolk'll tear you to pieces, like good dogs. But this is not fer their sake. It's fer mine."

The woman looked at her house with its yellow door, and nodded.

They got into the cruiser and drove away, beyond the dying forest, up the hill where the sign with the town's name used to be, and to the town's outskirts. They left the cruiser within sight of Main Street and made their way on foot so that news of their arrival would precede them. The woman went first. A length of rope was tied around her neck, the Sheriff holding the other end.

Doors and windows opened and the townsfolk gawked at their new Sheriff and the woman.

For all her efforts, the Sheriff couldn't take pleasure from it. Curiosity lined the townsfolk's faces. Interest. More, there was something closer to excitement, and an animal's agitation too, and that bothered her. It bothered her that she was about to add one more stain to the town's soul. Still, she didn't stop. Not even at this point could she lie to herself that what she was doing was noble. It wasn't. But, she'd see it through.

A small procession followed them until they arrived below the only traffic lights in town. The Sheriff nodded at the woman.

"I…" the woman started and cleared her throat. "I have betrayed you."

The words echoed through the silent street. It bounced off the pharmacy's walls, off the bar.

"I've ratted. On people. And the Party took them. I have betrayed you."

Those closest to the woman covered their ears and ran away. Those who were farthest stared with incredulous looks. The woman repeated those words again and again, as the Sheriff had commanded her to.

One hundred and fifty eight people had disappeared during the last three years. Reported as agents of Division. Marked as potential troublemakers and instigators. In a town this small, any one of them was a neighbor's wife, a husband, daughter, son, family. One hundred and fifty eight stones were missing from the graveyard up on church hill. Better to never have a name, she thought. Better to be no one.

The Sheriff dropped the rope. *For my family*, she thought, and rushed into the crowd. Grabbed the townsfolk by the cuffs, shoved them in the woman's direction. With outrage in her eyes, she exaggerated her movements, just as Red had done. She worked the crowd, spat on the ground. Pointed at the woman, *Look at her, Look at her. She speaks.*

Someone walked up and punched the woman in the gut. She gasped for air and doubled over, falling to her knees. A man approached and landed a fist against her ear. A boot kicked her. Then, another, and another.

The townsfolk rushed forward. They pulled at the woman's hair, tore at her.

The Sheriff felt a clasp on her shoulder and the pharmacist nodded with approval. More hands reached out and touched her. The townsfolk brushed their fingers against her arms, paying their respects, before joining the fray.

Pieces of the Sheriff's soul wilted with every strike and every acknowledgment. She saw the woman's eyes roll back into her skull as she collapsed. Hands propped her up. One of them carried a knife. Without a sound, she came to and stared at the hilt protruding from her body. Tears streamed down her face.

She was no longer a woman, but a girl with piss and blood dripping down her legs. The Sheriff tried to force herself to hold eye contact. To watch the cosmic balance even out. She couldn't. Breaking her gaze away, the Sheriff tried to flee, but felt bodies behind her forming a wall, pressing together, pushing her closer. She heard the child that would never become a woman whimper for her Ma and Pa and, when they didn't appear to save her, for someone, anyone, to help her, and still the bodies behind the Sheriff forced her closer and she felt their hands on her shoulders shaking her in approval for all the good she had done, while her nostrils filled with the sour stench of piss and blood mixing with the dust.

26.

T HE SHERIFF LEANED back on the familiar pew. She raised her head and took in the empty church.

She studied the figures of saints, carved deep into alcoves on either side of the altar or perched high atop thin latticework columns. From where she was sitting in the front row, she could make out their pained eyes, raised up to the sky. She liked to think they were being courageous, holding dignity like a shield against their suffering. *And what else could they do*, the Sheriff thought as she studied their filed-down mouths. *What else could they do other than hold out?*

Or perhaps, they're averting their eyes from this earth and the mess we've made of it.

Chisel grooves scored and struck through the lower part of their faces. Below the destruction, there were hints of what once were lips. All gone now. On some of the saints, only the faces from the nose up remained.

The same faces looked down from the wall murals. Faces with eyes, a nose, and cheekbones shaped by famine and martyrdom. No lips, no mouth. Those had skin-colored paint slathered over them.

Even the inscriptions on the tombstones outside had

been stricken off. The Sheriff assumed the next step would be to gag the dead to ensure their silence in the afterlife.

Her eyes drifted from saint to saint and she named each of them in turn. And when she had noted them all, she looked straight ahead at the far wall behind the altar. The Son on the crucifix, gazing away from the heavens. His eyes fixed upon the suffering earth. It seemed to her that the resin that had been poured over His mouth smothered Him, suffocated Him. She wanted to say, *Look away. Look away. We don't deserve salvation. We don't deserve your pity. Not us.*

On the pulpit, the priest stood silent with his head bowed and his hands hanging by his sides. His lips quivered, reciting scripture from memory that they couldn't speak out loud, his Bibles long-since wrenched away from him. Instead of making the sign of the cross, he lifted his hands, then let them drop again.

Amen, thought the Sheriff every time.

She became aware of a distant burning smell. Steps echoed in the empty church, heavy and without urgency. She didn't pay attention. With some difficulty, she had instructed the boy with the shaved head to stay close to the farmhouse and keep an eye out for the girl. The boy, though, wouldn't seek her out at the church. Few people had use for it anymore. It provided quiet and that was the only thing remaining in abundance in this world.

A hand touched her shoulder. The pharmacist stood behind her. Farther back, framed by the entrance and backlit by a setting vermilion sun, a dozen silhouettes had gathered. There was a nervous energy about them. They curled and uncurled their fists, looked over their shoulders, and jostled in the narrow space. From where she sat, their features were indistinct, vague. In their midst, the boy with the shaved head. And in the boy's arms, a black mass that fell apart into ash as he shifted. It settled on the pews and on the saints, on the pulpit and the priest's face. A piece landed closed to her. Burned paper.

The pharmacist reached down and palmed it. Then, he crushed it, wiping his hand against his trousers. He stood aside for her and pointed to the exit with a polite gesture. The Sheriff took one last look at the crucifix and stood. From the corner of her eye, she noted the priest lifting his hands, then bowing his head.

A handful of vehicles sat idle outside. Pockmarked with rust streaks along their sides, banged up with shattered windows. The town spread out below the hill where the church sat and up the opposite hill where the sign with the town's name used to be. She eyed the black mass in the boy's hands. Pages blackened by fire, fused together. Letters still stood out. They formed words that broke apart and floated away as the pages crumbled.

Her damn book. After all this time?

The Sheriff looked at the boy and the boy returned the gaze. There was no guilt in those blank eyes, no understanding. She tried to keep a neutral face. *It's not your fault*, she thought and resisted the urge to slap him. *I should have known better.*

The pharmacist lifted a hand and pointed at the road leading away from the church, merging with Main Street and continuing to the South, and held two fingers up. The second house outside town. The teacher's house. He stepped aside for the Sheriff and gestured at her cruiser, asking her to take lead.

"No," she said, and waves of tension swept over the townsfolk around her. Her molars grinding, she leaned into the pharmacist's ear. "You hear? I'm the law here, I represent the Party and I forbid it. I'll arrest them mahself. You won't lay a finger on them."

The pharmacist frowned and winced, and moved his face away as if she had bellowed. Straightened his back, unfolding his gangly limbs. He appeared disappointed.

"I'll arrest them," the Sheriff repeated.

He shook his head, disappointment turning to anger. She could see it in his posture, in how he tried to make himself appear taller, menacing. The Sheriff felt her control slipping away. She opened her mouth but the pharmacist laid a finger on her lips before turning away. With a wave from his hand, the townsfolk climbed in their cars and trucks. The engines started.

"Gets back here," she said. "Show respeccct, mongrels. I'm the Sheriff, goddamit. I forbid it. They're mmmine. You won't touch them."

A condescending look from the pharmacist as he passed by her on his way to his own car. She could tell what he was thinking. Language was created to deceive, the Party had told them. And now, the one person in their midst who talked couldn't be trusted. He reached down and patted the boy with the shaved head on the shoulder. With a backwards glance, the boy got into the car with the burned manuscript in his arms and they followed the convoy.

"I run this town," she called after them as the cars rode away, sending plumes of red dust up in the air.

The Sheriff cursed herself and entered the cruiser, following the others.

When she reached the farmhouse, the townsfolk were already on foot, their cars lined up outside the driveway to prevent escape. They had gathered in a half-circle in the middle of the street. Some were smoking, others were drinking from bottles. Someone uncoiled a length of rope.

The pharmacist stepped out of his car together with the boy. He popped the trunk open and retrieved his hunting rifle. To the boy, he handed a knife, and holding the half-burned manuscript high above his head, he began walking towards the house. The others followed him.

That feeling of blackness again washed over her. That same feeling as when the transient had pulled a gun on her and she thought she was dead. Through a dirty window, the Sheriff could see the farmer staring out. *Run,* she waved at him. *They're coming for you. Run.*

Before the mob reached the house, the front door blasted open and the farmer charged outside, his member card held high in the air. He closed in fast and pushed the card into the pharmacist's face. With his free hand, he pointed at the townsfolk and then pointed away, demanding they leave.

The pharmacist took the member card. Examined it. And tore it in half.

The farmer punched the pharmacist on his throat's star-shaped scar, sending him on his back rasping for air without sound. The mob closed in on the farmer.

A man kicked the farmer behind the knee and sent him to the ground over the pharmacist. Ash exploded by the impact, the burned pages came undone. A flash of metal and the farmer lurched forward wincing, his shirt over the shoulder blooming red. Behind him the boy stood with the knife held aloft. The mob kicked and spat and punched. Blood flowed into his eyes from a split forehead. The townfolk's hatred for the farmer poured out. For his wealth and good fortune. For still having his farm when they didn't. For helping them when they needed it, because to them there was no greater insult than forced charity.

"No!" a yell came from behind. The teacher descended the stairs in an unsteady gait. She tossed her books to the ground. They tumbled and opened and the townsfolk averted their gaze from their pages. "No!" she repeated in a broken voice. "No!" and her broken voice was loud and desperate. "No". One word, small and unimportant as a crack in a building's foundations.

You stupid woman, what are you doing, the Sheriff thought.

"Mine," the teacher continued and pointed at the heap of ash. "Mine. All mine."

The mob let go of the farmer and closed in on the teacher.

"Let go," the Sheriff said as she tried to get to the teacher first, but a dozen arms grabbed her and slammed her to the ground, pinning her down. "How dare ya, mongrels," she said before she felt hands muffling her.

She tried to free herself, but no matter how much she pushed, she couldn't move. She grunted with impotent rage, her mind going blank. *I refuse,* was the only thought that went through her head. *I refuse.*

A shot rang out.

The hands froze in place. Then, one by one, they pulled back. The wall of human bodies opened. The Sheriff rose from the ground, her shirt torn apart, a finger hooped through her gun trigger in the holster. In front of her, a man stared at his bleeding belly with confusion.

With two steps, the Sheriff reached the teacher and grabbed her by the arm. With an almost imperceptible nod, she pointed the farmer towards the house and he obeyed, leaving behind him a trail of red.

Holding the teacher by the arm, she led her to the cruiser and sat her at the back. The mob approached her, uncertain.

As she sat in the driver's seat, she glanced back through the driver's mirror.

"This ain't mah intention."

The cruiser peeled away. In the fields, she saw the farmer escaping with the girl behind him, running away from the farmhouse to the sound of the mob smashing its windows. Past the tractor, past the scarecrow, towards the poisoned stream.

"Not mah intention," she repeated.

27.

O F THE RIDE, the teacher remembered the dust-choked fields giving way to desert. Mangled plants folded in half by the dust storm gave way to desolation in a manner so gradual that there never seemed to be a true boundary between the two. In years to come, the teacher was certain that the desert would continue its inexorable march until it reached the town of the twin hills. It'd be as if nothing had ever existed there.

But it was beautiful as it was harsh. Dead trees like charred hands fell away behind the car and she spread her fingers out from behind the window as if to touch them. It was this crossing beyond the boundary that made the teacher's heart rest. She felt lighter.

This is it, the monster in her guts said.

This is it, the teacher agreed.

The rhythm of wheels on the road together with the heat lulled her into a meditative state, where the world seemed to fray at the edge of her vision. As the Sheriff drove on, the teacher tried to memorize every blade of brittle weed, every splintered tree trunk. The savage sun. How, except for the road, there were no traces of humanity.

She breathed without effort and tried to imprint into her mind what it felt like not being afraid.

She turned in the seat and looked down the road behind them. She hoped her husband and the girl had escaped the mob. *They're on their own now*, she thought, and for a moment the ache made her heart skip a beat. She leaned back and sighed, half-closing her eyes. *Don't think of them*, she told herself. *They will be fine. Where you're going, they can't follow, not even as memories.*

An hour passed. The deeper they drove into the desert, the more the town seemed like an illusion, something that had happened in a previous life. Soon, the teacher felt like she had always been riding in the cruiser's back seat on this empty road. That everything that had happened to her since she'd arrived in the town all those years ago had been a fever dream.

No cars had followed them from the town. She felt the engine's pitch drop, shaking her out of her languor. As the cruiser came to a rolling stop, it pulled over at the side of the road, crushing chaparral beneath the wheels. The Sheriff killed the engine and opened the driver's door.

Here, the incessant chorus of field insects was a distant memory. There was no rustling of corn and grass, no meadowlark warbling or crow squawking. Only the low, constant hum of a hot western wind that stung the eyes. A wind that never dropped, never rose. It made the desert feel lonelier.

It took long minutes before the Sheriff spoke.

"I took an oath once, mmm" she said and examined her torn shirt, her wounds. "No arrestin fer talkin. Done a fine job keepin mah oath. Til now."

Had the Sheriff grown older during the ride? Her face

was tired, crisscrossed by lines that hadn't been there before. She wondered how much she herself had changed in the Sheriff's eyes. Whether she was the villain in the Sheriff's story. She licked her parched lips and examined her handcuffed wrists.

"You can't return to town, mmm," the Sheriff said.

The teacher sighed. There was so much power in 'No', and it had spilled from her lips without thinking, without hesitation, without the slightest hint of regret. If the alphabet was born in pain, language was born out of frustration and anger and fear and a savage refusal to accept the world. There's never been a more powerful word, never will be. Fitting that it had been her first word in years.

It mattered little what more she said and to whom.

"You can't return."

"I know," the teacher said.

The Sheriff raised her eyebrows. "So good to hear you," she said and her eyes watered. "I've mmmissed you so much."

The teacher nodded.

"Place I'm takin you. It's a rehab facility." The Sheriff turned away and wiped her eyes. A sob escaped. "Not a facility, no. Words lie. A prison. Fer talkers. Be safe there."

"But… I'm dying."

"Better to die in prison than in their hands."

The teacher looked away. The ancients believed a person's soul materialized in the sounds made during speaking. I speak, therefore I am. Was this what her soul was now, then? Death? First words out of her mouth in years and they were about her end. Her heart yearned for the comfort of silence. It was too late for that, though. Too late.

"The girl that talks," the Sheriff said. "How many can

there be out there?"

The teacher hesitated, swallowed hard. "Few," she said. "None." She started coughing. Already she had spoken too much and the dust made it worse. The Sheriff reached for a bottle of water in the glove compartment. After taking a sip, she stepped out of the car, opened the back door and handed it to the teacher.

"I'll find her and raise her," the Sheriff continued once back to her seat, while the teacher drank. "Her parents are dead. I'll raise her as mah own. Mah son, she'll fix him. Make him normmmal. Not like," she waved her hand over her face. "Not like *this*. You've never met him. Great boy. Deserves better than this world. This is no place fer a boy."

The Sheriff's son must have been eleven or twelve. Almost the same age as Corvo.

"No place. For. A girl. Either," the teacher said.

"No. It's not."

"North."

"What's that?"

"Refugee. Must get. North."

The Sheriff didn't respond. Instead, she nudged a stone with her foot, getting it tangled in a ball of gossamer. A spider tried crawling up the cuff of her leg in fits and starts. She brushed it aside with her hand and watched it as it scampered towards the empty desert beyond.

"I need her. He needs her. You hear? I won't be round forever."

The teacher tried to imagine what it must have been like for the Sheriff. Something had happened to them all when they adopted the silence. Minds went loose. Rotted out. Not everyone survived being confined to their own minds. Not everyone who survived did so intact. But the loneliness the

Sheriff had endured was a different kind of torture, the torture of the talking in the valley of the mute.

"What's her name?" the Sheriff asked finally.

The teacher remained silent.

"She must have a name." she said again and exhaustion laced her voice. "Won't you tell me? Tell me, and you can walk away and die in peace. I prommmise. Mmm?"

The teacher didn't reply. She had nothing more to say.

The Sheriff's eyes remained pinned on the road. The teacher could hear her molars grinding over the sound of the wind.

"This silence has driven you mad," the Sheriff said. "I've had a hand in this mess. What I did to this town. I admit it. Fer this, I apologize, but there's no need fer you to suffer. Last chance. Her name is important to me. Gimme it. Please."

The teacher breathed in and held her breath, counted to four, and exhaled.

There the two of them remained for a long time after, each drowning in her own thoughts. Ahead of them, the road disappeared below the horizon, splitting the desert in two.

Finally, the Sheriff started the engine and brought the cruiser back onto the road. Neither of them spoke again for the rest of the trip, everything that mattered having already been settled. Outside, the setting sun turned the desert red and the dead trees appeared to immolate.

28.

THEY RAN WITH their heads lowered, the farmer ahead of the girl.

Their feet sank into the soft ground and their lungs filled with grit, so that they both coughed through the handkerchiefs that covered their faces.

When they reached the poisoned stream, the farmer spat into it. The girl scrunched her face, though she said nothing. In fact, the girl had remained silent since they'd started running. Small mercy. The farmer's mind had chaos enough without the girl adding to it.

And it hurt. Goddamn, it all hurt. Where the little bastard had stabbed him in the shoulder that he couldn't lift now, where his ribs were broken from the kicks. The fields were red, the stream was red, the skies no longer burned blue because the blood in his eyes painted it all the same crimson.

Every few seconds he looked over his hurt shoulder at the girl and she kept her mouth shut unless it was to cough.

She too looked back. There was still hope in her, the farmer expected. Hope that she would catch a glimpse of his wife on the horizon, running after them. She limp-sprinted ahead of him and stood on tiptoes on the tallest dust mount she could find. He didn't have it in him to explain to her that it was pointless. Not because he felt sorry for the girl, but because he didn't want to deal with the next question. *What are you going to do now?*

The farmer motioned at her to keep moving. The girl peered one last time in the distance and hopped off the mount on her good leg.

They ran until the farmer got winded, then walked, but they never stopped. He wouldn't let them. The girl scowled and sulked the more tired she became, her limp becoming worse. He caught her looking at him askance several times. Even when the girl started lagging behind, he didn't slow down. She stumbled after him, while he got farther ahead.

"Enough," she finally yelled. "Stop! Stop it! Just stop! I can't do this anymore, my foot hurts. Where are we going? *Say something!*"

The farmer took a few more steps and lowered himself down to one knee, but didn't look back. He could feel blood running down his shirt, through his pants and into his boots. There was something off about the way he breathed, he realized. Air came out of his lungs in a whistle.

"Are you hurt?" she asked when she caught up with him. "You're not dying, are you? I can't find a safe place for both of us," she said. "I got blisters, can't we please stop for a bit?"

He didn't turn, but raised a hand and pointed at the neighbor's house. The door hung open just as he had left it. Off to the right, the horses milled about in their corral. As they caught the farmer and the girl's scent, they raised their necks and looked in their direction. The farmer stood and the girl followed.

"Are those horses?" she asked. "They're bigger than in pictures."

The farmer nodded.

The farmer moved to the corral. One of the chestnut horses came up to him and he ran his bloody fingers through its tangled mane.

The girl went to the broken door. Stood with her hands on her hips, waiting for him while he slumped against the corral's fence. When he didn't make any signs of moving, she entered alone. The other horses milled around the farmer. The scent of blood triggered something in them and they snorted with agitation. The farmer covered his head with his arms and took deep helpless breaths, feeling his wounds throbbing.

I've lost her, he thought. *Damn everything, I've lost her. All because of that girl.*

He worked the water pump with his good arm until his hand blistered, and, when the trough filled with water, he dunked his head in it.

You stubborn woman, he thought and bit his lips.

When the farmer went inside, he found the girl in the kitchen. She was perched on the counter eating from a can of apricots with a fork. He trudged through the house, up the stairs and into the master bedroom. The window creaked with dust, but he got it opened.

Out there, beyond the horizon, was his house. He imagined the townsfolk invading it and punched the window frame in anger, making his shoulder ache. In the opposite direction was the town, where he reckoned the Sheriff had taken his wife. He weighed his options.

What am I supposed to do?

At another time, he would have laughed at the act of tearing the neighbor's bed sheets apart. Unable to lift his arms, he laid the strips on the floor and rolled on them, getting enough of the fabric around his body. He tightened the improvised bandages. It was only going to get worse from there.

He found an old shotgun in a box underneath the bed. That, he leaned against the sill and dragged a chair close to the window. He sat there until the sun came down, scanning into the distance for anyone approaching the house.

Dusk covered the land sooner than he had expected. The farmer tried turning the light switches on. The house, however, remained bathed in a lazy half-darkness. Flies buzzing around the empty can of apricots and the stink of drying syrup greeted him in the kitchen. He hurled the can out of a window. Searching through the drawers yielded a handful of thick candles but no matches. He pulled the lighter out of his cigarette pack. Lit one of the candles and set it on the kitchen counter, then turned and whistled loudly. When nothing happened, he whistled again.

"I'm not a dog."

The girl sat in one of the old armchairs in the living room, the cracked leather creaking every time she shifted. In her hands, she still held the fork from earlier and she stabbed a pillow with it in slow, lazy moves. Her dust-covered shoes lay discarded on the floor.

"Hey," she protested as the farmer took the fork from her. He lit a candle and handed it to her.

"Can I have the lighter?" she asked.

The farmer stared at her without expression.

"What will I do if the candle goes out?"

I don't care, he thought and turned to leave.

"What will happen to her?" she asked with concern.

He stopped in his tracks.

"She never told me her name. Do mutes have names?"

The farmer tried to search for her name in his memory.

"Everyone's born with a name."

He tried to remember his own.

"What are we going to do?"

The farmer half-turned and words at the edge of his lips threatened to spill out. Instead, he walked to the front door and locked it. Then, he went upstairs and spent the night staring out through the window before he fell into a dreamless sleep.

HE AWOKE THE next morning to find the armchair empty. A blanket lay in a pile on the floor with the stabbed pillow. His body felt capable of only moving in slow motion. His back was on fire and his shoulder was numb. Every muscle ached and he felt that if he moved too fast he would vomit his insides.

A noise came from the basement, paper rustling. With the shotgun propped over one shoulder, he went down the stairs.

He found her sitting cross-legged on the ground with several open carton boxes next to her. In front of her lay a pile of magazines displaying pictures of naked men. He stood watching, as the girl went through them, not realizing she was being watched. He stamped his foot.

"The box was open I just looked inside," she said without pause between the words and dropped the magazine she held. When he didn't react, she ran past him and disappeared up the stairs and into one of the rooms, slamming the door behind her. The farmer remained unmoving. *The neighbor had a wife*, he thought. *Yes, the neighbor did have a wife, but she's gone. A long time ago. What the hell is this?*

He opened more of the boxes. Old family pictures, toys. A stack of books. Agricultural manuals, legal texts. A dozen versions of the Bible.

In the back of the basement, there was a small pantry.

The farmer went through it. He thought, *come on you old queer, don't you have anything in this house to eat?* But the words felt hollow. He gave it another go, picking choice insults, everything he remembered. The slurs left a bitter taste in his mouth, even if he didn't utter them out loud. He tried to justify it to himself by thinking the neighbor didn't matter anymore. That he had bigger things to worry about. Soon, he thought of nothing else other than food.

An old can of meat emerged behind empty cereal boxes. It was long past its due date, but it wasn't swollen like cans of spoiled food are. In the kitchen, he filled a pot with water. To his surprise the gas stove still worked and soon he had a boil going. He opened the can and, with a plop, he upturned it into the rolling water. The house filled with the smell and the door to the room where the girl had escaped cracked open.

HE STOOD OUTSIDE and looked over the dead fields. Looked far beyond the horizon where he knew his house lay. *I can't even see the scarecrow from here*, he thought.

"What will happen to her?" the girl asked from the front door. This time, there was something else in her tone besides concern. Accusation and anger that she didn't bother concealing.

"What are we going to do?"

Instead of an answer, he headed towards the garage.

"Hey, where are you going?" she shouted as she followed him. "What are you going to do?"

When he didn't answer, she cursed at him. She raged and kicked at stones and her voice broke. "What are you going to do?"

And the more she asked, the more he retreated, so that her curses and her pleading came through to him as if he were underwater.

He looked in the town's direction. His wife would be safe with the Sheriff. She wouldn't hurt her. Wouldn't let others hurt her. He found the neighbor's car and checked it for gas.

"What are you going to do, you coward?" the girl insisted in a voice becoming shrill in its desperation.

He ignored her and went back inside. He looked at the neighbor's pictures on the wall. As a boy, as a young man, then as a husband next to that smiling woman. *Did she know what she was marrying?* he asked himself, but let the question fade.

The girl had stopped her questions and was following him from a distance, curious and hopeful by the activity.

First was the living room. He opened the cupboards and the drawers, emptying them on the floor. When he didn't find what he was looking for, he moved to the bedroom. He upended a few shoe boxes on the bed and sorted through coins and postcards without words on them, postcards with images of smiling soldiers and farmers, images of fists raised together and of determined masses framed by grand Unities painted on giant walls.

In the end, he found the car keys. He pocketed them and headed downstairs to the basement with the girl still following.

Coiled in a corner of the basement was a length of rope, which he shouldered and brought back upstairs. He let it drop in the middle of the living room and looked around him.

"What are you going to do with this?" she asked.

The farmer marched to the girl and grabbed her by the arm.

29.

THE FARMER PLACED the girl's picture on the Sheriff's desk next to that of his wife. He pointed at each of them, and stepped away from the desk, waiting for the Sheriff to consider the offer.

"Where is she?" the Sheriff asked and tapped the girl's picture.

On the palm-sized Polaroid, the girl was tied on a wooden chair in the neighbor's basement, surrounded by carton boxes and junk. By the looks of her, the Sheriff figured she must have put up a fight. Hair stuck out at odd angles, traces of tears marked her cheeks. Even in defeat, defiance lined her face. She clung to her fury well.

Angry girl, the Sheriff thought. *A strong girl. One that will survive no matter what.* She tapped again, pointing a demanding finger at the picture.

The farmer shook his head and pointed at his wife's picture instead, twice for emphasis. It was an older one, from before the Hush. Without the wrinkles and the streaks of gray hair, but the serene eyes remained the same.

"Her. Back," the farmer said. His fake confidence wasn't fooling the Sheriff.

"You talkkk, mmm," the Sheriff said and ground her molars.

Neither of the two Deputies were at the station, both had gone off on her say so. They were sitting in a cruiser outside the pharmacy, not far from there, waiting for the pharmacist to do something wrong.

Her body still hurt. Black and blue covered her legs, her arms. As long as the town believed she was holding its leash, she could protect herself, she could protect Zachariah. She could protect the girl. But the town had turned around and tried to take a bite out of her. She could still feel hands holding her down, gagging her. The town's leash was slipping out of her hands. The pharmacist had to go.

"Where you hid her, mmm? Your house is gone. Where you hid her?"

She watched him flinch and recoil.

"You don't know? Your house," she fluttered her fingers in the air. "Gone. Torched. Where you hidin now, mmm?"

Watching him trying to maintain his composure bothered her. It bothered her that she couldn't take pleasure from his suffering. Couldn't, wouldn't gloat. By the time she had returned, the house's embers were already dying down.

Instead of making her way to town, she had remained there for a few hours, watching beams collapse and feeling the heat, so different to that of the sun. It hadn't been her fault. Yet, she felt she needed to pay her respects to lives ruined. In a way, that house had been a part of her, too.

She let him ride the waves of shock and doubt. Watched his face contort in his effort to hide what he was going through. He tapped at the teacher's picture again.

"Ex-change," the farmer said, the X sticking in his throat.

The Sheriff picked up the girl's picture and studied it.

What kind of a monster tortures a girl like that, she thought. Then, memories of another girl from another time whose death was on her hands bubbled up and she had to push them back down. Couldn't afford to be distracted now.

"I'll meet you at your house, what's left of it. In three days."

"Tonight," the farmer slammed his fist on the desk, making his wife's picture jump and fall by the side of the desk.

"Tonight, shit. Need time fer that, mmm. Three days. Three days, goddammit, or you can rot in a cell while the poor girl starves to death."

The farmer lowered his eyes and his lips mouthed a reply, but nothing came out.

In the end, he leaned over the side of the desk and picked up his wife's photo. He held it up for a second, catching the light that came in through a high window, and then pocketed it.

"Three days. If you hurt her—"

"Sssh. Big man. Big speech. Go hide," the Sheriff waved him off. "Three days."

THE FARMER SLINKED out through the Sheriff station's back door, just as he had gotten inside.

He ducked through the back streets, keeping his head low. Fire spread from his wounds. Instead of healing, the cut on his shoulder spread further open, splitting him into pieces.

He had once known the names of the people who had tried to tear him apart, although he no longer remembered them. He had drunk with some of them. He had given them work when the bank came for their fields, just as his father had done before him. In the past, they would approach him in the street with a smile and a kind word or well-wishes for his mother. After she had passed, they told him how sorry they were for his loss in hushed tones.

Even if he got his wife back, what future was there for them in this town? Their home was gone. The townsfolk wanted them dead. And, one way or another, she wouldn't be with him for much longer.

The last of the town houses fell behind. He found the car where he'd left it, hidden in an abandoned wood yard behind the foreman's cabin. Instead of joining the road, he turned to the dirt trails. There was no way of knowing if the townsfolk were still after him. No way to know if the roads were blocked. He'd return to the neighbor's house the same way he arrived, through the back-country.

As he drove, he looked North. North, where people could speak. Where he would be allowed to speak to her and where she wouldn't avoid him. He had so much he needed to tell her. About how he had never felt the same after their baby's death. That the silence was an abyss between them, despite him being comfortable in it. His burning shame about trying to force on her the only language he thought he had left. The shame.

So much to say. Silence had eaten away at his ability to bare his soul. And there was so little time left.

Once he arrived at the neighbor's house, he went straight to the basement where he'd left the girl still tied to the chair. She refused to look at him and he found he could live with her hatred if it meant he would get his wife back. Once he made sure her bindings were still tight, he went back upstairs.

From a cupboard, he retrieved a dusty glass which he filled with water. For food, he took a couple of apples out of his pocket that he had stolen from the Sheriff's office. These, he sliced in wedges and placed them on a plate.

There was no posturing from the girl. She ate the offered apples and drank with greed from the glass until she coughed.

The farmer hesitated, then asked. "Bathroom?"

The girl nodded. He untied her and, with a hand on her cuff, he guided her up the stairs to the first floor. He opened the bathroom door and let her through, then closed it and leaned against it.

For a long moment, no sound reached his ears other than the horses from outside. Then, as if the girl had overcome her modesty, the clink of the toilet seat came through.

He wasn't certain how, but he became aware of the exact moment the Sheriff entered the house. He didn't move right away. Instead, he let the feeling of defeat sink in. It paralyzed him with a despair he had known only once before, when the obstetrician had presented him with his dead son.

He picked up the shotgun from the window sill and walked down the creaking stairs. The Sheriff stood in the living room taking in the surroundings, arms behind her back.

"I remmmember him," she said and pointed at the neighbor's pictures.

From behind him, the farmer could hear the Deputies closing in. He set the shotgun against the wall and let his arms drop by his side.

"He got arrested months ago. He had a…" she paused, looking for the right word. "Radio console. Short range. Very illegal, mmm. Party got him before the townsfolk did, luckkky fer him, mmm. Man's suffered nough. Whole fambly gone. Wife got taken away years ago. Someone reckkkoned she was too dangerous for Unity."

There was no irony in her words. No mockery. The Sheriff approached and searched him and, when he resisted, she kneed him in the groin. Her hands went through his pockets and found the teacher's picture.

"The neighbor and you don't see eye to eye. I remember, mmm. Your wife told me the stories. But it's the closest house to yours and you made lots of dust though the backroads. Easy to follow. Makes it easy that you take mmme fer an idjit. Where's the girl?"

The farmer nodded downstairs. The Sheriff rushed down the staircase into the basement, while the Deputies remained with him.

As the basement door slammed open and shut, the farmer turned around and faced them. A hope that, by drawing their attention, the girl might slip away. Also, a need to know who they were. Everyone in this town had become his enemy and he needed to understand how it had gotten to that.

The man and the woman stared back with blank eyes. They were both young, much younger than him. They were probably the girl's age when speech was outlawed. It seemed the madness that inflicted those who went silent manifested on their faces too. For a moment, he was tempted to say something to them, just to see their reaction.

Then, a terrible thought. He ran his fingers through his greasy tangled hair, felt the unruly stubble over his lips. The madness inside *him*. The words festering inside like a cancer. He stared at the Deputies staring at his own misshapen face and felt heavy, as heavy as Sisyphus must have felt when he first shoved against the stone. Such arrogance from his part to think the silence hadn't ruined him like everyone else. That he had a right to immunity.

The Sheriff came upstairs, her steps slower and heavier than before. He hoped Corvo had done the smart thing and left him behind. He would have.

"Where she gone?" the Sheriff asked with tired irritation.

The farmer shook his head.

The Sheriff drew her gun and pointed at the floor. Excitement in her voice that she struggled to hide.

"Where is she?"

The farmer didn't answer. He couldn't. He had frozen in place, unable to think anything other than a single phrase over and over.

There won't be no next year.

The Sheriff squeezed the trigger. The bullet punched through the floor, exploded splinters flying upwards. The farmer shielded his eyes. From outside, he could hear the horses jostling and neighing.

When the noise died down, she brought her arm level and put a bullet into each of the walls. Finding his senses again, the farmer lunged at the Sheriff, but a knock on his back sent him to his knees. Under his shirt, he could feel blood gushing down from his wounds again.

"And you still take mmme fer an idjit." she said with disdain. "These bullets don't go through shit, mmm."

The Sheriff turned the gun to a different point and pulled the trigger again.

When nothing happened, she raised her gun and fired three shots into the ceiling, sending plaster crashing down.

A muffled scream reached them from above.

The Sheriff holstered and followed the scream to the first floor. The farmer closed his eyes. *Stupid girl,* he cursed her. *Stupid, stupid girl.*

When she returned, she held the squirming girl's wrists in one hand.

"The girl that talks," the Sheriff said with admiration. "No reason to cry, darlin."

The Sheriff gave the girl to the female Deputy and sent them away "Put her in the cruiser. I'll handle her, make sure a doccctor cuts that voice of hers outta her throat." To the male Deputy, she said "Rope."

When the male Deputy returned he had a rope coiled over his shoulder. He handed it to the Sheriff and left.

"I thought bout kkkillin mahself," the Sheriff said as she let the rope drop to the ground and started uncoiling it. "Many times. Not mah proudest mmmoments.

"We've had 'nough exhortations to be silent. 'Cry out wit a thousand tongues—I see the world is rotten cause of silence.' That's Saint Catherine. Beautiful, mmm. It helps me survive. When mah man was taken, I was ready to quit. Do away wit mmmahself and go and meet him. But that wouldn't be brave. No, sir. That woulda been damn cowardice, in fact."

As she talked, her hands worked the rope, freeing it of twists. When she got to its end, she tied a noose.

"Felt lousy jes thinkkkin bout it. So, I didn't. I figured, I still have mah voice." She leaned into his ear and he could hear her molars grinding. "That's somepin to live fer."

She took the noose end and threw it over the rafters, letting it dangle, and pushed it at him.

"But, from where I sit," she said over her shoulder as she left, "I figures ya have nopin ta live fer anymore."

30.

T HE FARMER OBSERVED the silver-haired woman sitting
next to him in the back seat of the government car.
Passing streetlights bathed her face in waves. Now it was
dark, now it was light, until they were so far out in the
country that the only source of illumination was the half-
moon above. Dead trees rose on either side. And then, they
reached the desert.

He caught her smiling at him often. An attempt to make
him feel more comfortable, he knew. Instead of
reciprocating, he lowered his eyes and concentrated on the
sound of the air-conditioning.

"You're too harsh on yourself, you know," she broke the
silence and adjusted her ruby Unity pin. "I am well aware
you're not allowed to talk, not like that stopped you when
you came to me for help, but would it kill you to at least
smile?" she asked. He looked up and averted his gaze again
once he caught her mirthful eyes.

An opaque pane separated them from the driver and he
had no doubt it was soundproof, but he kept his mouth shut
regardless, despite the silver-haired woman's coaxing.

"This place you want to visit. There is a proper name for

places like them, but I find it vulgar," she said and twisted her mouth. "These facilities, gulags, whatever you want to call them, are not run by the government. Not in the strict sense of the word, you understand. I know you're not allowed to speak, but I would appreciate it if you would promise to keep what I'm about to say to yourself, regardless. Yes?"

The farmer nodded and sank his head again.

"I knew I could count on you," the silver-haired woman smiled. "You've always been easy to trust."

Her chirpy voice and constant chattering, the two things that had attracted him to her when no one else could talk, were now grating on him. It made him wish she would stop and it surprised him. *Me, wanting quiet*, he thought. *Me. What a damn world. After all these years, it still doesn't make a lick of sense. Soon, I'll be wishing for corn to wither and for rats in my fields.*

"See, these places have existed for quite some time, I believe they were re-purposed from old prison complexes. The people at the top are not stupid. 'You must know thyself to be successful', or so the saying goes, don't you think it rings true? Obviously, they do nothing at random, everything is carefully calculated. That's why they've remained at the top as long as they have."

They. As if she wasn't part of Them. As if he wasn't a member himself. Talking about Them as if they were a faceless entity. He wrung his hands and shifted in his seat.

"The Hush Laws, the so-called *war* against the North..." she said and rolled her eyes. "All those necessary measures would cause a backlash and, of course, the Party was expecting a certain degree of animosity and conflict. But the amount of support they ended up receiving! My heavens, it seems odd enough talking about it now, but they didn't always enjoy such universal acceptance. I mean, things were quite rough in those early days, believe it or not! What the regime was not prepared for, though, were the sheer numbers of volunteers that appeared one day out of the blue, reporting for duty."

She pulled back her lips in a toothy grin.

For as long as he had known her, she'd had the same silver hair in a sharp professional bob and the same laissez-fair attitude towards the world. She was among the fortunate few and questioning her privilege was to invite disaster. So, she didn't. The farmer had been surprised when she agreed to help him. Why not, she had said. For your wife's sake.

"Therein lies the problem. The guards are useful to the Party, because they're fanatics. It can be quite a challenge, bribing a fanatic. Which is why I hope you appreciate what I'm doing here for you, and the amount of risk I am taking. If my dim-witted assistant knew about this, he'd have a field day parading me up and down the Party headquarters, before cutting off my tongue for high treason," she said and erupted into a shrill laugh.

The farmer looked outside at the sun-burned trees. Were there cabals within the Party? This world of his, this world in which he suffered and bled must have been so dull and monotonous to Them. Them, who were like kings. The only way to alleviate Their boredom would be to turn on each other. To fight wars like the ancient gods used to when They got tired of their perfect world in the skies.

"Thankfully, you don't have to worry about any of this. And, truth be told, I enjoy helping you. It's a nice feeling, helping someone who needs it. Even if it's a little dangerous." She paused and, in the half-darkness of the car, he thought he saw a shadow pass over her eyes, and the grin died.

During those past few years, he had avoided letting his thoughts stray into matters of right and wrong, of what was fair and of who deserved what. He had learned fast. There was no point in trying to find an internal logic in who was allowed to talk and who wasn't. Were there other Party members like him who, although aware of the injustice, didn't protest because they knew they were on the winning side? He was certain of it. In the end, the people had the rulers they deserved.

They had never discussed the silver-haired woman's background or how she had earned that red ruby on her Unity. She never offered to tell him that story.

Now, she reached into her bag and pulled out a manila envelope that she set on her lap. The farmer guessed it couldn't contain more than a single sheet of paper. Or maybe a plastic card.

"I know your wife is not... well. She doesn't have much time. I could get her out. Secure her release. Somehow. Not myself, as I said, my clout only extends so far, though I know some people, and they know some people, you know how it goes. But... It might not be fast enough. If you had reached out to me sooner instead of showing up at my office out of the blue like that, I could have done something. Please, believe me," she said and took his hands, but he retreated deeper into his corner. If this insulted or bothered her, she didn't make a show of it.

"We're going to be there soon," she said. "Walk to the gate. A guard will meet you there, though he won't look like one. Don't let it trouble you. Let me handle him. You go and see your wife. I've bought you ten minutes. Make them count, won't you, dear?"

The farmer didn't know how the silver-haired woman

had arranged this in such a short time. He didn't want to ask. Didn't feel he had the head space to understand. Only his wife mattered now.

There was deceleration and the feel of the car wheels crunching gravel. He looked out just in time to observe the prison's eastern guard tower coming into view.

"Well. Here we are," the silver-haired woman announced. "I would like to wish you good luck but, somehow, that seems inappropriate. As I said, you have ten minutes. Then we'll be heading back. Alright?"

She squeezed his knee and the farmer nodded.

He stepped outside and the sudden dryness of the desert air made it hard to breathe. Ahead of him, about fifty yards from where the car had stopped, he saw a white rectangle cut into the cement wall. A door. Framed in it, was the guard who moved towards him.

The guard didn't wear a uniform. Just a shirt and jeans. The crude cordectomy had left a hole in his throat. He pointed behind him and stepped aside for the farmer.

Once through, the door closed behind him. It took a few seconds for his vision to adjust. The more he stared, the more the blur resolved. Concrete walls, halogen lights, and hidden niches formed by overlapping shadows.

From one of those niches, the teacher's ghost stepped out.

Part of his mind refused to recognize her. Doing so would have meant admitting that the woman he once knew was capable of being torn down. The person standing in front of him was a puppet made of paper skin stretched tight over a skeleton. Not a person. Sheared hair. Sunken eyes.

Her moves were small. Imperceptible. When she followed him with her eyes, she did so with lethargy and a delay that unnerved him. He didn't rush to her. Nor did he call out to her, as he imagined he would.

Once the initial shock dissipated, he took timid steps towards the ghost. He embraced her. The familiar body next to which he had slept every night for years was diminished. Eroded. He held her close and felt her weakness, how her body struggled to hold itself together, as if she'd collapse into nothingness if he dared to look away.

He brought his lips close to her ear so that no one would hear them.

"Your hair," he whispered. "Gone."

She brought a hand up to his cheeks.

"You talk… What are you doing here?" she said with a sound of crunched leaves. He hugged her, savoring her minor key words.

"Silly woman. Why? Why take the blame?"

"My decision," she said and, for the first time, a spark lit behind her eyes. "Done with writing. Nothing left to say."

"I have much. To tell you."

"Oh?" She opened her parched mouth and let out a long slow sigh. "But. I'm dying. We're out of time."

"I'mma take you away."

The teacher's ghost shuddered and exhaled again, resting her head against his shoulder.

"How'd you get here?"

"I'll get you out. Then, we'll leave. Go someplace else. Wherever. The ocean, maybe. Or the North. Anywhere. And then, we'll talk."

"Mmm."

"We'll talk there."

The teacher nodded against his shoulder.

"The girl?" she asked.

"Safe."

"Where?"

"Home."

She looked up at him and raised her eyebrows.

"Safe," the farmer said again. "Safe."

The teacher didn't react for a long time. On his cheek, the farmer could feel her breath, coming out between her teeth. Long, drawn-out exhalations between long, drawn-out pauses.

"Listen…" she said and he could feel her bracing with effort. "You asked, who will read my book. The book's burned. Gone. Wrote something else. Figured it out. Figured it out."

The farmer felt the teacher swallow and her legs buckled. He held onto her weightless form.

"In the basement. Give it to the girl. Take her North. Take her away." She closed her eyes and gathered her strength. "Don't let her become a mute."

Flushed with shame, he didn't reply.

She sighed and pulled back enough to face him.

"Everything I am. Is in those pages."

The farmer avoided looking at her in the eyes.

"Don't let me fade away."

He nodded and she felt the slightest pressure from her hands in response.

"Strange life we've had. The last thing we said? To each other? Before our hush? What was it?"

"Can't remember."

"You're awful at lying."

"Not lying."

"What was it about? Our last fight? Our last words?"

"Don't know."

"There's. Beauty in dissonance. But. We saw each other. As enemies."

"Stop."

"Tore each other to pieces."

"Stop."

"Was the silence worth it?"

The farmer didn't respond.

"We could have chosen to be happy," she said. "Together or apart. Peace be damned. But we chose silence instead."

The ghost pushed herself away from him with a whimper, almost tripping over her own skeletal legs. He reached out to steady her. Once she regained her balance, she limped away towards the far end of the white room. With slumped shoulders, she put distance between them and, little by little, she disappeared into the niches the shadows formed. In the end, he could only see her silhouette. A bang came from the door.

"Go," she said and looked down. "I got nothing more to say."

As she turned her shoulder, she disappeared from his view. Bled into the shadows.

He walked out of the prison into the night air and, keeping his head down, continued walking. Past the guard who now held the manila envelope in his hands. Past the silver-haired woman, ignoring her questions. He continued down the gravel road that led away from the prison, ignoring the car that accompanied him, her requests through the window, then her pleading to join her in the car because the town was far and it was the middle of the night in the middle of a desert and who knows what animals were out there. He continued walking even when, with a sigh and a moan, she ordered the driver to take her away.

He walked until the prison disappeared behind him and the sun went up and then down again, even when his eyes went blind, even when the scorpions stung his feet, even when the poison creosote scratched his arms.

He walked and didn't stop, because he knew that, if he did, he would be rooted in place and crumble away into nothing.

31.

Many years ago.

T HEY DROVE FOR hours in a straight line that took them away from the town and into the woods. Farmland became interspersed with groves that grew in the long stretches between houses. Then, the farmhouses were left behind, wheat and barley receded into the distance, and the trees grew so tall their branches intertwined over the road, blocking the sun.

Once they entered the national park, the rest of the world hid behind a green curtain. They rolled the windows down and took it slow, their minds wandering into a road trance that went on for miles.

At a sharp turn behind a thicket of trees, the farmer moved the car onto a dirt road. When they reached its end after fifteen minutes, he parked next to a grand cedar and killed the engine. They picked up the backpacks and the yellow tent from the trunk, and made their way deeper into the forest. Soon, their car disappeared behind them.

He and the teacher hiked in single file for three hours down a trail buried by burnished gold leaves and crisscrossed by ancient roots. The smell of pine needles and forest floor saturated the air.

During their hike, they didn't talk much. Often, the farmer, who led the way, pointed at a hidden rock that was easy to stumble over, or a colony of bright yellow Jack o' Lantern mushrooms on a tree trunk. When a rain crow or a shrike called out from the canopy, he nodded in their direction and glanced back at her. She would then smile at him. Nothing more was needed, because those plain gestures said everything that was needed.

Clouds blanketed the sky. Despite the birds and the swaying of branches in the breeze, the forest felt quiet in the manner of large cathedrals, where silence itself had a presence, echoing back from the high ceilings and the painted walls.

They felt the lake before they saw it. The humidity on their skin and the smell of water. The way the air became sharper. And then, the lake itself appeared before them in slices between the firs until they got out of the woods and into a small clearing that formed a natural beach. Under their feet was a mosaic of smooth pebbles in blues and greens.

He stood aside and let her take in the sight. A thick wall of trees lined the lake, while on the horizon the mountains that rode along the Northern border rose into permanent white caps. Light rain formed patterns on the water.

As she let her backpack slide down, she sighed her marvel and it made him smile.

They set up the tent together. Then, while he built a fire, she stripped off her clothes and jumped into the lake. The water was warm, so different to the rude shock of the ocean that she was used to. She swam out, away from their beach, to the lake's center. There, she closed her eyes and let the water cover her ears, muting all sounds. The water carried her body as it carried her thoughts. The shore ebbed away, the clouds covered the world.

Later that night, lying naked inside the tent, he ran his fingernails along the fuzz of her unscarred belly while she read her leather-bound copy of Yeats' poems. With a voice hoarse by not having spoken in a while, she recited.

"Where dips the rocky highland

Of Sleuth Wood in the lake,

There lies a leafy island

Where flapping herons wake

The drowsy water rats;

There we've hid our faery vats,

Full of berrys

And of reddest stolen cherries.

Come away, O human child.

To the waters and the wild

With a faery, hand in hand,

For the world's more full of weeping than you can
    understand."

She let the words hang in the air. She could still taste them when they turned off the lantern and fell asleep.

The next morning, she woke up to find him outside preparing breakfast. The skies had taken on a charcoal color that made her feel they were isolated inside their own little terrarium. Between that word's imposing T and the m that brought it to an end, she could fit this whole temporary world of theirs. This lake, this beach, this isolation.

She approached him and he smiled as he handed her a tin mug, steaming with hot coffee.

He spent the rest of the morning fishing, while she stayed back at the beach and read. From time to time, the teacher looked up to check on him as he stood in the water up to his waist, unmoving. Feeling at ease with himself and the world.

While his attention was on the water, she fingered the offer letter for a teaching position that was folded inside her book, between the pages with Yeats' words.

A small but well-funded college back on the coast. She was being offered the luxury to teach what she cared about to people who would lap up her words. To not feel that she was being mocked by a class of teenagers every time she turned to the blackboard. To not struggle against non-existent budgets. Or guidelines about which authors she was or wasn't allowed to teach. *No, not a luxury*, she corrected herself. Never that. But a need. An honest need. And one she didn't know if she wanted to sacrifice for his sake.

It had taken her almost a year of sending inquiries, of reaching out to her old professors, of doubt. The town of the twin hills would become a parenthesis. An embarrassing story she would tell at parties. The coast was wide and endless and full of opportunity.

But what about him?

The farmer waved at her from the lake, his sleeves rolled over his forearms. She waved back and smiled, but her smile faded as he turned around. One thing she was certain of was that he was an intelligent man. He knew something was wrong. Since she had received the offer, a distance had begun to grow between them. When they talked, she was content to just nod. Hearing, but not listening. Their small daily rituals lost their charm for her, the morning and night kisses that bookended their day. She recognized this behavior in herself. The prelude to cutting loose. No doubt he was picking up on it.

That was around the time he had started bringing up this lake his father had taken him to as a kid. It was a peaceful place, he had insisted, where they could spend a couple of days alone. And, in between the lines, he was worried. About what her behavior meant for him. For them.

Instead of feeling grateful, she felt cornered.

She had insisted that they wouldn't wander into sensitive topics. Politics. Her family. The boyfriend back at the coast who she once thought she would spend her life with and who still checked up on her now and then. And the farmer respected those boundaries, though this respect came with loud and constant complaints. If we can't talk about anything, he had argued, there's something wrong with us. She disagreed. To her, this silence was a survival mechanism that they both needed in order to coexist, even if he didn't see it that way.

In silence, there is eloquence, Rumi had written centuries ago. And his silence now spoke volumes.

It made her anxious to think of this conversation he was goading her into. And, following that, the dissension. The passive aggressive snipes that would follow. And, in the end, the random acts of kindness, the caring words meant to bridge the distance again. They had gone through the cycle dozens of times. This one wouldn't be any different.

She tucked the letter into the book and slipped into her shoes. Taking one last look at him standing in the water, she stepped into the tree line.

She walked for a while without direction. Her mind went down a thousand different futures. One where she packed her bags the moment they returned and left, not giving him a chance to argue. Another where she stayed in the town, forever defined by her association with a man. Another future where she kept wandering the forests and the mountains, never meeting another living soul.

Would it be so bad? Just vanishing?

Just off the hiking path, the trees opened up to form a narrow corridor deeper into the forest. She left the path and followed the corridor, stepping over a felled trunk and running her fingertips over the furry lichen on its branches. Farther down the corridor, she found a patch of berries and jumped over it.

When she asked herself why she accepted this constant cycle of squaring off and reconciliation, she couldn't answer, because the pain of compromising had somehow seemed petty compared to not having him in her life anymore.

This was not something she was prepared to admit to herself. There wasn't any one thing she could point to and claim as the sole reason for her affection, but rather that life seemed right with him in it. And because of that, all those futures that didn't include him felt false. She scratched at the bark of a tree that grew out into two trunks and cursed under her breath.

Asking him to come with her wouldn't work. For four generations, his family had lived and died in these parts. His land was his livelihood. And, even though he didn't talk about it much, she knew his mother was sick. Cancer. No point in even starting that discussion.

And assuming they did talk and he managed to convince her to stay? Or she convinced him to come with her, and it all ended up exploding in their faces? The resentment would break them. Her guts tightened thinking about it, the act of opening her mouth and starting that discussion, and her throat closed. She sighed, a long drawn out exhalation, until the feeling went away.

Soon, she had walked so far she couldn't see the path anymore. *It doesn't matter*, she told herself. *Keep going. There are more paths up ahead. So many more. One foot, then the next, until going forward is easier than going back.* She'd leap and turn into a many-hoofed animal that would melt into the undergrowth, never to be captured again, never to be seen again.

Try to find me, she thought. *I'll be gone. Vanished.*

But, in the end, she circled back and made her way to the beach. From inside the tree line, she could make out their camp. No sight of him. Walking as quiet as she could on the pebbles, she entered the tent, read the offer letter in her book again, and then stashed it in her backpack.

Splashing came from outside. The farmer made his way to the shore with two trout slung over his shoulder and a huge grin on his face. He took off his rubber overalls and went to work on the fish, scaling and gutting them on a flat rock.

Was this the existence she longed for? Sitting in a tent while a man caught fish for her? She could see herself becoming trapped between the town's twin hills. Never becoming anything more than the local school's literature teacher.

There is freedom in rootlessness, she thought. *But, here, everything grows roots. Just stay long enough…* It was the space between destinations where she felt alive. Between airports and bus terminals. Leaving the coast and that old boyfriend was meant to set her free. Not lead her to a different sort of ennui.

She looked out of the tent to the lake and thought, *I'll never travel to new places again on the local school teacher's salary.* And then she replied to herself, *but wouldn't all this be worth it? Wouldn't he?* The one person she couldn't imagine herself without?

Later that day, he motioned for her to follow him. She put down her book, careful not to let the letter fall out, and lifted an eyebrow. He just smiled and nodded towards the woods.

Close to their beach, the ground angled upwards in a slope that hugged the lake. They climbed it and, at some point, the farmer pulled the teacher towards a thicket. Once they got through the other side, the lake opened up below them. Between them and the mountains, forest covered the rolling land. Thin rock columns pierced through the forest, pillars hundreds of feet tall. Above them, falcons rode thermals.

They sat on a rock and she grabbed his hand. Part of it was vertigo, and part of it was awe.

Do you ever get tired of this, she wanted to ask, even though she knew that he wouldn't answer, that he would only bury his face into her neck and inhale her.

NIGHT FELL. FIREFLIES skimmed across the water and lit the edge of the lake, pulsing away and matching the flames that danced from the bonfire in front of their tent.

They both stared into the burning logs and she wondered how many of her thoughts he could pick up as she leaned against his shoulder. He didn't say anything and neither did she.

If only he could read her mind. Understand without her having to open her mouth. She didn't want to say anything, because, once the words came out, he'd have words of his own and she'd have to deal with them.

Their terrarium seemed too perfect for thoughts such as these. So, she let them drift away. She closed her mind to them and instead breathed in the burning pine, wishing they could remain frozen in their own world, comfortable in each other's silence for a while longer, for as long as they could. Silence didn't need to explain. Silence didn't have expectations. Silence just had to be.

32.

THE FARMER HAD no memory of getting back to the neighbor's house. Sores and sunburns covered his body, though, and he recalled stumbling blind through the desert. His head felt close to splitting open. He tried to touch his forehead and recoiled in shock at the pain caused by the cut there.

Still half-blind, he dragged himself to the horse corral and dunked his head into the water trough. He drank with greed. Then, his stomach clenched up and he vomited all the water back out, making his head explode with pain. Dripping, he walked back into the house and collapsed onto the couch. There, he closed his eyes and slept without dreams.

When he woke up again, the sun was sinking beneath the horizon and he couldn't tell if it was the same day or a week later. His shoulder burned with the knife wound and he couldn't move. Nothing came out of his mouth when he started crying, not even a dried out rasp.

I've lost her, he realized. *God, I've lost them both.*

There, on the couch in his enemy's house, he cried without tears and screamed without a sound. He could try to apologize in all the languages of the world and it wouldn't have made a difference.

Dawn came, then dusk, then dawn again. The swelling on his forehead lessened, but he felt feverish. From the walls, the neighbor's family looked down with cheerful faces. It took slow, careful moves to push himself up while fighting off a wave of nausea. *Get lost*, he mouthed at the photos. *Stop staring.* He pushed one of his shoes off and hurled it, knocking a couple of them off the wall. Outside, the horses snorted.

He remained there in a fog of suffering. From the rafters, the noose hung unmoving. Bullet holes gaped in the walls, the floor and the ceiling where the Sheriff had fired.

I messed it up, he thought and buried his face into his hands. *You can't trust the Sheriff any more than you can trust a snake. She played me for a fool and I obliged her.*

Everything became deep burning shame and he wished the earth would swallow him.

He drank in the pain, let it wash over him in waves, wishing for them to drown him so he wouldn't have to feel unmoored by the shame anymore.

At some point, he couldn't tell when, the Sheriff appeared at the front door. She carried a carton box in her hands, wrapped in brown paper. Without rushing, she took the seat across from him. *If she's here to finish me off*, he thought, *I won't fight her. I'm tired.*

But the Sheriff didn't fight him, only stared at him with eyes that had gone red. She tore the wrapping, dropping long strips to the floor, and opened the box. The things his wife had been taken away in came out one at a time, as the Sheriff placed them side by side on the floor. Clothes, her scent still clinging to them. Her reading glasses, one of the arms bent so that the frame tilted to one side. Her wedding band.

When the Sheriff finished, she stood and wiped her eyes. She pointed her chin at the noose still hanging from the rafters, and left the house.

A car engine started, wheels rolled away. It took a long time before the sound of the cruiser disappeared altogether and the house settled back into silence.

It took several minutes more before he managed to push himself off the couch. He blinked to clear his vision. There it was. Everything he had left of her, and not a body to bury. He looked around at the neighbor's walls, outside at the buried fields.

She's gone. She's gone. There is nothing left, he thought as he dragged a chair underneath the noose. *Nothing left.*

He stepped onto the chair.

Placed the noose over his neck. Tightened it.

Then, without a pause, without hesitation, he kicked the chair away.

This will be over soon. This will be over soon.

The rope groaned and its dry threads came apart, then snapped.

He collapsed on the floor, the noose still tight around his neck. He remained there in a heap, confused and disassociated, his breathing a labored whistle. His mind broke off. It wandered, no longer able to process the here and now. It left him in a heap on the floor, an empty vessel with empty lungs.

When the old man entered the house, the farmer didn't react.

The old man sat in front of the farmer, lowering himself on one of the chairs. One knee bent with a jerky move, then the other. On his bald head, tape held a piece of cloth, and dirt and blood caked his face. The two looked at each other, yet neither reacted.

The old man stood and went behind the farmer. With clumsy and uncertain moves, he worked the noose. The old man's fingers felt strange on his skin, somehow wrong in their texture and their structure. More flippers than digits. He heard the old man mumble something full of throaty O's and tight-lipped M's. Once, his wife had told him that Om was the only word that could be spoken without a tongue. The sound the universe made when all other sounds went quiet.

The noose lost tension and released its grip on his throat. The old man tossed it away. Then, he brought a glass of water to the farmer and pushed it into his hands with his odd-shaped flippers, helping him clutch it and raise it to his lips.

An air of defeat hung about the old man. He looked stretched thin, almost transparent. Smelled of piss and sweat and suffering.

Come on, come on, drink, the old man mouthed to him and tipped the glass. Inside the old man's toothless mouth, half a tongue wagged like a gangrenous tail stump.

When the farmer finished the water, the old man sat on the couch next to him and closed his eyes. He remained like that for long moments, his chest moving up and down in a quiet cycle. The farmer reached over him and thought, *is he not furious to find me in his house? Is he not scared I might hurt him? We've hated each other for so long*. Then, lifting the neighbor's picture from the ground, he thought, *a man should not be afraid in his own home. A man should not be scared of those underneath his own roof.*

33.

THE FARMER HAD gone through every cupboard in the house at least three times. That didn't stop him from searching them again, hoping he had missed something behind the empty dust-covered boxes and the rat shit. He hoped for a can of baked beans or maybe a box of stale crackers. Anything. Even a rotten potato would do.

Standing in the middle of the kitchen, he rubbed his neck where the rope had burned his skin. There had to be something.

He found a trowel in the basement and, with it, he went around the outside of house, past the corral. How he envied the horses as they chewed on the yellow grass blades poking through the sand. Even if their bones showed through their flanks and flies tortured them. Hunger pains competed with the sharp ache on his shoulder.

Pain, pain, nothing but pain. This is what my world has transfigured into, the farmer thought with self-pity, then hung his head.

Man up, he thought while gripping the trowel. "Man up," he said out loud and the horses stared at him, startled.

Behind the house he found the poles, coming out of the

ground at odd angles, which marked the neighbor's old vegetable garden. Now, it was all covered by sand, yet he hoped something remained underneath. Dry tomato stalks rose like dead fingers. Vole teeth marks covered the skin of half-chewed roots and tubers. He dug deeper. Despite the wound burning, despite his joints threatening to snap from the toll of the last few days, he dug. A farmer's way of dealing with losing his world without losing his mind. Work to distract. Work to stay sane.

All rotten. He cursed as he unearthed another decomposed head of lettuce, another ruined bunch of cow beans. Bad water. He threw them away in disgust and wiped his hands on the soil. It all started with the water and that damn poisoned stream. He wouldn't feed this to pigs.

It took him some time to spot the white and purple flowers growing amongst the thistles and the barnyard grass that had taken over one of the house corners. He crawled to them on his aching knees and tossed the trowel away. Little by little, he scooped the soil away with his fingers, until he unearthed the delicate wild onion bulbs.

Back inside the house, he cleared a surface on the kitchen counter and placed his harvest on it. Five egg-sized bulbs. Three times he boiled the tap water, just in case. He then chopped up the bulbs with a dull knife and threw them into the pot with a bit of salt, filling the house with the scent of a soup that would never be thick enough.

When it was done, he took a bowl upstairs to the master bedroom.

He leaned against the bedroom's door frame. The neighbor was asleep. Lying on his back, his breathing was so quiet that the farmer had to watch his chest to tell if he was still alive.

The neighbor had the skin of someone who had once been fat and which had never settled right during the lean times. It aged him more than the patchy hair and the liver spots, more than the dark circles around the eyes.

When was the last time he had seen this man from so close? He remembered the two of them screaming at each other at the top of their lungs, pushing and shoving and baring teeth. He remembered the two of them exchanging death stares from across the Main Street and wishing the neighbor and his whole family would die in a fire. And here they were now.

But he doesn't look like himself, he thought as he put the bowl on the nightstand next to the bed. *Is this even the same person?*

Beyond the signs of age, the farmer could read a story on the neighbor's collapsed cheekbones and on the nose that bent into two opposite angles. On the cauliflower ears that were almost swollen shut and the thick scars on his forehead.

Who broke you, the farmer asked the sleeping man.

He observed him and remembered what the Sheriff had said. That the neighbor had been found using a radio console. Had been arrested months ago. Could he have been taken to the same prison as his wife?

His wife. She was gone. Gone.

He rubbed his eyes. The rope burn around his throat hurt. Tears streamed down his face and he swallowed a sob.

That moment had been coming for some time. Since the cancer appeared, he knew he'd have to face the moment when she wouldn't be part of his world anymore. He knew that, when it came, it'd feel like the stars disappearing from the night sky or the sun rising from the west.

When he opened his eyes, the neighbor was staring at

him from the bed. The farmer half-turned and wiped his face with the back of his hand. He felt like he was expected to say something. As with the past decade, no words came out.

The tongueless man raised himself on his elbows. Falling back on instinct, the farmer grimaced and left. It was hard being near him. Hard to undo generations of hatred.

In the living room, the noose remained where the neighbor had tossed it. The farmer reached underneath the couch and pulled it out. It seemed smaller than before. Much lighter, now that it wasn't wrapped around his neck. He felt ashamed. Suicide is for fags, his father would grumble whenever someone they knew took their own life, like one of the other farmers who had lost everything. Real men dig in. Real men keep on fighting.

He hurled the rope at the wall, ignoring the pain lighting up his nerve endings. The sound of the soup bowl shattering on the floor came from upstairs, followed by a heavy thud. He strode up the staircase. There, he found the neighbor on his knees in front of the bowl's remains, the soup pooling out over the floor. He rushed to help him up to his bed. A sound escaped the neighbor's torn lips, something between a wheeze and a sigh. Looking away, he held his hands up. Instead of pointing to the ceiling, his fingers lay sideways at an impossible angle. They turned along the wrong plane, stuck forever in the direction they were broken, knotted tendons crisscrossing underneath his skin. There was anguish in the neighbor's face as he pushed his mangled fingers into the farmer's chest. *Look at them*, he seemed to be saying. *Just look at them.*

The farmer touched the flippers. Their sandpaper texture, their lines. The calluses that were so similar to his own. And then, the stiff fused joints. *How did I not see them,* he contemplated. *And, yet, you took the noose off with these mangled things.*

He let them go and motioned for him to wait.

When the farmer returned a minute later, he held a new bowl. He sat next to the neighbor, dipped a spoon in it and waited.

The neighbor made a disgusted sound and screwed up his face and, for a moment, he looked like the man the farmer used to know. Full of loathing. The neighbor raised his useless hands up in protest and the farmer thought he would strike him.

"Enough," the farmer said. His words froze the neighbor.

"Eat, damn you," the farmer said again without malice in his voice. "Eat."

The neighbor's resistance lessened. His face softened. The two of them remained unmoving, sitting on the edge of the bed, avoiding each other's gaze.

Just look at you, the farmer thought and raised a spoonful of soup to the neighbor's lips. *Took a noose off my neck with those flippers, but can't even feed yourself. And look at me. Just look at me. Lost everything except my enemy.*

The farmer fed the neighbor until the soup was gone.

In his enemy's house, there was not much left of anything. Some gauze and boiled water to treat the wounds. Antiseptic. The farmer couldn't do much about the neighbor's broken fingers. He couldn't do anything about the neighbor's severed tongue.

He helped him take off his soiled clothes and, with a clenched jaw, he observed the torture wounds that covered his back. He applied the antiseptic in awkward heavy-handed dabs, but the neighbor didn't flinch, didn't react, nerve endings gone dead. Without a glance, the farmer helped the neighbor up and guided him to the bathroom. He used a wet towel to clean the rest of his body as best he could. Layers of filth came off. *There is not much left in this house*, the farmer thought. *No pride. No anger.*

When he finished, the farmer left to tend to the horses. The sun went down and, when there was nothing else to occupy his time, he laid on the couch in the living room, though he couldn't sleep. His eyes went over the pictures on the wall, including those he'd re-hung. The neighbor's son and daughter looked down at him from their broken frames. They had left the farm to study in the city, he knew, and had stayed there. There were pictures of the children with their father, pictures with both their parents. The neighbor's wife beamed with that huge smile of hers. The farmer had never spoken to her. Never met her, though he'd probably told the neighbor how he'd fuck her to rile him up in one of their many fights.

The farmer shook his head. He stared out of the open door into the fields that were half-buried in sand and the stars rotating over them. And he asked himself, *what now? What remains to do?*

He sighed and let his eyes wander across the constellations and the nebulae that colored the night sky. Despite his efforts, his wife's face wouldn't let him sleep. And what now? He had nothing left. And she… She was no longer in this world.

I can't even kill myself properly, he thought.

In the morning, the neighbor came downstairs. He paused to stare at a bullet hole in the wall and then continued into the basement. The farmer went to investigate the sounds of heavy things being rearranged, making sure his steps were loud enough to announce his presence. The neighbor came into his view, walking away from an old dresser, a notepad and a pencil in his mangled hands. He motioned to the farmer to come closer.

The neighbor moved towards a corner of the basement, stepping with care over boxes. Something in the measured way he put weight on his feet made the farmer wonder what other bones had been broken. From one of the open boxes, the magazines with the naked men on their covers spilled out. It gave the neighbor pause. He looked up at the farmer and studied his face with fear, waiting for a reaction.

A few months ago, I would have destroyed you for this, the farmer thought. "Do I look like I give a goddamn?" he said instead with weariness in his voice and stepped over the box.

The neighbor nudged a few cardboard boxes around. He half-sat, half-collapsed on them. Now was the hard part. With the notepad on his lap, he studied the pencil. He tried to hold it with one hand, but dropped it. Then, with both hands. It took some experimenting, but in the end he found a position that allowed him to move the pencil without losing it by squeezing it between both palms. He started scribbling. Out came a few words that resembled barbed wire and he then turned the notepad around for the farmer to read.

brok hnds

The farmer nodded.
The neighbor took his time pondering the next words.

"rehab"
now gud citzen
let m go
but took my tong

He tore the page away, not waiting for acknowledgment before he started writing again. He looked at his words, hesitating, then closed his eyes and turned the notepad over, as if the very action took mountains of effort.

yr womn…

The farmer read the words and replied, "Gone."

The neighbor's eyes opened wide in surprise. The air in the basement felt thicker, like before a heavy rain, back when heavy rain was still something that happened. The neighbor turned the notepad around again and wrote.

Im sorry

The farmer nodded.

The neighbor had nothing more to say and he stood, letting the notepad and the pencil slide off his lap onto the floor. He took in the basement and walked around without purpose.

"Did you see mah wife? Where they took you?" the farmer said, his voice full of emotion.

The neighbor nodded.

"In the prison?"

The neighbor nodded again.

The farmer approached, making the neighbor flinch and raise his destroyed hands up in defense. Instead of striking him, though, instead of shoving him, the farmer opened his arms and embraced him, burying his face into his shoulders. There they remained, unmoving, and everything the farmer wanted to say was said without him opening his mouth.

✕

THE HORSES DIDN'T resist the farmer. They let him saddle them and try his balance on top of each. In the end, he settled on a chestnut that took well to him. He went slowly through the fields, suspecting that the horse wasn't capable of more than a careful walk. Better than chancing the car again, and risking bringing the townsfolk on him.

He took the horse past the poisoned stream without letting it drink and up a gently sloping hill where he paused to take in the horizon. Mourning had emptied his mind of all thought. Only the sound of hoof on dirt and his own breath underneath the handkerchief occupied him.

Grass was finding its way out of the sand. As he got closer to his destination, he noticed corn stalks that broke the surface. Before long, they were brushing against the horse's underbelly.

As the sun came down, though, and touched the horizon, he laid eyes on his house that resembled a fistful of burned sticks stabbed into the earth. He took it in and his chest tightened. There had been the porch and the chairs. There had been the kitchen, and the unbreakable mahogany table that was no more, and that jagged lump full of edges over there looked like their bed. Home.

He pulled the reins to one side and forced the horse to circle the house's remains a few times. He had to observe the destruction from all angles for it to sink in, every burned splinter, every cracked beam, the skeletons of a lifetime and of several generations before, now collapsed out there in the open.

The horse snorted in irritation, sending buzzards flying away from deep within the house's exposed guts. He dismounted and wrapped the reins around a corner of the porch that still stood. With a half-charred stick in his hands, he made his way through the debris, shifting through the ashes. Here was a steak knife from the dinner set, bent out of shape. Here was a spring from the spare room couch, and this layered accordion-like mass must have been her books, fed to the fire by the mob.

He stood in the middle of it all.

Nothing. There was nothing there. What he had left of her was ashes. Her words were gone, burned.

He started to walk back to the horse and the ground underneath his foot made a hollow sound. He paused and tapped with the ball of his foot. The ground creaked. He pushed the ash aside, then lowered to his knees and cleared the debris with his hands, getting his palms black. He recognized the swirls and lines of wood grain. Sure enough, the brass handle was there. Grabbing it with both hands, he pulled the heavy oak door free from the ground, ignoring the pain shooting through his body. Below, the stairs led into the basement.

Steps covered with gray soot disappeared below into the cool earth. One foot hovered over the chasm and, as he held his breath, he lowered himself down and out of sight.

In the darkness, he spread his arms out to his sides and let the walls guide him. Only a patch of burning sky from above lit the way. Any moment and he'd reach out into nothingness, where he knew he'd fall forever.

The basement was intact. The old smells of isolation and mold and mothballs were gone, replaced by the acrid stench of ash, but everything else was in its place. The girl's bed remained in its corner. His wife's writing station stood next to it. With timid steps, he approached the armoire against the wall. It opened without resistance. Inside, in the hole behind the fake back, was her manuscript.

It looked different than how he remembered it. Her book had been several hundred pages long and this was only a small handful. This was something he had never seen before.

A gust of air made the manuscript's pages shiver. They fluttered and the farmer moved to grab them, but they escaped his fingers and peeled off, filling the basement. He watched them somersault and swirl, disappearing into dark corners. The basement felt the size of a matchbox. Breathing became hard. He almost ran up the stairs, slipping and hitting his knees on the way.

He emerged through the floor's remains, gasping with effort. Above, the first stars were coming out. Grazing sounds came from close by and he felt a sliver more relaxed in the horse's presence.

Taking a few steps into where the porch would have been, he reached into a heap and with a few pulls he unearthed a chair without a back. He shook the dirt off of it, then turned it the right way up and sat, his head in his ash-covered hands.

He didn't notice the rustling, the flashes of matted fur, and the hungry panting. The horse stomped its hooves and snorted.

The dogs attacked without snarling, without barking. They were on the horse, all five of them. Taking chunks off the legs, they brought it down. One of them, a black mastiff, got pinned underneath the horse, red foam frothing at the mouth. The rest sank their teeth into the horse's throat and shook their heads, tearing its jugular. Blood soaked the ground beneath and its eyes rolled back into its head.

The farmer jumped up and tossed the chair in their direction. The dogs turned their attention to him, muzzles wet with gore. The horse's thrashing decreased. They turned back and continued tearing the horse apart, ignoring their companion pinned beneath it.

Not seeing a way out, the farmer retreated back into the basement. He pulled the old door over the gap, the door his wife had once used as a barrier against him when he had begged her to talk. There, he gathered the pages. Too afraid to read what was on them, he pressed them against his chest. Long ago, he learned that words could shatter the world or put it back together. He would read them. Just not then. Not there.

He only surfaced when the sun came up. Having filled their bellies, the dogs were gone. The horse lay with its neck twisted backwards. Its intestines spilled out onto the ground, torn to pieces. Underneath it, the mastiff lay with its mouth still open. With the pages held in tight fists, the farmer started walking.

When he reached the neighbor's house, he entered and collapsed exhausted and starved.

The neighbor came hobbling down the stairs. He shuffled to him and stared, waiting for an explanation.

"Both our famblies are gone," the farmer said. "Nopin left. For us here. Do you. Want to leave. This place?" the farmer said.

The neighbor leaned back. He looked at the pictures of his family on the wall, then his broken hands, and seemed to consider his options. He nodded yes.

"North. We go North."

Another nod.

"Got the car still. It works. Can ride up North. They'll take us. There."

Yes.

"Tomorrow."

The neighbor squeezed the farmer's hands with his flippers and nodded.

34.

CORVO STARED AT the boy sitting across from her. His mom had said that his name was Zachariah and he seemed to be around the same age as her.

Drool hung from the boy's lopsided mouth. Staring out of the window at the town's streets, Zachariah seemed fascinated by the wind creating dust eddies and made excited sounds that rarely coalesced into words. One of his hands pressed against the window and tried to grab the miniature dust devils. In his other, he held an apple.

"You can have an apple too," his mom said. "In exchange for your name. Fair trade, mmm."

Corvo continued to observe the boy. His face was kinder than his mom's, though it scrunched from time to time as if he was trying to remember something important. When he smiled though, which was often, he did so with warmth. The wind rose and formed a short-lived twister that tossed broken bottles up in the air. The boy turned to Corvo full of excitement and gave her a huge grin. Corvo smiled back. Despite feeling trapped in the boy's house, she didn't have it in her to let him down.

There was no one else in the house with them, just his

mom. She wore a crisp tan uniform, so Corvo figured she must have been the town's Sheriff and that this was her home. Her face wasn't the same as the rest of the mutes. She did, however, grind her teeth constantly.

"Why can you talk but no one else does?" Corvo asked the boy's mother.

"I proteccct the law here. I need to be doin the talkin."

"But no one else is allowed to talk."

"Mayor is, though he's gone. No one knows where. The others don't need to talk. Come on. Tell me your name."

"What if they want to?"

The Sheriff shook her head. "Still not allowed."

"It doesn't seem right."

"What's right ain't always legal. What's legal ain't always right, specially these days. Look… Givin names is important. When you give your name, you show respeccct and you stop bein strangers. Can start bein friends. Mah name is Chastity."

Corvo didn't react. Instead she continued staring at Zachariah, if only to avoid the Sheriff's gaze. Neither the farmer nor the teacher had given her their names. Both of them were gone, though. The teacher taken away. The farmer… he was dead to her the moment he'd tied her to that chair with a mumbled apology.

The Sheriff took the apple from Zachariah, sending the boy into a fit. When he started hitting himself over the head, the Sheriff grabbed his hands and cooed to him until he stopped struggling.

The boy didn't talk much. There was "ello" and "how do" and other memorized expressions empty of substance or intention. An automated courtesy. Unlike the other mutes, though, there was a calm about the boy. An aura that let her know he was comfortable with not saying much. He didn't need to. Not like the farmer. In fact, she was certain the farmer was bursting to the brim with things he needed to say.

"Don't seem right," the Sheriff said to herself as she took a folding knife from her pocket. She cut the apple and gave a slice to Zachariah. "Sheriffs can talk, but not their sons. How's it fair? How's it right? It's the law, is what. What's right don't play into it."

"I talk. Am I allowed to talk?"

"Are you a Party member? One of the immmportant ones?"

"No."

"How bout a Sheriff or a Mayor?"

"No."

"Mmm," the Sheriff shrugged. "Then, I reckkkon you're not allowed to talk."

"What will you do to me?"

"Do to you?"

"Will you put me in jail? Huh?" she asked, tilting her chin up. "Are you going to kill me and hang me from the traffic light out there? Just like Mom and Ali?"

The Sheriff gave Corvo a venomous stare that scared her silent. She cut another slice of apple and handed it to Zachariah, pushing his arms away when he reached for the knife.

"I don't enjoy hurtin little girls, mmm," she said with a voice that quivered and she tossed the rest of the apple to Corvo. The Sheriff looked away and sighed, her shoulders shuddering. "No. I don't enjoy it one bit. What will I do to you? Nopin. You don't believe me, but it's the truth. Mah deputies think I've had you sent away to have your voice fixed. That won't happen."

"Tell you what will happen, you'll live with us. You'll be

my son's friend. In time, you'll have a fambly, your own children that talk and then this world might start makin sense again, mmm."

Corvo shifted in her chair and looked outside the window to the road. A woman wearing a cardigan full of holes stared at her from the street. She was squinting at the window but her eyes were not focused on the people behind it. Corvo realized that she could see the woman, but somehow the woman couldn't see them. She snapped her fingers in front of the woman's face. Zachariah winced and stared at Corvo with a half-chewed piece of apple in his mouth, but the woman behind the window didn't react.

His Mom leaned over his shoulder and placed her hand on his back.

"Lookkk at them, mmm. Every day, they have a choice. Only thing they have to do is say, no more. We disobey. And every day, they choose not to choose. They choose to keep their mmmouths shut. No one in hell can force them to keep quiet, mmm. Only themselves. Yet, they stay quiet, cause life's easier that way.

"In 'bout a generation, there won't be anyone left who talks. Don't you know? When you're born, they give you a snip right here," she tapped her throat with the apple knife, "and that's it. No mmmore talkin. You and him are the only children who can talk in this town. The whole county, far as I knows. The whole world, far as I care."

Zachariah's throat was as smooth and unblemished as the apple's skin. The boy was now observing the woman on the street too, his face glued to the window. Every move the cardiganed woman made, Zachariah repeated and giggled.

"Hid mah belly fer nine months. I brought him to life without screammmin once. Not once. Ground mah teeth till they almost fell out. Just to spare him from some doccctor takin his voice away. Almost lost him. Almost. Didn't breathe at first, turned all blue. Longest ten mmminutes of mah life. But he's a fighter."

With practiced moves, she took a handkerchief out of her pocket and wiped his drooling mouth.

"Almost kkkilled me. I'd do it all a hundred times over if I had to. This silence… No talkin. No writin. It does a nummmber on you. Won't let im turns like them out there. I won't."

Zachariah turned to her and smiled. His mom tussled his hair, making him titter.

"Stop it," he giggled.

Corvo bolted towards the door and crossed the short distance in two leaps, too scared to look behind, expecting the woman's wiry hands to grab her, but no one did, no one yanked her back into the chair. She reached the door and pushed, but the door didn't budge. She rattled the door knob but it, too, remained in place.

The Sheriff pointed at the chair and Corvo returned to it. From the window, the cardiganed woman stared at the door with confusion.

"There's nopin out there fer you. We're your fambly now, little girl. We proteccct you. Don't go pullin a stunt like that again. Understand?"

Corvo nodded.

"And I still want your name. Mmm?"

As the Sheriff went back to working on an ancient computer terminal and Zachariah back to watching the now empty street, Corvo tried to imagine her life with them but couldn't.

All those thoughts must have been plain to see on her

face, her resolve painted on her skin like words written in ink. The Sheriff stared at her and the muscles on her forearms tensed. Yet, Corvo refused to break eye contact. *I don't care*, she thought. *Hurt me if you want, I made up my mind. At least I'll get to see Mom and Ali again and you'll be stuck here, all alone with no one to talk to. Go ahead, do something. I win no matter what.*

The sound of a car parking outside just out of view made Corvo sit up. The Sheriff noticed too and her body stiffened in response.

A car horn bellowed for long seconds, piercing their ears.

The knock that came after felt leaden. The Sheriff half-stood, opened a drawer, and retrieved her gun. On his seat, Zachariah toyed with an apple slice. Corvo observed the Sheriff's troubled look, which went from the door to her son. She seemed to be considering her options. She marched to the door, unlocked it and opened, keeping her gun aiming at him behind the door.

The farmer stood in the frame with a shotgun in his hands trained towards the Sheriff's belly. They faced each other. Him with his torn clothes and stubble and curved shoulders. Her with every muscle in her body tensing. Behind him, a crowd began gathering in the street, first attracted by the horn, then picking up the promise of violence in the air. Recognition dawned on the faces of a few, who pointed at the farmer. There's the man whose wife writes.

The farmer looked inside the Sheriff's house and spotted Corvo. He motioned for the Sheriff to move farther inside with the shotgun.

Windows opened along the road. Bodies leaned over to catch a better glimpse.

The Sheriff turned and glanced at both children.

One step back. Then another, and the farmer was inside the office, locking the door behind him. He disarmed the Sheriff and motioned for her to sit behind her desk, taking the seat across her and resting the shotgun on his knees. He reached out towards the girl and squeezed her hand, sighing when she refused to squeeze back. When he saw Zachariah, his eyes darkened.

"We need to talk," he said.

The Sheriff sat and crossed her arms.

"You're bringin those mongrels here. You'll get us kkkilled. Do you know what they'll do to us, what they'll do to them?" she pointed at Corvo and Zachariah.

"Won't take long. You'll have time. To leave. Jes want to talk."

"So, talk," she said and leaned forward. "Speak your piece. Then, get the hell outta mah house."

"I'll take her wit me."

"There's not a fuckkkin—"

"Not askin."

"You know, I thought it proper," the Sheriff said with a frown. "Takkkin someone from you. Finally, forcin some balance to this world."

"And now, we're here."

The Sheriff smiled with bitterness. "And now, we're here. You won't takkke her."

"Listen. I need to talk to you. *We* need to talk."

"After all this time?"

The farmer nodded.

Corvo went to sit next to Zachariah who was starting to become agitated. Outside, the townsfolk stared through the window, unable to see them on the other side. One of them, a tall thin man with a mustache she recognized, leaned in and cupped his hands against the glass. Zachariah pointed and his face scrunched again. She squeezed his hands and it helped sooth him.

"Will you kkkill me when this is over wit?" the Sheriff asked. "Are you here to take revenge?"

The farmer shook his head. "No."

"Pardon me if I find it hard to believe you, mmm."

"I'm here fer the girl. And to talk."

"Talk? You want to *talk*?" the Sheriff said. The muscles on her forearms tensed with anger, the artery in her throat pulsed as she ground her molars. "Then take the girl and keep your talkkkin for yourself, I preferred you better silent."

"I… need to make," he paused and concentrated on the words. "Amends."

"Amends?" she barked, making Zachariah jump. When she talked again, her voice came out thick with emotion. "They ruined mah life. Mah fambly. You coulda helped me. You knew folks in the Party. Your Pa."

The farmer lowered his gaze and his voice came out small. "I'm sorry. I'm really sorry."

"I begged you," she growled. "Mmme."

"It wasn't that simple."

A hand slammed against the window and a face approached trying to see through. Someone began to scratch at the door. Zachariah squeezed Corvo's hands and closed his eyes and she cooed at him the way his mom did.

"He was. A good man," the farmer continued. "But. What was I supposed to do?"

"You could have done somepin."

"Too dangerous. For mah fambly."

"And you were okay wit it."

The farmer hesitated. Then, he lifted his head. "I was."

The Sheriff sneered. "Everone else in this cccountry had exactly the same thought. Nopin I can do. Better keep mah mouth shut, keep mah fambly safe, mmm? I used to lie awake at night, starin at the ceilin and wonderin how I could reach out to the townsfolk. How to get them to see. But naw. This is exaccctly where they want to be. Head bowed and mouth shut. And when a man cries his pain in the open, *bammm*. They lynch him and nod and pat each other on the back. You belong here. Now, you're takin her away. To where? There's nopin out there. You have nopin left. Wit me, she had a chance. Now, you've blown it, same wit everypin in your life."

A kick rattled the door in its hinges. Outside the window, sharp things had started to appear in the in the crowd's hands, and righteous rage in their eyes.

The farmer sighed. "I did you wrong. No makin up fer it. But you're the one lying to yourself. You brought the silence to this town. You helped them." He paused and licked his lips, searching for a word. "Hypocrite."

The Sheriff stared at the farmer, her face blank. The door shook harder. Then, as realization set in and the rage with it, her jaws clenched and her teeth cracked and her eyes turned red. "Ya did me wrong… Go tell it ta the dust."

Corvo caught only flashes of what happened. The Sheriff leaping over her desk with the apple knife in both hands held like a sword. The farmer leaning back and raising the shotgun. Bodies colliding. Arms and fists and kicks as they rolled on the ground, the shotgun pressed between them.

The gunshot was so loud that Corvo doubled over and screamed with her hands over her ears. When she realized she couldn't hear her own voice, she screamed louder. The world was painted red. Blinded, she touched her face and, when she pulled her trembling fingers away, they were coated in slick gore.

"Blood," she said and gasped, unable to breathe. "There's blood in my hair."

"Not your blood," the farmer rushed to her and muttered. "Not your blood. You're good, sweetheart. You're good."

At the other side of the room the Sheriff stared, stunned, from the floor. Her face was full of shock and her eyes were searching for Zachariah.

"Mah boy," she huffed and tried to stand up.

Squeezed in a corner, Zachariah had his head between his knees. "Shh," he whispered to himself. "Shh."

The gunshot sent the crowd outside into a frenzy. The door splintered and hands appeared through a gap.

"We're gone. Don't follow us," the farmer said. He reached out and grabbed Corvo's hand and, despite her resistance, dragged her along to the back door.

They went through it and, keeping their heads low, ran through the back streets, past fences, past windows. Behind them, a door snapped and dozens of feet stomped into the Sheriff's house.

A turn, then another turn, and they came face-to-face with an old man waiting in a car. The farmer opened the back door and shoved Corvo inside. From the driver's seat, the old man stared at her with the balls of his crooked hands on the steering wheel.

The car started. Soon, they were out of the town of the twin hills.

"Whose blood is this?" Corvo hissed and patted her hair. "Whose freaking blood is this?"

The farmer looked ahead and settled back as the old man

drove on. "No one's," he said as he bled on his seat.

✗

A DOZEN TOWNSFOLK rushed inside.

They didn't go for the Sheriff at first. Instead, the pharmacist, his face bandaged and swollen, pointed at Zachariah hiding underneath a desk. Then, he pointed at Zachariah's smooth throat with a long claw of a finger.

The townsfolk fell on the Sheriff and pinned her to the floor, two at each arm. She kicked and growled and tried to command them to let her go but all that came out of her mouth were animalistic grunts.

The pharmacist picked up the folding knife and cleaned off the apple juices on his pants. Then, he approached Zachariah and offered him a hand.

"Ma?" Zachariah uttered as he came out from under the desk.

The pharmacist sat him on the desk and patted the boy's back until his posture relaxed. He smiled at him. Then, he gently pushed his forehead and made him lie on the desk.

"Ma?"

The pharmacist passed the knife to the boy with the shaved head. The boy leaned over Zachariah, touched the knife tip low on his throat where the vocal cords were. His eyes looked back to the pharmacist with uncertainty and he hesitated.

"Ma?"

The pharmacist put his hands over the boy's and pushed the blade in.

35.

CORVO BID THE horses farewell. Leaning against the car, she raised her hand at them as they approached the open corral gate.

"There was one more. Where's the other horse?" she asked.

The farmer didn't answer. Instead he fumbled with a bandage. The gut wound still bled, sticky and warm, onto the car seat.

"Will they be safe? There's wild dogs out there," Corvo continued.

"Better out there," the farmer replied. "Have a chance."

They watched together as the neighbor led them out. When the white one hesitated, the neighbor shoved it with his shoulder, sending it trotting. The horses milled about as if expecting instructions. When the neighbor turned his back on them and headed towards the house, they took small, uncertain moves towards the distant hazy mountains. Before long, they were the size of pin heads on the landscape, and, a blink later, they were gone.

"What's wrong with his fingers?" Corvo asked, following the neighbor with her eyes.

"They broke them."

"The same ones who took her?"

The farmer nodded.

Corvo didn't know what to think of the old man with the mangled fingers and the stiff gait. He had driven them through the town, steering with the balls of his hands. Then, without warning, he had plunged the car into the back roads. Only when they got back to the house did she connect him to the face in the pictures.

Seeing the farmer struggle with the bandage, she snatched it from his hands and applied it to the wound, wiping the blood off on her pants. "I hate you, you know."

"I know."

"Who knows if Zachariah and his Mom are still alive. She's nuts, but he's just a boy like Isaiah. You're no better than the mutes. Do you know that?"

"I know."

The bandage slowed the bleeding. The girl stole another glance at the house. She could hear drawers and cabinets slamming shut.

"I should let you die," she said.

"Got hit with birdshot. It'll take time. Wait til we're safe. Then do what you want."

"You're the worst shit I've ever met."

The farmer shook his head. "Didn't know," he said. He looked in the direction of the town and let his head drop. "Didn't know. That her son was still alive. They won't hurt him. She's the Sheriff."

Corvo didn't answer, tired of the town and its people. Resisting the urge to lean into his wounds and hurt him, she finished dressing the farmer's injuries and stood. This town and its surroundings had branded her to the point she could scarce remember anything else. When she thought of the compound now, details escaped her. Her room, her home right next to the fence. The library and the mess hall. All the people who lived there. She longed for the smell of generators. Everything was fading away, leaving only a feeling of safety connected to those memories she felt she would never be able to capture again.

"Where are we going?" she asked, her eyes shut. Behind the darkness of her eyelids, she chased patterns and afterimages, unwilling to face the world around her.

"Your parents. Had the right idea," the farmer said without elaborating.

Still with her eyes closed, Corvo listened to him shifting and groaning.

"Ali wasn't my parent," she said. "He met my Mom when I was a baby. But I wish he was."

There was a long pause before the farmer said anything.

"Wish I coulda met him."

"The TV said there's war in the North."

"Yeah."

"Will it be dangerous?"

"No."

"How do you know?"

"Trust me."

"Trust you?" Corvo finally opened her eyes. "You want me to *trust* you?"

The farmer didn't answer.

The neighbor appeared again at the broken door, carrying a backpack over his shoulder. He smiled, patted the bag and limped towards the car, then stopped as if a thought had struck him. He turned and stared at the house, his shoulders sagging. With its open windows and broken door, the house stared back at the neighbor, the two of them saying their farewells.

Then, shaking his head, the old man turned around and made a beeline for the car. He gave the backpack to the girl, took the driver's seat and didn't look back again.

The car struggled to find traction through the dirt, but managed to reach the street. There, the neighbor paused. He gestured outside the windscreen and raised his eyebrows in question.

"That way," the farmer said and pointed. "North."

They passed the few farms that lay farther down the road, as well as a mill and a junkyard that had been reclaimed by weeds. The road turned rough and the vegetation by its side grew taller, though no less fragile, and it seemed to the girl that the car grew lighter with every yard it put between itself and the town. She stared through the window at the asphalt and the cracks running through it that grew deeper and wider, feeling the cadence of the wheels change as they rolled over them.

Buried farms turned to desiccated trees. Trees turned to dead forests, stripped and sun-torched.

They drove for hours in silence without making eye contact with each other, without acknowledging that the farmer's time was running low. Once, Corvo wanted to ask how long it would take them to reach the North, but thought better of it. The neighbor couldn't answer, only shrug. As for the farmer, she preferred if he didn't talk to her at all.

Night fell. They stopped at a shoulder of the road underneath the stilts of what must once have been a billboard. Save for an abandoned gas station several miles behind them, they were far away from anything and anyone.

She and the neighbor with his broken fingers did not

sleep inside the car, but offered it to the farmer. It wasn't to keep him comfortable through his injuries. That first night, the farmer tossed and turned and grunted as fever set in, making sleep for them impossible. His wounds emanated a sharp odor.

Corvo covered her head with her arms, finding a sense of comfort in the way she smothered her eyes and ears. Once, when she looked over at the neighbor, she found him staring at the sky with a vacant expression.

"Hey," she said. "Did you see her? His wife?" But the neighbor was far gone into his own world, galaxies and distant nebulae reflected on his unfocused eyes.

"Do you think he's going to make it?" she continued. "He's hurt bad."

There was no reply.

Much later but still before dawn, a pair of headlights appeared in the distance. They crested a hill and came down towards them, two bright orbs floating over the asphalt like will o' wisps, soundless, throwing long shadows around them. The girl felt the neighbor nudging her. Without a word, they opened the car door and pulled the farmer out, dragging him away to a nearby ditch. They scampered down and waited.

The lights stopped a dozen yards away from their car, shining towards them and destroying their night vision, so that they couldn't tell whether it was the Sheriff's cruiser. The person that came out turned on a torch and pointed it in their direction before sweeping the area. She, by her body shape they could tell it was a woman, leaned through the open window of their car, inspecting its interior. Both the neighbor and Corvo held their breaths hoping that the farmer would not give them away, and, if he did, that the person bathed in blinding light would not harm them.

They watched as she reached to her hip and unbuttoned a holster carrying the silhouette of a gun.

Corvo swore none of them had made a sound, but the woman turned and headed straight towards the ditch. Twenty short steps separated them. At the ditch's edge, she shone the torch straight at the group and stared in shock. Her fingers fumbled to unholster her gun. Corvo felt the neighbor's broken hands pushing her away. He rose up with a grunt, a rock between his forearms, and she heard the shattering crunch it made as it came down on the woman's skull.

The woman collapsed and convulsed, blood spilling onto sand. With effort, the neighbor bent and picked up the rock again, lifting it high. He brought it down with a throaty grunt, the tongue stump visible as he opened his mouth. The silence that followed shocked Corvo as much as the sudden violence. The woman's legs went rigid. Only the car engine's ticks and the whine from the lights broke the stillness, together with the neighbor trying to catch his breath.

Corvo could tell it wasn't the Sheriff, though she was dressed in a similar outfit. The star on her chest was different. This one had a blue stone instead of a red one, and the metal was a dull gray compared to the Sheriff's golden badge. Still huffing with the exertion, the neighbor turned to her and studied her face with concern. He touched her shoulder with a flipper.

"I've seen worse," she said.

Corvo and the neighbor lifted the farmer, and she felt the fever on his skin. Together, they moved him back into the car, then they pulled the gun from the dead woman's holster and dumped her into the ditch, covering her with loose sand

and stones that they kicked from above.

"What about her car?" Corvo asked.

The neighbor nodded. He pointed at the handbrake through the open window and Corvo released it. Little by little, they pushed it, too, into the ditch, close to where they had buried the woman who wasn't the Sheriff.

They got inside their own car and, keeping the lights turned off, drove away as fast as they dared.

In the morning, the farmer came to. Overnight, he had lost his color and his lips had appeared sickly blue in the daylight. His hair clung to his sweaty forehead. The stench from his wound had become closer to ammonia and bitter almonds and they had to drive with the windows down.

When they took a break to refill the gas tank from a canister, Corvo observed the neighbor treat the wound.

"There's no point taking him to a hospital. Is there?"

The neighbor shook his head. He peeled the dressings off, pulling parts of deceased skin away.

"Will he make it North?"

The neighbor glanced at her and raised his eyebrows, sighing. In his seat, the farmer squinted with pain.

"Not far, now," he said. "One day's road?"

The neighbor bobbed his head left to right in uncertainty.

"Thereabouts," the farmer concluded and closed his eyes.

She walked away, kicking stones.

Her path took her towards the burned forest off to one side of the road. Trees resembled thin coal shards that smudged her hands with ash as she brushed against them. The ground was covered in sand, but it had an odd quality. Hard as stone. A rough, sandpaper surface, unlike the fine loose dust that covered the fields.

Corvo scrambled up a ridge and descended the other side. She found a wide charred tree whose trunk had split and splintered and sat under its shadow.

She wished she could dig a hole into this rough ground and burrow inside to sleep for a century. And she wished for a slumber heavy and dreamless. Free of mutes. She longed for the compound. They should have never left the compound. Everything had gone to hell after they had left. Then, embarrassed by her own outburst, she thought, *stop being such a freaking baby.*

She rubbed her eyes and smudged her face with ash. *There's no compound anymore, get used to it.* She looked back towards the car. That was all the home she had now. An old wreck on wheels, a man without a tongue, and a terrible man running out of time.

From her pocket, she brought out a tiny leather-bound book without a title. It was small enough to fit into an adult's open hand. The teacher had given it to her. She had said it belonged to one of her favorite poets, a man named Yeats who had lived two centuries ago. He couldn't read until much later than other children, and not without a lot of help from his family. Letters danced when he looked at them, words didn't make sense. Still, not only had he gotten better at reading, but his writings were salve for the soul. Corvo felt she needed this now.

She opened to a random page and read out loud to the burned trees.

"I had this thought awhile ago,

'My darling cannot understand

What I have done, or what would do

In this blind bitter land.'

And I grew weary of the sun
Until my thoughts cleared up again,
Remembering that the best I have done
Was done to make it plain;
That every year I have cried, 'At length
My darling understands it all,
Because I have come into my strength,
And words obey my call.'
That had she done so who can say
What would have shaken from the sieve?
I might have thrown poor words away
And been content to live."

The poem came out slow, but uninterrupted. It soothed her to listen to its timbre as the wind carried it. It raced across the burned forest floor, though the sandpaper ground, and Corvo felt lighter. On the page, her thumb print remained, formed in ash.

She practiced her breathing.

Four seconds breathing in. Four seconds holding it. Four seconds breathing out. Four seconds of peace.

When she felt ready to continue, she got up and headed towards the car again. As she neared the burnt forest's edge, a sound like running water came to her ears. She stood and listened. It perplexed her as she hadn't noticed any brooks or creeks close by, like the one between the farmer and the neighbor's houses.

When she reached the car, she dropped to the ground. The neighbor was on his knees, the dead woman's gun on the ground out of reach, and the Sheriff, her crisp uniform in shreds and her skin covered in swollen bruises and cuts, stood above him. With one hand she held his chin up. With the other, she sawed at his throat with her apple knife. The neighbor gargled blood and clawed at her with useless hands.

Behind them, the farmer writhed in pain on the ground. When he spat, teeth rattled on the ground. He tried to crawl towards the Sheriff, leaving behind a dark red trail that seeped into the dry ground.

Corvo felt vomit rise up her throat. She wanted to retreat to the forest, into the hole where she could sleep forever. She wanted to become small, as small as possible, and disappear from this world.

Instead, she rose and shouted.

"Hey."

The Sheriff looked up. At once, she let go of the neighbor and marched after her.

"Git here," she yelled with tears in her eyes. "Everypin's ruined."

Corvo ran deeper into the forest that couldn't hide her. Even from a distance, she could see the Sheriff following her, mad with anguish. There was a limp in her run, but she didn't show pain. Only rage.

"Git back here," the Sheriff howled. The clipped sounds that came out of her mouth were more barks than words. She breathed with a wheeze through clenched teeth. It terrified Corvo. To her, the Sheriff seemed gone, turned into an animal that inhabited her skin, and it was then that she knew Zachariah's fate. Her terror ebbed and she felt an ocean of sorrow spreading inside her. Sorrow for Zachariah. Sorrow for the farmer and the people they had all lost. For the poor neighbor that had wanted to help them.

Corvo led the Sheriff deeper into the forest, away from the neighbor, away from the farmer. She twisted her hurt ankle on the uneven forest floor. An old dried out stream bank cut deep through the ground and she climbed inside it. Before the Sheriff came into view, she dropped into a cavity in the ground and pressed herself against its sides, willing her body to become one with the dirt, to become invisible. She felt the sand scratch the skin on her cheek, rootlets and insects caress her eyelashes. She pressed harder and harder, willing the earth to take her in.

I'm tired, she thought. *I'm tired.*

Footsteps approached. The Sheriff's shadow fell across the stream bank, her fist wrapped around the apple knife. She breathed hard between her desperate sobs.

"Git back here," the Sheriff wailed again. "Everypin's ruined. Ruined."

The words came out with difficulty between desperate gulps of air. Corvo saw the shadow hold her head, pull at her hair.

"He's gone."

The Sheriff came into view at the edge of the bank, sticking her head up as if sniffing the air. She shifted the apple knife from hand to hand, the skin on her palms torn open where they rubbed against the hilt. The uniform's tattered remains were soaked in blood, though most of it appeared not to be her own. Where her badge was meant to be pinned, there was a hole with frayed edges.

"I'll cut your cccords out with mmm-mmmah own hands. Leave you out here to bleed. They kkkilled him. The boy I almost died for."

She walked along the bank, hitting herself over the head. She howled and retched, then darted up and down the stream bank without direction.

"What right d'they have touchin mmmah son? What right?"

She stalked, skulking and barking "Git here," like a curse

over and over again until it all turned into a cough. "Ght ere. Ght ere." Stones and dirt came loose and rained down as she moved.

Corvo rushed from one cavity to another, certain every time that the Sheriff could see her, that she was toying with her. Several times, she heard her walk over her head and stop. She heard the Sheriff's knees pop as she squatted and her wet drooling huffs as she surveyed the stream bank before she moved to a different spot. Inside Corvo's pocket, the leather-bound book pressed against her thigh.

The Sheriff rushed up the opposite bank, scampering on hands and knees. She walked now along the bank's lip towards Corvo's spot. Corvo switched sides and tried to remain unseen.

"Please, cccommme out," the Sheriff said. "I have no one now. Cccommme out. Won't you go backkk wit mmme? Mmm? Go backkk wit mmme and kkkeep mmme cccommmpany? Mmm? Won't you cccommme out and tell mmme your nammme?"

As she reached the spot where Corvo was hiding, the girl reached out and pulled her leg. The Sheriff lost her balance. There was a wet sound as her head hit a stone and her body rolled to the bottom of the bank, where she remained motionless. In her hands, she still clutched the knife.

Corvo climbed over the bank's lip and glanced down. Sharp bone fragments emerged through both the Sheriff's thighs. Blood flowed from her nose. Her eyes caught her and she followed Corvo without moving her head. There was no pain in her expression. Just fury and grief. Fury and grief. Corvo expected her to yell, to curse her. Nothing came out. Only the sound of the Sheriff's molars grinding to dust. Corvo walked away backwards to keep the Sheriff in her sight, and the Sheriff shimmered in the heat waves until the bank's edge obstructed her and she was gone.

Corvo arrived at the car to find the neighbor staring at the sky with lifeless eyes. His broken hands lay crossed over his chest.

When the farmer spotted her, he reached out from the ground. Corvo went to him and helped him stand. She let him lean on her and helped him to the car's passenger seat. He didn't ask her what had happened, where the Sheriff was. There was no need.

When Corvo turned to look at the neighbor's body, the farmer sighed.

"Leave him. It's okay. It's okay. He's gone. Just an empty body, now. Gone."

Corvo searched the car and found a bottle of water. Ignoring the farmer's questions, she grabbed it and went back to the stream bank. There, she got on her belly and crawled on the ground. When she got close enough, she peaked over the lip and prepared to throw it at the Sheriff. One last mercy. But the Sheriff lay with a cut along her throat in the shape of a gaping C. In her still-clenched fist, the knife was smothered in her own blood.

Corvo returned to the car, ignoring the gun on the ground, not daring to come close to it. She shut the passenger door before moving to the driver's seat without hesitation. Adjusted the seat and the mirrors, then put her hands on the wheel. There she remained for a few minutes, eyes on the road, arms tense with over-gripping.

The farmer reached over with a shaking hand and turned the ignition.

"This steers," he touched the wheel. "This makes us go faster," he touched her right leg, "and this stops us. So go easy on it."

Corvo waited for more instructions. She pointed with her chin at the levers sticking behind the wheel, the buttons on the dashboard, the dials. Instead, the farmer breathed with labor and shook his head. He squeezed her arm and guided it into putting the car in drive.

"Go," he said. "Don't have much time."

36.

BEYOND THE TOWN, beyond the countryside, traces of others became sparse. Gone were the stilts on which signs with town names used to stand. Communication towers on distant mountain tops laid collapsed and bridges that once spanned across rivers rusted where they stood.

As Corvo and the farmer drove on, even those structures vanished. Only the rolling road provided evidence of humanity. It led them ever North, the girl at the wheel and the farmer slowly bleeding out next to her on the passenger seat.

The engine was a hypnotic murmur, unchanging in tone except for when the girl had to slow down to drive around a fallen trunk or husks of other cars. She had a steady foot, the farmer told her. It was true, he said, because the ride was making him drowsy. Corvo kept her eyes fixed on the road, not saying much.

The farmer had his eyes closed most of the time, one hand over his belly keeping pressure on the wound and his head leaning against the window. Even the bleeding had stopped, he complained that his insides felt wrong.

"Like I've swallowed a frozen boulder," he described it.

Before long, they encountered forest again. Not tree remains this time, but tall firs and elms that crowded both sides of the motorway.

Through the open window, Corvo felt a drop in temperature. Next to her the farmer remained sleeping with a sheaf of paper clutched in his hands, just as a rain cloud covered the sun.

37.

T HE FARMER DREAMED.

Of lakes and mountains.

Of comfortable silences and meaningful stares.

Of a gut wound in the shape of disappointment.

If there was an afterlife, he was scared of who would wait for him there.

With what words he would be greeted.

You did well.

You did your best.

You did me and everyone around you wrong.

In his sleep, he clutched the words she had bled on the pages with graphite.

38.

T HE WALL ROSE up on the horizon.

The single continuous concrete structure towered over the firs like a curse. It was the same dirty gray as the clouds covering the sky. Glanced at in a hurry, the wall created the illusion that it extended up to infinity.

It covered the entire length of the mountain pass. Framed by cliffs and thick vegetation, it was monolithic, shaped to make those who looked upon it lose their courage and turn back. Even now, with the wall still far off, she felt its weight over her. Stay away, it screamed. Leave at once.

But that's where the farmer had pointed her to. Straight up the mountain road, he had said before falling asleep again.

With careful moves, Corvo pulled the car over, crunching leaves underneath the tires. The car had taken them as far as it could. With the last drops of petrol sloshing in the tank and the road becoming more trail than asphalt, they would have to walk. She pulled her feet off the pedals and the car coughed and lurched before the engine died. She rushed around the car to help the farmer and noticed with surprise her breath condensing in the crisp air.

The farmer almost fell out when she opened the door.

She caught him with her shoulder and pushed him back in place, then slapped him a few times to wake him up.

"We're walking," she announced. "Stop being such a baby, I'm not carrying you," she continued. Throughout their ride to the border, she was preparing herself for the eventuality that she would have to cross it by herself. Despite her mental preparation, though, dismay crept in the longer the farmer remained still.

She knew nothing of the North. What little Mom and Ali had told her about the Northerners, about their willingness to take in anyone who would ask for help, always ended with the same phrase. That was a long time ago. Would things be the same now? No news came into the compound from the outside world. For all she knew, it could have also turned into a country of mutes. Or worse. What kind of people raise a wall this ugly, this absolute, that makes you want to turn back to the hell you just escaped from? Still, for Mom and Ali, the risk was worth it. Trying to get there had cost them their lives. Now, with every step she took, she wanted the North to be worth it.

When I get there, I'll do anything they ask of me, Corvo decided. *And, if that fails, I'll beg, or steal. Anything, as long as I'm over there and not over here.*

Another slap and the farmer opened his eyes with weariness. He stared at the border wall, confusion on his face.

"Here, already?" he said with surprise.

"Come on," Corvo said and pulled one his legs out of the car.

"So much green."

"There's no one here. There's no war."

"Never was any war."

"But I saw it on the TV. Explosions, helicopters. There

were soldiers."

The farmer shook his head.

"No war. Lies. To keep people away."

"How did you know?"

But the farmer didn't reply. He continued taking in the evergreens, the wall, the verdant desolation that surrounded them. All around them, the forest was untouched and unspoiled by the war the Party had promised was raging.

"So quiet," the farmer said and his chest rattled. He didn't sound right. Corvo pulled at his arm, forcing him to move.

"That's the North?" she nodded at the wall.

"It is."

"Can we get through the wall?"

"Yes. There was a border crossing here. Once."

"Then, move."

Once out of the car, he leaned against her. She felt she could take him to the wall, farther even, if it got down to that. They headed towards the mountain pass.

Up ahead, a road sign had been replaced by a warning. No words on it, no instructions.

"That's bad, right?" Corvo asked and regarded the black skull against the red background. "That means danger, is that what it means? Does that mean war?"

She watched him regard the sign and clench his fists with what little energy he had in him.

"Don't mean a thing," he replied after a long pause. "Empty threats. Is all."

The path wound upwards. Once the forest grew thicker, the tree tops hid the wall from their view. It took time to negotiate the mountain side, but in the end they settled into a steady cadence. Long stretches fell away behind them. Where the ground turned rocky and rough, Corvo went first and helped the farmer across, or stayed a few steps behind, supporting him when he faltered and lost his balance.

For his part, the farmer accepted the help without complaining. There was no fussing. He walked with a stoop that increased as time went by, doubling over his wound.

They reached a field of boulders gutted out of the mountain where they decided to rest. There, the farmer let Corvo change his bandages.

His skin had turned black and hard to the touch where the shot had hit him, like burned tree bark. Corvo didn't flinch. She threw away the bandage and quickly wrapped a new one around his torso.

"Can't feel a thing," the farmer whispered.

When the girl finished, they sat and stared at the boulders, curved into strange sculptures by the winds. Curves and loops and wavy surfaces covered by moss.

"First time you see somepin like this?" the farmer asked with one eye open. Above them, tree branches intertwined to create a natural cave out of the forest canopy.

The girl nodded.

"Damn shame," the farmer said and shut his eye again.

Corvo wished the teacher could have been here with them. So close to the end of the line, she wished she could share it with her.

The teacher had once revealed to Corvo that she had had an epiphany some time ago. She saw a man get hurt. Someone that must have suffered a lot. Suffering resembles water piling up behind a dam. Too much of it will spill over and drown everything in its path. That man had suffered so much the words just burst out of him. It was then that she knew. Not what the first word was, but what the first word must have been about.

At other times, she wondered what the last word would be. What great tragedy would shock us into speaking one last time and then hold our tongues forever, because there wouldn't be anything left to say after that.

"What do you think was the first word ever spoken?" the girl asked the farmer.

The farmer considered the question. "Hell if I know," he shrugged. Then, after some more thinking, he added. "A warning. It'd be a warning. Or asking fer help. Somepin desperate."

"Something desperate," Corvo said, thinking of the teacher yelling No. "I think so too."

When the rain drop hit her arm, she thought it was an insect. She lifted her eyes to the sky just as the drizzle started. Next to her, the farmer was still deep in thought. She shook his shoulder, careful not to hurt him, and pointed up. His smile... Had she ever seen him smile? He ran his hands through his hair and stared at his wet palms as if he were watching the world's greatest magic trick.

There they remained for a long time, their faces turned to the sky as if in prayer, welcoming the rain. When they decided to move, they did so without hurry.

At first, Corvo mistook the music for leaves rustling under the rain. As they got closer to the wall, she could make out words weaved between the notes. The girl picked up the pace the louder the music became, trying to urge the farmer onward, though he was becoming hard to support.

It was an odd kind of music, one full of soulful trumpets and mellow violins. Not an anthem, the kind that would come out of the TV that could not be turned off. It made Corvo think it was old. She had never listened to music like that at the compound.

The voice that crooned over the notes spoke of quiet lives, content lives. It reverberated off the wall and the trees, seemed that it came from everywhere at once. Corvo looked at the farmer saw confusion in his face.

They rushed ahead as fast as the farmer's injuries allowed them. The wall was not far. Between it and the tree line lay a wide strip cleared of vegetation and, once there, they could take in the wall in all its tyranny. The music continued.

The farmer was the first to curse when it stopped, as if someone had pulled a plug.

"No," he shouted, then slipped to the ground and coughed blood onto the wet leaves. Corvo put an impotent hand on his back. *Please, don't die now*, she thought.

Words blared out of the speakers, drowning out his heaving, tinged with a coarse accent.

"Attention, asylum seekers. The group, and the man with the girl. Do not attempt to scale the wall, you will be shot. Do not attempt to dig underneath the wall, you will be shot. Do not attempt to write on the wall. You will be shot."

Every "Do not" seemed to blend into each other until it became a long litany of prohibition. Then, nothing. The speakers went dead.

"It's fine, it'll be fine," the farmer said. "Least they know we're here. Oh, but they're clever. Using music. To draw us out. And there's someone else here too."

Corvo didn't answer. Instead, she marched towards the wall, lifting a fist as she went.

"We need help," she yelled. "Stop hiding behind that wall and help us."

But the wall remained silent. A surveillance camera, perched on top of the wall, swung in her direction, then another, and another. Corvo continued raging against the wall, even picked up a stone and cocked her hand back. With strength she didn't imagine the farmer still had, he yanked her back and forced her to drop it.

"Empty threats, that's what you said."

"From our side. These people, I don't know."

He waved her towards the tree line. Despite her reluctance, Corvo obeyed and watched him shuffle up to the wall in his lurching manner, hands over his gut. The cameras along the wall focused on him. He raised his shirt to reveal the bloody gauze. He stared at the cameras and the cameras stared back at him until they grew tired and went back to pointing elsewhere along the wall.

The farmer looked around him with disappointment, then dropped his arms and shuffled back.

"Let's find the gate," he said.

There had once been another wall, surrounding the compound she had grown up in and keeping her safe from the mutes. And behind its gate, Mom and Ali and the others had argued about whether to let in the stranger that showed up one day. But that was different. Wasn't it? Corvo looked up at the cameras following them. Imagined people sitting on the other side, arguing amongst each other, about whether they should let the man and the girl in.

Look at him, he's hurt, one would say.

Then another would reply, but this is how they get you.

But he's bleeding.

But he's faking it.

"How do you know there's a gate?" Corvo asked. "How do you know there's anything here but the wall? How did you know there was no war?"

"A friend," he answered. "In the Party. She helped me.

Over the years. Walls everywhere long the border. Every one of them has a gate. How they agreed it. With the North."

"Agreed it? Why?"

But the farmer sighed and became heavier. Corvo felt his breathing slow. She stopped the questions and focused on supporting him.

"This country's a prison," he whispered. "All prisons have doors."

They continued at a safe distance along the wall. Corvo scanned every inch of it, looking for gaps that would indicate an opening. There was nothing. Only concrete studded with cameras disappearing into the distance, until it turned into mountain. *But we're not like the stranger*, she wanted to shout. *We just need help.*

The smell of cooked meat came to their nostrils. It hurt Corvo to think of food, but she could see the farmer staring deep into the forest, looking for the smell's source with something more urgent than hunger in his eyes. Could this be another trick of the people behind the wall?

"This way," the farmer nodded.

"What if they're mutes? Like those that hurt us?"

The farmer thought for a second with his chin on his chest.

"So close to freedom. Even a wild dog would behave."

Corvo seemed to consider his words, then shook her head. "Can we trust them?"

The farmer shrugged, but moved towards the smell all the same.

They were three, four counting the baby. They huddled around a small fire pit just inside the tree line, their features covered by dark green ponchos. One of the figures, a woman, held the baby close to her chest. The farmer knelt behind a tree and pointed at her.

"They're running too," Corvo said.

From where they hid, they could hear low murmurs, conversations taking place in clipped sentences. They could hear the baby's babbling and gurgling as it reached out at the woman's chopped blond hair. Beside her, two men squatted side by side and tended to a couple of skewered rabbits.

The farmer didn't say anything to Corvo. As one, they rose and he cleared his throat loud enough so that the group turned their heads in their direction. They ceased their talking and observed them, the only sounds coming from the crackling fire and the baby.

Their resemblance told Corvo that this was a family. One of the men had a bearded face, while the other was too young to grow one yet. Their faces, though, lacked the strangeness of mutes. There were no drooping eyes or twisted mouths, no misshapen ears.

The woman pulled the baby closer to her chest. They all wore too many clothes, shirts layered on top of blouses and t-shirts, like vagabonds who carry all of their belongings on them. They had all kinds of practical things sticking out of bed sheets tied together, and other things that had no use. Fishing rods and family portraits. Blankets and jewelry boxes. Empty packs of flour with flower patterns on them. There were no guns, but a long, curving knife stuck into the ground that the older man now wrapped his fist around.

Once they got closer, she noticed the young man didn't have a scar on his throat like a lot of people his age did. And the baby didn't sound like it had one either.

"That's close enough," the matriarch said and the baby fussed in her arms. Behind her, the older man jerked the knife out of the ground and rose up.

Without stopping, the farmer lifted his shirt.

"Let us by the fire. It's cold."

There was no answer. The two men's eyes gave nothing away, but the matriarch appeared alarmed.

"Throw away your guns," the older man ordered and took a step forward while raising the knife.

"We got none," the farmer said and pushed Corvo behind him. "Put that pig sticker away. Or I'mma shove it up your ass."

The matriarch let out a tired sigh and nodded at the older man. She pointed at a spot on the other side of the fire pit and signaled them to sit.

"Much obliged, ma'am." the farmer muttered as he dropped to the ground. "Pardon mah words. Been some time. Since I used them right. Been a bitch of a week, too."

"I hear you," the matriarch said. Another sigh, one full of long days and cold nights and endless marching. Her gaze went to the farmer's gut. "How bad?" she asked.

He shook his head. "Bad enough."

"Knife?"

"Birdshot. Up close."

"Smells like you should be in a hospital."

"Feels like it, too."

The matriarch's lips broke into a crooked smile and she nodded.

"And that?" she rubbed her throat as she eyed the rope-burned skin on his.

"Accdent."

Corvo studied the family. The dirt on their faces, the open wounds on their hands. She hadn't noticed them earlier. There was a long slash on the younger man's forehead and his lip was split with such violence that it would never heal properly. The older man's knuckles were bloody and one of the bones in his right hand bent at an odd angle. When she studied the matriarch, she noticed she shifted her weight every few minutes with a wince and a groan. She talked with calculated effort. If the farmer noticed it too, he didn't make any sign of it.

"Fixing to go through the wall?" the farmer asked.

"Through it, over it, under," the matriarch said and waved a hand at the grey mass. "Any way we can, we're goin'."

"How long have you been hiding? Out here?"

"Coupla days."

"Have you seen the war?" Corvo asked.

The family stared at Corvo with shock.

"Ain't been no war round these parts, far as we can tell," the older man said with a gravel voice. "Ground's unspoiled. No waste in the water. And the trees look healthy to me. If there was fruit on them, I'd eat it."

"Are you sure? No war?"

The matriarch sighed.

"Girl, we haven't been here long, but if you're lookin fer war, this don't seem like the right place," she said with weariness. Then, her face softened and she added, "We watched the same news on the TV. Said a whole lotta things. Said a whole lotta nothing. Don't feel bad. You made it this far and now can see the truth fer yourselves."

Corvo nodded.

"Say…" the matriarch hesitated. "Where have you two been hiding? The girl talks. Ain't got no scar on her throat. That's mighty unusual."

"Away from any towns," Corvo said and immediately regretted it.

"Y'ain't her Pa," the matriarch stated and pointed at the farmer.

"I ain't."

"Where's her Pa?"

"Dead, I reckon. The girl don't know fer sure."

"And her Ma?"

"She's dead. The mutes killed her and my step-dad."

"The mutes..." the matriarch said with sadness. "We were mutes."

"We want to get over to the other side. You won't give us any trouble, will you?" Corvo continued.

"Trouble?" the matriarch raised her eyebrows. "No. No trouble. We want to get through too. Through it, over it, under. As I said. Any way we can, we're going."

The matriarch stepped up now. As she did, the two men rose to flank her.

"May have a couple of extra blankets, I reckon," the matriarch said. "Help yourselves ta some food, though there ain't much."

Corvo covered the farmer with one of the offered blankets, and then wrapped herself in the other. Now that the matriarch had accepted them, the older man stuck his knife back into the ground and leaned back.

"He's hurt bad," the younger man said pointing at the farmer. "Shouldn't be out here."

"I'll be fine," the farmer said. "Jes need ta get through that wall. I'll be fine then. Found the gate yet?"

"There ain't no gate, mister" the older man said. "Least, none we can git through."

"Then how are you planning. On getting to the other side? Flying?" the farmer sneered.

"We got a baby. We ain't a threat. They'll see that and let us in."

"But the voice on the speakers—" Corvo said.

"Jes have to be patient."

"We don't have time."

The family looked at her with tired sympathy. Instead of arguing, instead of explaining, they turned to the fire. The older man cut a hunk of meat and offered it to Corvo, which she wolfed down with a heel of bread. The farmer nursed his portion and, when Corvo was done, he gave it her.

"Eat," he said when she protested, "Got a whole lotta carrying to do still."

No more words passed between any of them. No small talk. No questions about where they came from or their story. Corvo and the farmer didn't ask them either.

The matriarch breastfed the baby while the two men tended to the fire, glancing back at the wall now and then. Corvo found she didn't feel bored. She continued staring into the fire, mulling over the puzzle of the first word in her mind. In time, she felt her mind pulling away.

She changed the farmer's bandages and felt the family observing them, studying the wound and wrinkling their noses at the smell, but she didn't pay them any attention. After that, they avoided looking her in the eyes. The farmer, they avoided looking at altogether.

There they remained in silence until night fell and they each turned to their sides, making themselves comfortable on the damp forest floor. Corvo helped the farmer get settled in. She stayed over him and stared until he asked her if something was wrong.

"No, nothing," she said and wrapped herself in her blanket. "Good night."

✕

WHEN HE WAS certain the others were asleep, the farmer shook the blanket off him. Without help, he struggled to stand. He could no longer feel his own body, as if he had already petrified. Only his will kept him bound to this world. *Just a little while longer*, he thought as he clutched the teacher's manuscript in his hands. *Just a little while longer. Then, I'll let go.*

Beside him, curled up by the fire, Corvo slept. She didn't stir, not even when the farmer coughed.

Am I leaving her with decent folks?

The matriarch lay on her side with the baby in the crook of her body, while the man and the boy leaned against nearby trees. The ache in his gut reminded him he didn't have much time. He had lost a lot of blood and, despite the girl's efforts, the wound had gotten infected. He'd be lucky to survive the night, he knew.

Now was the time.

The elephant starts his journey to the graveyard, he thought. He made a torch out of burning branches from the fire pit and a strip of bloody gauze pulled off his own skin. Then, with a final look at the girl, he turned and shuffled deeper into the forest.

It was strange to move without feeling his legs, or to clutch his wife's manuscript without feeling his fingers. It didn't bother him. On the contrary, he was relieved. The stab wound to his shoulder, the rope burn, the gunshot wound. He had been in pain for such a long time, he welcomed the respite.

Other wounds persisted. The loss. The shame. The stab wounds that were her last words. Those, he couldn't get rid of.

After a short walk, he found a clearing, a grassy patch

strewn with felled tree trunks not thirty feet wide. From there, he had a good view of the wall on either side. A part of him was bothered he wouldn't be able to cross it. He would never see what lay beyond the wall. Would never get to see the North.

And the girl?

He looked back towards where she slept, where flames flickered and threw long shadows along the forest floor.

"Take care of yourself," he whispered.

He made his way around the tree trunks, then found a short flat rock and sat on it. With hands that surprised him with their steadiness, he smoothed out the pages on his lap, smearing blood. The torch's light was enough to read them.

There they lay, his wife's words. Hesitation gnawed at him. A fear of what he'd read, her final condemnation. He looked at the lines and curves of the familiar handwriting.

Time's running out, he thought.

He took a deep breath and started to read.

✕

CORVO FELT HANDS rustling her, pulling her out of her sleep. She opened her eyes and saw the matriarch standing over her with clouds the color of graphite behind her, rain dripping off her hair. To the side, the rest of the family watched with quiet tension, the younger man holding the baby. Corvo could tell from the pity on their faces that the farmer was gone.

She sat up and rubbed her eyes, breathing in pine and sap and the smell of ground after it has rained, wrapping the blanket tighter around her body. With slow moves she stood.

"Where is he?" she asked.

The older man pointed in the direction of a nearby clearing.

"Haven't touched him," the matriarch said. "Thought you should be the one to see him first."

Corvo nodded.

"Want the men to come with you?"

"No. I'll be fine."

Corvo stood and sighed. *Now, I am alone*, she thought.

As she walked to the clearing, she felt the family's eyes on her. Looking for signs that she was breaking apart, no doubt. *Stand a little straighter, a little taller*, she told herself. *Let them know you'll be alright.*

When Corvo arrived at the clearing, she saw the farmer's body sitting on a rock. His head was hanging between his slumped shoulders, water dripping from his hair, and on the ground between his legs lay loose pages that were smudged with muddy, bloody fingerprints. She stood in front of him and watched his closed eyes. There was the urge to reach out to him, to shake him and wake him up, appearing as he did to only be sleeping. Instead, she knelt and picked up the manuscript pages that had scattered around him. She cleared the pages of the mud and leaves and the blood, careful not to tear the soaked pages. Then, she rolled them and hid them up her sleeve.

Was there anything to say? Any meaningful gesture to make, not for his sake, but for her own, for the sake of the living? She climbed up the rock and sat next to him. Staring out at the tree branches that formed the canopy and hearing rain drops hit the leaves made her feel peaceful. She turned to the farmer. Before leaving him behind, she wanted to make sure she memorized on the map of his face, every line, scar and half-healed wound.

"I'll remember you," she said and squeezed his hand before leaving him behind on the rock.

When she returned to their camp, the two men were arguing with the matriarch who had returned to her seated position near the fire pit. The baby in the younger man's arms seemed undisturbed by the hissed whispers that passed between the adults.

"You're killing her," the younger man said. "She can forage. She can help. She don't hafta be a burden."

"She's just a girl," the matriarch said.

"So's so mah sister's daughter," the older man said and pointed at the baby. "How 'bout her? Mmm? Are you puttin a stranger over her?"

"Now, wait jes a minute," the matriarch seemed offended. The older man turned his face away in anger. "What if the gate don't open cause of her?"

"Christ, man. You sound like the people we're running away from."

"They," he pointed at the wall, "are watching us. To see if we're decent folk. Don't know if she is."

"It's thanks to strangers like her that we're here at all."

"And it's because of strangers like her that only the four of us made it here."

"A girl. No more than twelve."

"Younger girls have gone and done worse."

The matriarch threw up her arms in exasperation. The argument went on. Neither of them would let up, while the younger man sat down and held the baby against his chest.

Corvo turned around and walked away, pulling the blanket around her tight. She started shivering, but didn't stop. She didn't stop, not when the younger man called out after her, not when the older man feigned remorse. No one ran after her to bring her back to the camp. There was no sadness in Corvo, just numbness that spread from her chest. No hatred either. She continued, past the tree line. All nearby cameras swiveled to concentrate on her. She walked up to the wall and rested her forehead against it, feeling the cold concrete on her skin.

"Open up," she uttered with a steady voice. From her sleeves, she pulled out the manuscript. "I got something to say. So, open up."

She unrolled the manuscript and read it out loud. Twenty pages in all. Wet and falling into pieces. The teacher's now familiar letters, smudged in places, unfurled on their surface, expansive and wild like horses galloping in a valley, even as the paper disintegrated. Words flowed out in long unbroken streams, making her feel lighter as they left her mouth. There was solace in hearing the teacher again, even in this manner. Louder now. *Let everyone beyond the wall hear me*, she thought. *The family, too. I don't care.*

She read the manuscript out loud and then she read it again. Her own voice seemed to be coming from everywhere now, the wall amplifying it as it had done with the singing the previous day. It told the story of the farmer and the teacher.

Of the silence between them. From the moment they met until her decision to burn her book and everything in between. Their gradual falling out. The death of their baby. Their estrangement. Her thoughts of leaving him, the divorce she had in motion, and then finally the peace the Hush had brought into their lives. An account of their lives of quiet desperation and of their shared tragedies. Of all her regrets and resentments.

"Open up," she yelled when she finished reading. "He's dead. There's a family with a baby here. We're not a threat. Open up."

She took a step back and the cameras pivoted to match her movement. In the sky above, rain turned into snow. The words were dissolving, becoming harder to read, the pages slipped from her hands as she shivered harder.

"Open up," she said again and again and her voice began to become hoarse, breaking at the edges. She went louder.

"Open up.

Open up."

She shouted and yelled until something snapped deep inside her vocal cords. When she opened her mouth again, she spat blood on the snow that was beginning to cover the ground. She went into a coughing fit. It lasted for long moments, a wet hacking that left her breathless. She almost fell to her knees, but refused to show weakness, even as her eyes watered and fear overtook her.

"Open up," she shouted again and held the manuscript over her head for the cameras to see.

"Open up.

Open up.

Open up.

I got something to say."

She coughed and she knew she had lost her voice.

Music played over the speakers. The same song as before, and its promise of a simple life lived well.

In the distance, a gate opened without sound.

Dear Reader

Thank you for reading *The Hush*. If you enjoyed this book (or even if you didn't) please consider leaving a star rating or review online. Your feedback is important, and will help other readers to find the book and decide whether to read it, too.

Acknowledgements

Without the continuing and unwavering support of a tribe of amazing humans, this book would have remained a bundle of loose pages hidden in a hole in a wall.

Sarah Rahmeh, Marilag Dimatulac, and Marianne Hansen, for the love and endless sparring over red wine and hummus.

The Crazy Monkeys crew for keeping me sane; Kamila Piotrowska, Hristo Valev, Tomas Cydik, Mireia Marè Badalló, Oksana Lukjancenko, Gyula Szathmary.

Stefania Mylona, and the Antonakou, Nosek, and Kyzewettr clans for their unconditional backing.

Sara-Jayne Slack and the Inspired Quill team, for believing in the success of The Hush and for doing what heroes do best; making the world a better place one book at a time.

Constance Renfrow, whose understanding of what I wanted to say helped me write what I needed to say.

The good folks at Beta Boulders, for providing me with a safe haven where this book didn't exist for a few hours.

Melina Mattheou, Katerina Mavroudi, and Petros Moraitis, whose support doesn't recognize time or distance.

Freddo B. Frederiksen, First of his Name, the Watcher on the Porch, King of Catfolk, for being the best friend any human could wish for.

Essi Valo, mi media naranja. A new language would have to be invented to describe the love you gave me.

Last, but not least, I'd like to thank the trails of Kalvebod Faelled. Within the silence of the birches and the ashes, I found all the words I needed.

About the Author

Evangelos is a photographer, writer and author of the speculative fiction novel *The Hush*.

Originally from Athens, Greece, he has spent the last couple of decades travelling and working through the world. In that time, he's tended to wounded loggerhead turtles, baked bread for a Michelin-star restaurant and written dialogues for video games.

An environmental scientist by training, he is an advocate for the climate cause, sustainable living and anti-corporatism, which inspire his unique brand of literary sci-fi set twenty minutes into the future.

He currently resides in Copenhagen, Denmark, on the spot where the city ends and the forest begins. He spends his time trail-running, hiking and rock climbing.

Find the author via their website: eamylonas.com

Or tweet at them: @ea_mylonas